The Blood Miracles

Also by Lisa McInerney

The Glorious Heresies

The Blood Miracles

Lisa McInerney

JOHN MURRAY

First published in Great Britain in 2017 by John Murray (Publishers)
An Hachette UK Company

2

© Lisa McInerney 2017

A CIP catalogue record for this title is available from the British Library

ISBN 978-1-444-79889-0
Trade paperback ISBN 978-1-444-79890-6
Ebook ISBN 978-1-444-79891-3

Typeset in Sabon MT by Hewer Text UK Ltd, Edinburgh
Printed and bound by Clays Ltd, St Ives plc

John Murray policy is to use papers that are natural, renewable and
recyclable products and made from wood grown in sustainable forests.
The logging and manufacturing processes are expected to conform
to the environmental regulations of the country of origin.

John Murray (Publishers)
Carmelite House
50 Victoria Embankment
London EC4Y 0DZ

www.johnmurray.co.uk

For Caroline

I

This, like so many of Ryan Cusack's fuck-ups, begins with ecstasy.

It begins in Rotterdam, like so much ecstasy does, where Daniel Kane, frustrated from months feeling like his supplier's afterthought, strikes up an acquaintance with a couple of lads from Naples. Dan bonds with them, in so far as these kinds of boys can bond, over Dutch draw and contempt for the Rotterdammer dignitaries.

It escalates when Ryan returns from a summer's week in Naples with a throwaway observation about how their yokes are so much better, based on two nights out and zero hangovers. It's a thought that germinates in Dan's head until it becomes a strategy. By autumn he is making preliminary, private enquiries. By winter he is arranging a visit.

Finding ecstasy is no easy task. The market offers so many MDMA knock-offs: PMA, NBOMe, MDE, alphabet broths of second-rate stimulants developed in Chinese laboratories. The black market is not a free market. Consumers take what they can get. They cannot always get methylenedioxymethamphetamine. Access to the proper stuff depends on the capacities or whims of the dealers and the dealers cannot truly be trusted; they're in it for the money; the satisfaction of the end user matters only in the context of how much the end user is willing to pay.

But Dan Kane believes that because he will never be the man importing the most pills, he has to be the man sourcing the finest. The profit margins aren't as magnificent as they are for alphabet broth rubbish, but good yokes move fast, so Dan's developed a reputation for artisanal pharmaceuticals. It makes sense for him to switch from one producer to another if there are better yokes available. His enterprise is small enough that he can manage the shift. His ambitions are broad enough that he will cope with the upheaval. And Naples, well. It turns out there are better yokes in Naples. *Is that not serendipitous?* he asks.

Because, of course, there's the matter of Ryan's blood.

At the start of December, about three months before Ryan is to turn twenty-one, about five and a half years into his relationship with his girlfriend Karine, about seven years after he first met Dan, he and Dan stand in a corridor on the third floor of a Cork City hotel. Dan, fidgety on the way over, has dedicated himself to cold lucidity; only once in this corridor does Ryan see him waver, and that's in exhalation, a deliberate expelling of breath as you might see in a long-distance runner.

Dan tilts his head and in response Ryan bows his own. 'Get every nuance,' Dan says, and Ryan nods faintly, so diminished is the space between them. 'This is not,' Dan goes on, 'a deal to be done in simple English.'

Ryan knows it's too late to say it but he says it anyway.

'You know if you're opening routes there, you're dealing with the Camorra. You know that, right?'

'What difference does it make?' Dan asks. What separates gang from clan from syndicate? It's all business. Dan's dealt with English top boys, Dutch producers, Russian smugglers, 'and if I can manage Russians, Ryan, I can manage Italians.'

Ryan knows you don't manage the Camorra. He cannot say how he learned this or when he accepted it; he just knows it, maybe from his mother's muttered oaths or maybe because he is sane, underneath it all.

Dan tilts his head the other way. 'Tell me you're all right.'

'I'm all right,' Ryan lies.

2

In a corner room Ryan sits with a lone Neapolitan and they converse as the city below them darkens. The MDMA will be manufactured in Estonia, pressed in Naples and shipped to Cork while Dan's money goes the other way. Accountants will whir about in the background, making what's illegal legal; they will obscure details and arrange bribes, put thick skin on the bones of it. Dan directs Ryan's questions. The rest of the inner circle – Shakespeare, Pender, Cooney and Feehily – sprawl on armchairs or lean on walls. The Neapolitan doesn't flinch.

Ecstasy, a taster batch of fifty thousand for fifty thousand, just to test the route, all grade upfront, a fifty-thousand-euro risk for a brand-new channel, and Ryan's misgivings are months too late.

I'm all right, he tells himself, though he is not all right. He is nervous and he is rusty. He has been out of action since the October bank holiday weekend.

The Neapolitan asks him to clarify a statement. It's Ryan's pronunciation or an ending sliced off a word or he slips into Napulitano. The Neapolitan's eyes widen. The smell of blood: his nostrils flare. His mouth stretches. He identifies Ryan as one of his own.

I'm all right, Ryan tells himself. *This is all right.*

Dan carefully structures the fortnight following this meeting. He sends Shakespeare – Shane O'Sullivan, enforcer, adviser, right-hand man – to go over complexities with his customs guy. He evaluates an old rental on Watercourse Road as a potential base for storing the batch, checking it for damp and draughts, sizing up the neighbours. He goes through two dummy runs with Cooney and Feehily and fabricates solid reasons for them to be at the Port of Cork in Ringaskiddy for the days leading up to the delivery. The pills are due on the last container in from Salerno before Christmas: the 23rd of December.

He looks beyond the best case scenario: the delivery is a success, the pills are immediately sold, and the Neapolitans agree on a price per pill appropriate for a long-term partnership. Half of Ireland will want in on it. The Shades and the shams, all looking for a cut. Handling such interest will take strong nerves. He will need to be totally confident in his abilities, his men's loyalties, and his belonging to his city. The one he is most worried about is the robber baron Jimmy Phelan – often referred to by initials only, abbreviation sprung from jitters and dismay – the man who thinks everything in Cork is his by default. When Jimmy Phelan finds out about the route, he will almost certainly make a move towards seizing it. Dan knows it is imperative that the route is established before this happens. The longer he can keep Phelan from finding out, the easier it will be to manage his megalomania. If it means selling outside of the city for the time being, so be it.

He explains such thoughts to Ryan over and over again in Ryan's sitting room in the early afternoons of the first half of December. Dan is excited, Dan is nervous, Dan is determined, optimistic and desperate.

He seems surprised that Ryan's appointment as translator didn't lead to instant relief from his depression, as if he'd expected Ryan to emerge from the meeting with the Neapolitan his old self.

At the end of that preparatory fortnight he says, 'You'd want to get your arse in gear,' not altogether unkindly.

It is only in terms of Ryan's new melancholy Dan has any real right to be frustrated. Ryan has kept earning. During his weeks indoors his brother Cian brought him chips and bad news in exchange for directions – to clients, pick-up points, debtors, underlings. The dealers whom Ryan supplies have not run low; Dan has heard no complaints. But then Dan needs more from Ryan than a line of income, more, even, than an Italian tongue and Neapolitan blood. Dan Kane, a disciplined eater who lifts weights and reads and plucks what he likes best from Buddhism and believes in balance and fucks around and is proud of the

4

quality of his cocaine, needs an apostle. He needs walking, talking reassurance that he is up to snuff.

Daniel Kane has put a lot of work into Ryan Cusack being all right.

Mere days before the pills are due, Dan has need of Ryan's words again.

It is late on a Saturday afternoon, and Ryan is at home with Karine, who has come over, as she does when she can spare the time away from studying, to remind him of the various things he needs to do to be alive. *You should eat, you should talk, you should go for a walk, you should have sex with me.* Today she's told him to have a shower. Ryan's natural attributes are such that he is easily inclined towards vanity – *septic* is the old Corkonian term he hears from his dad – but since the bank holiday he's been forgetting himself and, in so doing, remembering himself again with mild surprise. His beard grows pretty quickly, it turns out.

Dan texts:

I need you to talk to someone for me.
So get moving, little man.

This message comes through while Ryan is in the bathroom, and Karine intercepts it. When he comes back in she's on his bed, boots off and legs curled beneath her, holding his phone and staring into space.

She says, 'Dan's looking for you.'

She lets him take the phone. He reads the message. It has come through at a very bad time, for Karine doesn't know that Ryan's been talking to Neapolitan exporters and so is not prepared for Dan demanding his company now. He knows he should sit, gather his thoughts and call Dan to ask for an hour's grace; he needs to explain his return from exile to a girl who believes exile fits him. He leaves his phone on his desk and picks out dark jeans, a slim-fit T-shirt, boots. Going-out clothes.

This is a creaky sort of enterprise. He's slow in dressing and she watches him as if assessing a rehabilitation. She runs her hands over him; she rearranges the short waves of his hair, she pulls her fingertips along his jaw, she opens a palm over each lung.

'D'you not know you're a mess?' she says.

A mess in blood and in deed. The oldest son of Tony Cusack and Maria Cattaneo is Cork City born and bred and in its sing-song accent speaks fluent Italian, shaky Neapolitan and rough and rapid Hiberno. His eyes are the colour of black treacle and his olive skin is paled by adjacency to the Atlantic; his nonna, with varying degrees of sincerity, blames everything from draughts to the *malocchio* for his pallor. He takes up just under six feet and a good bit less across the chest than he should, exile being the kind of thing that makes a man skinny. His is the business of fledgling savages the world over: he facilitates the movement of illegal inebriants from his foolhardy class into the hands and mouths and nostrils of those who should know better. He feigns a swagger to hide the fact that he doesn't breathe easy and doesn't sleep well. He has notions about his future; he feels violently inadequate sometimes; he hasn't had enough practice to be a good shot.

In front of him now is his girlfriend of nearly six years, as blonde and bright as he's dark and bloodless. She withdraws her hands and purses her lips and takes a breath.

'You're a mess,' she repeats, 'and if you go out there after Dan now you'll fall to pieces.'

'I have to go back to work, girl.'

'Why do you have to go back to work? You've done nothing for the past six weeks, Ryan. And guess what, he managed without you.'

Ryan cannot correct her. For the past six weeks he has been still and quiet and he's mostly stayed indoors but it goes to show, he thinks, how innocent his girlfriend is that she doesn't suspect he was up to no good at the same time. Only in outline is Karine aware of what her boyfriend does when he's not with her. She knows Dan because Ryan has been with Dan even longer than he's been with her. She knows Ryan sells enough to make decent grade. Lately this has bothered her. She could consent to his carry-on when he would otherwise have gone hungry. Now he's flush and enjoys a sort of reputation and that doesn't sit right with her at all.

Ryan says, 'Staying in is doing me more damage than going out.'

'And how do you make that out?'

She looks tired, he thinks, but then, she's doing exams. A trying life each, at odds and opposites.

He says, 'I feel better, like. The last few weeks . . . It's over, I got my head together.'

'You got your head together? Ryan, you tried to kill yourself.'

'I didn't.'

'You say you're out of the pit and you still haven't faced up to what put you there.' She stands back. 'Oh God,' she breathes, and blinks at the ceiling.

'I know what it looked like.' Ryan reaches for her hand and she holds both up and pouts. 'But that's not what it was. I have a hard enough time going without you for a couple of days, Karine. Why would I want to stretch that?'

'Guilt? You weren't exactly thinking straight.'

Ryan rubs his eyes. 'I'll make it up to you,' he says.

'Right. I had to drag you out of an early grave, but that's just something you can pay me back for. Like it's part and parcel of being with you. Oh yeah, my boyfriend's deep. So deep he was nearly six feet down.'

Her hostility is justified. He proved incapable of containing what should have been a common-or-garden October bank holiday binge, falling instead to overindulgence: a few drinks too many for a constitution weakened by secrets, apostasy and self-medication. The anxiety was there to begin with. Everyone tells Ryan he's the bulb off Tony, the living spit, his father's son, as if after nearly twenty-one years it could be news to him. It was always going to happen. Tony burst out of him, not just the dark hair and the dark eyes and the slow smile but the wrath, the tears, the knuckles. Ryan was fighting with his girlfriend; she turned him inside out and he raised his fist to her. He didn't hit her but he came close. He pinned her to the wall and aimed at the plaster.

'What's gotten into you?' she wept, and some short hours afterwards emergency department doctors had an answer. Cocaine, they said. Alcohol. Paracetamol.

This was the makings of his six weeks of stupor: Ryan was dissociated by half-memories and stunned by having made so dire a mistake. He is reasonably sure that he never meant to overdose. He knows how long paracetamol takes to kill, so it makes no sense to him that he'd choose it.

He assumes that he was drunk and melancholy after another fight with the ould doll, but he never blamed her, not even in the darkest moments; Karine had no hand in his blotting out the beautiful lore of him and her and the million things she always does right. He's torn her apart; she hovers, tearful and tender, and her complicity makes her angry, and her anger makes her ashamed. There have been doctors echoing sinister words like 'episode' and referrals to a psychiatrist or a psychologist or whatever, and Karine has to take it seriously because she's almost a nurse. She stood with him at the pharmacy, waiting for a paper bag of the kind of drugs they don't want him to take recreationally, drugs he hasn't taken and won't take. She bought him a notebook and pleads with him to write down those agonies he cannot otherwise express. *Write down what you're feeling*, she directs. *I dunno, write about songs that make you feel things. If you won't talk to me, write to me; write to someone, anyone.* She tries to put him back together.

I am a mess, he wants to tell her, I am a mess and I want you to put me back together, I want to change direction, I want to leave the country, I want to take back what I did to you, I want to bury it on Vesuvio.

But instead he moves towards her and in his actions tries to simulate health and normality; he kisses her insistently and secures her cooperation; he wraps her arms around his neck.

Heat, skin, sweat. She chides him even as their bodies start to slip. She tells him she can't fix him if he doesn't get the legwork done. She reminds him that she's graduating next year. Their paths threaten to diverge; doesn't he know that? Celestial in the pale glow of the floor lamp beside his bed, she tells him she loves him. Past her shoulders glint the bits of herself she's left on his chest of drawers. A hairbrush, a can of deodorant, make-up remover, cotton balls. Two pots of pastel nail varnish. There's more tucked away in one of the drawers – fluffy socks and T-shirts and tampons and a hair-dryer. The most obvious stuff here belongs to Ryan – decks, a digital piano, black, blocky, blokey hardware – but the room is as much her space as his.

Between deeper and slower breaths he says he loves her too, he loves her more.

'If you love me, you'll stop. Like, straight away.'

'Stop what?'

'Stop dealing.'

He pushes his mouth against her neck and tastes salt.

His phone rings when he's catching his breath against her shoulder as she draws circles on the back of his neck. Outside someone bellows *OK love!* and a car door slams and a van rumbles past and the hum starts at the back of the house as the central heating kicks in. Ryan rolls away. Karine clings to his side.

'Don't answer,' she says. 'Just leave it.'

But he must answer, because normality demands that of him.

Mam,

Maybe I'm not mad. Maybe I'm not suicidal. Maybe I'm restless.

I might be 1300 miles away but I have Neapolitan blood and Neapolitan blood is restless. San Gennaro was beheaded but his blood is still flowing. Naples takes a couple of vials of it out every so often and it keeps on liquefying. Only it dawned on me that Neapolitan blood doesn't need a body and so deep down I mustn't care whether I live or die. I'm restless and reckless and this blood will kill me before it keeps me alive.

Did I ever tell you my earliest memory? Me burying my face in my dad's neck because lunging at us was a blind monster the same colour as the stone.

I don't remember how you explained it to me but I knew I was looking at a dead body and it burned into my brain then that that's what happens when people die: they turn the colour of stone and their eyes fall out. You shouldn't have brought me to Pompeii when I wasn't old enough to cope with monsters. Though I wonder now if that was the plan. Did you think bringing me there when I was small and easily scared would do the trick? That I'd steer clear if I associated Italy with death?

Like volcanoes. In Ireland we barely have mountains, in Napoli the mountain can kill you. And obviously Pompeii goes with Vesuvio. I found out years later that the bodies were just plaster casts, but it didn't make a difference. Death, death every-where, souvenirs of an explosive mountain.

Remember the wan you used to sing with at weddings? Stephanie? Once you were in the kitchen and it was bucketing down out and she said, I don't know why you'd live here, Maria, when you could live in Italy where it's hot, and you said, Raise sons in Napule? Jesus, girl, I'm not crazy. I asked Dad after what was so murderous about Napoli anyway, apart from the moun-tain? He said it had more than its share of head-the-balls. This would have been around the time of the Scampia thing. Don't live in Napoli, the place can kill you in a hape of different ways.

And you were from there, so I always knew you were going to die too.

Thing is, after you died the frequency of visits to Napoli was dictated by your mam and dad and their need to pinch our cheeks eclipsed your deserter's logic. Usually I went when the option was there. I was last over in the summer. I went to see you but I didn't do any talking coz Karine was with me and we'd just done a week in Ibiza and were both fucking goosed. So maybe you didn't notice me there. I was though.

Karine was quiet too but I didn't think much of it. I mean, she speaks only English, why wouldn't she be quiet? But on the second day we went out for a poke around and some proper pizza, and she said to me:

Ryan, this is so weird.

I thought she meant the mess. She kept gawping, as if Napoli was a bedroom I'd forgotten to tidy before inviting her round. In a narrow lane between crumbling walls tagged over and over again she told me, It's so weird that you're talking and I can't understand you.

She'd never thought of me as anything but a Corkonian, and now all of a sudden I was a Neapolitan, gibbering and kissing fellas. It was a part of me she'd glimpsed only during long-distance phone calls or Napoli matches. Front-and-centre, she

12

had to accept that I'd never been a whole person, just two torn halves.

It's a fucked up thing to feel drawn to somewhere you don't really belong. I think you'd get that, you felt that way about Cork. You spoke English with a Cork accent, you collected Irish legends, you gave us Irish names. And me: I shout for Napoli, I gesture even when I know no one will understand, I've got Il Mattino on my phone.

See, I have a nose for corpses and quaking ground.

That's why my dad would lose it whenever I was arrested. Your mam tried to keep you from this kind of shit, and look, you went and found it anyway.

But where'd I get the restless blood in the first place, Mam?

2

Dan Kane says that a man makes his own luck, that fate is cruel when left unchallenged, that fortune is a thing to be managed. And so it is Ryan's second-hand conviction that he, too, knows what he's doing, that he cannot expect anyone to wring hands on his behalf. And Dan has done a lot for him.

Ryan fell in with him years ago. Bonna night, trouble in the smoke and Ryan belting away from it – he can't remember what the rírá was about now – Dan pulled up in a black 5-series.

'Hassle, little man?'

Ryan gave him his standard 'Fuck off' and Dan laughed.

'The doonshie dealer,' he said. 'I've been told all about you. What's the matter, don't you recognise the source of your merchandise?'

Dan is the man, all right. Of unremarkable height but a strapping build underplayed by well-chosen duds, grey-eyed with greying hair clipped tight, he looks indifferent to the stress involved in pulling off deals in a city run by the dangerous. This is due in part to masterful manipulation of his drug intake to numb or stoke as needed; his dosages are medically precise. The only thing out of place on him is an oversized bottom lip, which gives him the look of a sulky boxer when he forgets to flatten it against his teeth.

Back then he could get his hands on the loveliest pills, and he needed to share the wealth. At fourteen Ryan was looking for any place beyond home to rest his head and fed up with having no bobs except what he could salvage from his father's benefits. Selling yokes to a base of enthusiastic vibe-gobblers never felt like the society-warping enterprise the *Six One News* liked to lament. And so Dan Kane took him on.

That in itself is remarkable – other savages have remarked on it – as one doesn't tend to take apprentices in the trade. Why put time and effort into raising a rival? If the little fucker doesn't rat you out, he'll take you on. Those marked for making money will pick up the game as they play; there is little room for patient instruction.

Remarkable, noticeable. Ryan has drawn attention by dint of his early ascension. From guards – why wouldn't there be guards? – who know that youth means fragility, who have put Ryan away, who bother him on the street and pat him down in public. From other fledgling savages, the boys Ryan started out with, who have stayed stagnant in dirty sitting rooms, playing Battlefield in their jocks and selling grams and half-rolls to randomers while he climbed the ladder and got himself staff and a GTI. From associates much longer in the tooth who watch Ryan rack up promotions and feel hard done by, who mutter that he's a wunderkind hand-reared only to take a bullet for his keeper.

And worse. From professional savages, the likes of whom Dan Kane is only trotting after. Ryan's career has roused interest in his city's masters.

Dan has asked that Ryan meet him now in one of the many flats he has access to, a spotless, uninhabited two-bed above a city centre bar.

Ryan parks on the quay and gets through most of a spliff as he does Oliver Plunkett Street. A black sky pushes down on amber flare after amber flare; the street lights glow, the shop windows glow, the pavement glows. Cork City holds up the night and its people shiver and cough under its canopy: Ryan feels the contrast of cover and exposure, the cramped streets as shelter from spinning space, and both make him nervous. He dodges ball-hoppers admiring each other's Christmas jumpers, dawdling middle-aged couples, deadpan young wans whose phone screens are cyclically lit and doused under their chins. Already he's breathing too fast.

Dan is in the best of form. The task he has for Ryan is a simple one, involving the transfer of funds from one bank account to another. Ryan takes the relevant details and strict instructions for their use from a male voice in Italy. Then Dan passes over a throwaway handset so that Ryan can relay these details to a female voice in Ireland.

He thinks first that he is speaking to Dan's girlfriend Gina, for while Dan likes to surround himself with young wans, to intrigue them with hammy tales that span the breadth of Europe till they allow him to de-stress between their legs, he doesn't tend to employ them. But this woman is not Gina, as Ryan realises when she responds to his soft tone with a bored one. He modifies his in response.

'Like, are you getting this?'

'You're literally just giving me an IBAN,' she says, and it's as if he can hear the eye-roll.

Fuck it, Dan says to this minor annoyance, she got it, it's fine. They go downstairs to the bar and Dan buys Ryan a pint and a tumbler of Jameson in a remodelled snug decked out in LEDs and a scavenger's haul of kitschy artefacts.

Ryan has been dry this past while. An idea of Karine's: if his constitution is weak then he must stop testing it. But it occurs to him now that the drinking needs doing if he intends to rejoin the race, and so he will take the poison, bare his chest on the altar, dare the gods to take him. He's not yet fucked on the drink. It made a monster of his mother and his father and there are times he considers denying it its chance to make a monster of him, but not drinking is admitting you're broken. He is not ready for that. Certainly not in front of Dan.

Two pints, one Jameson in, Ryan goes to the beer garden for a cigarette and to phone Karine. To reassure her, because if he makes today his first official day back at work then he feels it went well.

She can hear the merriment around him. 'Jesus, Ryan, are you out?'

'I'm done for the day,' he tells her. He is giddy; he wants her here with him; nothing would constitute normality better than that. She is usually up for a Saturday night out. He tries to remember how many exams she has left. 'I'm having a couple with Dan.'

'And did you tell him?'

'Tell him what?'

'Ryan, don't play the prick. That you're done with him!'

'No,' Ryan says. He points his cigarette at the sky and rubs his forehead with the flat of his thumb.

'So you won't quit.'

'It's not that I won't . . . He's not going to let me walk away, that's not how this works.'

'So what you're saying is I'm being pure silly because once you get into this shit they don't let you out again, and you're a lost cause, Ryan, and I should stop trying. Yeah?'

'That's simplifying it,' he says. 'It's not a simple thing. I earn for him, y'know . . . Stuff like this can't be done overnight.'

'A lot of things can change in a night, Ryan.'

'What's that supposed to mean?'

'There was a night not so long ago when I thought we were just having a row and suddenly you were someone else entirely.' She hangs up.

He phones her back but she doesn't answer. He lets the call run into her voicemail.

'C'mere, girl. I know what's bothering you. I can fix it. I just have shit to do in the meantime. You just need a bit of patience, like.'

He sees Dan come through the back door of the pub and the man looks content.

Ryan says, 'Just wait for me, Karine. Please.'

Dan approaches, a tumbler in each hand.

'Such great things ahead of us. And behind,' as he looks over his shoulder at their fellow smokers. There are fellas dotted throughout, holding pint glasses through which the light refracts, making little lanterns, but it's mostly girls, two dozen maybe, bare-legged, in pale dresses with flat, glossy hair. Ryan catches the eye of a brunette with feathered eyelashes and cherry lips. She smiles. He looks away.

In the far corner of the beer garden Dan arranges lines on the tabletop behind the crook of his arm. He points once the lines are drawn and Ryan knows that this is a test more than it is a kindness, that if he wants to insist he is all right then Dan will expect him to show it, snort a rail, prove he's able for it. He does not want to accept. He is well on the way to drunkenness and with that may come panic: disintegration, a jumble of limbs, lung spasms, tears. *Between a rock and a hard place*, he thinks, and thinks then of camorristi and the manifest peculiarities of the Neapolitan language.

He takes the line. He concentrates on holding himself together.

Such great things, Dan elaborates. His interest is not just in money but in the by-product of money. He wishes autonomy for himself. He is not, he reiterates, interested in paying homage to robber barons. He has spent long enough bringing offerings to the likes of Jimmy Phelan, whose only real advantage is that he came of age a decade before Dan. The cocaine spurs him; his eyes bore into Ryan's as he delivers his sermon. Oh they will prosper, they will dominate trade in the city and while only the very best will know their names, everyone will intimately know their product. Entrepreneurs, thespians, stay-at-home dads, models. 'Look around,' Dan says, 'at the good people here, with their degrees and their careers and their ways and means and all the things they hope no one sees are wrong with them. They all want it, and soon they'll all want it from us. Look at all the ould dolls. They're halfway there.

18

'How a man like me gets here,' he continues, 'is down to balls, and patience, and knowing, fucking *knowing* he'd get here. And having the right lads around him,' he adds, generously. 'How would you go about that, Ryan? How would you pick the right feens for the jobs you want done?' But he does not want an answer, and Ryan has heard versions of this speech before. 'It's not luck,' Dan goes on, tapping his fingers on the tabletop, contorting his bottom lip, fixing and re-fixing his field of vision over Ryan's shoulder. 'It's being able to spot the qualities you want and then having the capacity to sculpt them. I'm never wrong about character.'

He curves his hand around the left side of Ryan's neck.

'All that time you spent getting your shit together and I never once doubted you, Ryan.'

Dan doesn't doubt Ryan because Dan doesn't know Ryan's been doing favours for Jimmy Phelan.

This is a memory Ryan can't risk reviving. Whatever about his inconvenient holiday, or losing his temper with his girlfriend, the guilt of treachery could crumple him. He thinks about his dad, only briefly, and that's on the edge of too much.

Dan squeezes open Ryan's palm. He produces a few pills stamped with a curved shape coming to sharp points at either end.

'A phoenix,' he says. 'You never got a taste.'

Ryan closes his fist around the sample and presses the pills into his palm. Dan brings his hand back to Ryan's neck. Forehead-to-forehead, Ryan closes his eyes. Dan flexes his fingers.

'It's good as fucking anything to have you back, little man,' he says.

Cork is a small city of one hundred and twenty thousand souls. Its residents live overlapping lives so there is nothing remarkable in Ryan sharing a background with people whose deeds are darker than any of his. It is not remarkable that Jimmy 'J.P.' Phelan, the most successful of this city's mistakes, grew up with Tony Cusack, or that the connection endured until Tony's son grew old enough to be useful. So it is not remarkable that Phelan sought to enlist Ryan, whose apprenticeship was such a notable thing. And it is not remarkable that Ryan was bound to bow under the man whose word is sacrosanct on the streets, especially since the penalty was orphanhood.

Six months back Ryan Cusack did a favour for Jimmy Phelan.

There was a girl. Georgie. Midway through her twenties, bones sewn together in a slutty dress. Ryan was her dealer for a time when he was fifteen or sixteen; she was raven-haired, giggly and jumpy, too brittle to manage grown-up outlaws. Whatever disrespect she threw at Jimmy Phelan, it was big enough to necessitate her passing. Phelan waded into Tony's home one damp day and asked Tony, the dampest man in Cork, to do the job, but Tony being weak the job was left to his first-born. Ryan took the girl back to her den to do the deed. Acting on his father's behalf, and under the thumb of the most belligerent man he'd ever met, there was no room for error, but Ryan failed and failed gloriously. He put the girl on a plane instead and told her to fuck away off and never come back, but he couldn't trust her to comply, he didn't even demand her word of honour.

But this is how the city works.

There are the boys on the top, and knowing their names is a curse. Villains for the most part, but sometimes cloaked in virtue – senior guards, customs officers. Ryan doesn't know who they are but he knows they're there. A circle-jerk revolves elsewhere, ad infinitum, and Ryan knows because occasionally he claws gains from their takings or finds himself fucked when things don't proceed to their liking. Which is the way the world works, he suspects, whether you're a rock star or a McDonald's dogsbody or a mid-ladder dealer.

This is how Ryan works. He took the task set for him by Phelan because he was not big enough to refuse him. He hid the request from Dan because to Dan, Phelan is as much an oppressor as the Garda Commissioner; Phelan suppresses Dan's activities, curbs commercial initiative, adheres too closely to archaic ideas about territories. Jimmy Phelan was never Ryan's confidant or friend, but Dan won't distinguish between confidant or friend or tyrant; it won't matter to him how the treachery was constructed, only that it was.

But look, Ryan tells himself, *if in feeling guilty I betray myself then I've to stop feeling guilty.* This is how the city works, after all. It's not like their relationship has always been defined by respect and fraternity. He has put up with a lot from Dan. There have been slaps – education administered across the back of the head or to the jaw, in pubs, in corridors, on waste ground. There've been rude orders barked and bullish shows of Dan's superiority. Ryan has always weathered them, and even when things went to shit the shit was always a means to an end. In it for the money and in it for the leg-up, Ryan is never going to be one of those gnarled fuckers down the Flying Bottle on a Tuesday night, looking sinister with tattoos up both arms and an ould doll with big hair and only one fucking eye.

Last orders, and there are hours still to knock out of the nighttime. Dan is tightrope-walking the long white line between drunkenness and clarity. Ryan is clumsier on this threshold; things have gotten away from him a little bit, but Dan's mood is such that he either doesn't notice or doesn't care.

'Let's see what's happening elsewhere,' Dan says, and chooses a club called Room.

Six weeks in his room and Ryan escapes to Room. This ugly consistency does nothing for his mood. The place is hardly buzzing, but hefty beats supplement pills or coke or whatever artificial good humour's nudged the crowd onto the dance floor. Ryan wants a double whiskey. He wants a double drop.

'This gaff's gone to the dogs,' Dan says, but he says that no matter the venue; the surest sign of a man approaching his late thirties. 'Get me a gin,' he says, and heads behind the DJ booth and up to the balcony – the VIP room, a space used by middle-aged bouncers to impress disingenuous girls in uncomfortable shoes. Ryan heads to the bar. Rachel's serving. A couple of years back, Ryan had a one-night thing with her. He was pissy with Karine at the time – wounded, half insane with it – and there was a house party, and these things happen.

She mouths, Hey Ryan.

He takes a gin and a Jameson and her smile up to the balcony, where Dan has already found three girls to shit-talk. Ryan hands him his drink. There are times when Dan is happy to have his company during the preliminaries – after he has decided which girl he likes best and is in need of a distraction for her friends. Now he seems not to notice Ryan, and so Ryan moves to the railing and looks down at the dance floor, and feels like resting his head against the brushed steel, closing his eyes, rolling forward. Climbing over.

But across the dance floor comes Colm McArdle, Promoter, Manager, Ringmaster General and the stature for it, a good six-two, a good span to his shoulders, a good flush to his cheeks. He holds both arms over his head, each hand directed at Ryan and ending in what Colm knows as the sign of the horns and Ryan, having Neapolitan blood, knows as something else entirely. Colm nods to the beat as he parts the crowd.

'Just the fucking man,' he shouts, once he gets to the balcony. A Belfast stretch on the last word: Ryan Cusack's just the fucking *mawn*. 'Were you in England for a bit or something?'

'Naw,' Ryan says, and though he'd do well to make clear that his disappearance had nothing to do with the law, there are no details to go into from there; what details from the hollow?

'Thought you'd gone to London. The Dam, even. I heard you were keeping the head down.'

Ryan smiles and shakes his head again, and Colm is smart enough to change the subject. 'I have a wee proposition for you,' he says.

He folds his arms on the railing beside Ryan and they eyeball the fifty or so on the dance floor below.

Colm says, 'What a shithole.'

The balcony's ice-blue lighting highlights his flaxen hair and gives his colourless eyelashes an alien glow.

'Starving interns swaying to music the DJ doesn't care about,' he says, 'drinking pitchers of piss and nosing for some pleb with more gak than sense to hang off. Witness a scene dying and no one here with the wherewithal to save it.'

He asks if Ryan remembers when clubbing used to be the only thing that mattered, when they'd spend all week only waiting for the weekend so they could get mashed and feel like they were part of something. For a twenty-five-year-old, this is fervent and dubious nostalgia. Ryan tells him he remembers, though he doesn't. The scene choked on its vomit well before he was legal. Well before Colm was legal.

'Money won,' Colm says. 'DJs started charging a king's ransom just to turn up for an hour on a Friday night, like there's something noble in coaxing idiots to dance to bad trance. So why would you bleed two hundred euro subsidising . . .' His nose wrinkles. '. . . EDfuckingM when you can gather your mates and the same shite you were listening to two years ago and get blasted in the comfort of your own home? Meanwhile I try to convince my overseers that they need to put enough on the table to book a few decent names and all they do is get ornery and tell me there's no room for risk. No room for risk! In fucking dance music? Oh aye, dead on. So I'm setting up my own night for those of us who still want to get fucked on music without over-priced drinks and overfuckinghyped DJs.'

He stands up straight. He drums his palms off the railing and spins to watch Dan.

'I'm going to get him a drink,' he says, and heads off again, and Ryan uses this time to gobble the first of Dan's pills and then, as Colm makes his way back, the second. Ryan knows he should not be out in this mood, but out is what he's stuck with, stuck here on account of duty and of the chemicals already in his body. He is in dire need of contentment, or if not contentment then a sort of oblivious swell. He wants respite from the anxiety of his fermenting hangover.

Colm gives Dan his complimentary drink and Dan claps him absent-mindedly on the arm.

Colm returns to Ryan and says, earnestly, 'Are you in?'

'Am I . . . ha?'

'In. With me. On my venture.'

'I know nothing about running nights, boy.'

'I've heard your mixes. You're better than you think you are. C'mon, I'm hundreds of miles from home and you're my wee local genius.'

The LED beams kick up. The rays cut through the gloom and the strobe goes on. The dancers jerk and the DJ pulls in a massive breakdown, Tiësto-like, contrived for maximum messiness from people who have no clue how to let go.

'OK, I'll be honest with you,' says Colm. 'I've put thousands of my own money into this project. I've sorted a venue, I've sorted a licence, it's all lined up. But the guy who was supposed to be my partner has fucked off on me, and I have to admit it, I'm in dire straits, Cusack.'

'Why'd he fuck off?'

'He fucking emigrated, the cunt.'

Below them, dancers hold their wrists over their heads and drag the lights back and forth.

'What d'you think I can do for you?' Ryan says.

'I need someone with me on this, and you're as gifted as you are connected. I know that sounds mad cheeky, so it does, but the time for diplomacy passed weeks ago. And honestly, I would have asked you to play a few sets even if the other lad hadn't fucked off to Canada. If I'd have seen you at all in the last few weeks I'd have been bending your ear about it.'

'Did you ever hear of a Credit Union, Colm?'

'Listen, everything happens for a reason,' says Colm. 'I think this was always how it was supposed to go. I'm not looking for a loan; I'm looking for accomplices.'

'You're looking for an introduction,' Ryan says.

They watch Dan charm his little audience.

'Aye, well, no flies on you,' Colm says.

One of Dan's girls breaks rank and settles onto one of the balcony's leather couches, and in this brief disorder Ryan re-enters; he stands beside Dan, he leans in to him, he says, 'McArdle's got something he wants to run by you,' and though they cannot hear these words, the girls – tipsy and effervescent – seem interested in the dynamic.

Colm's is a short pitch. Ryan does not hear the details. Even after the talk of gifts and genius, the pitch is not his concern. Dan will be interested, or he will not; he will ask for Ryan's opinion, or he will not.

Now he feels it at the back of his head. The pills are coming up on him.

Colm is counting something on his fingers for Dan and Dan is nodding along.

Ryan blinks. He feels his lashes lift from his skin. His throat relaxes. His pupils flood. The euphoria surges from the floor to his calves, to his thighs, to his groin, his belly, his shoulders. Dan grasps Colm's shoulder and turns back to the girls. Colm, smiling, whirls a wrist with the music. Ryan chews the notes and forces them down, like they might moor him, like the music might stop him spinning back into the dark. He is alarmed at how quickly he's coming up. This goes past euphoria; this is a wild loss of perspective and parameter.

'You're fucked, are you?' Colm roars in his ear.

Ryan drags a hand over his mouth and holds on to his jaw.

'It's looking good,' Colm goes on. 'The thing with Dan, I mean. Though whatever's done this to you is looking good too, just saying.'

'I'm going out for a fag,' Ryan says.

'Aye, I'll go with you,' Colm says, and apparently does; Ryan has lost the capacity to notice. He finds himself out on the smoking area, fighting the flame of his lighter; he finds a girl rubbing his back; he finds himself being told by a bouncer to get himself some water; he finds himself convinced he is going to die; he is impressionable and defenceless; he is concerned only with the shapelessness of this experience. 'Dan was looking for you,' Colm says, at some point; the dance floor is clearing; there are people fetching their trodden coats. Ryan is holding a bottle of beer then, in a corner booth with all of the lights on. 'There better be a party now,' Rachel is saying; Ryan's hand is in hers, on her lap. A taxi spin, during which Ryan closes his eyes and Rachel puts her head on his chest; he cannot mind; his body doesn't feel like his own. A party, then, or some bleak gathering. Ryan has never been so lost.

'I don't know what I'm doing wrong,' Rachel says.

'What?' he says.

They are in a bathroom, standing very close. Ryan moves her hand away and does his jeans back up. 'Fuck,' he says, and looks into the mirror over the sink and it seems everything is outlined in the thinnest silver strip. 'We could just go to my house,' Rachel says.

'I need to go,' Ryan tells her.

'OK, let me just get my coat.'

He does not wait for her. He walks, holding his jaw and rubbing the palm of his other hand over his thigh.

He comes to the footbridge at the end of Bachelor's Quay, where the river twists to take its final run through the heart of a sodden city, still fading in and out of reality, as if the air is thin here and he can move between a Cork in which he must deal with camorristi and drug routes, and no Cork, no Cork at all.

He climbs onto the steel parapet of the footbridge. He creeps out to the halfway point and stands with his toes poking out over the swollen December water. Behind him there's the night, empty buildings and gutted townhouses and the hush of those dreaming and dead drunk. In front of him, the lights of the hub, far enough away that if anyone was up and wandering they wouldn't see him, a shadow on the steel.

And bad enough he's here. Bad enough the gloom that bested him at the October bank holiday weekend endured through the winter, through his girlfriend's placation, through cannabis smoke and his own lost patience. Bad enough to be taken by surprise by his own product. But now he's singing, like a lad who had something to sing about.

Aimless mash-ups: Patrick Wolf, Sam Cooke, Murder by Death, Joe Goddard. His mind is wandering like his centre of gravity. *If I fall*, he thinks, *I'll end up very wet.*

Or very dead, and it's the either-or that stalls him. He can swim like a fish and if he falls in and does the clockwork front crawl out again, all he'll get is a sopping walk home, coming-down-slash-coming-down-with-pneumonia. He doesn't feel like swimming. He feels like creeping out of his skin, casting off his past; they'll find him propped against the parapet in the morning, peaceful, papery-thin, and go, 'Ah, poor Ryan. But wasn't he always losing bits of himself?'

The air has teeth and his feet are numb. He makes fists and tucks them into the sleeves of his jacket. He is singing. Under his breath or at the top of his lungs; he doesn't know.

'What do you think you're doing?'

Ryan turns his head. There's someone behind him, and she is not made out of whiskey and chemicals, nor does she look as if she's come through where the air is thin. He thinks he might ask her to prove it, but his tongue sticks to the roof of his mouth and in sliding his jaw to free it he loses his balance and there's a moment where the steel shakes and his stomach flies up his gullet and then he falls flat on his back on the bridge, hitting his head and sending the night sky spinning.

She stands over him and frowns.

He sits up so fast against the parapet he bangs his head again and she sighs and repeats,

'What do you think you're doing?'

He pushes himself vertical, scraping shoulder blades on the latticed parapet, and the woman traipsing city streets in the middle of the night scowls so hard her brow falls down on top of her eyes.

'Well?' she says.

'Well what?'

'Well, what do you think you're doing?'

'Nawthin'.'

She honks. 'Oh yes. Great times we're having, when you meet young fellas making eyes at the Lee in the early hours. Doing nothing. What would your mother say?'

Ryan thinks it unlikely his mother would be up for a conversation, being almost a decade dead. He starts telling the woman that he's not here swaying because of his mam, then gets sideswiped thinking that he is here because of his mam coz that's the point of mams, and his jaw hangs open halfway through the sentence and he rolls it and remembers to shut up, being, as he is, knee-deep in fucked.

'What's your name?' she says.

Ryan once had a fine portfolio of mocking identities built before the guards started recognising him and the social workers stopped trying with him, but with his head pounding so, he cannot remember even one.

28

So, 'Ryan,' he says, and she waits till he follows up with 'Cusack'.

'What in God's name are you at, Ryan Cusack?'

She has a voice stung by thousands of cigarettes and this face on her like some heavy hand started at her forehead and wiped her downwards. *Oh grandmaw, what big teeth you have.*

He hopes to Christ he didn't just say that out loud.

He might have. She glowers.

'Come on,' she says.

And she starts walking.

3

It is still dark when Ryan gets home; the first of the morning buses passes him at his front door, its windows glowing, the heads of its few inhabitants bobbing as if their necks have snapped. Ryan gets to his bedroom, lies down and shuts his eyes. This is loss of consciousness, but not rest. He sees shadows of a nightclub crowd, grasping hands, fag ash on the kerb, an older stranger who led and berated him. The images lose form and ebb as the chemicals do and slowly he realises that his phone is ringing. He opens his eyes. It stops. He rolls onto his side. His phone starts ringing again.

It's Karine, and she is fit to murder him.

'Where are you?' she says.

'In bed. At home.'

'Are you sure?'

This via a sarcastic howl, but he raises himself onto one elbow and looks around with one eye closed, just in case this is not his room in the two-bed terraced house he rents with his first cousin, Joseph, who has a job, a daughter and nineteen months on Ryan.

'You know I have an exam on Monday?' Karine says.

'Yeah,' rubbing his eye.

'So why were you ringing me at two in the morning, literally bloody speechless, Ryan? Do you know how much energy I wasted gathering the cop on not to go looking for you to bring you home? Oh my God,' she says, then 'Oh my God' again.

'I'm really sorry, girl,' he says. 'The drink went to my head.'

'That was drink, was it?'

Ryan lies down again.

'I just want to get back to normal,' he says.

But what's normality, he asks himself some hours later, if it's not a capacity for dealing with the fact that nothing's normal? No situation is trustworthy, no condition is fixed. Normality: I can take what's thrown at me and laugh hard doing it. I can take drugs I can down shots I can fuck ould dolls I can talk shite I can walk through my own fucking city without checking both shoulders every five fucking steps.

He sits in his father's kitchen just after lunchtime with his phone in his right hand and his right hand on his lap, staring down at Karine's last message.

So what will it take? Physical threats?

So he has to sit now and wonder what she means. Like, is she talking about his father? Knowing, with preternatural intuition, where he is, is she trying to drag him backwards five years so she can shame him into compliance? As if Ryan wasn't clutching the walls already.

'Don't get me wrong,' Tony says, roughly. 'I'm happy to see you out and about.'

Across the table he pauses, looks at Ryan, then back down at his cigarette papers.

Ryan taps his mobile screen to keep it active.

'It's just you should be taking it easy,' his father says.

'Spa breaks, that kind of thing?' There's physical effort in being a smartarse today.

'There's nothing wrong in wanting you to be all right, is there?' asks Tony.

'I am all right.'

Tony shakes his head.

Behind Tony, on the kitchen windowsill, is the electricity bill Ryan's come to take care of. Its letterhead is unfolded and propped against the glass. There is something deliberate about this; it's been days waiting for him.

Ryan rests his forehead on his hand.

'God knows I don't get to tell you what to do,' says Tony. He sparks up his joint. Ryan's eye falls to a robust smudge of forest green in the middle of the tabletop: the baggie he's just brought his father. Ah, Ryan's dopey dad. Giving out to Ryan for being a drug-dealing scumbag while smoking all his weed.

'But that said,' Tony goes on, 'you hit a brick wall at Halloween and that shouldn't slow you down, it should stop you.'

At this point Ryan might once have reassured his father that all he does is buy a little bit extra and pass it on to his buddies, and that he stretches to his car insurance through DJing and barely passable stock music production. Post-Phelan, such tender falsehoods are pointless.

'I'm fine, Dad,' he says, automatically, though he is not fine. He's hungover. Beautiful pills won't kick too hard the day after, but whiskey and lager and cannabis and tobacco and a double drop of something of yesteryear quality – that's the kind of carry-on that will fuck a man up.

The problem with beautiful pills is that the city isn't used to them, the city won't be ready for them.

'None of this is fine,' says Tony. 'It's not normal.'

'What's normal?' asks Ryan, who has just made his own definition, and suspects his father might, given appropriate time and space to think about it, agree with him.

Tony exhales. They accidentally make eye-contact through the smoke and look away again, like two lights flicked off at the same time.

'You were such a smart young fella.'

But now Ryan can't help frowning at him, for a horrible, twirling moment cut loose from the ballast of his disintegration.

'You'd run rings around anyone, Ryan, and all you want to do is chase your fucking tail.'

Tony looks to the kitchen door over his son's right shoulder. His eyes narrow as he takes another drag. Ryan wonders sometimes when he watches his father smoke if that's what he looks like when he makes his way down a joint – inappropriately stern and focused. It seems such a bitter thing to Tony. And aren't they the same, him and his dad? Aren't they both ebony-topped bruisers disposed towards sullenness with a capacity for dragging down with them women they don't deserve?

'I think of you out there . . .' Tony says, and shakes his head.

Ryan puts his phone in his pocket and his head in both hands and stares at the kitchen table.

'And what would I do without you, Rocky?'

And isn't that it? Tony Cusack could yet again get himself tangled up in some Phelan-driven catastrophe and where would he be without a son at whom to lob the problem? Sure as far as he knows Ryan's a willing murderer.

At least it concerns him. He struggles, he is agonised, and to his son his anguish is both bitter pleasure and a kick to the nuts.

Ryan wants to confess to him. He wants it as much as he's ever wanted anything; he can feel the weight of it. But he can't confess to him. His father thinks he's a killer and he has to let him, because the reality is worse: he's a failure. Jimmy Phelan handed Ryan a task in an ultimatum: Ryan gets rid of the girl or Phelan gets rid of his father. Ryan hates Tony Cusack, he hates him with a passion that keeps him up nights, but he loves him more than he hates him and he hates himself for that.

'So many stories in this city,' says Tony, 'of young fellas . . . taking their own lives and headlines then about who had theirs taken from them and all I can think is that I could still be one of those fathers making statements to the *Echo*, couldn't I? I'm

33

glad to see you out and about, Ryan. But I was more glad to see you locked in.'

Ryan pushes his chair back and crosses behind Tony to get to the bill on the window.

Tony's embarrassed. The back of his neck is red below his wavy dark hair. He hasn't yet got much grey, despite his hand-knotting, his insomniac episodes, the many flus brought on by worry and whiskey.

Ryan takes the bill back to the table and lays it flat and counts notes onto it.

'Are you not going to talk to me, boy?' says his father.

'I'm all right.'

'Don't you tell me you're all right, when six weeks ago I was holding your fucking hand while you slept off an overdose!'

They stare at each other. Tony thinks he sees defiance and so he yields, but really Ryan just doesn't know what to say to him. Tony won't believe him if he tells him he doesn't think he meant to overdose. All the sorries in the world won't stack against it, in any case.

He leaves his dad to his weed.

As soon as he passes through the gate outside an imp, shorn-headed, freckled and glowering, skitters up and says, 'Ryan, I minded your car for you.'

'Aren't you the berries?'

He scrunches his nose. 'You've to pay me,' he says.

'I do yeah.'

He pulls a face and runs off and when he's a safe distance away he shouts, 'I'll bust your tyres next time!', snaps his teeth together and hunches down at the kerb.

In the driver's seat, Ryan taps:

Charming

Karine returns fast as a slap.

34

You put up with threats from Dan to keep you
in line but it's a travesty when anyone else
does it, is that it?

Logical fallacy

You think you're so clever.
No one's laughing Ryan.

The small fella is still by the kerb, staring, one hand knocked to
his forehead in an unintentional salute.

Ryan sits for a minute, a minute and a half, staring back.

Cian comes out of the house, down the driveway and into the
passenger seat. He's as dark as Ryan is, taller and already broader,
though he's almost three full years behind his brother. He's culti-
vating a bit of a beard; Tony has taken to calling him *Fuckin'*
Pirlo, which Cian is pleased with. His are wide-set, lively eyes,
those of a boy acquainted with many private scandals. He reaches
for the clasp that slides the seat back and says, 'Story, boy?' and
through back-and-forths they determine there's no real story but
their father and their business. The latter is knocked out of the
way first. Ryan has to be concise. Cian's Italian isn't as good as
his; the young fella needs the practice. Collection points and
times are identified as Cian rolls a joint. They sit there then,
watching the light contract, smoking, sporting till the words run
out. Ryan loves his brother but he's in no mood for banter.

'Did I tell you there's new yokes coming in?' he says.

Cian opens his mouth and the smoke bulges. 'What're they like?'

'Savage.'

Cian is pleased. 'Daycent,' he says.

Ryan corrects him. 'Savage.'

The double meaning is a portent, but maybe Ryan's overthink-
ing it. So the city is unused to such chemical riches, grand, nine
times out of ten the quality will be a nice surprise.

35

He reminds himself it's not his problem, checks Karine's last message again and texts back:

> Ok I'm being a cunt. This isn't doing either of us any good. See you later on?

She doesn't answer.

A catalyst, Colm explains, is something that starts a chemical reaction while staying itself on standby. That's what his night is all about – throwing people together, giving them space to lose themselves. Catalyst, Cork's edgiest club night, every second Saturday in the refurbished function room of the old Riverbank Inn on the quay. They'll kick off the hedonism just as soon as they're solvent enough.

This is where Dan comes in. 'It's great timing,' he says. 'New pills, new market, new laundry. Have I ever told you' – he puts an arm around Ryan, laughs and squeezes – 'how fucking delighted I am that people tend to like you? They'll give you the freedom of the city yet.' He does not mention their night out, Ryan's inebriation; Ryan takes it to mean he didn't look as mashed as he was, or that Dan was too busy making the moves on one of his young wans to care. And there is no real need for alert security yet. Later, when the Shades and the shams get wind. Later, when the robber baron circles.

On Tuesday Ryan pokes about in the Riverbank Inn's DJ booth as Colm tells Dan about the strings he had to pull and promises made with fingers crossed behind his back. He tells him about negotiations with DJs both hot and coasting on sagging reputations, young guns he's bringing in from the UK to play for four blistering hours, Dublin legends who seem up to travelling to the Real Capital for a taste of high-living down south. He leaves room for Ryan to conceive of warm-up sets and website mixes. While Dan structures the enterprise so that he can pump money through it, Ryan can be its soul. Its resident artist. Its in-house dreamer.

'Kane is the banker but we are the catalyst,' Colm says, back at his own gaff. 'We're going to set the spark on this city and sit back and watch it blow.'

Ryan can't concentrate on the chemistry lesson. He stands by the window in Colm's living room, hoping cannabis will calm him enough to think positively about Karine's insistence on him switching careers.

I'm a DJ so, he imagines telling her. *How's that? Just, I need to keep dealing till the DJing funds itself and funds me and funds my dad and funds my car insurance and funds every holiday you've ever been on as a grown-up.*

The city's got its Christmas coat on, an extra layer of colour, another line of defence against the dark. The lights below trigger notions of fixing things with more things; Ryan has some bits and pieces bought already, ordered online before the haze swallowed him. He could do with buying more. A hotel suite, a pair of shoes, something sparkly. He conjures his girlfriend, bright-eyed and beaming, surrounded by wrapping paper.

The Christmas lights should trigger his wanting to go on the tear. A few pints, a few shots of Jamie, a few rough scratches for this itch. He doesn't want to go out but neither does he want to sit talking shite with Colm, whose own stoned state is of the inventive kind. Ryan takes his leave, promising to mull on strategies but feeling a bit unglued.

He cannot retire from dealing and DJ at Catalyst. He cannot retire and stay in Cork. *Once you get into this shit they don't let you out again.* He smiles, involuntarily, as he remembers his grandmother complaining very recently that it was a terrible thing that young people couldn't expect a job for life anymore. His Irish grandmother. He doesn't know what the other one complains about: she makes the most of what time she gets with her first grandson; she tells him he's beautiful and sends him struffoli at Christmas.

He knows that if he did turn his back on Dan, he could take off to Italy and his mother's family would welcome him, at least till they discovered the extent of his moral corrosion. When his nonna asks what, precisely, he's doing with himself, he always tells her he's engaged in making eminently passable stock music and assures her he hasn't given up on his piano and can in fact play Rachmaninoff, blindfolded, with just his elbows.

But Karine can't call Ryan a mess in Italian, and he doubts she'd be keen on his teaching her.

Maybe there is a perfect token out there. Maybe if he finds it and brings it home to her she'll understand, she'll wait for him. He knows it's a ludicrous notion. But maybe. *Stupidity tries*, he tells himself, and then he can't remember where he heard the term, whether it was a dream or a retort.

He drives home but has to pull in some yards from his front door to watch a gaggle of neighbours cluster round men in hi-vis vests and hard hats. Irish Water meter-installers, accompanied by Gardaí, opposed by round-bellied compatriots sick of bearing new burdens. There are people with cameras and mics. Stoned and supine, Ryan gazes out at the rírá and decides to make himself scarce. He can't see the guards' faces, but there are those locals who get off on pulling him over and wasting his time. There is, too, the menace of vigilantism, a mood easily stirred by any spot of community activism; he hears it sometimes in the pub or on the radio, or reads it in Facebook comments, *pushers need nothing but a kneecapping, let's arm ourselves with iron bars, let's fucking do something about it*. He knows some of those round-bellied sentinels, and they know him.

He drives in the opposite direction. When he reaches St Luke's he gets out of the car and stands with his elbows on the roof.

Tony used to bring Ryan here when he was small; there's a big green and benches; the streets are especially steep. He watches

38

his city sparkle, the hills spill into a lake of light. He knows he is meant to look at Cork and feel great hunger; he is expected, in his line of work, to have ambitions of ownership.

He thinks about the new pills. He imagines himself telling his buyers to warn the users *Go easy, this is good stuff, Balearic-level stuff.* He'll have done then all he's able to do. He'll wash his hands. He'll get richer.

When he gets home the workers and guards and protesters have moved on. He sticks on a saucepan of ravioli and eats it going from the kitchen to the sitting room to his bedroom. He cannot sit still. He tries fiddling about with a track he was building earlier in the year but he can't lock into whatever groove inspired it. He has a joint. He clicks through YouTube.

He picks up the notebook Karine bought him. It's mostly empty still, bar the notes of a sequence he wanted to capture for his track, the beginnings of playlists, and, in the back, a kind of he-doesn't-know-what to his mother or about his mother. But he doesn't want to look at that.

He only starts to go under after three in the morning. He lies with his hands curled on the pillow in front of his face. He drifts off and jerks awake again. Falls under, catches himself falling. He worries about Karine and the worry becomes a dramatic piece; she turns to him and snaps and he dreams how he feels about it. He wakes again. He gazes at his hands and thinks about songs falling asunder. Hammers, keys and strings warp and splinter while his fingers left-click and right-click and he wonders why he can't build tunes out of bad samples and cyclic glimpses of Reddit. He fails his musician's hands.

But you're not playing, are you?

Freefall, a sudden fluttering in his chest. He's wide awake.

You're the musician, says a crone all-knowing. *But you're not playing, are you?*

39

4

Ryan decides the next day that he's grand. Why wouldn't he be grand? Coming back to work after a period of coke-born malaise would tangle anyone's grey matter. Clearly whatever it was that powered his capacity for building tracks has been remapped to his late-night imagination, which is why he's conjuring reproachful old dears from yoke dust. The final, manic visions of his post-depressive state; that's it, that's all it is.

In this span he stretches old muscles and revives bad habits. He conducts the sale of half a kilo from one of the many flats Dan has access to. They are usually suburban one-bedroom boxes; work has started again on the previously derelict site across from this one, and Ryan takes twelve-and-a-half grand from a lower-rung dealer over the sounds of heavy machinery and shouting.

He meets Dan in the Watercourse Road house to deposit his twelve-and-a-half grand for laundering. Dan is there with Shakespeare, who has a minor update from the customs guy, mostly involving a hint for a few extra quid. Dan is still in good form. 'Suppose it's worth it,' he says. He counts Ryan's notes and takes all but a slim sheaf. 'A bit of pocket money,' he says. 'Enough to keep you going till I can sort the rest.'

'Though the mills of God grind slowly . . .' drones Shakespeare.

On Friday night Ryan meets Colm at Union Studios, where Colm is running a Room-sponsored service that involves taking the ragged dreams of the talentless and stitching them into a couple of hours' studio time, five commemorative professional photos and a keepsake CD. 'Give your beloved the gift of delusion this Christmas,' he grumps.

They bump into Triona outside the control room. 'Hey, Ryan,' she says, evenly; this city is littered with the bodies of women he accidentally fucked.

'Story, Triona?'

'Usual craic. What are you up to?'

'Being led up the garden path by this fella.'

'He'll do that.' The indoor heat has made her heavy-eyed; she rubs her palms over her cheeks and one of her earrings catches a strand of hair. She's got five or six years on Ryan. It's been two since they had their thirty-minute rapture; he doesn't recall much of it, only that it was the culmination of a drunken night of eye-contact and innuendo and that she'd just come back from Santa Ponsa and had tan lines on her arse.

'Are you around the day after Stephen's?' she asks.

'Probably.'

'I'll have a little remix for you. Something trancey. Generic. We had a singer-songwriter in this past fortnight. Her manager wants the lead to come with a bouncier option. Right up your street.'

'What, trancey and generic? I think the world of you too, Triona.'

She makes a face. 'Call down then. I'll be here all day. Happy Christmas.'

Ryan and Colm sit in the control room and discuss setlists. Colm's mind is on tech-trance, touches of progressive house for warmth. Deep is in, Ryan tells him. He fucking *knows* that. Deep is fine for Saturday night dollies but it's not going to engender radicalisation in anyone, is it? Colm doesn't want customers; he wants disciples.

He enquires as to the chances of Ryan throwing together a quick-and-dirty mix that he can promote on the new website.

'Even if you have something already that might suit,' he says. 'From the last six months, maybe.' Ryan hasn't been hearing all that much since Halloween, and so this is a timely challenge.

But these are just short bursts of hustle to break up long hours of waiting for orders, deliveries, go-aheads; his days stay manic and depressed in cycles.

So it comes to the 23rd of December, the night the pills are due. Karine wishes to unwind, post-exams, so she is heading out with her friends. Ryan tells her that he'll be there. He makes this promise in the early afternoon without knowing whether or not he'll be able to keep it, but Dan is happy to give him a few hours' grace. 'It's not like you can courier,' he says. 'Too many guards too fond of you. Go to Karine. Give her her last ever ride with a man of middling prospects.'

Colm, too, has been on at Ryan about going out, insisting they should be making their intentions known to the jaded city. This is a thing to be done without Dan Kane; Dan can never be the face of Catalyst. This is how the city works.

Karine and Ryan meet encircled by her heavenly host in a Grand Parade pub draped with twinkling white lights and green boughs. She glitters in pale patterned pink. Her hair is sunlight on snow. She kisses him and rests her head on his chest and he knots his hands through her loose curls and moves his lips to her forehead and shuts his eyes and inhales.

They stand in a thicket of old school friends, people Ryan sees all year round and people who've left for fairer shores. The former ask him how he is and for updates on their favourite inebriants. Smoke, coke and yokes: St Paddy's modern trinity. The rest do a lot of whooping. Between the three-bodies-deep bar and the floor-to-ceiling windows there are stories, jokes and flippancy wrapped in basslines of a lazy DJ's choosing. Ryan buys a round. He downs a Jameson at the bar and brings a second back with the rest of the drinks.

'I'm,' trills a man clutching the bar in a stiff polo shirt. 'Dreaming.' He straightens and spreads his arms. 'Of a white. Christmas!'

'And you'll fucking stay dreaming!' someone roars.

Karine rolls her eyes and smiles. Ryan smiles back.

Colm comes in, spots Ryan and pushes over, grinning, focused. 'Bout ye, comrade!'

He makes his own introductions to those who don't know or don't remember him. He tells them about Catalyst. Karine turns to Ryan.

'What did I just hear?'

'Yeah. He's starting a night. I'm giving him a hand.'

'Musically, you mean?'

'Yeah.' There'll be a better time to tell her the whole truth. When she looks less angelic and feels less like she belongs to him. He watches her pull the concept apart and appraise it. 'I have to do something with myself,' he says. She cocks her head. 'So I'm told,' he adds.

'Why would you keep this a secret?'

'I wasn't trying to.'

She bestows on him a thin smile.

His phone vibrates. He pulls it out, intending to kill the call, but it's Dan's name on the screen. Karine is staring at Colm. Ryan squeezes her side and goes to the door.

'Where are you, little man?'

Ryan lights a cigarette. 'Out. Having a couple in the Annex.'

'What's it like down there?'

Ryan looks behind at the open door. 'Fairly mental, like.'

'Stay where you are,' Dan says. 'I need you to do one small thing for me and then, d'you know what? We should have a drink, because the occasion demands it.'

When Ryan goes back inside Karine is still staring at Colm like he's a scout from an army advancing on her sideways.

Ryan orders another whiskey and joins her. He watches the door and she notices.

'What's wrong with you?'

'Nawthin'.'

Under his palm her side is smooth and warm. He flexes his fingers and feels her give way to him and tries to record how that feels because as soon as Dan walks through those doors she is going to fucking kill him.

Dan arrives with Shakespeare twenty minutes later. He locks on to Ryan's eyes as he walks past and Ryan exhales; it feels like he's been holding his breath for hours.

Karine stiffens.

'What?'

Anger stills her against a bright and swimming background. 'You brought Dan down?'

'I can't stop him coming here, girl.'

She shrinks from him and folds her arms.

'Don't overreact,' he says, softly, for around them their cohorts strain to hear the details of the row.

'To the man who nearly killed you?' she says.

'Ah now.'

She chops at the air between them. 'He represents something that nearly killed you, Ryan. And you bring him out with us?'

'Just let me say hello to the man. I'm still with you. I'm here with you,' Ryan says, and waits until she snaps, 'Do what you like.'

He pushes through to the stairs at the end of the bar. There's a smoking terrace on the first floor, filled with space heaters and wicker tables. Dan stands at the far end with Shakespeare at his side. 'They're in,' he says. He hands Ryan a phone. 'Call our buddy in Italy. Tell him the stuff is through.'

Ryan goes out to the lane at the side of the pub and makes the call. He relays the message in Italian. His new colleague replies in Neapolitan, and this is fine, Ryan tells himself, sure why wouldn't you add another layer of obfuscation to such a dangerous conversation if you had the means to do so?

'What now?' he asks Dan, once he returns, though the what-now is evident; both Dan and Shakespeare are holding drinks, standing by a small group at one of the wicker tables. The hand of a girl with cartoonish red hair rests on Dan's. Perhaps this is one of the girls from Room, perhaps not. Ryan cannot remember.

'Cooney and Feehily are at the port,' Dan says. 'Once they give me the all-clear we'll get the stuff here. Gina'll do the job, nice and quiet. So we raise a glass, and when Pender gets here we'll raise another one.' He presents Ryan with a tumbler of whiskey from the table behind him. 'A very surreptitious "to us",' he says, and there is wary acknowledgement in Shakespeare's expression, a quick glimpse of the man's teeth.

They drink.

Colm appears at the door of the smoking area and Dan nods at him and says to Ryan, 'Not now, tell him,' and so Ryan finishes his whiskey and joins Colm to put him off. Colm doesn't take exception. He doesn't seem to want to prod or take great stands; he might do all right out of this partnership, Ryan thinks.

They go into the toilets and squish into a silver cubicle. There are no cisterns, for prudent reasons. Colm slides a bankcard out of his wallet and with its corner scoops a dose from a baggie.

'Everything all right?' He puts the bankcard to his nose and sniffs.

'Up here it is. When I go back to my ould doll she's gonna blow me out of it, though.'

'Aye, she's cold as,' Colm chokes. 'I don't know what you did but she's got a face on her.'

He pushes the bankcard at Ryan.

'What didn't I do?' Ryan says, and does a bit more.

He goes down to the main bar with Colm but hangs back from the horde, and even from behind a mass of strangers and another tumbler of Jamie he can tell the mood's changed. Their friends gather around Karine, moved by her beautiful eyes and her trembling lips. Ryan's in the wrong again.

Pender arrives.

Jason Pender, a long-time client turned collaborator, is full sure he's now important enough to run with his suppliers. Custodian of so much of the trade in West Cork, he's been known to disappear between the hillocks whenever his grand-standing tests the patience of men bigger and scarier than he is. A volatile prick, but a prosperous one, and that's an attribute that's gotten him further than should ever have been allowed. In Ryan's opinion, anyway. It doesn't escape him that it might be loathing swollen by ego; Pender thinks of Dan and Shakespeare as partners, but Ryan's only a grunt to him and it's plain he can't fathom a reason why Ryan would be privy to their pacts if he wasn't acting as Dan's bodyguard or, very lately, translator.

Ryan goes with him to the smoking room. Dan flashes his canines and sends Ryan back to the bar to get another round. Ryan orders and swallows a final – and he means it – Jameson.

Ryan suspects that he is not a natural reveller. It is not that a dealer's life is lived in pubs and clubs as a matter of course, but Dan is happy around night-time glories, and Ryan follows Dan. More than this, though; making music in this sphere seems most doable, whereas making music in a concert hall is unthinkable, in that if Ryan thinks about it he becomes tense and resentful and indefensibly sad. It does not escape his notice that he was set for something other than this, that his mother had laid such foundations. Instead of playing and composing on piano Ryan does it on a monitor; instead of practising he is out on the lash.

Shakespeare, too, is uncomfortable in pubs and clubs. Pender looks awkward in the city. Ryan is more than a decade younger than both of them and looks so much more like he belongs in places like this but it is hard to live up to it sometimes. *Tense little fucker*, Shakespeare has called him, more than once and to his face.

He gets back up to the smoking terrace with the drinks, and something has gone wrong. Pender and Dan stand in each other's space. The tip of Dan's forefinger bends back against the centre of Pender's chest. A confidence has been badly twisted.

Ryan puts the drinks down. He tries to catch Shakespeare's eye but the other is immersed.

'Nothing gets into Cork without J.P.'s say-so,' Pender is stressing. 'We give him the nod now, we get access to his markets, his contacts in the ports.'

'Clearly plenty gets into Cork without J.P.'s say-so,' Dan says. 'I just went and fucking proved it.'

'The big lads come down on top of us and we are going to lose, boy.'

'If I wanted to collaborate with old men like Jimmy Phelan,' Dan says, 'I wouldn't have opened this channel at all. Are you so thick as to not recognise that?'

'Are you so thick as to think it's a climpy task from here?'

'There must be something wrong with my ears,' says Dan, 'because I'd swear you just called me thick.'

'Just a notion,' Pender says. He slouches, but Dan is riled now; he takes a swing at thin air. Shakespeare holds a calming hand up for the rest of the room, though he does not look back. He continues staring at Dan and Pender. It is Ryan's task to look around, and some people have noticed, one girl in particular who makes exaggerated expressions to her two friends, but no one is gawping, and no one looks too disturbed.

'Just a notion,' Dan says. 'A thought suspiciously cautious for a reckless tool like you, Pender.'

'What's that supposed to mean?' Pender says.

'It means I've to ask myself who you've been talking to already, boy.'

'No one,' says Pender. 'Who'd I be talking to?'

'Who'd listen to you, is what I'd ask under normal circumstances. But then, after what I've just done, I'd imagine there'd be a lot of shams out there willing to listen to you. Get the fuck,' he says. 'Get the fuck out away from me. I've no more to say to you, boy.'

Pender begins to state his case. He steps up to Dan; Dan turns his back. 'What the fuck, Dan,' Pender says. 'I've never said anything against you.'

'Get him out of my face,' Dan growls at Ryan.

This is done with no small exertion. Shakespeare must get involved too and in tandem they get Pender out of the door and down the stairs. Pender turns on Ryan at the bottom. He's an ugly creature. Husky, provisionally normal in the clothes his ould doll buys him, bristle-chinned and dopey-eyed. 'Cusack,' he says, 'you can't think that made any sense.' He does not address Shakespeare; he knows entreating Shakespeare would be a waste of time. And when Ryan is undemonstrative he changes his tune; he snaps, 'Or didn't he teach you to think, Cusack?'

Shakespeare raises his eyebrows, points Pender to the side door, and heads back up the stairs.

'Job done, is it?' Pender says.

He turns back to Ryan.

'Is this "job done", lap dog? Right so, fuck off back to your sugar daddy, coz one more step and I'll personally help your balls drop for yeh, how's that?'

Ryan pushes his nose to Pender's.

'Say that again.'

Pender pushes Ryan and Ryan lashes out, but Shakespeare, rushing back in, catches his arms and tugs him backwards. Off-balance, Ryan slaps the wall and Pender stretches as if he had something to do with it.

Dan comes down the stairs, his steps heavy and slow.

'Don't think I don't appreciate your devotion,' Dan murmurs, 'even when you choose to show it in a city centre pub, in front of half the county.'

48

Ryan doesn't even say he's sorry. He feels like he's about to cry, and that is profoundly embarrassing, profoundly Tony-Cusack-inspired, profoundly Ryan-but-not-Ryan. He and Dan stand by the fire exit in the lane running at the side of the pub. At the end of the lane, where it joins the footpath near the front door, is the flame-haired girl. She poses impatiently, one leg stretched and hands on her hips.

'I tell you to walk Pender out and you challenge him to a duel on the staircase? What the fuck's gotten into you, Ryan?'

'Nawthin'.'

'Don't tell me that,' Dan warns.

'Karine's scrapping with me, is all.'

'Why would you let that intrude on shit between you and me?'

'I don't,' Ryan says. 'I wouldn't.'

Shakespeare comes out the fire exit and bumps its door off the wall. He flakes past, professionally heedless. Ryan starts to bring his hand to his mouth to chew his nails, catches the action, makes a fist instead and drums it off his thigh.

'You can't let these young wans throw little apocalypses at you whenever they feel like it,' Dan says. 'D'you need a minute to stick your hand down your jocks and feel around for your balls?'

'It's not that.'

'It is that. So many places I could have been tonight but I came here, because I trusted you to look after me. Don't tell me I was wrong.'

Through bricks and mortar Ryan can hear bass; its tempo times the swelling and shrinking of his chest. 'You weren't wrong.'

'And yet I continue to have to bend the fucking rules for you.'

'I've had a couple of drinks,' Ryan mutters.

'Ah yeah, blame the sauce. Look, little man. If I'm out for the night, whether socialising or jawing with certain or sundry snakey pricks, I take solace in the fact that you will always back me up. If the drink jeopardises that, then don't drink. Of all people you should know that.' And there. He hauls Tony Cusack out of Ryan's head and into his bollocking.

There's only the hint of a grin. 'Ah. You don't like that, do you?'

'It doesn't matter what I like or don't like,' Ryan says.

Dan draws away. 'I'll talk to you tomorrow,' he says. 'I need to get my head together, so on that note I have things to be doing. Specifically, things that are pouting because her counterpart, and my second helping, is after getting the hump because of Pender's conniptions, and fucking off in a taxi. Go back in there and sort shit out with Herself. I can't be dealing with your hormones.'

Herself. Light of Ryan's life. He thrusts through braying obstacles – fellas with sleeves rolled up to show off bad tattoos, girls who bulge out of neon dresses, scowls and winks and elbows in profusion – and the surplus of seasonal lights picks out every grubby prospect from this end of the bar to the other. She is where he left her, but now there's a new man at her side, not one of the group, not someone's boyfriend or brother or a stray friend drifting in from the periphery; Ryan can tell. He's on the same course Ryan would be, if he were out trying to reel in something tasty.

He moves closer to talk in her ear. He puts a hand on her back.

Ryan lands beside them and the stranger's hand twitches and falls.

She just watches.

'D'you want something?' Ryan says to the hunter.

He has the sense to look self-conscious. 'What?'

'You've got your paws on my ould doll there, boy.'

The stranger puts his hands up. 'Jesus, it's not like she's wearing a badge.'

Karine turns on her heel. Ryan catches her just beyond the door, in the chamber between the bar and the bouncers. Her fist closes as he takes her wrist; she purses her lips and flops back against the wall. There's a poster to her right advertising a New Year's shindig. Stock images of ould dolls dancing in purple silhouette. 'See, you get possessive,' Karine says, 'but you have no right to.'

'Era no, I don't. Who the fuck is that langer?'

'Just a boy. Y'know? Boys? They sometimes try to make friends on nights out?'

'You think he was trying to befriend you? That's fucking comical.'

'Well I guess you'd know how to spot a prick's skill set, wouldn't you?'

Ryan places his left palm on the purple dancing girls and leans over Karine and she pouts at him.

'I was only gone a few fucking minutes,' he says.

'It was not a few minutes.'

'It was work. It was necessary. And I'm meant to be able to trust that you won't go advertising as soon as my back's turned.'

'You're a fucking scumbag,' she smiles. 'You are a real fucking shit. D'you know what you can do now? Go scuttle after Dan and see if he has a shoulder to cry on, because I'm done with you. I'm fucking done with you.'

She tries to slide past him but he brings his right hand to the wall, the other side of her head, and stares her down, and figures out that she means it. Her eyes flare. She rips him open, reaches into his belly, gets her hand around his stomach and squeezes.

'This is how it is?' He coughs out a laugh. 'On the 23rd of December? After a rake of drink?'

'I've had two, Ryan. How many have you had?'

'What's it matter, if you're finished with me?'

'Oh, right. I forgot that me worrying myself sick was just an inconvenience to you. You're right. I'm not your nurse. You keep self-harming, Ryan. I'll get out of your way.'

'See, this is more of it!' She tosses her head and Ryan slaps the brickwork. 'Everything's over the fucking top now, Karine. I did the dog on it, OK? I stuck the GNP of Bolivia up my snout. But it's done. I told you. And all I'm getting from you is one fucking declaration after another on how hopeless I am and how I need to change every single fucking thing about myself to make you happy. And OK, look, I'll fucking admit this too: I nearly belted you.' Her shoulders drop. 'And you'll never let me forget it,' he continues. 'I didn't belt you. But for fuck's sake, the way you go on, I might as well have.'

'What is that supposed to mean?'

'Just what I said,' he says. 'You need to let me move on from it.' But he's fucked it and he knows it. She pushes his chest and he falls back. 'Karine,' he says. His arms hang at his sides. She rushes to the bar door and stops.

'We're done, Ryan. But don't let that stop the spiral. Have another Jamie, sure. Or another line. Or another slut. Or . . .' She rolls her eyes theatrically; the tears are coming. 'Or are you just going to go home and kill yourself?'

She disappears into the throng and he goes the other way, out past the bouncers and onto the street.

And stands then. And mouths. And makes fists.

He stands for maybe fifteen minutes before he thinks *I need a drink and I need a line*. Just to mitigate the shock. Colm's still inside, chatting up the wall-eyed masses on their supposed joint behalf. Like Ryan cares for engineering the city's debauchery now.

He moves to the side of the building and the top of the lane. He looks along its black and tan path. The city makes its racket around him. He wants to run and he's afraid to run while she's still in there.

He glances back at the door and there's a girl side-on to the bouncers, her hands hidden by the waist-height barrier behind her, looking at him.

'Are you OK?' she says.

Ryan tilts his head.

52

'No,' she says. 'You don't know me.'

She reels him in. Smoky eyes under strong brows, a blood-red cupid's bow, mocha hair curling over her shoulders. She watches him watch her and she chuckles and sighs as if it's all very amusing. 'Hi,' she says.

'Story,' Ryan says back.

'Are you OK?' she says again.

His hands are embarrassed out of fists. '. . . No.'

'Something told me you need to be asked. I'm Natalie,' she says.

His jaw drops a second before the sound comes out. 'Ryan.'

5

Sometimes Ryan wants to remind Cork City that it can't hide its nature from him. He wants to stand on Patrick's Bridge and roar at both north and south banks *Don't think I don't have the bones of you!*

This city, like all cities, hates its natives. It would rather be in a constant state of replenishment than own up to what it has warped. Ryan sees it well enough: the tribes in town, hipster baristas and skinny suits and the tides of students pushing the rest of them back up the hills. Ryan gets it: who'd want the likes of him who sullies all he sells to, except those who need to buy? But the men who sleep on the street are alcoholics, the girls who stop you and ask for money are alcoholics; that's Cork's damage, Ryan thinks, he didn't do that. People lose their jobs, people can't pay their rent; he didn't do that either. And still when his compatriots see the veneer of the city crack they peer through only to identify him as the culprit. He is too blatantly urban, his accent's too strong, his gatch is too arrogant.

But this girl Natalie is from another Cork, a glossy, artsy, vibrant Cork and she skips down its streets.

He follows her because she tells him to and she asks him, huskily, why he's so sad. He tells her his girlfriend's had it up to here with his shit and she says *Fuuccck* so he looks at her with his mouth open, hoping in a wild and dangerous way that she'll clutch his hand. They get a paper cup of coffee in one of the late-night Centras and sit in the sharp air by the river at the end of the Parade. Ryan gets the feeling that one day someone will ask him, 'What did you talk about?' and he'll barely remember. You talk enough and soon enough none of it matters; it's all just words, pauses, silence-and-sound. Especially if you've had a dab and you'd tell her anything to stop her leaving. Not that he's lying to her: Catalyst, Colm, Karine, the failing heart in a half-finished tune. Not the full truth, either. He might be locked but he's not crazy.

She turns towards him on the bench and plays with her hair. She gathers it behind her head, leaves it go to swing loose, gathers it again. She's a landscape expertly composed, an hourglass accentuated by a high neckline and a pinched waist. She conducts an interview. The right words in the right places, the right tone to bowl him over.

She asks how long he's been with Karine and he tells her next March would make it six years.

'Wow,' she goes. 'That's forever.'

He thinks of eternities as the air crystallises and the pubs start to close. Far behind them, at the other end of the Parade, his ceremonial sometime-buddies may well be spilling onto the paths, shrugging coats onto their shoulders, deciding on after-parties. He thinks of Karine among them and on her sharply perfect face he sets an underbite of sullen fury.

What's left of his coffee is at the temperature of saliva. He squashes the paper cup.

In danger of sobriety and with no shortage of words left to tell each other, Natalie picks a late bar and they go there, still at fingertips' length. The place is made up like a burlesque house. The smell of old velvet, polish and hops. The lights down low. He buys her a brandy. She checks her phone and laughs that her friends have gone home without her. He texts Colm and asks him what's happening. Parties, he's thinking. Chaos to hide and feed the hunger. And she smiles at him. She moves closer and she smiles at him.

They stand by a wall decked with mahogany picture frames holding photos of cellists and brooding guitarists and busty singers with their heads thrown back. She leans in to his ear. 'You seem a lot happier.'

'Was I that miserable-looking?'

'A beautiful tragedy,' she says. 'Lost on a footpath.'

He buys her another brandy.

Whiskey-drenched laments about his girlfriend and stop-start assertions about running club nights taper off. She comes with him to Colm's party. As ould dolls dance and Colm rakes out lines on the surface of his iPad, they talk about music. She goes on about Nina Simone and asks if he thinks EDM is the new classical. She doesn't believe him when he tells her he plays piano. She sits forward on the thin leather of Colm's landlord's couch and examines his hands.

'They're far too nice to be musician's hands.'

There's that term again – *musician's hands* – but he's too fucked to focus on it.

'What were you expecting? Claws?'

'I don't know. Maybe. All knuckles and veins.'

He traces his middle finger down the length of her palm.

Colm drops carefully to his haunches in front of them, present-ing the iPad. 'Ladies first,' he says, and Natalie takes the offering. It's a forthright action that bypasses the usual dance – *D'you do drugs? Are you OK with this?* – and Ryan is glad for it. He settles into his own line and wonders if she feels the same relief.

An hour after that he stands with her in the wan light of the apartment complex hallway and takes her hands. She tilts her head back. 'Are you going to kiss me?' she whispers.

'Yeah. Are you going to come home with me?'

'Yeah.'

From there to a taxi backseat charged with greed to the hall-way at home where coats are yanked off each other's shoulders. Her kisses are hungry; her teeth clip his. In his bedroom she pulls his shirt over his head, she dances fingertips over the end of his spine, she goes for the top button of his jeans. He unwraps her with rough regard; her body is soft where his is firm; he grips her arse and pushes his mouth into the side of her neck. Behind her his bed lies unmade. The duvet folded up and curled back on itself. The sheet puckered.

'Aren't you worried at all,' she asks, 'when you've only just met me? When you don't know what kind of girl I am?' Her eyes are ocean-blue in the brown and orange shadows of his bedroom. She stands in a puddle of their clothes, her hands on his chest. 'Don't you think you should ask me,' she whispers, 'whether I'm likely to return you to your girlfriend?'

He leans forward and she lies back on the bed under his weight; he rests one knee between hers and an arm either side of her head; she sinks; fabric is tugged down over their hips; she reaches for him, closes her hand around him; he probes; he pushes her thighs apart; she pants, 'You have got a condom, right?' and the temporary focus of this lust collapses and she can see it in his dopey pause.

Joseph's not home. Out on his own campaign, Ryan supposes. Naked and clumsy, he hunts through the chest of drawers in his cousin's bedroom. Ryan doesn't have a problem with the concept of safe sex; it's just that he rarely has to have any. Long-term girlfriend benefit; it's Her Thing.

Her Thing, his loss. He finds a box of Durex. He catches his breath. He just stands for a minute. He figures Natalie is currently bolt upright thinking of ways she can escape from the man who's so ill-equipped to deal with his own reality he doesn't even keep condoms in his room. The humiliation rides on the wallop from withdrawal and he curses the loss of momentum; he asks himself what he's doing; he reminds himself he's doing whatever he fucking likes. He scowls and makes fists. He hastens back to his bedroom and she looks at him from the dusk of his sometime-prison and his bad decisions.

'I just noticed your tattoo,' she says.

'Oh.'

'It's sexy. How long have you had it?'

'Couple of years.' He gets some tunes on, a bit of 65daysof-static, something to spit the emotion back into the room. That she mentioned the tatt is a secret catastrophe. It's a brushstroke dragon which stretches across his shoulders and whose tail ends in the twin forks of a flicked 'K'. Karine on Ryan's spine.

'It makes you look like a UFC fighter,' Natalie says.

She sits up. His duvet slips down onto her lap. She slides her hands over his hips and brings him to her mouth. Catastrophe evaporates. He closes his eyes and hears conflicting rhythms: the pounding of keys over drums – *pesante*, *fortissimo* – his breathing, his heartbeat.

She pulls back then and waits for him to prep and follow. Once he's lying down she slides on top of him; she encourages him to yield; she straightens. He catches her elbows.

'No,' he says.

She blinks.

'I don't like that,' he says.

He rolls her onto her back. He holds her hips. He pulls her against him and looks into her eyes and her gaze flickers away. She looks at his throat, at his mouth, back at his eyes. Her lips part.

And so this, like so many of Ryan's fuck-ups, begins with ecstasy.

You'd probably think you're too strong an Italian mother to like Karine D'Arcy. Stereotypically speaking, you'd have hated her. You'd have thought she was a pale bitch who couldn't cook. But you can't hide behind stereotypes now that you're dead. It's hard enough to find you as it is.

Just I have a confession for you. Dad only realised I had a girlfriend after I turned down Italy to be with her.

We got together on the night of my fifteenth birthday and three weeks and two days afterwards

We. Fucking. Did it.

I know, you'd have reddened me, I was too young, I know, I know.

Know how I know? Coz it was fine for a couple of days after that, and then she got really, really odd with me. She was convinced now that we'd Done It that It was all I'd want from then on, so she pushed me away every time I got near her. She kept this up for over a month, happy one minute, eating the head off me the next. And sure I couldn't work out what was going on, I was fifteen, I knew nothing about anything. Joseph cottoned on to it and made it worse, he knew I'd gotten in once and then been locked out and he said I was either lying about having done it at all or too young to know whether I'd actually gotten all the way in or that I was so shite at it that she'd gone frigid on me. He had my fucking head wrecked.

We had this blazing row in the end and she actually went far enough with it to make me cry, which I thought at the time was going to kill me. It's the most embarrassing thing, breaking down when you're fifteen. But instead it fixed everything. She knew then that what I said I felt for her was real. Like I was in love. She made me go Bam! All over my body. All the time.

Anyway, Dad didn't know about it until the end of the Junior Cert and the start of the summer holidays, when we'd been together nearly three months. My nonna phoned my dad with the usual invitation and he came in then to me and Kelly in the sitting room and asked if I was doing Napoli for the summer (the offer would have been open to Kelly too, but she was well on her way to becoming a heritage-evading megagowl at that point). And I had to say, I don't think I will this year.

My dad nearly passed out and then Kelly jumped in with He doesn't want to go coz he's got a gurrrrrlfriennnnnd.

Dad took it well. It's no odds to the dads, is it, whether their sons have ould dolls or not? You though? I can't imagine you'd have taken to her so quick, because she was the girl I was giving up my Italian summers for. But then, you were gone long before I was old enough to have a girlfriend, so I don't really know how you'd have taken it. I mean, you were odd with Italy, I remember that, so maybe you'd have been happy I was too busy meeting Karine to go over. I don't know. That's the problem, isn't it? I have to make it up based on stereotypes.

6

They come down sharing a couple of joints, engaging in sparse chat. Natalie tells him about her Masters in accounting and her adventures thus far on her year off. She's just home from London, where she'd finished her trip with a twenty-fourth birthday Shoreditch blowout. She spent last summer travelling across the continent. She tells him about her older brother in Melbourne, who's an accountant, and her parents, who are both accountants, and Alf, her golden retriever, who's probably an accountant too. He tells her about Italy, about DJing, about trying to catch the melodies in his head.

She orders a taxi just after seven and dresses, smoothing down creases, combing her fingers through her hair. He pulls on a pair of trackies. They draw a line under their rendezvous. She holds his left hand, plays with his fingers.

'I really respect what you and Colm are trying to do,' she says. 'Everyone else I know is freaking about their Masters or their internship and that kind of thing doesn't even register with you, does it?' She hangs back and smiles. 'Show me your phone,' she says, and sways her hand under his chin.

He places his phone in her palm and she gets her own, calls up his number in a couple of taps and types it onto her screen.

'There,' she says.

He walks her to the front door and kisses her goodbye. She holds on to his waist. 'I had a really good time,' she says. And then, 'Are you OK?'

'Yeah,' he says, 'course I am.'

'Nearly six years, though,' she says. 'Wow.'

Inebriation ebbs and its detritus knocks its code on the back of his skull.

Ryan wakes alone at lunchtime on Christmas Eve, stretches, breathes deep, remembers, deals reverently with his erection. He showers. Back in his bedroom, he opens his half-finished track on a whim and a way forward flickers. He tries to feel fortunate. He tells himself that it would make perfect sense to feel fortunate, but his conscience will not be hemmed in by convenient, perfect sense.

Karine, bright-eyed and beaming, surrounded by wrapping paper.

Don't call her, he tells himself. *Don't fucking call her.*

Jesus, he tells himself. *Jesus Christ, she told me to go home and kill myself.*

He flexes his fingers and plays a full piece on his digital piano for the first time since his shell cracked and the blood and guts of Tony Cusack came through swinging and he used his musician's hands to pin his beautiful Karine to the wall by his bedroom door and tear the wings off what they had.

He calls her. He turns his back on the bed in which he's fucked a surrogate and waits for the ringing to cut to voicemail, and he leaves her a message made up of sorries and deep breaths.

On his computer screen that spark stirs, waiting for him to breathe life into it.

His phone rings and he jumps, relieved that Karine's resolve has collapsed so quickly.

But it's Shakespeare, who says, 'Who were you talking to?'

'What?'

'I rang you just there and it went straight to voicemail. Who were you talking to?'

Shakespeare does not usually ask such questions – if he did, Ryan would usually tell him to mind his own fucking business

– but there is an odd nip in his voice, and so Ryan replies, 'My ould doll. What's the matter, boy?'

'You better not know.'

'What are you on about?'

'I'm on about the present your Italian friends sent us.'

'Yeah?'

'Because it's been fucking pinched.'

All fifty thousand units. Shakespeare spells out the details slowly, as if he's had to practise relaying this bad news several times to be sure of maintaining composure: Gina drove down this morning, picked up the packages and took the back roads into the city, but just before hitting Rochestown she was pulled over by three fellas in balaclavas and relieved of the entire batch.

'Fuck.'

'Fuck is right,' Shakespeare says. 'So you better get over here.'

It's not everyone who gets an invitation to Dan's house; it's open only to confidant-bodyguards, men in whose presence Gina feels safe and Dan feels important. Even of these chosen few Ryan is a special case. He has slept on Dan's couch when he was hiding from his father, he has been fed and watered here, commiserated with, minded.

Gina's been with Dan at least as long as Ryan has, at least seven years. She couriers only when it's important; Dan doesn't like to put her in jeopardy. She opens the door of their city centre gated development home with a sweet, 'Hello, stranger.' She looks calm, but she's had some hours now to calm down, Ryan supposes. She's in leggings and flats and a loose bun. Gina loves her comfort; it's rare he sees her out of pyjamas. She's been good to him. If she ever objected to Dan taking him on and taking him in, she never let it show.

'Are you back to yourself, hon?' she asks, as he steps in. Her meaning's apparent in her gently troubled expression. It's hardly a surprise to Ryan that Dan tells her shit, but he's embarrassed.

'Ah yeah. It was only a breather; you know how it goes.'

She squeezes his forearm.

'Are you all right?' he asks.

'Oh, no harm done to me. It's Dan who was targeted, really.'

She points him to the kitchen and she goes into the sitting room. There are sounds of merriment when she opens the door; she has pals over. Moral support while the men wage war. In last night's cruel words Karine may have saved herself from such a life: growing used to threats from the world her man moves in, putting his business ahead of her peace.

Ryan joins Dan and Shakespeare in the kitchen. There's a pan of mulled wine simmering on the hob. It smells warm and rich so Ryan thinks of drunkenness and the spice in an unexpected and illicit fuck. This is an involuntary reflex; he is green from drink and sick with nerves.

'You took your fucking time,' Shakespeare says.

'It's Christmas Eve,' Ryan says. 'It's busy out.'

'Fucking wind your neck in,' Dan says to Shakespeare; he, too, has had time to calm down.

He adds little flesh to the bare bones Shakespeare offered. He draws out Gina's route and identifies the spot she was held up. He describes the packaging the pills came in and confirms that Cooney and Feehily were the ones who checked them over.

'No one but us knew the route was there,' says Dan. 'Me. You. Shakespeare. Cooney. Feehily. My customs guy, but he's a rogue for the high stool, not for this kind of shit. And Pender. So you tell me, Ryan. Which of our nominees is going to get a bullet to the brain?'

Ryan winces.

'Yeah, you have an idea,' Dan says.

'That being the case,' Shakespeare says, 'I don't know why we're sitting around here talking about it. Unless, Dan, you're wondering if we don't have a choice of suspects. Pender, coz you kicked the cunt out. Or Cusack, coz you let the cunt back in.'

Ryan gapes. 'Are you for fucking real?'

'As for fucking real as I am with anything in this game, Cusack.'

'Ryan has nothing to do with this,' Dan says. 'I'm as sure Ryan's clean as I am Pender's a dirty thief.'

'And see,' says Shakespeare, 'that's where I think you're soft in the head, because I don't be sure about anyone.'

'You wouldn't be trying to out-think me?' Dan says. 'Has that ever worked out in your favour before?'

This shuts Shakespeare up; Ryan doesn't know why. This is one of the many secrets of his and Dan's relationship, dredged up when either needs to make a point.

'Don't take me for a fool,' Dan warns Shakespeare.

'Let's say you're spot on, boy.' Shakespeare slaps the table. 'Point remains, what the fuck are we doing sitting around here?'

'Maybe I don't get my hands dirty on Christmas fucking Eve, boy.'

Dan goes to the hob and stirs the wine. From the sitting room there comes a sudden chorus of 'Stand By Your Man', replete with piercing twangs and ended with a sole, ridiculous hiccup. A beat, then ferocious laughter. Shakespeare's nostrils flare.

'Or maybe,' Dan goes on, 'I want to see who moves next.'

'Ah, fuck off,' Shakespeare cries. 'Nicking our stuff isn't enough of a move for you?'

'I want to know if the next step is an effort to take the route.'

'Pender? That gowl has a hard enough time taking a shit, let alone a fucking route.'

'Which is exactly what gives me pause for thought.'

'My thought is I want my fucking stuff back,' Shakespeare says.

'You'll get your fucking stuff back,' Dan says. 'And when you do, you'll know exactly what kind of landscape you'll be selling it in. Doesn't that make sense to you?'

Shakespeare stands and tugs his jacket on. 'This is fucking mental.'

'Have I ever steered you wrong before?' Dan asks.

Shakespeare doesn't reply. He stalks out. Ryan makes to follow him but Dan beckons, tilting his head. 'Let him go,' he says. 'I need to run something by you.'

They wait until the front door closes and a bit more after that, till Ryan's throat dries up and he begins to swallow in pulses. Dan leans against the kitchen worktop. His gaze drifts; he is a man having a conversation in his own head. Finally he turns to Ryan.

'He went sparring with you on the way out the door last night,' he says. 'Pender.'

'He was fairly pissy, like.'

'Coz I was on to him, wouldn't you say?'

Ryan nods.

'Remember,' Dan says, 'I told Pender last night that his sudden grá for Jimmy Phelan was a bit suspiciously cautious?'

'Yeah.'

'D'you think I was right?'

'This shit's proved it really, boy.'

'Yeah,' Dan says. 'But would you have thought it of him before this shit?'

Ryan says, slowly, 'I wouldn't have thought he'd be able to think that far ahead.'

'So J.P. knows about our route, would you say?'

'I dunno, boy.'

'Jesus, Ryan, do I pay you to stand around looking pretty?'

Ryan throws his head back. 'I can't speculate on what J.P. knows or doesn't know but I wouldn't have thought he'd make subtle advances through Pender if he did know. Like he'd come out swinging.'

'Unless he had only half a story. Unless he was trying to get more out of Pender and Pender was shitting himself, hence coming to me, trying to pass it on before he got burned. This is bothering me, boy. This kept me up last night.'

'You were right.'

'Yeah. Yeah.'

Dan straightens. He runs a hand over his head.

'Look, I'm going to bury Pender,' he says, 'but before I bury him I have to find out if the fool, so suspiciously cautious, is working independently. I'm certain Cooney and Feehily would have neither incentive nor balls to try me. But still, do me a favour, get the lay of the land. So long as you don't let on to Shakespeare. I don't want him knowing I have cause to think twice about him.'

'You're hardly doubting Shakespeare, boy?' Shakespeare's been Dan's partner for a decade, more even.

'That's fucking good of you, Ryan, because Shakespeare wasn't at all reluctant about doubting you.'

Ryan turns this over in his head and finds the truth in it. He says nothing.

'I need to know whether I'm dealing with a pair of secessionists before I do anything else,' Dan says. 'Then there'll be bridges to cross. And fuckers to drown under them.'

The double doors to the sitting room open and Gina comes through holding three glass mugs. She smiles and says loudly that she's only in for the refill.

Dan pats Ryan's cheek. 'Don't you lose the head on me,' he says, softly. 'We sit tight. We'll know the score soon.'

Gina leaves the mugs on the worktop by the hob. 'Are you having a drink, Ryan?'

'Thanks, girl, but I've to scoot on.'

She gives him a hug instead. 'Happy Christmas, honey.'

Ryan has plans beyond happy Christmases. Whatever about late nights and lie-ins, or occasional crumblings, a man of twenty years cannot achieve what Ryan has achieved without some savvy – he is doing all right for himself, and Dan tells him this often. One day there'll be enough of a nest egg to assist his evolution from brute to rascal. There'll be music, live hopefully, maybe synthesised, depending on how lucky he is. There'll be Karine. There'll be a gaff of their own once she graduates – they've talked about it many times. There'll be a ring after that. Or a baby; the order's unimportant, only that it happens, and Ryan believes it will.

On Christmas morning he showers and shaves and dresses in snappy gear and stands in his hallway for a couple of minutes with his eyes closed, breathing through his nose. Then he drives himself around the bend to his old terrace with two bottles of Jameson, a slab of Carling and a bunch of presents for his siblings, even the one who thinks he's the greatest fuck-up to ever blaze a trail through a brittle home.

She's in the kitchen, grinding salt over spuds in a roasting dish. The promise of roast poppies is scant reward for an afternoon of Kelly Cusack's verbal carnage, but today her brother is a masochist.

'Good of you to get out of bed,' she sniffs.

Ryan slaps two fifties on the worktop and slides them towards her and she says, 'What's that?' to which he replies, 'What's it look like?' to which she retorts, 'Ah, a bribe?' to which he suggests, 'Donate it to the charity of your choice then' to which she huffs, 'Make yourself useful and peel those parsnips.'

Tony's already been drinking, as is his tradition, but today Ryan, Kelly and Cian keep him company. Cathal sneaks a can of lager. Everyone pretends not to notice. Niamh and Ronan pour Coke into wine glasses and dance in their chairs. Cian talks with his mouth full. Kelly glares at Ryan and Ryan counts patterns on his plate and his dad, his poor dopey dad, sits and swigs and occasionally suffers a forkful of turkey and though Christmas in this house has been shit since Ryan was eleven and newly motherless it's worse again this year because Kelly thinks

68

he's selfish enough for suicide and his father thinks he's a murderer.

He slips his phone in and out of his pocket in ritual, watching the clock on the screen, and when the dinner's done he goes out and sits on the front wall, sparks up and calls Karine.

The air sets freezing beads around car windows and gate latches, and Ryan's joint takes neatly, and the smoke tastes just right.

'I was wondering when you'd call,' she says.

'I called yesterday. You didn't call me back.'

There might be truce in the sound she makes in reply.

They meet an hour later over at his grandmother's house for the post-feast assembly. Karine is a favourite of Ryan's grandmother because she's nothing like him and Nana Cusack hopes that might be catching. She gets a glass of wine and a kiss on the cheek. Ryan gets nothing; he brought his own alcohol.

In his nana's hall Ryan gives Karine her presents.

'I know you're after breaking up with me,' he says, 'but . . .' Shrug. An inchoate smile.

He waits for her to say *About that* but she doesn't. She tries on her bracelet and smiles at her perfume and hugs her iPad to her chest. In the living room his extended family put up with indigestion and each other. *She's a lovely girl*, Ryan imagines his grandmother confiding. *Much too good for him.*

'I got you something too,' Karine says, and as he unwraps it she sighs, 'A book. For a boy who doesn't read.'

It's a heavy yoke. Daunting.

Sound and Silence: A Human Obsession.

Ryan turns it over.

'This is great, D'Arcy.'

'You don't have to be nice about it. It's supposed to do you good.'

The story of music – it says on the back – *history, science, and culture.*

'No,' he says. 'It's really great.'

'It wouldn't have been right not to give it to you.'

He puts it gently on his nana's hall table. Karine allows him to slip his arms around her. 'I'm sorry,' he says.

'For what this time?'

'For the other night. For Dan being there.'

He rests his forehead on hers and closes his eyes.

'I'm sorry for saying what I said,' she whispers. 'About you going home and . . .'

'It's all right. I was acting the maggot.'

'No, Ryan . . . I had to see you today because it would have felt horrible otherwise but . . . I'm sorry for how I spoke to you but that's just the little problem. The big problem hasn't gone away.'

He's afraid to open his eyes. He stretches one of his arms up her back, to her neck. Their noses touch. He feels her breath on his lips. He forms the beginnings of appeals that wither with the drink and her melancholy. This isn't how it was meant to go.

7

Halfway through St Stephen's Day, Dan texts:

Nothing happening little man. Keep the head.

So Ryan digs out a mix he'd been playing around with just before Halloween. He takes it apart on the computer monitor and over the next few hours rebuilds the thing. *Tech-trance*, he reminds himself, *and disciples*. He scrawls the words in his notebook. He builds the thing and it is a beautiful thing: a ninety-minute taster of rhythm and heart. Whatever Karine might say about him, Ryan can paint night-times from palettes of other people's songs.

His mouth is dry. He drinks a pint of water by the kitchen sink and brings a mug of tea back to his room. An intro passes a baton of beats. It gets persuasive. Ryan sits on his bed and starts rolling a joint because whether it's the tea or the hangover he's threatening to break out in a sweat. Behind his ears is hot, a point too on either temple.

He wraps up the mix and opens his half-finished track. Then he stands back from his desk and phones Karine.

No answer.

'This shit again,' he mutters, and sits back down and sups his tea and gets to building lines and arcs. The silence opposite needles, though.

Are you around

71

Back to the bassline. He tweaks the riff but his imagination struggles against the stillness of her anger. He phones her again and an hour later she texts back.

Not really.

That's your fucking response

Jesus Ryan what else do you expect me to tell you?

and he's desperate to come back with *Are you sending these from your iPad?* but he thinks better of it. In his head, his track reels off in a new direction. He holds his fingers a hair's breadth over his MIDI keyboard and mimes a new riff.

Are you going out

Yeah. But to someplace not Ryanish.

What's ryanish

Heavy bass + drugs + sweaty shirtless dickheads
trying to stick their hands up my dress
+ toilets with slugs on the walls + Garda raids.

Funny

Its not really. You have a good night.

'Oh, I fucking will,' he says, to his empty room.

He taps his fingers against his desk and his mind turns back to cocaine. He has enough to spend the rest of the day holed up with Cian and Joseph, snorting rails and talking shite. Though there are advantages to hitting the town. He's a free agent, apparently.

72

'Fuck.'

He can't afford another dreadful bout, not now the music's flowing.

His mobile rings. A flutter between his ribs and he grabs the phone, but it's an unknown number, not Karine's. Though what did he think she was going to say? *Oh Ryan! I'm so terribly sorry for calling you out on your failings! Can you ever forgive me for noticing how irredeemably fucked you are?*

So he answers with a 'Yeah?'

There's a pause, and then she says, 'Hi, Ryan.'

'It's so lucky I demanded your number,' Natalie says, round-eyed. 'Because all I could think about was how desperate you were to see me and I simply couldn't deal with the guilt for another moment.'

Ryan's response sounds more like a polite sneeze than laughter; this seems to please her.

They're at the merries in the Showgrounds. Her idea, and he was feeling suggestible. She wants to wander with him around the lights and the green-faced smallies and those things that are ninety per cent scarf and ten per cent student. She wants to watch him over twirling beams and between the ruddy features of the festive horde. And he is all for it, one hundred per cent on the side of opportune disruption with an implied, undressed conclusion.

'Also,' Natalie says, seriously. 'I was worried your girlfriend might have torn you to shreds, which is even more guilt. And once recovered, you'd expect me to be your rebound girl. My God, you're such an opportunist.'

'You're mad,' he grins, and she agrees. 'I stole you from a street corner,' she says. 'We are doomed to madness.'

She takes his hand and after a fidgety sconse three-sixty he settles into her touch. People whirl in the air above them, prisoners of mechanical beasts weaving webs from happy howls.

There's the smell of popcorn and the throb of bass. There are promises in neon.

'Ah,' Natalie says. 'This is it.'

This is a small caravan with crimson lights and silver beads in the window and a sign that says 'Fortunes Told' by its open door. He hangs back as she starts to walk over; their arms stretch as far as he'll let her go, and she falls back against him, giggling.

'Don't tell me you're nervous,' she says.

'Not a bit of it, girl. It's a load of crap.'

'Is it, Rebound Boy?' She widens her eyes. 'Who's to say I wouldn't like some reassurance as to whether I'm doing the right thing, allowing you and your fuck-me eyes to lay siege to my common sense? Madame might have some valuable insights.'

'Into the contents of my pocket, yeah.'

'She has the right to make a bit of money, and I have the right to be enlightened on your doubtlessly impure intentions.' Her head bobs and she looks up at him. 'Are you afraid that your dark purpose will be exposed, Ryan?'

'I think you already have the measure of me.'

'We'll see, won't we?'

Madame's eyes are lined with indigo; her fingernails, long and pointed, are painted to match. She is impressed by the length of Natalie's lifeline. Ryan supposes everyone who listens to this shite has a very long lifeline. That, and the likelihood of travel and fulfilment and everything else hazy enough to mark Madame as gifted in the ancient arts of commerce.

Natalie makes the expected noises. Her expressions make her giddiness evident; her eyebrows dart upwards, her ruby lips form perfect Os.

Ryan thinks about Madame's taxes. He wonders if one can register as a self-employed swindler or, if the transactions are cash-based, if one could launder enough through the gullibility of hen parties and the recently bereaved to make being a part-time waffler a cloak thick enough for full-time criminal

74

enterprise. But he's distracting himself from a leftover of his most recent blackout. He's chewing nails he bit beyond reaching years ago. There's a surge once again from that binge, words on a steel footbridge.

You're the musician, echoes an ould wan, thumb pressing down on his hand. *But you're not playing, are you?*

'Now,' yaps Madame, and she juts a palm towards him.

'You're grand,' Ryan says. 'Don't I already know I'm fucked?'

Madame is sourly triumphant. 'I get this a lot.'

'Do you?' asks Natalie. 'Boys who are absolutely zero craic?' and as the barb stalls Ryan, Madame grasps his hand a little too hard. 'Ooh!' she breathes, squinting. 'You're a derk horse.'

Two sets of winged eyes stare Ryan down. 'I'm not,' he says.

'You are. Ent you are a very private person. Not surprising to me that you come from a big femily.' Madame waits. Ryan says nothing. Madame squeezes. 'You don't want to reveal, do you? You hev a lot of secrets.'

'Sure I'm an open book.'

'You are . . .' She leans closer. '. . . a very inkry person.'

'I . . .' He leans closer again. '. . . am a model of compassion.'

'You think you are so clever,' she says, 'but no one's liffing.'

It takes Ryan a moment to recognise that this rebuke echoes Karine's, by which time Natalie has gently removed his hand from Madame's. 'Sometimes,' she says soothingly, 'people feel uncomfortable when the . . . mysteries of the future . . . are revealed! You must have seen this kind of thing before, Madame. Boys get nervous and then they show off.'

Madame sits up. 'People who hev secrets alveys get upset when they are beink found out. So missy, you vatch this one. He is a derk horse.'

They tumble out of the caravan. Natalie marches with one hand on his arm, the other in front of her mouth, and when they're no longer close enough to Madame's place of business to be overheard she lets go and hoots, 'Oh my God, did you *hear* her accent? I think she learned it from Red in *Orange is the New Black*!'

Ryan heads towards the car park and Natalie walks with him, punning and laughing as he tells himself *Calm down, you fucking idiot* and pulls tobacco smoke into his lungs. There's nothing Madame could have pointed out about him that he'd hidden. She deduced the scope of his family from his accent; he can't pretend he's from anywhere but the arse end of the welfare class. Dark horse? *She's the chatty one, he's got black hair . . . That's it, I'll call him a dark horse.* Explicable, not worth the jump. He uses the cigarette smoke as an excuse to turn his face away.

'Have you secrets, Ryan?' Natalie teases, as he looks out over the lights. 'It's OK. I have secrets too.'

She turns on the stereo when they get to the car and finds a station she wants to listen to. She settles into the space Karine left. She stretches, pushing that space out of shape. She flips the sun visor and peers into the vanity mirror, dabbing at her bottom lip. Ryan breathes in through his nose, out through his mouth, and pinches his forehead. Natalie opens her coat. She's in slim trousers and an embellished top that's skimming over her breasts, hinting at all sorts, and inside his head he pleads with her to let him in again tonight, knock him out and keep him there, safe from his secrets. She says something about the song she's singing along to, and it takes Ryan too long to realise she's expecting a reply. 'What?' he says. 'Sorry . . . What?'

'It doesn't matter. Hey.' She turns down the stereo. 'Are you OK?'

'Course I'm OK.'

'You've gone really quiet.'

'I am really quiet. I'm a dark horse.'

She cuts her laughter short when she realises it's a solo effort.

'Oh,' she says. 'Oh God. Did that *upset* you?'

'Course it didn't upset me.' In his head the scene splits into two and a parallel Ryan and a parallel Natalie peel off to the right and drive on the wrong side of the road back into the city. *For fuck's sake*, contradicts Parallel Ryan, *of course it fucking upset me. Didn't that bitch draw fucking stark attention to the fact that I appear to be somewhere far, far below you on the ladder, with my big fucking* femily *that she pulled right out of my thick fucking accent?*

Well, that's true, I couldn't help but notice that, sighs Parallel Natalie. *Also those secrets she claimed to spot on your open hand; what might those have been?*

None of your business, Natalie. Are we gonna have more sex now or what?

Oh, I don't think so, croons Parallel Natalie, with significant sympathy for the blueish tint in Parallel Ryan's Parallel Balls.

The real Natalie slides her palm onto his thigh.

'You never took me for a birthday drink.' Her fingers dance upwards. 'How about your local?'

'That's way up the Northside, girl.' And he's only half-talking about the pub.

'So? Will my plumminess insult them or something?'

'We're in town now, is all.' Ryan doesn't want to get it in the ear from a parliament of outraged mutual friends when it's discovered he's taken Karine's break-up too swiftly and literally. 'Besides, it's a long way home from the Northside.'

'What, you're going to send me home again?'

He looks over at Natalie but on the street to the right of her head there's a ghost. Ryan lamps her disappearing through a wide gate before he swings onto the path.

Natalie gasps. 'What—'

He opens his door and turns back with one leg on the road. 'Stay here, I have to check something out.'

'Check what out?'

But he's closed the door behind him and is flaking up the pavement.

The street hums with revelry but once he passes through the gate the bass fades and the rhythm ends. Tidy apartments around a tidy courtyard, leaves and branches clipped back from the paving bricks, not the kind of place left open to gawpers and gurriers. She should have closed the gate behind her. No doubt there'll be an earful pitched if anyone finds Ryan here. *See what happens, Missus Seer, when you leave the place wide open? Knackers skulking through our sculpted briars, dropping fag butts, scaring the cats.*

He sees her entering a doorway on the furthest ground-floor apartment on his left and he hurries, imagining screams. *God only knows what he might have done to you, girl! Great long weasel of a thing, and, I heard since, as known to the Gardaí as we're known to the bingo halls.* Her front door is open. *Bold as brass, the pup, walked straight through the door after her, Godsaveusandpreserveus.*

There's a whiff of cigarette smoke in the hall. She's through an open door to his right: a woman with salt-and-pepper hair and a fag between her fingers, wearing a beige expression and a beige coat, an extension of the grand bland couch she's sitting in the middle of.

'Well, Ryan Cusack. You got through the Christmas.'

The couch she's perched on faces the door and the wall behind her is covered in shelves, the shelves covered in jumble: books, ornaments, old records, baskets. The room stretches into an open kitchen. The worktops are scattered with shopping bags, cigarette butts, food.

'Oh for God's sake,' says its warden. 'Don't tell me the season's ripped out your tongue?'

'What?'

'Small mercies. How have you been?'

'All . . . right.'

She nods and smiles encouragingly and off his silence she heaves an exasperated sigh and says, 'And-how-are-you-Maureen.'

'You know me.' It's more question than statement of fact.

She gets it. 'Yes.'

'But I can't place you.'

'But sure you must have some idea, if you're following me in off the road?'

'No, I mean . . . I know we spoke. I know when. I just don't remember what about.'

She chuckles. 'Well, that doesn't surprise me.'

'Yeah. Look, I might have been a little bit out of sorts.'

'Is that what the young fellas are calling it nowadays?' she marvels.

'I mean, I could've been . . .'

'Rude?' she guesses. 'Aggressive?' She shifts on the couch and consents to a small comfort. 'You weren't. But you're a silly boy, Ryan.'

'Why am I a silly boy?'

'Threatening to throw yourself off a bridge strikes me as a pretty silly way to carry on.'

'Oh.'

Oh, she echoes.

'Things got on top of me for a bit there. I wouldn't have done it, though.'

'Would you not?'

'No. I mean . . . Look, obviously I owe you a debt of gratitude, like. And I'm sorry if I gave you a land. But there's stuff you knew. About me. Stuff I wouldn't tell you in a hape of fits.'

She doesn't even twitch an eye for him. He starts to massage his forehead.

'I've no idea who you are,' he says, weakly. 'But you scared the shit out of me.'

'Come in,' she says. 'What's the point in you standing there by the door?'

He edges into the room and stands with his back to the wall.

'Is this your place?' he asks. It's a nice apartment, but up in a heap.

'My son moved me in here,' she says, 'and no one's going to throw me out again. Is that enough of an answer for you?'

'Is your son here with you?'

'No.'

'Is anyone?'

'Not a soul,' she says. 'And I don't need anyone to be, either.'

'I didn't say anything.'

'You were going to.'

'I wasn't.'

'Not that it's any of your business, but this . . .' She spins her hand over her head. '. . . is part of a stand-off. Don't judge what you don't have the measure of.'

'I don't give a shit why you're living in a kip, all I want to know is how . . . Look, you said stuff about me.'

'What stuff?'

'Like that you thought I was . . . a bit of a scut.'

'Ah, get out of it. I called you a little gangster.'

'That, then,' Ryan croaks. 'How'd you know that?'

'Sure I can see right through you, boy.'

'You can't,' he tells her. 'I'm a dark horse.'

She throws her head back, then her chin tips downwards and her eyes come to fix on his. Hers are pale and staunchly narrowed; she rescinds her laughter. 'Who,' she says, 'told you that?'

'I might have been being a bit smart there.'

'Well I hope so. I wouldn't like to be running around the town thinking I was a mystery if I was as transparent as you are.'

'What's that mean?'

'It means,' she says, as if he's just come to after a head injury, 'that I can see right through you.'

80

'Yeah, I mean *how* can you see right through me? I'm not literally fucking transparent, am I?'

'You're crotchety is what you are.'

They gape at each other. Her face implies enduring scowls, deep lines either side of her nose stretching onto her chin, rippling out at the corners of her mouth. She's got his accent.

'I'm sorry.' He's not sure why he's apologising. It seems like the right punctuation. 'I need to know how you knew the stuff you said. It's wrecking my head, like.'

'I'll tell you what I told you the other night.' She stands and brushes down her lap. 'I know things.'

'Yeah, it's *how* you know things that's—'

'What if I told you it's a gift I got from a higher power?'

'What's a higher power?' There's a trick in there somewhere. 'A judge? My dad?'

'Oh, 'tis more than half-Irish you are,' she laughs. 'Are they the highest powers, when you're a little gangster? I suppose they would be.'

Hesitantly, he asks, 'What's half-Irish?'

Her reply is a solid, 'You are.'

She moves into her kitchen. Over her shoulder she shoots, 'You were a lot more receptive the other night.'

'I was a lot further off my face the other night.'

'Well, that's true. The fact remains that I know things because I know things. There's no science to it.'

'Are you trying to tell me you're fucking psychic?'

She fills the kettle and clicks it on.

'This isn't funny,' he says.

'Do you hear me laughing?' she asks. 'Though I don't mind telling you, Ryan, I'm very pleased to see you bright-eyed and bushy-tailed. I've been worrying about you. I'm not going to tell you I was up all night saying the rosary, but it's good to see you didn't go swimming. You know I went to the bridge on the two nights following our chat, just in case?'

Thanks is the automatic response but he sucks it back.

She throws a teabag into a mug. 'So I suppose you heeded what I told you, even if you can't remember it now.'

'Listen!' She looks on as he pushes himself off the wall and extends a warning finger. 'You don't go around telling fellas you think they're gangsters and expect them to be compensated in fucking fairy tales, d'you understand me? If you don't tell me where you got these notions you're forcing me into a corner and I am not likely to react well, am I?'

She smiles. Smiles!

'How would I be afraid of a musician?' she says.

He could have told her that; it's his favourite delusion. But he didn't tell her that. He remembers flashes and one was a flash of confusion as she told him *You're not playing, are you? You're not playing, little gangster boy.*

'Listen,' he starts again, but something's caught her attention. He looks over at the door and Natalie's standing there watching him, his car keys in her hand.

8

Trancey and generic.

The night after Stephen's, Ryan sits in his room building that remix for Triona. Like fortifying a castle with rubbish. Like spray-painting a butterfly. He wonders if the artist wanted this interference or if a manager inflicted on her his expertise. *Here's the thing* – he checks the file name – *Aimee. We must cover all the angles. Dance is huge. Sure the Americans can't get enough of it. And the drugs!* Molly, *they call the stuff. They don't even bother pressing it, they're in such a hurry.*

Trancey and generic is all Ryan can muster. His head's clouded.

There was little he could do. He'd made some small move towards losing the rag with Maureen and then Natalie came in after him and made shit of his temper. At which Maureen stood, mouth all to one side like she couldn't bring herself to scoff at such a simpleton.

'I'm coming back,' he warned, as Natalie stepped out the front door again.

'Sure I,' said Maureen, 'will keep the home fires burning.'

Little he could do there and then, because even though crazy seers may take him for an open book, well, a puzzle like that is a pursuit for the mind and Ryan was still up for the physical chase. Natalie came home with him, her curiosity too stoked for pub atmospherics.

'Who was that lady?'

He shrugged. 'Met her a few nights before Christmas. I was on the way home from a party and she was wandering around the city. Just wanted to make sure she was all right.'

His compassion proved quite the aphrodisiac.

Afterwards they had a smoke. Natalie sat on his bed with his duvet wrapped across her chest and draped between her legs. 'So, Ryan,' she said. 'So. Ryan.'

She slung out questions and was cursed with the occasional truth for her trouble.

'What did you do after school?'

'What I'm doing now. Bit of production. Bit of DJing.'

'Did you do a course in that?'

'Self-taught.'

'Did you do any courses at all?'

'I couldn't go for third-level. Didn't do my Leaving.'

A plume, exhaled thoughtfully, hung in the air. 'That's so Irish,' she said. 'When people don't engage with the curriculum, the procedure is, just let them fail.'

He looked up and she maintained her gaze, even after his furrowing his brow and shaking his head.

'Naw, listen, I *could* have done my Leaving. I didn't do it coz I got turfed out, not because I was too thick.'

Eyebrows raised and lips pursed. Then, 'You got expelled?'

'Yeah.'

'How did you manage that?'

'Drugs.'

Head back, mouth open. Curled smoke. A throaty laugh. 'I'm *sooo* glad you learned your lesson.' A slip of the duvet as she coddled the joint, just enough to expose one pale-rose nipple.

'Do you have any babies?' she asked.

A negative answer, obviously, and a short distraction as he wondered if she'd entirely forgotten he was only twenty. But only a short distraction because even after fucking her, her bare breast was doing him in.

So he thinks now, as he's taking such a cheap shot at her heart-felt song, about what kind of tits Aimee has. And that lazy notion takes him from his workstation to the internet, and that open landscape takes him to a couple of short films. Ah, this is the reason Ryan never gets a damn thing done. The ould dolls'll be the death of him.

After Natalie's interview he played her a portion of the Catalyst mix, and off her approval he played her his two-thirds of a track, and off her rapture he found the balls to play for real. He took to his keys and made a minor hames of Pieczonka's Tarantella; he started out rigid and nervous; he had to close his eyes to the task, drop his shoulders, roll his neck. Natalie was undone. She curled back on the bed with her arms over her head. 'You must have been playing your whole life,' she said.

'My mam taught me.'

'Lucky. My mum taught me nothing.'

'She taught you how to be an accountant. That's more lucrative.'

'As if a soul like yours is into filthy lucre. Oh God, I just keep corrupting you. Your poor girlfriend, Ryan.'

Aimee sings of falling for someone she never thought she'd fall for. Her voice, fragile and gutless, strains for an emotional wallop that cannot land. Her song's growing on Ryan, but it's killing him that she's not reaching where she needs to go with it. He plays along. He pushes her up with the piano and gives blood to her whispers. After a while something starts coming together that has little to do with Aimee's voice or her sentiments and it breaks away from the tune it was meant to cushion and begins to exist on its own.

He snuffs out Aimee's voice. He keeps playing.

It's coming up on midnight when there's a rap on the front door – one blunt thud, made by the flat of a fist, not the knuckles. Ryan lifts his hands from the keys. He listens. No guard knocks like that. He checks his phone for missed messages. No friend or dad or brother, either.

He goes down the stairs, hands in pockets.

It's Shakespeare, and he too has his hands in his pockets, though when he steps in the effect is not of nonchalance but of snake-like elasticity. This is a consequence of Shakespeare's gauntness; the man has learned how to carry himself, and he is stronger than he looks.

'Story, boy?' says Ryan.

'What's Dan said to you about these yokes?'

Shakespeare, at the bottom of the stairs, doesn't move towards another room, so Ryan shuts and leans back against the door. 'No more than he said on Christmas Eve.'

'Why's that?'

Ryan shrugs. 'Didn't he say it's to see what happens next?'

'And you think that makes sense, Cusack?'

'I think he knows what he's doing,' Ryan says. He is watching Shakespeare now for signs of treachery, though he is not sure what treachery might look like. Ryan, after all, would never have fancied himself so capable of hiding its twitches and tics; maybe treachery is a symptomless disorder.

'See,' Shakespeare says, 'that strikes me as odd.'

'That he wants to see what happens next?'

'No, boy. That you're as fucking mellow as he is.'

'I didn't invest. Don't think it's my right to get pissy before Dan does.'

'Bullshit, Cusack. It's a loss of potential income, and you should be raging. You should be out there tearing the town apart. You should be halfway down to West Cork, gunning for Pender, but you're not. You're sitting on your hole again. You're out of action for weeks, you come back just to talk to a fella in words we can't understand, everything goes to shit and you go stagnant again. D'you see, Cusack, a fucking pattern?'

'Didn't Dan put you straight on that the other night?'

86

'Dan has some sort of horn for you I've never understood, boy. So maybe he can't bring himself to suspect you, or maybe he does suspect you but he can't bring himself to kneecap you. See, Christmas and all, I can't fathom why Dan isn't going after Pender if he's sure Pender's the problem,' and he comes in hands first, catches Ryan's T-shirt at his chest and slams him back against the door. Ryan splutters. He grabs Shakespeare's arms and pushes up but Shakespeare is budged only briefly. 'If those yokes don't turn up, Cusack,' he rasps. 'If I find out you had a hand in this, Italians or no Italians I will slit your fucking throat.'

'Let go of me,' Ryan grunts.

'Are you gonna tell me something worthwhile if I do?'

'What, am I supposed to make shit up? Let fucking go of me!'

Shakespeare rams Ryan against the door again before letting go and moving back.

'All right.' Ryan smooths down his T-shirt. 'Here's a worthwhile thing for you, you prick.' He recognises a surge of belligerence. Assessment of emotion is a habit Dan has nagged him into; *acknowledge it, evaluate it, if it's negative you'll likely find it serves no purpose, swallow it*. But he doesn't want to tame this.

'It's you Dan has the problem with,' he says.

'Me?' says Shakespeare.

'Yeah, you're a dodgy cunt.'

'You better be codding me.'

'I'm not codding you,' says Ryan.

Ryan didn't really know anger till he hit his teens, and then it frequently got the better of him. He was known for fighting, chastised twice for banging his head off a brick wall, bawled out of it once when he made three cuts across the inside of his left arm at the kitchen table.

What would you expect with your constitution? Nana Cusack once sniffed, like temper's a disease boiled up in his mongrel's blood. That was part of the evaluation once he came home from nine months in Saint Patrick's Institution, like in being caught with controlled substances for sale or supply he was only falling prey to genetic defects; same colour heart as hair, further outbursts expected if he even raised his voice. Sure Irish men don't get cross at all, naw. Irish men don't bate their young fellas up and down the fucking hall because there's no sliced pan for the morning.

Ryan plays his temper by ear now. Sometimes he funnels it into his job, sometimes he rolls it into a joint, sometimes he fucks it out. Sometimes he gives it power over his mouth.

'See, Dan thinks, just like you and I think, that Pender's too useless to nick those pills on his own. So either he didn't do it, or he had help. You think it's me, because clearly you're a dope who can't see that I can no more stand Pender than he can stand me. Dan thinks it's you, coz which of us has the capacity for being such a dodgy cunt, ha?'

'That cokehead fuck,' Shakespeare says, and catches his chin and looks at the ceiling.

'Take it as a compliment, boy,' Ryan says. 'Pender's too thick and I'm too in awe of him; that only leaves you on equal footing.'

'It doesn't feel like much of a fucking compliment.'

Ryan isn't sure if this is what Shakespeare looks like shocked. He strokes his beard, pinching at his chin. His shoulders are stiff. Otherwise he is as he always is: like he cannot spare the energy to bite you.

'Doubtless you're not supposed to be telling me any of this,' he says. 'So why are you?'

'Coz you had nothing to do with it. You were pretty convincing there in how you went to batter me.'

'Still no guarantee that you're not behind all of this.'

'Oh fucking . . .' Ryan shakes his head. He is very tired now; he is fit for nothing but panning out. 'Whatever. Lead your own investigation, then. Ask Dan how keen I was to build bridges with the fucking Camorra. Ask away.'

'Except I can't ask, can I, Cusack? I can't let on that I know any of this, coz then we'll be fucking conspirators' – he gestures – 'and we'll spend months trying to quench that flame in the fucker's mind, while someone else sells all our yokes.' He slaps the wall beside him. 'Fuck me. Whether Pender did it or J.P. did it or Rory fucking Gallagher did it, doesn't matter, now we know the route isn't safe.'

'The route's fine. The yokes got in. Cooney and Feehily saw them. They passed them to Gina.'

'Then maybe Dan should be looking at Cooney and Feehily.'

'Are you serious? Cooney's head just holds his ears apart and if Feehily had two brains he'd be twice as stupid.'

'You'd want to be fucking stupid to rob me,' Shakespeare says.

'It was Pender,' Ryan says. 'Just remains to be seen if he has J.P. backing him.'

'Yeah, and the only thing to do is haul him up on it, because the longer we wait, the poorer we get. Dan won't proceed with the second part of the purchase until he finds the first, and where does that leave us, ha, me and you? We're gonna run out if he keeps the warehouse empty. And the boys abroad, they're not going to be impressed if we suddenly clam up.'

Oh, Ryan says, under his breath.

'So if Dan's confiding in you, Cusack, then you're in the right position for talking him down and getting him moving. Whether Pender's done this off his own steam or with J.P.'s blessing makes no difference. We make the move and we move on. I have bills to pay.'

'I'm not in a position to browbeat, boy,' Ryan says.

'Well what can I say to him? I can't tell him I learned what's going on through flaking into you, not after he told me you were in the clear. Naw, the task of putting straight the paranoid fucker's yours.'

Ryan bristles. 'It's not paranoia if the fucking things are gone.'

'Everything's paranoia with Dan,' Shakespeare says, 'because Dan is getting altogether too fond of the marching powder. Maybe because of the time you tried to do yourself in. Maybe you gave him that much of a shock. Maybe all of this *is* your fault, whether you helped lift those yokes or not. Maybe on that basis it's only right you take the brunt of it.'

He goes for the door and Ryan barely has time to get out of his way.

'Sort it out,' Shakespeare says, from over his shoulder out on the street.

This is easier said than done. Insomnia being a frequent nuisance, Ryan doesn't wholly blame Shakespeare's visit for the restless night following, though he turns the man's challenge over and over in his head, in the dark. Shakespeare had nothing to do with the pills' disappearance, and he is not in cahoots with J.P.. Moreover, he is aghast and hurt that Dan thinks him capable of defection. Ryan imagines Shakespeare nursing hurt feelings, unburdening on his ould doll over a cup of strong tea; even wretchedly tired, it makes him grin. Shakespeare does not deserve Dan's suspicion and Ryan can't figure out how to advise Dan without admitting that he told Shakespeare everything. At best, he'd get a dawk. At worst . . . well. Who knows, now, what Dan is capable of, Dan who kicked out one of his shareholders for suggesting partnership with J.P., Dan, who is *too fond of the marching powder.*

Though Ryan remembers his intake as measured specifically and strictly, as if Dan knew where in his nervous system to direct every last grain.

Ryan has some poor options. The next day he sits with Dan in the Watercourse Road house, listening to him direct dogsbodies; Dan wants word from Pender's pack, and he wants to know what kind of rustlings are coming from J.P.'s camp. Ryan realises that he could follow both avenues of enquiry himself. This thought makes him rub the back of his neck unhappily. He has sort of an in with J.P. There could be a way of gauging Phelan's intent without risking Dan's harvest and his own life. He remembers his father telling him he'd run rings around anyone. Ryan doesn't know if he's ever done such a thing before.

It edges closer to New Year's Eve, and no one manages to find the pills, hear Pender's confession, or draw out Phelan. Ryan, tasked still with proving Shakespeare's loyalty, tries his word out on Dan: his word is not enough.

'How d'you know he had nothing to do with it?' Dan presses.

'He's like a lunatic over it, that's how.'

'What's throwing your weight around prove?' Dan asks. 'Nothing. Can't you fathom possible ulterior motives? You've to always see three moves ahead. You've to pay heed to potentials. For fuck's sake, I hope you don't play snooker.'

'All I'm saying is we should just haul Pender in. I don't think being crafty will do us much good in the long run.'

'You're right there,' Dan says. 'You *don't* think.'

So Ryan, having done his thinking but unsure of a way to present it, keeps working on his remix and his track; between sessions coloured by cannabis and tea he visits the Riverbank Inn with Colm to tinker and survey. All the while Natalie texts him. She likes him; he gives the quandary its due and concludes that it's either the sex or the music. Maybe even both. Ould dolls like to lay lies over lust, pretending they're not really as into sex as fellas are, but Natalie's not up for denying it. Ryan likes her bluntness. She's not giving him much to work with in terms of the hunt, but her honesty is intoxicating.

Turn on Sky Arts, Piano Man. Jarvis Cocker's
playing Common People on this weenie little keyboard.

I just this minute realised you can get
vape pens especially designed for blow but

> Oh My God is the dirtiness of a joint not
> kinda part of it?

> Do you ever hear Philip Glass when you cum?
> You can tell me, I think it's kinda hot.

That last one led, a few texts later, to a beautifully indecent selfie that captured her only from mouth to ribs.

Ryan's not sure what he's gotten himself into but he's finding it increasingly difficult to be ashamed of it, seeing as December looks like thawing before Karine. She grants one reply to every three of his texts, an answer to none of his phone calls.

> You can at least fucking say your grand

> I'm grand.

This is how it is till the night Joseph comes home from the pub with Crowley, Sheehan, Emma, Louise, and sure where there's Louise there's Karine, and Ryan is up off the couch like it's spring-loaded. She's the last in and she goes straight through and into the kitchen as if she owns the place.

He follows. 'What are you doing here?'

She removes her mug from the press. 'We share a social circle, don't we?' She puts the kettle on. 'Avoiding you entirely would mean me having to move halfway up a mountain.'

He nods at the mug. 'You're not up for the party so.'

'I'm flahed out from partying.'

She turns, back to the worktop, hands on the counter either side of her, and pouts at him.

'You've been odd with me all week,' he says.

'It's Christmas and I'm allergic.'

They watch each other, the floor and the walls in turn.

'Are you drinking?' she asks, once the kettle clicks off.

He admits to his bottle of beer in the sitting room.

She goes up to his room as Joseph and the gang settle into a playlist and Ryan grabs his beer and follows. She's changing into one of his T-shirts and he catches just a glimpse of her breasts as the fabric falls. She goes over to the chest of drawers and rummages. His shirt reaches just to the curve of her arse, not enough to hide the flash of pink knickers. She brushes past and out to the bathroom and leaves him to talk down a very speculative semi.

Ten minutes later she gets into bed and turns onto her side. He sits at his desk and swings gently on the chair, sipping his beer, watching her fall asleep. He could, once she's under, slip his headphones on and hone what he's done on the remix. The aspiration caves in; he gets into bed beside her and the bass and laughter from downstairs keep him awake and wondering for ages.

They're still up, their social circle, by the time Karine and Ryan stir. It's fire in the frost; he wakes with his arm over her, his body pressed against hers. She sighs and he hugs her tighter, drowsy, drifting. The rise and fall of her ribcage. A tress of her hair on his shoulder.

She softly complains of feeling terrible and tells him that she's sorry she went to bed so early if she was never going to get reprieve from the hangover. They brush their teeth and get back into bed. There's tentative effort at conversation, and then a kiss, and then he slips his T-shirt up over her shoulders and onto the floor.

She asks the questions at the points where he can't answer. 'Why did I come here when I knew this is all you'd want?' with his mouth between her legs and his hand on the softness of the inside of her thigh, 'Why can't you just let it go?' as he slides inside her, and she moves with him and holds him so tightly that he feels like they're fused and maybe they are, maybe that's it, for a beautiful span he knows it all makes sense, that his is a body that's whole only in hers, and he concludes that he doesn't hear Philip Glass.

He pulls on his trackies and goes down to the kitchen to make her a coffee.

'Was that a good idea, now?' A wobbling Joseph, behind him.

'Was what a good idea?'

'You know, Cusack. You fucking know.'

Ryan directs him to fuck off and goes back up to his girlfriend who is sitting upright on his bed, mauve-cheeked and wet-eyed.

'Who the *fuck* is this?'

She holds his phone out. Natalie's unclothed self-portrait fills the screen.

'*Do you*,' bawls Karine, '*hear Philip Glass when you cum?*'

It's all Ryan can do to put the coffee down on the desk.

'How could you?' Karine screams.

'You broke up with—'

'Days ago, Ryan! Days ago! It doesn't drop off from neglect, like!'

'You didn't specify a fucking moratorium.'

'A *fucking* moratorium?'

'Not a *fucking* moratorium, a fucking . . . Christ.'

Sex has fixed her hair in darkened strands. One frames her left cheek and sticks to her skin when she wipes her eyes.

'You told me you didn't want to be with me,' Ryan says.

'You'd think you'd give us a chance to get our heads around that before you go out picking up sluts. Though maybe this isn't recent, ha? I mean if she's bloody sexting you!' She lobs his phone at the wall; there's a thud as it smacks the plasterboard, a drier clatter when it hits the laminate floor. 'How long have you been seeing her? The whole time you were telling me you couldn't leave the house?'

'I only met her last week, I swear to you.'

She bounds out of bed and hurls herself into her clothes. 'Last week? Last bloody week? I tell you we need a break and you immediately find a replacement?'

94

'You didn't tell me we needed a break, girl. You told me to go home and kill myself.'

'I *said* if you were going to kill yourself to just do it because I can't live between your moods anymore!'

'That's not what you said at all!'

He follows her down the stairs. She flings the front door open so hard it bounces off the wall and leaves a black mark on the paint.

'I don't know what you want!' he cries after her.

He goes as far as the gate and watches her storm into the grey, afraid to follow and loath to turn to the concern of their mutual, fucked friends.

9

Because Ryan's not very good at interrogating the elderly, his crabby sage takes the reins. The place in which her son bought her apartment is called Larne Court and it is, she tells Ryan, full of the kind of people who'd neither greet nor mourn you. Maureen's the oldest resident by at least a decade. She brings her black bags down to the communal skip once a week and no one ever stops to help her. Neighbours stand outside her front window to smoke and speak carelessly about their lives. There are no secrets worth knowing at Larne Court, she complains.

She tells him her story. She's Cork to the core; years in London couldn't strip her of her accent. She found foreknowledge on her travels, because hauling up your anchor makes your judgement keen and your eyes second-sighted. Loneliness can do that to a soul, she says. People aren't meant to exist outside of their tribes and so sometimes they go mad and sometimes that madness manifests in psychic sensitivity. Madness loves madness as much as loneliness craves company, and so she was drawn to Ryan, and so his character was revealed to her and she saw it was frayed at the edges. She could no more ignore him than walk through him.

Naturally he doesn't believe a word of it, but there's nothing he can do to prise the story open. He goes to her flat with fire in his belly and she pisses it straight out.

'That kind of carry-on might fly with the hotbloods in Italy,' she chides, 'but it won't work on me, boy.'

'What, the oracle specified Italy?'

'No.' At the sink to fill the kettle, she opens crumpled hands with short, clear nails, no rings. 'You did.'

He could have. It could be that the awe he remembers feeling was tied more to the drink and drugs than it was to her claim to clairvoyance. He is chatty on yokes. So tea is made for him by a woman who knows he's bad as rancid butter and crooked as a dog's back leg, and there is nothing he can do but drink up.

She settles on the couch and says, 'You're hardly ready to talk to me.'

'About what?'

'I didn't think so,' she sighs.

She pushes on instead with her own history. He picks at each sentence. She's around his grandmother's age so he listens for street names, common enemies. She's definitely from the Northside.

'Talk to me about music instead so,' she says, suddenly, before her yarn is finished to his satisfaction.

'What do you want me to tell you about music?'

'Sure how would I know? You're the musician, aren't you?'

'I'm the musician,' he confirms, softly.

'And still not playing?'

'I play.'

'I'd be glad to think I was wrong on that. What do you play?'

'Piano.'

She looks over his head and says, 'Piano. Now I could have told you that,' and clears her throat and asks, 'Are there many little gangsters who play piano?'

'You have to stop saying that.'

'What? That you're a little gangster or that you play piano?'

She takes the mugs and empties their dregs. She rinses them, then stacks them carefully on the draining board. There's what looks like a fortnight's worth of ware to the right of the sink.

'You'll get rats,' Ryan says.

'I will not.'

It's pushing up on eight o'clock, and he has a dozen things he should be doing instead of sitting with a crackawly, listening to lies.

'Tell me about the piano,' she says, back on the couch. She's wearing a blue knitted jumper; she pulls a piece of tissue from one of the sleeves and knocks it swiftly across her nose.

'It's a hobby, is all.'

'Is being a gangster a hobby too, or is that a vocation?'

'I'm not a gangster.' Ryan sits forward. 'I'm not in a gang. I don't start turf wars.'

'Do you have a criminal record?'

'No.'

'You do.' She's delighted with herself.

'Where would you get that idea?'

'Same place I got all the other ones.'

'If I was a gangster, would I be sitting here?'

'Yes,' she says. 'Because a little gangster would be worried about my mouth, and asking me where I get my ideas.'

'A gangster'd be a lot crosser than I am.'

'Unless he was the piano-playing kind.' She laughs and the laughter folds from the arrogant tilt of her chin down to the creases of her lap. She sighs happily. 'Tell me about the piano,' she says again. 'When did you start playing?'

When he was three. An hour a day with his mother, countless hours by himself, stringing together cacophonies slowly rounded into melodies by her patience. They started grading him when he was eight, and he'd just gotten his distinction in Grade 4 when his mother decided to take herself out of the picture. That was as far as he got in terms of the formalities. His father assumed passing Junior Cert music was substitute enough. As soon as Ryan had done his practical exam . . .

He mimes a slit throat.

'What?' Maureen presses.

'He sold the piano.'

She's generous enough to blanch.

'My granddaughter plays piano,' she says.

'Yeah?'

She grimaces. 'Don't ask me what grade or what exams because I haven't a notion. But everything she plays sounds like the funeral march.'

'Which one?'

'Now you're being cheeky,' she says.

Defying his better judgement, Ryan's mouth stretches.

'So that's when you stopped playing?' Maureen extracts a cigarette from the packet on the coffee table between them but doesn't light it, holding it instead between her thumb and first finger and tapping it off her bottom lip.

'For a long while.'

'How long?'

Ryan shrugs. He'd found equivalents at that stage: sex, drugs, blood. Music wasn't the only thing capable of stirring him. The piano was gone but he had a girlfriend, access to all the stimulants he could want, and a dawning realisation of his own strength, though he knew he must never use it against his father. He thought about it, of course. Late at night, in the bedroom he shared with his brothers, he imagined how he would take his revenge on the shrinking sire safe inside his head, where his anger had nowhere to go.

It might have been when the anger dwindled that the need for music came back, but by then he'd become afraid of it, worried that his talent could exist only in competition with the drugs and the blood and the sex when he couldn't be doing without his job, his attitude or his girlfriend. So for a while there were sets spun by DJs that blew his mind: Danny Howells, Steve Lawler, John Digweed. He taught himself to mix, then to craft songs out of samples, then to record his own. He bought a second-hand MIDI keyboard from a fella who'd belatedly realised that making music is hard, but fucking around with the keyboard only amplified the deficit so he ended up dropping almost a grand on a Yamaha digital piano, carefully setting it up in his room and staring resentfully at it for far longer than makes any sense to him now.

And of course there was the silence between his intentional-slash-unintentional overdose and his accidentally charming the knickers off Natalie. But he leaves that out. As he does with the bit where he's behind bars for nine months with nothing to take rhythm from but his stuttering heartbeat.

'Are you any good?' asks Maureen.

'Woeful.'

'G'wan outta that, you couldn't be that bad if you've been doing it since you were a child.'

'Yeah, but I haven't, have I? I played from three to eleven and then half-played from eleven to fifteen and then I didn't play properly for years. Negligence kills it, like. So you were right when you guessed I wasn't playing. I played a tarantella the other day and it sounded like . . . Fuck.' He pushes a hand over his forehead. 'Crows shitting on a corrugated roof.'

'Ah, I'm sure you're only being hard on yourself. You'll have to play for me.'

'I will yeah.'

'You should. I have a great ear.'

'A great ear and a third eye. I suppose you can touch smells too. And taste dinners before you make them.'

'God but you've some lip on you. I suppose that's right and proper for a little gangster. Have you a car?'

He frowns. 'Why?'

'Because I need a spin.'

'*Stall an ball*, will yeh? I'm not a taxi.'

'I know you're not a taxi. But I know too you're a decent boy and that you're aware it's freezing out.'

'Decent? Didn't you only tell me I was a gangster?'

100

'You're at the age yet where you can be both,' she says. 'But it won't be long before I'm crossing the road to avoid you.'

He grins. 'Who said I had a car, anyway?'

'Well I'm hoping that's your keys bulging there in your jeans pocket.'

The grin evaporates. 'What?'

'Is it your car keys or not?'

'Jesus Christ, what a thing to say to me.'

She takes her coat from the back of the couch. 'Come on,' she says, 'I don't have all night.'

She lets him out the front door ahead of her.

'I was courting in the seventies,' she explains. 'And the fellas then wore their pants very tight too.'

'Ah, d'you mind not fucking perving on me, like?'

'You've a grand opinion of yourself. I'm afraid you're a little underdone for my liking.'

She follows him to the car. 'Very nice,' she says, settling in. 'You must be doing all right for yourself with your jigacting.'

'Actually, I got a rare deal coz the lad who owned it was going to Australia, and still I was lucky I had the bobs, so . . .' He nearly finishes with 'fuck off'.

She's going to Glanmire, which is handy for him, she says, though he can't recall mentioning where he lives. Add that to the list of things he told the mocking stranger that she wishes now to sell back to him, coated in lies.

'Your mother,' she says, as they cross the river. 'Did she teach?'

'Only me. She tried with my brothers and sisters but none of them really had the grá.'

'So you were Mammy's Boy, were you?'

'Couldn't have been, she wasn't a mammy.'

'She was what, so? A mamma? Such a pity she's not around to see you . . .'

He thinks for a white-hot moment she's going to say *engaging in organised crime* but she continues . . .

'. . . stepping out with girlfriends. Don't the mammas usually have plenty to say about that?'

'You're talking about the girl that was with me the last night? She's not my girlfriend.'

'Ah, but someone else is.'

Maybe the nuance was there in the gruffness of his setting her straight. They halt at the traffic lights. Maureen looks over but he keeps staring ahead. Artificial lights hang patterns on the black; dense at eye level and spread out above him, like the last buoys before the open sea.

'My mam,' he says, flatly, 'wouldn't have given a fuck either way. She wasn't a stereotype.'

Maureen sniggers. 'Is it not an Italian thing to have two girl-friends? It explains the jeans, I suppose.'

'They're not even fucking tight, they're . . .' He comes to his senses and trails away. She makes the delighted sounds of a canary that's just spotted her reflection in a dangling mirror.

'You're off your game,' he tells her.

'Sure don't I know that?'

Ten minutes later they pull into the drive of a detached pile in a well-tended estate. The house is dark but for a glow in the hall and the Christmas lights framing the downstairs windows and draped over the tidy tree in the middle of the lawn.

'No one home,' says Maureen.

Not what Ryan wanted to hear. He doesn't want to have to drive back into the middle of town. He has two tracks to be finishing, a girl to plead with and another whose photography he needs to commend.

'Do you need to go back again, so?' he huffs, and Maureen turns with an expression of mild vexation and says, 'After making you drive all the way out here? I have a key. Come on.'

'Come on where?'

'It's my daughter-in-law's house.'

'So?'

She gets out of the car and stands by the passenger door, fixing her coat. Ryan stays where he is. She crouches to glare in at him.

'Come on,' she says, muffled.

He opens the window.

'Come on where, I said?' He assumes she thinks she's befriended a tough bastard and, coincidentally, has some wicked task too big a sin for one set of hands.

She shakes her head as if she's explained the plan twice before.

'This is my daughter-in-law's house,' she says. 'The mother of my grandchildren, you see?'

It dawns on him. 'You're hardly still on about the piano?'

'I have to hear you play,' she says.

'You want me to break into your daughter-in-law's house to play a piano for you?'

'Indeed I do not. I have a key. Jesus for a musician you're awful fecking deaf.'

'I'm not going into a stranger's house with some ould wan I just met to give a fucking recital. Are you on fucking drugs?'

'Deirdre and the kids are in Spain for the New Year,' she says, 'and my son doesn't live here anymore, sure she turfed him out. So there's no one here to critique you but me.'

'Critique me? D'you think you're Simon Cowell or something?'

'I do,' she says. 'That's it.' She turns and walks to the front door and he sits shaking his head at her retreating back and eventually gets out and follows her.

The hall is of bright wood and white walls bare but for matching paintings of one muted colour dripping onto another. Maureen opens the door to the left – 'Now' – and a flick of her wrist directs him to the upright in the corner.

The fallboard's down and the ebony finish polished and on top someone's placed a glass bowl of blue and grey pebbles. The stool has been reupholstered to match the room's colour scheme. It's cream, just like the couch, just like the armchairs.

Ryan lifts the fallboard.

It's been five years but it hasn't taken anything but polish and the odd new keytop.

'This is my piano.'

Hmm? from behind him.

He tries to repeat himself and falters. He thinks he must be wrong. He thinks that the evening's gentle chaos has him telling himself lies. The truth tucks his hands into fists and turns his stomach.

Every scratch and chip still there, treated with nothing more camouflaging than a smear of Pledge.

'This is my fucking piano.'

He sits heavily on the stool.

'It's my daughter-in-law Deirdre's piano,' says Maureen, quietly.

Ryan turns to face her. She's unsmiling, but soft. Her cheeks seem fuller. Her hair curls over her collar.

'Deirdre who?'

'Deirdre Allen is her name.'

'Well, she has my fucking piano.'

'Small city,' she says.

He jumps up. 'How did you know this was mine?'

Maureen raises her eyes to the ceiling. She begins to speak. She spreads her hands, kicks off with contrite burbling.

Ryan doesn't wait to hear it. He hurries out onto the driveway and pushes his way to his car and sees his piano being driven into this yard, sees it being carelessly pushed over the threshold and left angled in the hall as some stuck-up wagon dictates where it needs to go to best support her fucking jar of fucking pebbles.

The day his mother's piano was taken creeps up on him. His eyes water.

The hours after this are an agitation of fury and grief. The hours after those are spent mostly asleep; he wakes on more than one

104

occasion, stressed even in the spaces his subconscious mind inhabits. He gets up in the late morning and sits around, seething, then sad; he decides to go to his father.

He skirts around it for a bit, because they are good at skirting around shit, Ryan and Tony. Nothing ever said except in shrugs and knuckles. So when Ryan says, 'D'you remember who you sold my piano to?' he's still omitting mountains: *d'you remember who you sold my mother's piano to? And why you were so pissed off that I was bent out of shape by its loss?*

Tony doesn't remember. It was that long ago. A woman, yeah, definitely a woman.

'Why are you asking me that now, boy?'

'Dunno. Maybe I'd like it back.'

Tony doesn't like that. He suddenly believes sentimentality to be the privilege of the minted. He coughs and folds his arms and looks mournfully at his son, as if this conversation makes him ill.

'It was my mam's piano,' Ryan says. 'It means more to me than to anyone else on this fucking rock.'

'Yeah, it was your mam's piano.' Tony struggles with this simple admission; the corners of his mouth pucker. 'But so what, like? We got that only when we got the house. Before that her piano was the one in your grandparents' gaff in Naples. And before there was that one, there was another one. No point going out of your way to track down something so . . .'

Fundamentally pointless is what Ryan thinks he's going for. Tony is mortified at the questioning; he doesn't like being reminded of how he cut off his son's hands. Ryan could ask him, *Does the name Deirdre Allen mean anything to you?* but he doesn't. His father's poor memory wears him out and he knows he can't stand another twenty minutes of his shaking, hawing.

Besides, the night's broken sleep has left Ryan mostly convinced that he was imagining things. There's no guarantee he could tell two U3s apart standing side by side, let alone two separated by half a decade. He must have been inventing histories. It was a weird evening to begin with.

So he goes to say sorry.

She heaves a warm sigh when she opens the door and steps back so as to let him pass.

'I'm not staying,' Ryan says. 'I just wanted to . . . There's an apology owed.'

'Is there?'

'For storming off on you like that. And leaving you in Glanmire.'

She sighs again. 'You're awful soft,' she says.

'I'm not soft. Just . . .' He glances back at the courtyard and finds the rest of the lie in the shrubbery. 'Raised right.'

'No, you're soft. And in a game where it's a terrible handicap.'

'Listen,' he says. He doesn't have time to feed the charlatans. He has plans to nestle into the post-Christmas revelry, based around such matters as his wounded boss and his wounded girlfriend. Ex-girlfriend. Girlfriend. 'My mam's piano meant a lot to me. So I might have overreacted when I saw your daughter-in-law's one. It's the same model. But it couldn't be the same—'

'It might be,' she says. 'There can't be that many of them in Cork.'

'But sure lookit . . .' He takes his phone out of his pocket and slides between screens. 'Even if it is, what difference does it make? I just came to say sorry for being a prick. And I know you were good to me when you first met me, so thanks. I don't think I'll ever get out of you that you're my nana's bingo buddy or whatever, so well done for maintaining the mystery. So, y'know . . . I'll see you around.'

He turns and she says, 'Deirdre's not back until the tenth, so if you want to take another look just let me know.'

'It's OK.' He raises a hand and keeps his eyes to his screen and walks down the path.

'I'll see you when you're ready to talk,' she calls. 'You know where I am.'

He raises his hand again and back in his car he thinks, *Well, girl, I'm in no need of half-chats and yarns.* He drives home. He puts the kettle on. He sits on the couch. And knows he'll go back, and fights with the knowing, and swears at himself for wanting it.

For ages I was hungry.

We can't really blame Tony Cusack. The man knew how to put a dinner on, but he'd drowned the knowing. He stuffed it into a bottle of Aldi whiskey and let it ferment. He didn't always get up in time because he didn't always go to bed. I was eleven, twelve, thirteen, fourteen, fifteen. I did what I could. I put down pots of pasta and spuds, I peeled carrots, I grated cheese. But that doesn't really compare with having proper, Mam-made dinners. Frittata and sartù di riso and parmigiana.

My dad had a few meltdowns, I dunno were you watching. One right after the funeral, so we were divided up between aunts. Another then when I was twelve, a scary one, and me and Cian ended up staying for four months with this family out in Carrigtwohill. We were only just all back together when Dad lost it again. I didn't go anywhere this time. Me and Kelly were left with him and I suppose we kind of minded him and kind of made him worse.

The point being that for the first while Dad was a mess, so Nana Cusack used to come over to help with dinners and stuff, and there were a lot of boiled spuds. I mean I like spuds and all, but Non si vive di solo spuds, like.

The thing I missed the most was the risotto. You used to fuck everything into it: salami, olives, chilli, leftovers. I asked Nana for it. 'She used to put it in a big pan and you could feed an army with it.' Well, said Nana, there's an army of you in it, so

108

that must have come in handy. Then she'd give me an extra spud.

I guess I cracked one day. I dunno.

I was fourteen. This was before Karine, but after Dan, so I had a little bit of pocket money. I was in town one Saturday on my own. I went through the English Market from the Grand Parade to Pana. Remember you were mad for the English Market? You said you could just do it all day, inhaling. The coffee, the sugar and chocolate and warm cakes, the rain kicked in on people's shoes, the cheese, the tang of olives, the butcher stalls at the ends, the smell of salted, raw, clean, cold meat, the air then that hits you from the street outside.

Remember the little shop with the pastas and sun-dried tomatoes and that? I went in for a nose that day and found myself standing in front of the rice and then there was this woman beside me taking a good long sconce. I guess I looked like I was about to knock shit over for kicks, or fill my pockets, and I probably had my hood up.

She said, Are you looking for something?

Mam, I wasn't the most forthcoming young fella. I definitely wasn't as you left me. I was barely playing, I was getting into fights, I was always on thin ice with my dad. So I don't know what made me say it, except maybe hunger.

What's the one for risotto? I asked the woman.

She was cross-looking with thick, brown-framed glasses. She looked like she'd clatter you for nothing at all, so when she smiled it seemed like a terrible effort, like she really had to heave-ho at the corners of her skinny lips.

She handed me a box.

I turned it over. I jerked my hand up and down and felt the weight of it.

Do you need anything else? yer wan asked.

And oh, if there was dirt there to kick.

Do you know how to make it? I asked.

She didn't know what to make of me.

So I had to explain, my mam used to make it all the time. She died though.

That made her have a think about it.

She said, C'mere timme, pet.

In between serving other customers she wrote down a recipe for a risotto, like the plain one, with butter and cheese and onions. She gave me this little tub of stock stuff as well, and she didn't charge me. I suppose there's something about a hungry young fella that charms the battleaxes.

The funny thing was that even though I went straight home with my box of Arborio and my stock and my recipe clutched tight, I never tried to make it. I thought I'd have killed for a taste but when the chance was there, I didn't take it. I was hungry but the hunger felt right. I needed to miss you more than I needed to eat.

IO

Dan decides not to open Catalyst until the beginning of February, January being too miserable a month to encourage hedonism. He and Colm put their heads together. They plan impressive guest DJs, a classier interior, a sound system upgrade.

January progresses. Ryan draws up a couple more big transactions. He's introduced to a fella in Kilkenny who runs a private-number hair salon and has an exclusive clientele, all of whom are mad for good coke and yokes. He's put out that Ryan doesn't deal in meth; Ryan tells him he'll see what he can do, then proceeds to do nothing. He's turned on too to a girl who sells single-use quantities online via proxy servers; smoke and mirrors she explains to him in great and futile depth. He thinks her methods are convoluted and he thinks it's gas that she can't operate her high-tech enterprise without conducting traditional codeword-based business with him; she's got the bobs but he's got the balls, and that's how it's always worked and how it will always work.

And Karine nails the coffin shut. She's the first person Ryan phones at New Year's, and she doesn't pick up. She freezes him out. Their friends flounder. She doesn't care. The girls stop interacting with Ryan altogether, which leads Joseph into a sequence of rants about how sisterhood is an awful conceit and how one shouldn't have to state loyalty to either party if a pair of friends decide to stop fucking each other.

They have one meeting on a damp Friday night. She arrives at his house spooked and pale. It has just occurred to her that she's left him curator of some of her most vulnerable moments. 'Nudes,' she says. 'Delete them.' She stands by the desk in his bedroom, arms folded, as he frowns and goes through folders on his computer and phone for her. 'What about cloud storage?' she says. 'What about backups?'

They argue. She wants them deleted; he's desperate not to delete them. The images are proof of what he had, their continued existence proof of mere hiatus.

'When we were together,' Karine says, 'and you were angry with me, you'd pin me to the wall, remember? So if you get angry with me now and I'm not around to pin to the wall, God knows what you'll do. Share these? Shame me?'

'I'd never do that to you,' he says. 'That's fucking horrible.'

'So was pinning me to the wall.'

But she's not gone on the taste of upsetting him. She brushes her hair back from her face.

'Y'know, you don't have to be so difficult,' she says. 'We might have to be friends one day.' Like friendship is something they could manage – platonic regard, shoulders to cry on, in-jokes and companionable lunches.

'I never want to be your friend, D'Arcy,' Ryan says.

But as his relationship with Karine decays, his acquaintance with Natalie blossoms. They spend their time together mostly in his bed; she calls him, and sometimes she gets a taxi over, and sometimes he picks her up from outside her parents' house. They drink hot whiskeys and talk about music. She listens to him play, or she finds him stuff to listen to; she digs up old recordings and new compositions and lines up links for them to consume. 'Tell me about your girlfriend,' she says at inopportune times; she starts him answering, then goes down on him. 'Is she unbelievably beautiful?' she enquires as she undresses for him. 'Do you think your girlfriend can forgive you?' she asks as his penis slips against her, inside her. 'D'you know, I think she's my ex,' Ryan says at last,

112

helplessly, giving in, all the way in. 'Is she?' Natalie smiles. 'Is she really?'

There's a date he's watching for this month: the 10th of January, when Maureen's daughter-in-law will arrive home from her holiday and proceed to barricade her front door against the likes of him. He goes to Larne Court on the evening of the 9th with his tail between his legs. And Maureen, beside herself with glee that another of her forecasts has come true, launches into the excursion, pulling on her coat before he has a chance to remove his own.

Once again they pull into the driveway of that handsome house in Glanmire and once again he hesitates to follow her in.

'Your daughter-in-law doesn't get cranky about you rooting around in her gaff when she's away?' he asks, in the hall.

To his discomfort Maureen reaches out and heartily rubs his arm.

'She doesn't mind me rooting around when I'm feeding the cat or watering the plants,' she says, and though she must have spotted the involuntary jerk her gesture provoked she ignores it, and flings the door open.

'Take a good close look now,' she says.

Ryan is as immediately sure as he was the first time; the moment he sees it he knows it, though he forces himself to ask if the scratches he spots here and there only match those in his memory through wishful thinking.

'This is mine,' he says.

He lays fingers on it. It's slightly out of tune.

'Go on,' says Maureen. Self-satisfaction has plumped her face again. She sinks into the armchair to his left. 'Play me something.'

'I don't know what to play.'

Ah, she sighs. 'Give it something familiar.'

He chances the tarantella and this time the only thing it lacks is the clarity of perfect tune; then again, he has been practising.

'Well,' says Maureen, when he finishes.

'Well what?'

'You're a lot better than you let on, aren't you?' She says this as if he's let her down.

'I told you I've been playing since I was a smallie.'

'You also told me the knack had up and left you. And me thinking I was doing you a great favour.' She pouts, and recovers then, and tells him, 'Now give it something new,' and so he shares 'Mosquito Song' and 'I Saw the Dead' and Einaudi's 'Fly' with his mother's piano.

They're there a couple of hours before he feels the need to pull back. She unlocks the patio door for him and he steps out for a smoke. Behind him, in the roomy kitchen, her shape moves from sink to countertop as she sets the kettle to boil. He makes sure the seat of the closest patio chair is dry, settles with his back to the sliding door and rolls a joint.

He's just sparked up when she stands out beside him.

She wrinkles her nose. 'Not that I should be surprised,' she says, as a suffix to an objection skipped over.

'I'm wound up,' he tells her. 'It's a big thing, playing that piano again.'

'At least you're not pretending I'm imagining things.'

'I don't think I'd get away with it. It's smelly stuff. Anyway, I have the notion you're a right rogue – maybe too much of a rogue to go to bingo with my nana, after all.'

She stands side-on to the lawn and looks at him out of the corner of her eye.

'Give me a puff, then,' she says.

'Fuck off, I don't want to be done for killing you.'

'Jesus, your generation seems to think you paved the world. That Bob Marley fella was closer to my age than yours, wasn't he?'

114

'He died in his thirties.'

'It must be great' – she sticks her hands on her hips – 'to know everything.'

Ryan laughs, and her forehead creases until he offers the joint. She takes it casually, drags, and emits a dignified hiccup.

It might be, Ryan thinks, that his getting reacquainted with his piano has fed a hunger in him. For a week or so after giving Maureen her recital his place in his city seems to make more sense. Natalie thinks of him as an entrepreneur musician who smokes too much dope and he decides that's something to aim at. In the meantime, he must placate his boss. So he talks to associates and makes a great show of turning over stones; he is diligence incarnate, hoping Dan will accept his assessment of Shakespeare's loyalty and exact revenge on Pender or come to an understanding with J.P., whatever applies, so that they can get moving on the second delivery.

A last hurrah, he tells himself: music will save him yet. And as soon as its influence is evident he intends to return to Karine and present her with his mended self.

But still Dan doesn't make his move. Shakespeare waits and Ryan waits, biting his nails till it hurts. He has a stash still, but barely enough to carry him, and he can see a couple of big orders on the horizon.

He wakes very early one Saturday towards the end of the month to a fingertip pressed under his left ear. Natalie is leaning over him. She retracts her finger as he stirs; she shifts her weight; she presses her finger underneath his right ear.

'What're you doing?' he asks.

'A spell,' she whispers. 'To ward off ex-girlfriends and pretty little chancers. They'll stay away when they can sense me, you'll see.'

The points she's touched dry almost instantly.

'I'm a witch,' she says. 'Go back to sleep before I tear your heart out.'

115

They wake again in the early afternoon. Ryan's due to meet Colm in the evening, with nothing to do before then but fuck the witch and smoke his mind wide open. So a phone call is a hassle, and a phone call from his father is an upset. Ryan answers with his other arm over his eyes and with his greeting he notes the sensation of the duvet being lifted from his belly, and her breath then, and her mouth after that.

'Will you call over?' says Tony.

Ryan slides his hand through Natalie's hair and holds on at the back of her head. 'I'm kind of in the middle of something.'

'It's important, boy,' says Tony.

'I'll be there at some stage, so.'

'Ryan, listen to me. It's important now.'

Ryan pushes himself up on his elbows and Natalie sits with him.

'What's happened, Dad?'

'Just come over,' Tony says. 'It's not something I can tell you on the phone.'

Love and loyalty; Tony stirs the fear. Ronan's been knocked down, or Niamh's been snatched, or Ryan's nonna's had a stroke. Or it's the guards. Maybe there's a summons. Scenarios pollute him; he becomes brusque and unchivalrous; he wards off the spell. He points Natalie to the bus stop and arrives home fifteen minutes after answering his father's phone call.

The kitchen door is open and so he sees his father straight away, leaning against the draining board, normal in a shirt and black jeans, Saturday-typical and breathing . . . Well, as long as the cunt's still breathing.

'What's up?'

As he goes through the kitchen door he sees.

To his left, comfortable at his father's table, is the man whose directive, seven months ago now, proved much too much for Ryan.

Jimmy Phelan says, 'Well, young Ryan?'

116

Ryan thinks *I'm fucking dead. He's found out that I'm a worse hitman than I am a liar.* Phelan stands up. 'You changed your phone number,' he says.

'I do that,' Ryan says.

'As well you should.'

Tony moves away from the draining board. Phelan turns to him.

'See you again, boy. Myself and the young fella are going for a pint.'

Tony looks at Ryan.

'Just a pint,' Phelan laughs. The sound is raucous – joyful, even. It's a trick of the trade Ryan has yet to master, cloaking intent in leisure, hiding evil in song.

They go to Tony's local on the Old Youghal Road. The walk is seven or eight minutes of high-intensity endurance. The air burns Ryan's throat. Phelan doesn't speak. The ignorant who pass them stretch their lips in feeble greeting and those who recognise Phelan quail or stare.

They sit at the bar. Phelan buys Ryan a Carling.

'A little birdie tells me you've gone legit,' he says.

Ryan translates this as a pop at his gutlessness. If a hitman can't pull off a hit it makes him law-abiding, in a perverse way.

Phelan takes a draught of his Murphy's.

'A new club night. What did you call it again? Cat's Piss or something?'

There is no room yet for relief. Phelan takes another sup and watches Ryan as he raises his glass and nips at the head.

'Catalyst,' Ryan says, when his throat is soothed.

'I must remember that one for my next Scrabble match,' says Phelan, and calls the barman to turn up the volume on the Manchester derby.

Ryan steadies his hand on the pint glass.

'It didn't concern me,' says Phelan, checking his phone, then staring back at the television screen, 'until I was told it was Dan

Kane's thing, and that you were in on it with him. Thought it best to check in with you, that's the long and short of it. Speaking of shorts.' He calls the barman again. 'What Scotch have you, Donie?'

He buys two glasses of neat Glenfiddich.

'Best of luck with it.'

He holds out his glass for a clink. Ryan obliges.

'Dan the Man's expanding,' Phelan continues. 'Took him long enough, but I always knew he had the itch and since our last collaboration . . .' He turns and his eyes bore into Ryan's. '. . . I knew you were good enough to scratch it.'

An almost-goal. A cry from the barman. A tut from a raw-boned woman with folded arms.

'Not just clubs either,' says Phelan. 'New pills in my city. What would you know about that?'

The traitor frozen out, the beast comes for Ryan. Pender's skulduggery culminates in this interrogation and Ryan wonders, bitterly, how he didn't see this coming.

He knocks back half his Scotch.

'That arrangement fell through,' he says. 'Didn't whoever's telling you tales tell you that much?'

'Tales?' Phelan says. 'No, boy. I hear whispers and I get mind to ask after them. My city hints at there being a new line of merchandise on offer from Kane. I remember that I have a man on the inside, bearing in mind, of course, that he has one foot yet in the schoolyard.'

He stretches.

'Tell me where Kane found these pills,' he says.

A mis-pitched pause in the lead up to Ryan's answer and Phelan doesn't deign to notice.

'Rotterdam,' Ryan says, and waits for Phelan's eyes to narrow.

Instead Phelan purses his lips.

'Expand on that for me.'

'New acquaintances with better stuff. Simple as.'

118

'How new?'

'Entirely new. This was a fresh market for them. Which was the risk, and it didn't pay off. The arrangement fell through, like I said.'

'Like you said,' Phelan intones. 'Except it fell through on this end, because there's no honour among thieves, isn't that right?'

'Either or,' Ryan says, 'the process wasn't safe and that's where the story ends.'

'Not at all,' Phelan says. 'I can't imagine you lot are so cautious as to derail at the first bump. Where did this purloined consignment come in?'

There's an elevated sneer to this and it boosts Ryan's bpm and cuts again the capacity of his lungs. Such a chance to take and he takes it, whether out of audacity or loyalty or his inclination towards self harm . . .

'I don't know,' he says.

'Come off it, Cusack. There's nary a fart produced by Kane that he doesn't have you assess for the stench of roses.'

'I'm in the doghouse,' Ryan says, thinking of six inert weeks, shows of savage devotion in city centre pubs.

'You?' Phelan says. 'But haven't I just heard about your hunting high and low for poor Dan's wares? You're making plenty noise.'

'A task given to me exactly because he's pissy with me.'

'Why's he pissy with you?'

'That's between me and him, isn't it?'

Phelan's mouth twitches. After an age he says, 'Until I decide to make it my business, yes. I've as much interest in your lovers' tiffs as I do faith in your sudden ignorance.'

Still the match goes on at normal speed in Manchester, and still the ignorant around them clap and holler. Phelan finishes his Scotch and pushes the tumbler to the edge of the bar. Ryan watches his fingers slide, stretch and retract.

'Y'know,' says Phelan, 'what first occurred to me? That the whole thing was a scam, that there was no new exporter, that there were no pills. You wouldn't put the scam past a man like Kane, would you?'

He brings the glass to his smiling mouth.

'But then, a new business arrangement would be a timely accompaniment to a new club, and if the yokes are good . . .'

He finishes his pint in three swigs.

'Get me a couple of those yokes, Ryan,' he says. 'I'll know better once I have a taste.'

'I can't. He had a few, yeah, but they're long gone.'

'Have a look for me. Kane's the shiftiest fucker I ever laid eyes on. I dare say he'll have kept himself a stash. Just the job for nightclubbing, boy.'

He stands. He asks for a pen. He writes a number on a beer mat.

'Call me when you've that done,' he says. 'But don't worry about giving me your new number. Don't I know exactly how to get you?'

Ryan even thinks, as he leaves the pub ten minutes after Phelan and turns once more towards his father's house, that he could come clean to Dan. Just to see what harm it would really do.

Pender may have nicked those pills but it seems Pender didn't go first to Phelan with the heads-up. Pender's a thief, but not a grass. And if Pender's cleared then so is Shakespeare and so the inner circle are as tight as they ever were and there is no way Ryan can tell Dan any of this without telling him how he knows it.

Ryan goes back to his father to tell-him-without-telling-him that he's OK. Without-telling-him, Tony tells him he's relieved. They have a joint. Ryan gives his father sparse particulars: the club, Phelan's interest, his congratulatory Scotch. On the way out the door again a pang is stirred by his smallest brother's joking. He's only just gone eleven. Ryan throws him over his shoulder and Ronan laughs so hard Ryan thinks he might puke.

He texts Natalie from his dad's driveway and tells her no one's died.

II

Ryan has his meeting with Colm, during which he breaks away to organise a delivery, and then he has an hour with Maureen, during which he asks if she could find out whether her daughter-in-law would have any interest in selling the piano. Maureen promises she'll ask. Ryan's at a loose end after that, owing to the fact that Natalie's got a friend thing that she can't get out of. He goes home to make sense of his new predicament. He plays an hour and a half of Forza, looking for dull repetition, minor wins. He comes to no useful conclusions outside of the game, but he keeps his hands busy till time runs out and his mobile rings in his pocket. Dan needs him.

Perhaps it was always Dan's plan to wait so long that he drove Pender insane. Perhaps Pender was tired of jumping at shadows and sleeping with one eye open. Maybe Dan's stillness was a clever precursor to revenge, after all. Pender went looking for trouble.

Unable to dig up Dan, he tailed one of Shakespeare's couriers and went ballistic on visual evidence of a small deal going down. In O'Connell's pub, north of the river, with an audience of curious nonentities, he rattled the courier's sockets. The young fella rang Shakespeare from the street outside. Shakespeare came down and confronted Pender. Pender said he'd get Dan's attention even if he had to kill every courier in Cork. Shakespeare ordered his courier to keep watch on the pub and went into the city centre to get Dan. Once alerted, Dan called Ryan. By the time Ryan gets into town both are fit to be tied.

122

They stand by the river railings at the top of the South Mall, between the boardwalk cafe and the memorial. 'Like I have time for this shit,' Dan says, then allocates himself time, watching the streets, ignoring Ryan and Shakespeare both. Lumbering men and girls in bulky coats and unstable heels get out of cars on either side of the Mall. They move towards restaurant doors or ATMs. Theirs is a shivering, joyless gait, infectious. Dan darkens further.

'Fuck does this prick expect from me?' he says. 'Is he J.P.'s runner now? I say when to go to war – we don't scrap on their terms.'

'Maybe he's giving you the yokes back,' Shakespeare says.

'Don't be fucking smart,' Dan snaps, but Shakespeare too looks like he is about to snap, and that this comment came from lack of patience rather than high spirits. 'What do I do?' Dan says to the boardwalk. 'What do I fucking do?'

Shakespeare takes his hands out of his pockets and holds them in front of him, curving them as if around a neck.

'You go in there,' he hisses, 'you drag him out, we find a nice quiet spot and we kill the cunt.'

'Yeah,' Dan says. 'Yeah.'

His doubt is unusual; everything about this response to the lifted yokes is unusual, Ryan thinks, Dan is an ardent force not given to dithering. Nor is he usually shifty – no more than any of them are shifty – and so Ryan feels safe enough dismissing Jimmy Phelan's assessment. Dan is not shifty but Dan is acting out of nerves and suspicion, Dan is paranoid, Dan is too fond of the marching powder . . .

He looks now at Dan's nose and it seems the right colour, his pupils the right size. He's looking at Shakespeare. *Is that relief?* Ryan could well be wrong but ah, wouldn't it be a fine thing if he was right, if Dan was finally convinced of Shakespeare's loyalty through the other's strangling thin air?

Ryan considers Pender. He considers the timing. In the wake of his earlier meeting with J.P. perhaps Pender has come to warn

Dan that Ryan is an informer. He folds his arms, impulsively, over his chest. He hunches his shoulders. No, no. J.P. had heard no tales; no way he would have accepted the lies about Rotterdam otherwise. It was Dan's own rírá about thieves and traitors that alerted J.P., not Pender's hints, nor anyone else's.

'Right,' Dan says. 'We're going after this fucker but you' – he points at Ryan – 'you do a job for me first. Back there' – he gestures at the restaurant on the corner – 'at the table in the snug, is where I had to leave the chickie I was all set to be flahing tonight. Go to her, tell her I'm sorry I had to cut our encounter short, pay the bill, get her a cab, and then follow us, all right?'

He heads off. Shakespeare follows, and with both their backs turned Ryan puts his hands on his head and throws his neck back and exhales.

Not that going to war is a good thing, he tells himself as he heads towards the restaurant. But at least something's happening, and it's not like he'll be made an accessory, even if Shakespeare's simplistic, bordering-on-stupid threat is carried out. *No, this is fine*, he tells himself. *It's moving but it's fine. Keep the head, keep the head.*

Ryan asks the girl at the restaurant till about the table in the snug and pays for Dan's dinner. Then he finds the snug, where Dan's chickie leans across the table, wearing a black dress, smoky eyes.

'What are you doing here?' she says.

'Might ask you the same thing,' Ryan says.

'Having dinner with a friend,' says Natalie. 'I told you.'

Ryan slumps into Dan's seat and stares, and Natalie wets her lips and stares back at him.

Ryan finishes Dan's wine. He pours what's left from the bottle and finishes that too. His throat warm, he's able to do more than grip the table. He leans across it.

'What the fuck's going on, girl?'

'What do you mean?'

'I mean,' Ryan says, quietly, careful not to push the limits imposed by fine dining and wide-eyed company, 'what *the fuck* are you doing here?'

'Having dinner with a friend.'

'Dan Kane is your friend?'

'Yeah.'

'Do I have to ask what kind of friend?'

She looks pained. 'It's not as simple as that.'

'You're seeing Dan Kane?'

'The plan was: up till tonight. You know him? Where is he?'

'He's gone. See, I'm his friend too. He's called away, he gets me to come in here to look after the chickie he's out with. I'm to pay her bill, get her home safe.'

Natalie picks up her wineglass and the rim strokes her bottom lip for a moment before she takes a sip.

'You didn't tell me you were seeing anyone,' Ryan says.

'Oh God,' she groans. 'He said we'd go to dinner and I agreed because I wanted to tell him that I didn't want to see him anymore. Because I want to be with you.'

'But you were with him while you figured that out?'

She glints. 'I wasn't with him while I figured it out. I was with you while I figured it out. And now it turns out I want to cut him out for his friend, but how could you be his friend, Ryan? What sort of friend gets tasks like this?'

Ryan puts his head in his hands. 'Where's your coat?'

She sits till he looks up and snaps 'Where's your coat?' again.

Out on the street he watches cars glide past. She pulls her coat across her shoulders and stands beside him. She is patient.

'How long's this been going on?' Ryan asks, once the asking is inevitable.

'Dan? I don't know. A few months?'

'D'you know what he does?'

'For a living? He's a letting agent or something.'

Ryan looks at her.

'Amongst other things, I suppose,' she concedes. 'I guess now I know you better, Ryan.'

She's being careful but the delivery doesn't have to be harsh to hurt. Though he knew he wouldn't be able to keep it from her for ever; dealing's not the most subtle profession. He turns.

'You know nothing about me, girl. And I know nothing about you. I didn't think you were this kind . . .'

'This kind of what?'

He walks. She follows. 'This kind of what?' she says again, but he does not answer, he says instead, 'So you were with him when me and you got together.'

'I wasn't with him, I was seeing him on occasion.'

'Did you know?'

'Know what?'

He stands in front of her and she walks into him. 'About me! That I was one of his fellas! Did you fucking know?'

She laughs. 'One of his fellas, what does that even mean?'

'It means did you see me with him?'

'No.'

'If he'd seen . . . Oh Jesus.'

He pushes his hands over his temples.

'Jesus Christ,' he says and repeats it under his breath and stands then with his head in his hands. 'Jesus fucking Christ!' he restates to his city.

He turns to her, hands still on his head. 'You were fucking him while you were fucking me,' he says. 'You were fucking him while you were fucking me, oh Christ. What the fuck else haven't you told me?'

'Are we talking secrets? You've got a few to get off your chest, right?'

He falls back against the shop window behind him. She steps closer.

'Don't come near me,' he says. 'I need to think. Oh Jesus, he's going to kill me.'

'Oh my God, relax! This is just a coincidence.'

'You don't get it, girl. They're going to find me in a field some-where with a nice neat hole in the back of my head.'

'Oh, come on.'

He sinks to his haunches and puts his face in his hands.

'Let me think,' he says. 'Let me think.'

She crouches beside him.

'You've got a thing for a bit of rough,' he says. 'You've a thing for scumbags. Yeah, that's all it is.'

'What is that supposed to mean?'

'It's a type,' he says, cupping his hands over his nose and mouth. 'You haven't brought me home or anything coz I'm a type. Why you like me is the same reason Karine's mam and dad hate me.' As he says this he pictures Gary and Jackie D'Arcy dancing jigs around their kitchen, whooping.

'Are you really telling me you think you're a fetish?' Natalie says.

'I'm wrong, am I? You were charmed by Dan's politics and my wit, was that it? What are you after, girl?'

'I'm not *after* anything. You must have massive self-esteem issues, Ryan. Why are you so suspicious?'

'I'm a dealer, girl. I'm always suspicious.'

He barely hears her sigh. She gets up and walks off.

He turns his head on folded arms and watches her. She doesn't look back. He swallows. He rubs his forehead off his forearm. He stands. 'Natalie!'

She waits.

When he stops in front of her she catches his hands. 'This is a mess, but that's all it is. I'm not as . . . I don't know, as manipula-tive? As weird as you seem to think?' She sniffs and looks down; it's clearly not enough to banjax his head, she wants to break his heart.

'Jesus, girl. What are you doing with a fella like Dan Kane?'

'Ryan, he's fun. You hang out with him, you know this. And yeah, maybe he walks the line a little bit. The world is a complex place. Who am I to judge?'

'You couldn't judge him as being a fucking headcase?'

'God, we went to dinner a few times. We talked about Dubrovnik and drugs. Not much scope for headcasery there.'

'You know he's thirty-seven.'

'So? Look, tonight was arranged so I could finish with him. Like, it's pretty obvious that you and I should be exclusive.'

'D'you normally fuck around while you make up your mind?'

'Right, so you decided not to encourage any other romantic interludes the second you met me?'

He tsks.

Natalie nods. 'Yeah, you know you're being unfair.'

'All that aside, girl. When I say I'm dead when he finds out, that's fucking literal. You'll have to go from witch to fucking necromancer. You OK with that?'

'But it was a misunderstanding!'

He tries to coax her out of her misunderstanding. He tells her that he and Dan go way back, that he looks after Dan and Dan looks after him, that he can't undermine him because that would be suicide.

She keeps shaking her head. She tells him she'd never felt a connection with anyone the way she had with him. That she'd never before slept with a fella the same night she met him. She tells him they could make a go of it. She rests her head on his chest. He catches her arms and moves her away.

'No, girl. This has to stop.'

She closes her eyes. 'Does he have to know?'

'What?'

'If you hadn't been summoned to his side tonight, Ryan, I'd have finished with him.'

'And I'd have gone on seeing you, and I'd have ended up six feet under.'

'But now we know.' She moves towards him again. 'Now we could be careful. It's not like he's in love with me. I know he's got

128

a girlfriend. You could go to him in a few weeks, say you met me again, ask him what he'd think if you asked me out. He doesn't need to know about now.'

'Listen, you don't get it, you don't know what this . . .' Life? Business? Ryan can't find the word. 'What this thing is like. But I know. And I have to be sensible.'

'Is ending this what you want?'

'Fuck what I want, Natalie. I'm going to end up dead.'

She pulls her arms around her and looks away. 'God, I'm so stupid. I knew I shouldn't have given in to you that first night. I knew you'd just think of me as an easy lay.'

Ryan could let Natalie go and drive to O'Connell's and do favours for the man who'll never know he took her from him. He could quit with a kiss and tell her *Who knows, sure we might bump into each other again, thanks for letting me finish inside you.* He could take her here. He could lift her in his arms and score her back on this wall. There are a lot of things Ryan could do.

Dan enters the lions' den alone and gladly, having stationed his battalion outside. Ryan leans with Shakespeare on the bonnet of his Civic, watching out of the corner of his eye the movements of dogsbodies like Dessie and Reidy, who hang out at the corner mumbling to one another, and the glances thrown in his direction by Feehily and Cooney, who sit in the front of Cooney's Avensis. In ludicrous paranoia he imagines that they've read a flash in his eye that exposes his treachery. But this could be it; what's reasonable doubt, in a city so small?

Shakespeare doesn't curl his lip or wrinkle his nose. If he can catch her perfume, the scent of Ryan's duplicity, he doesn't broadcast it.

Fewer people here. Those pedestrians that pass are ould fellas and flat-heeled wives. The drinkers who enter the pub are after only nightcaps. Ryan hunches his shoulders. There's motion hidden somewhere in the never-ending black above; Ryan feels it in the pit of his stomach; he sees it when he closes his eyes.

'What did the ould doll say?' Shakespeare asks.

'Not a lot.'

'Did she look impressed?' He forces a hollow laugh. 'Sometimes they look impressed.'

'She wasn't impressed, no.'

'Ah. A classy bird so.'

Dan emerges. Pender in his wake is growling, throwing shapes, until he sees that Dan has company. There's a harsh embrace as Dan walks Pender against the wall and puts his elbows on the fool's shoulders. Pender's few comrades seize up. Dan cocks his head and whispers something in Pender's ear. Pender sets his jaw.

With heated geniality, Dan taps Pender's cheek.

And that's it.

Dan walks towards Shakespeare and Ryan. Behind him, Pender swivels his neck, as if in cooldown from a much more balanced altercation.

'Come on,' Dan says, and Ryan takes a final look at Pender and his silent attendants and steps into line with his boss.

Dan crosses around to Ryan's passenger door. 'You can give me a spin,' he says, and to Shakespeare, 'Back to mine.'

Ryan sits in the driver's seat and turns over both engine and implications in that 'back to mine' directive. *Back to mine to be shot and killed, for Pender, still standing, has sold you out.*

For Dan doesn't offer details of his meeting. Ryan can guess some of the particulars. There would have been calm acknowledgements that turned, tightly, into low threats. Cold rage. Equal parts exasperating and frightening. And then what? What made Dan leave Pender there, breathing?

Dan opens the glove compartment. 'Have you a fag?'

Ryan tosses the packet and his lighter from his jacket pocket. Dan lights up.

'What did Pender want?' Ryan asks.

'What d'you think he wanted? To protest his expulsion. To make some shitty point about the future of the route.'

'As if he didn't nick the yokes?'

'As if he didn't nick them. Except he did.'

'I don't get it, boy. Why leave him there after what he did?'

'I don't know if you noticed but he's surrounded by his own boys tonight. Besides, he's approaching madness, let him stew. I'll get the fucker when he's least expecting it. Or perhaps I'll get my yokes back when I least expect it. Let Pender feel what the ground is like out of the trenches. Meanwhile I'm holding my cards . . .' Dan mimes, clasping both hands to his chest.

Ryan says, 'But when do we get moving on mark two?'

'I'm not moving till Phelan does.'

'It's been weeks, boy. There's fuck-all guarantee Phelan knows anything about Naples.'

Dan doesn't react. Instead, as they reach the corner and the quay he asks, 'What did my little chickie say?'

'Not all that much.'

'Oh she's well bred, that wan. The well-bred girls are the wildest. Everything's so easy in their lives that they want to be fucked hard and the rougher the fella the harder they want it. That's not a bad thing to know, Ryan.'

Ryan squeezes the steering wheel.

Back to mine does not involve Ryan being shot and killed, though it is a harrowing event: Dan explaining his reasons for seemingly letting Pender off the hook; Cooney and Feehily nodding, stopping, nodding again, reluctantly learning to agree; Shakespeare looking like he's about to shoot and kill someone, authorised or not.

'What do we do?' Dan says. 'Leave bodies, with a new route being established? Invite the law in on top of us? Have the jackeen tabloids in on top of us? Think past the weekend for once in your life. We are not animals.'

'We're fucking dumb enough,' Shakespeare says. 'Langers can lift what they like from us – we won't retaliate.'

'But I wouldn't be surprised,' Dan says, 'if we got those pills back yet.'

'Jesus Christ, Dan, whoever lifted them did so to sell the fuckers. D'you think they're in a fucking gallery somewhere?'

'Don't you think we'd know if they'd been sold? Little Phoenixes, blowing the heads off young wans up and down the county?'

'Grand,' says Shakespeare. 'Grand. Potent little Phoenixes, going down Italian throats while we pull fucking moths from our pockets. Move on the second delivery, boy. Chalk the loss down to experience or exact revenge or wait for them to be magically returned to you, do what you like, but give me something to sell in the meantime!'

It is only now Ryan sees Dan rattled; he bares his teeth.

'When I'm sure it's safe to do so,' he says. 'Then, and only fucking then.'

'How does it work?' Natalie asks.

'How does what work?'

Her head's on his belly, a tress of her hair twisted in his fingers. It's early enough that it's still dark; Ryan would be happy to nod off again.

'What you do when you're not with me,' she says. 'What you do with Dan.'

'The less you know about me, girl, the less likely you are to run for the hills.'

'But what I'm imagining is probably worse.'

'What are you imagining?'

She turns her head and her cheek rubs his belly. '*The Sopranos*,' she says.

'Jesus, far from *The Sopranos*.'

'OK. So how did you get into all this?'

132

'Grade, girl. There's an attractive salary.'

'There must be more to it than that.'

'Nope.'

She makes a face. 'Oh come on. Help me understand.'

'I was into yokes. And one day Dan asked if I'd sell some for him. So I did. And I made money. There.'

'What age were you?'

'Fourteen.'

'You little mercenary.'

Her embrace transmits acceptance, or at the very least pragmatic apathy. Still he doubts he can make her understand. He could tell her that working for Dan gave him something to give a fuck about, that Dan kept an eye on him for reasons other than he was afraid Ryan would nick his car. But what would be the point? Even in his head explanation sounds like excuse.

'I want to know you,' she says. 'And what you do is part of you.'

So she seeks gory details, stories about rebellious users and gangsters cleaning guns in underground strip clubs. Would she mind if he detailed reality? It's about moving around all day, scared shitless, talking shite and throwing shapes at those in the same boat but knowing it's all chestnuts and mottos and platitudes, like you're working off a script. It's meaningless so you're disassociated and with disassociation comes hangovers, a bad diet, a smoker's cough. It's a false and empty function and there's no point to it, no comfort in it; you're a boil on the arse of your own country. So you deflect reality with notions like brotherhood, loyalty, hierarchy. Stupid dick-clutching fantasies. Stories Natalie wants to hear.

This is not part of Ryan. It's something Ryan does to keep the wolf from the door, even though the bears are inside picking their teeth by the fire.

12

Ryan goes the next day to the Riverbank Inn, where Colm is sitting with Dan in the office allocated to them: a beige, windowless space behind the function room. Colm looks frazzled but Dan's relaxed, clear-headed after his unexpectedly early night.

'It's my manager,' Dan says.

'. . . come to join the party,' Colm adds, head in hands.

Ryan sits with his arms crossed over his knees and endeavours to look like he's paying attention while he contemplates the prospect of a confession, delivered in time this time. But that he doesn't have to confess is a tempting and muddling thing. Dan has his sweet, innocent counterpart already – what does he need another for?

Colm complains that it's hard to find dedicated helpers when his start-up is rather the iceberg – substantial, but not wholly above board. One cannot expect devotion from people only interested in a few hours' untaxed pay. Colm frets about this negatively affecting his door policy – he explains that he'd love to be socialist about this but ranking works, people like to feel special and having a doorman as well as bouncers gives off the impression that everyone who gets into his club is special. He presents a scenario in which employing a doorman is the only way they'll broadcast their belonging in a city stuffed with licensed venues and dolly birds.

Dan looks at Ryan and rolls his eyes.

134

He's still in this light-hearted mood as the meeting wraps up. He is kind enough to indulge Colm's notions of manipulating punters and parts promising he'll reflect on his vision. On the street outside the Riverbank Inn he stands, hands in coat pockets, looking out over the Lee. 'It's going well,' he says. He segues into orders for the coming week – who needs cocaine and who needs correction. Ryan nods and listens, watching the Lee as well, and movement in the water – an industrial spool barely breaking the surface, bobbing towards the bridge.

'One more thing, little man.'

This as an afterthought; Dan turns away, then turns back.

'You won't be playing,' he says.

'Playing?'

'For Catalyst. I told McArdle to find another DJ for the warm-ups. I can't have you doing it. I need you running things – that's what's important.'

'Are you serious, boy?' Ryan says, though he knows Dan is serious.

'You can't be so visible. That hotshot shit's not for you. Eventually I'll have more pressing matters and that's when you'll have to step in here. It'll be good for you.'

'Yeah, but Colm's plan—'

'Colm's already looking for a fella with nothing better to do. You don't fit the bill. Time to put away the toys,' Dan says, to the Lee, and walks away.

Ryan can handle this. He has weathered worse. He can see the logic in it. Art and business, incompatible. Running a late-night venue to make money, to build a front, oh yes, that is sensible. But one should not seek to direct the revels for artistic or altruistic reasons if one is not off one's fucking head. Ryan is not off his fucking head. Ryan knows his place and it is his responsibility to ensure he stays in his place. He does not have to like it to see the sense in it. He kicks the wall. He does not have to like it. He slaps the side of his fist off the wall. He rolls his forehead off the wall and breathes through his teeth. He does not have to like it.

He had still been in two minds about Natalie before this afternoon.

The start of the following week Ryan spends getting his hands dirty cutting down a delivery in the kitchen of a ground-floor apartment in an ill-planned housing estate in Ballincollig, he and Shakespeare, usually excused from such duties but temporarily reassigned because when yokes go missing, the circle must contract.

'So it goes,' Shakespeare mutters, under his respirator.

So it goes. Similar responses like 'This and that' and 'Here and there' sate a Natalie newly cognisant of how Ryan makes his money; the less he tells her, the more she pretends to know. She's delighted by dark clues, the thrill of speculation. There are many happy sighs, and when Ryan meets her on Wednesday evening she mauls him and waits neither for a bed nor for him to get his jeans off.

Ryan doesn't see Karine at all, though he looks for her in Joseph's narrow glances. Towards the weekend he asks, as coolly as he can manage, 'Story with Karine, anyway? Were you talking to Louise?' but whatever Louise is saying to Joseph doesn't translate into shrugs. Joseph says no one's really seen much of her, socially anyway, that she's throwing herself into her fourth year internship. There's a weird moment on Thursday evening when Ryan runs into Jackie D'Arcy in the shop and she stops to ask him how he is. Now that he's been jettisoned, she has mind to care about him.

There's an awkward phone call from Colm just after that.

'I've got this fella to do the warm-up,' he says. 'Kenneth Hourihan, from Hollyhill, I think. Goes by the name of Dante.

A lot of his old stuff is very commercial but he'll tone it down, he says.'

'Right,' says Ryan. 'Yeah.'

'D'you need to hear him?' Colm asks. 'Like you're still the musical director of this venue, you know?'

'Am I, boy?'

'I think you are.'

'Yeah.'

'He's very good,' Colm says, helpfully.

Colm plans a meeting for Friday night: Dan, Ryan and the little gang they've managed to gather round – moonlighting staffers from the Riverbank Inn, a few girls Colm knows from casual hours at Room, the security team Dan's assembled. Ryan gets up late and spends a couple of hours messing with Ableton Live and his Yamaha, before he decides to check in with his mystic and prod her on the acquisition of his mother's piano.

She lets him in grudgingly. She's annoyed about something; she sits on the couch, glaring, smoking one fag after another.

Ryan feels cheated by her silence. He wanders around her living space, poking at ornaments, turning over in his hands little remnants of whatever she was before. He returns to the kitchen and finds himself sweeping ashes off the worktop into his cupped hand. There's no bin, but there are plastic bags under the sink. He empties both ashtrays, cleans off the rest of the worktop and puts away the packages of food she's left out. All the while the soothsayer stares at him, and when she says 'Are you looking after yourself?' it's more accusation than query.

Ryan weighs out his response.

'I haven't crossed a footbridge all year, girl.'

Harrumph and glower and white flags in eyebrows eventually raised. She regards the emptied ashtray he places on the coffee table in front of her and finally, delicately tips her cigarette into the bowl.

Ryan rests against the cleaned kitchen worktop.

'D'you ask your daughter-in-law about the piano?'

Maureen looks put out all over again.

'Selling it would be hassle she's too lazy to deal with. She says she'd have to get it refurbished to get a decent return, and that who knows, the young wan might take to it again one day. I didn't tell her I already had a buyer for it. How would I have explained that I'd a young lad up in the house? She'd think I was up to something unsavoury. She'd report me to my son, and he only a fecking maggot.'

'He is?'

'He's only useful when it suits him to be useful. That mess you just cleared away. That was his mess.'

'Sorry for cleaning up the mess,' Ryan says.

She tuts and pats the couch beside her.

He sits down.

'I'll try and sort out the piano thing for you,' she says. 'I can't push too hard. Deirdre already thinks I'm mad.'

'You're not mad, Maureen.'

She gives him side-eye. 'Am I not?'

'Unless you mean pissy. You're in a bit of a mood, like.'

'Women,' she explains. 'Women are always moody.'

'Are they what.'

'Sure that's right,' she says. 'The boy with two girlfriends. How are they treating you?'

Ryan goes through the changing of the guard – his other half for a beautiful stranger with whom he can indulge his arty side. He doesn't mention that Natalie's been playing the field up to now, or that she chose his own boss as her plough.

Maureen decides that he believes Natalie to be above his station.

Ryan tells her that that's not really how the world works these days.

*

138

Friday night, just after eight o'clock, Colm stands on the dance floor of the Riverbank Inn and shouts a run-through to a team of people Ryan has belatedly realised he's meant to know how to direct.

Doors at eleven; anyone who's invited friends needs to have them in on the dot or they'll have to pay full whack. Colm wants the dance floor full by midnight. He's booked Sterry, a trance DJ who's crafted a couple of charting remixes, over from London for the grand opening; next week they have Belfast bigwig Charli Dare, who's never played south of Dublin. Last orders at two-thirty; if VIPs need watering after that – the DJ and his entourage, essentially – staff are to do it stealthily. Everyone is to be a bastard if they see blatant drug use, but sympathetic to the subtle. The ladies' toilets have to be checked every half hour, because ould dolls won't give the place a second shot if there's no sanitary area in which to have mashed heart-to-hearts. The rest of the gaff is to stay crude around the edges, a homage to Sir Henry's, a Mecca most of them aren't old enough to remember.

Nods all round and Ryan breaks away and slips out the main doors.

He stands between freshly painted walls, the building one side of him, the block boundary of a stubby lane on the other. He tests the block wall. The white's dry. Ryan leans against it, lights a cigarette and fires up Tetris.

He's building walls between walls when Dan's head juts past the corner from the street outside.

'Fuck're you doing there, little man?'

'Making a balls of things,' Ryan grumbles, as one of his tetrominoes falls across a gap.

Dan shakes his head. He stands at the street entrance, hands in pockets. 'I assume McArdle's in there?' he says.

'You assume right, boy.'

'Do I tell him you're hiding out here, then?'

'Do not.'

He looks to his left. 'I've brought him someone to attend to his precious door policy,' he says, and Natalie appears at his side. 'You know Ryan, don't you?' Dan asks her.

'Oh yeah,' says Natalie. 'I remember him from last weekend.'

13

In the windowless office Ryan watches it dawn on Colm. The open smile, then the dipped eyebrows, then the relaxing of the muscles around his mouth till his jaw falls and he finally recognises her.

Ryan paves the way to his silence with a cagey headshake behind Dan's back, and so he stands and stares at Natalie until Dan's removed his arm from round her waist and gone back out to his car, then he says,

'What the fuck is going on?'

Ryan asks too. He asks what she thinks she's doing and Natalie shrugs and tells him it was Dan's idea and Ryan tells her that, as someone who knew that idea was a very fucking bad one, she should have told Dan she didn't want dragging into it. Colm repeats his demand for an explanation. He wails when Natalie says that her seeing both Ryan and Dan is more complicated than it looks.

'How's it more complicated than it looks? They pass you around like a fucking joint – that's not complicated!'

'Watch your fucking mouth, boy,' Ryan says.

Colm reels on him, clasping his head. 'Cusack,' he cries, 'what the fuck are you doing?'

Natalie starts into an explanation. Colm, stressed now to the point of self-contradiction, tells her to shut the fuck up. Ryan squares up to him. Colm points a finger at Ryan. Ryan grabs Colm's collar and slams him backwards. Natalie catches Ryan's arm and pleads that she be allowed to tell them a story.

Ryan doesn't want to thump Colm. Colm doesn't want to thump Ryan. They look at Natalie.

She's well attired for this. A black pencil skirt hugging her rump, heels that bring her up to Ryan's nose; he doesn't know if she dolled up for him, or for Dan.

'What you guys are doing here is amazing,' she says. 'Like, dynamic. Ambitious.'

Colm throws up his arms and turns away.

'There's so much I could help with,' Natalie says. 'Coming here keeps Dan happy. He thinks he's sorting a problem for you and doing something nice for me. I want him to sink into thinking we're just friends. So I'm down here, working, having fun . . . with Ryan. I see Ryan, Dan sees me with Ryan. You know, Dan isn't in love with me. After a while he won't mind seeing me fall in love with Ryan.'

She rustles up a blush.

Colm says, 'Are you even listening to this, Cusack?'

'Don't you think I've asked myself whether coming down here was doing the right thing?' Natalie says. 'Every way I look at it this makes sense.'

'Not for me,' Colm says. 'No fucking way.'

'Weren't you telling Dan you didn't need staff, but collaborators? This really stokes my interest. I know I'll be good at this.'

'Are you also good at cleaning brain off span-new decks?'

'Dan won't find out anything till I let him,' she says. 'Look, I've got a Masters in accounting. I can be an asset to you. You'd be surprised what I know.'

'We've thrown away the rule books for that side of things, thanks.'

'No, Colm, you'd be surprised what I know.'

'I can't be part of this,' Colm says, after a pause long enough to germinate seeds of doubt. 'Maybe you don't want to admit it, but you're fucking him in more ways than one.'

142

He shakes a thumb at Ryan, then turns to plead. 'This is suicide, Cusack.'

'It's a mix-up that needs to be sorted.' Now Ryan pauses, puts his hands on his head, pivots. He looks back at Natalie and she smiles. 'This actually makes sense,' Ryan concludes.

Colm casts his arms wide. 'Cusack.' His hands come back together; he knots them against his chest. 'I know enough about Kane that I'd sprint screaming from every woman he blinks at, and you know him better than I do.'

Ryan says to Natalie, 'Give us a minute.'

She exits and as Colm watches her leave his forehead corrugates and his shoulders slump. 'Look,' he says, 'don't get me wrong. She's fucking nice. I said that the night you brought her back to my party. But no woman is that nice. Unless she has a second fanny, I fucking implore you to back off. Dan Kane is riding her. I mean, Jesus Christ.'

'He's not anymore.'

'Isn't he? He's fairly fucking hands-on if that's the case.'

'Naw, boy, she finished with him.'

'Aye, and forgot to tell him about it.'

'Listen, it's . . .' Ryan shakes his head. 'It's a tough one, like. There's a bit of delicacy required. This is the right approach. I hang out with his leftovers, and eventually I ask him if I can take a stab.'

'So I host the double-crossing because double-crossing's all you fuckers know? Oh dead on. Dead on. And if you get found out before he's lost the taste?'

'If it comes to pass that I'm found out you can say you know nothing,' Ryan says. 'I won't hold it against you.'

'That's not what I'm worried about.'

Ryan notes the sounds bleeding through from the dance floor, the exertions of the oblivious prepping for the great adventure. The noises encourage sincerity. He tells Colm, 'I don't know, boy. My ould doll spent Christmas crushing me. Natalie means something, is all.'

'She means trouble,' Colm says, but in a swift embrace he tells Ryan that that's his final word on the matter.

Just before Catalyst's grand opening, Ryan texts Karine. He asks if she's going to make it down for blast-off. He dawdles then in the shower, comes back to his room and picks up his phone gingerly.

> **The gang will be there but I can't promise anything.**
> **Good luck if I don't see you tho. x**

Ryan sits on his bed and sets about translating the casual windfall in that little x, then shakes his head and scowls and tells himself to cop on.

From there things progress in a rush: he meets Colm and greets Sterry, he runs a sound check, Hourihan starts a mix. From Hourihan's side Ryan watches the doors of Catalyst open. There is steady ingress. People have dressed up for the occasion. Drinks are procured and land staked out and every face turns towards the booth. Hourihan's set is well chosen. The crowd rewards him. Ryan stands and watches Hourihan bounce and pose and hates the fucker.

Sterry comes to a full dance floor and unleashes a set of flashy big-hitters. Ryan spots Joseph by the bar and ducks out of the booth and through the crowd. Sterry conducts thirty seconds of double-time and all around Ryan people holler and howl.

Joseph has crafted an expression like a camel ready to spit. 'Industrial fucking chic,' he bellows. 'I like it. Ditch the shitty trance and I might even come back.'

'You're comical, boy.'

Joseph removes his tumbler from the bar. He takes a sip as a shadow placed by the light show casts a hood from his forehead to his neck. He leans in to Ryan's ear.

144

'Natalie's at the door.'

Possibilities now, more fleeting shadows around the beams dancing across this space. 'Did you tell Louise that that was her?' Ryan asks.

Joseph's eyes dart left. 'No.'

'Joe, did you?'

'Yeah, I think I actually might have.'

'Karine's not coming down, though?'

'I don't think so, boy.'

It's not a bullet dodged. Natalie's new position will inflate her legend among the buddies Ryan and Karine lopsidedly share – the girl fucking him becomes the girl fucking him so well he has to have her around him all the time. 'It had nothing to do with me,' he says, and Joseph's eyebrows climb and dip. 'She's a buddy of Colm's.'

Joseph smiles at him like Ryan's a chimp who's just completed a vaguely ape-shaped finger-painting.

Beats build and crash, bass stirs blood rushes, melodies pull the dancers as strings pull puppets. Joseph and Ryan find their buddies. Ryan accepts round-eyed congratulations. Sober, he watches his friends' dispositions synthetically change, their hands begin to wander, their arms draw arcs in the colour-bombed dark. He wants to join them, so that he can explain.

He goes to find Dan.

Dan's at the bar, holding court with Colm and a couple of Sterry's people. Ryan stands with him and Dan tilts his head towards him, pontiff-like.

Ryan asks before it hits him what he's asking.

'You hardly have any more of those yokes, boy?'

'Well, funnily enough . . .'

Ryan has yokes of his own, of course. They're not terrible by any stretch of his yoke-stretched imagination, but they're nowhere near as potent as the beauties Dan used to whet his appetite back before Christmas. He had thought they'd be well gone; Dan has a habit of partaking privately with Gina, so Ryan can't imagine his personal stash could have lasted up to February. But look; he's wrong.

He follows Dan out the door behind the bar and through the bowels of the Riverbank Inn to the office. His ears ring with the sudden quiet.

Dan has an open roll. He doles out three, then shrugs and adds two more. He places these in Ryan's open palm and firmly closes his hand around them.

'Share or take home,' he says. 'You do them all tonight and you'll be fucked off your chops, and that's no good to me.'

'Can't believe you still have a few.'

'Let's just say they're so great it pains me to take 'em. Let's just say every time I see them I'm reminded of my loss. C'mon, how's about a rail while we're here?'

Back on the dance floor Ryan divides them: one for Joseph, one for himself, one tucked in a cigarette paper in the corner of his pocket for Natalie, and two for the man who knows sitting in his father's kitchen is a bat-signal personalised for Ryan in beating danger-red.

Sterry's songs, notched up feverishly, stoke his pulse.

Colm's booked Sterry and his buddies adjoining hotel suites and they go back there, Sterry and his crew, Hourihan and his mates, the girls they've hauled in, Colm and Dan, Natalie and Ryan.

It's not a good idea, but advice Ryan gave himself wilts as Dan's yoke, augmented by the rail and one of Ryan's own pills, conducts cyclical explosions under his skull. He stands at Sterry's window and looks down four floors onto a Lee oily under lamplight and hardly moving. No stars, so he refocuses and watches his reflection, pressing his forehead to the glass, touching fingertips to shadow. Dan is too blasted to notice his state; there is no hassle to be found up here, halfway to the

146

stars with a bunch of Englishmen and ould dolls in tight dresses mad for throwaway intimacy. There are beats, down low, and trays of bottles from the bar. There are words and cackles, abandoned stiletto heels, cocaine raked out chaotically, and Ryan sees it all through the golden tinge of his fuckedness. Sweat, shivers, shallow breaths. Natalie perches on the arm of a blood-red two-seater. On arrival there were ten minutes of anxiety over how she was going to avoid Dan's attention, looking, as she does, unreal in black, but now Ryan thinks Dan can have her if she wants him to; it's all good; he's too warm, too complete to care.

Sterry appears beside him and grinds out approval, cocking his head and scratching his scalp and chewing, tasting, spitting the air. 'Dan,' he hollers. He puts an arm around Ryan's shoulder. 'The owner? He's a fucking legend, bruh.'

'Chalk it down.' A smile threatens to separate Ryan's jaw from the rest of his head.

'Talk it down,' Sterry misquotes. 'I fucking love your accent. It's like you're singing football chants all the fucking time.'

Dan joins in. He removes Ryan's shoulder from under Sterry's arm. He crooks his arm around Ryan's neck, pulls him down against his chest, kisses his temple.

'There's my boy.'

There's his boy, watching from under his arm as Natalie's mouth curves and her head shakes gently, as if Dan and Ryan were endearingly wayward children. Ryan closes his eyes. He can feel Dan's heart beat.

The conversations around them sound suddenly clear and reckless.

Well yeah absolutely, but then I told her that if she didn't sort herself out . . . No, thank Christ, I got Monday off . . . I've had some fucked-up experiences . . .

'I fucked her.' But the sound stays safe in Ryan's throat.

*

14

Spring takes its time. Natalie and Ryan make the most of the darkness.

They see each other two, three times a week, not including the Catalyst sessions presided over by the emperor Kane. Natalie confirms that she's spoken to Dan and ended their relationship on the best of terms, and that's why he's so pleasant to her. On club nights he checks the guest list over her shoulder with his hand on her waist. He offers her lifts home and buys her glasses of Prosecco. He rests his fingertips on her arse and her arms and a couple of times on the back of her neck and Ryan can feel it coming: the point at which his humour will snap and so the point he has to intercept and circumvent by going to Dan, cap in hand, to tell him he'd like to take it further with Natalie in his stead, to ask for permission to give her what he's already giving her.

His feelings for her keep pace with the weather; the turbulence of winter calms into periods of serenity punctuated by here-and-there squalls, internal usually, stirred by something Dan said or did and demonstrated only in irritability. Ryan thinks she thinks he's occasionally difficult because pianists are supposed to be, drug dealers even more so. She has no patience with jealousy because she thinks Ryan has no reason to be jealous. Sure, Dan pats her sometimes on the arse. Sure, she smiles and tuts at him. What's she supposed to do, piss him off?

In between Catalyst weekends and midweek squalls there are nights watching movies on the laptop in bed, the analysis of sets over mellow smokes – Ryan's own sets and the sets of dead legends, upcoming Catalyst guests, modern icons. She tries to fight with him sometimes, before the smoke takes hold; she tells him he's too dismissive of some chart-topper, or makes an intentionally unjustifiable fuss over some poseur on *Jools Holland*. To which Ryan grins and keeps rolling.

There is something affected in her takeover. There are intermittent hints that she's reciting at him. She likes when he recites back at her; she melts for forecasts breathed into her ears. She poses even when he fucks her, like she's catching the light in her head, like she's emulating. She has a thing for tasteful smut – her own term – she has favourite photos and gifs found on vintage-filtered image banks online; she shows them to him. 'It's not porn,' she says. No, not porn. 'What kind of girl do you think I am?'

'I could just look at you sometimes,' she says. 'Oh my God, there is something about a lean boy.' She stares at his abdomen. She drags fingertips along his hips. Physically, he does it for her. Mentally. Musically. He's drunk on her attention. She doesn't look him in the eye when he's fucking her in case doing so would anchor them, but on occasion she lets him emulate images of his own choosing.

He thinks of Karine as he does so, and her inviolable limits, how she'd tease by allowing him to draw the tip of his cock along the cleft of her backside before the smiling, adamant *No*. He thinks of how she wasn't afraid that eye contact would ground the fantasy. He thinks of how that's in the past. Fantasy in nostalgia and the other way around. Karine still has a hand in turning him on.

Between such charged times he gets fond of Maureen's couch and her grumbling and it makes him feel better to have someone so alien to talk to. They drink tea and draw up plans for the piano handover. They play cards and twice Maureen cleans out his pockets. They tell each other stories. His are of girls in whose labyrinthine affections he's fond of getting lost. Hers are of Old Catholic Ireland, Magdalene laundries, the tyranny of faith. It becomes apparent to him why they get along so well. Something barely mended about Maureen. That raggedness qualified her to recognise his gawping into the pit, gave her the strength to haul him out again. When things are especially quiet, when between them is gregariousness and truce, he feels grateful, but he's too afraid of it to admit it.

Over it all Jimmy Phelan looms, then shrinks. Ryan figures the pills must not be that good to J.P.'s jaded mind, because he makes no move on them.

This is lucky, as Dan now preps for the second delivery. He concedes Shakespeare's point without once referring to it. 'Clear the decks for midweek,' he tells Ryan, and from there his colleagues seem to breathe a little easier, particularly Shakespeare, who shakes out his limbs and stretches, released at last from a terrible bind.

Dan pays for Ryan to take the seat beside him on a flight to Naples, where they check into a dull hotel ten minutes from the airport and meet with their suppliers' representatives: three thirtysomethings, suited, booted, grinning. The one who made the trip to Cork in November greets Ryan warmly. Ryan sits at the bar with them for fifteen minutes, plámásing in Italian and dithering in Neapolitan, before Dan's smile shatters and he tells Ryan that they need to put their heads together, that this isn't a fucking holiday.

So they get down to brass tacks. The route now proven, Dan is expected to pay upfront.

'Get them down to eighty a pill,' Dan murmurs.

Ryan shakes hands on seventy-five.

Trading closes. A delighted Dan tells the boys, through Ryan, that he'll start the transfer rolling with his accountant as soon as he gets home.

An hour later they're in Salerno, where they get a rapid walk-through of the basics of international trade, and Dan asks questions for which Ryan procures increasingly worrying answers: what's the cocaine situation, what kind of volumes would test absolute limits, what kind of products would test absolute limits? Guns, perhaps? People, hypothetically?

Restricted once again to each other's company back at the hotel, Dan triggers a sigh of relief when he says he has no real interest in heading into the city; Ryan sweats with the thought of accidentally meeting his grandmother and having to explain, in between clips round the ear, what kind of business he's conducting in Napule.

'Bit run-down, your gaff,' Dan sniffs. So instead they head back to the bar and get mouldy.

December's heist is at that moment reclassified as teething trouble: the whole thing was Pender's fault. The whole fucking thing: Dan's panic, Gina's victimhood, the suspicion shared with Ryan on Shakespeare's hidden motives, Ryan's subsequent anxiety. It feels like a wound bleeding out is treated with forgiveness instead of surgery.

It's early afternoon, Saturday, hours yet to go to the latest Catalyst outing, where Ryan is to direct and humour a deep house doyen before counting the takings and transporting them to Dan's gaff. He sits at home on the couch, watching his phone but otherwise engaged in nothing more stimulating than arguing with himself. *I'm going to tell him about Natalie and me. I'm going to ask him. Naw, fuck that, I'm going to tell him.* He's been composing such gambits all week.

There is a thud on the door that leads from the kitchen to the yard at the back of the house.

Ryan startles. There is another thud. He jumps off the couch and as he does so he begins to cycle through an inventory of what he has on his person or in his room or in his car out of panicked habit; he goes to the kitchen; another thud. This is someone getting in whether or not Ryan lets them in, but the door would be flat on the floor already if it was the guards.

Ryan opens the door and is pushed back by a broad and dour creature, grey-haired and red-faced, well into middle age, so fearless and presumptuous and sharpened by his own longevity. Ryan trips over his own feet and falls against the worktop and stays there as this man, whom he knows, oh knows too bloody well, stops in front of him, puts a thick hand on the worktop either side of him, and keeps him still.

Jimmy Phelan walks in behind him and Tim Dougan, his stalwart, doesn't move for four or five seconds after Phelan touches his shoulder.

Phelan goes towards the sitting room. Dougan falls back and nods after Phelan and then pushes Ryan after Phelan, so Ryan follows as directed. Dougan stays where he is.

In the sitting room Phelan takes a satisfied breath and looks around. He seems to grow in this small space and Ryan feels the skin around his Adam's apple contract.

'Y'know you could have just called me,' Ryan says.

'I don't trust you enough to wait for you to come to me,' Phelan replies. 'Luckily, Ryan, a man like me never has to wait. I was just that excited about the buzz around your latest catalogue.'

When Ryan doesn't reply he rests an elbow in its opposite palm and taps his knuckles against his chin. The action only partly obscures his neck. J.P. has some neck: a squat square of bristle and muscle protecting a windpipe so many men before Ryan have wanted to crush. You need some neck in this line of work.

'When do you launch?' he asks. 'The new range of empathogens?'

'Where'd you get that idea?'

'Ah, Ryan. I do nothing all day but tend my grapevine. I hear everything so I can choose for myself what to look at – I'm the closest thing to a psychic you'll find, if you're into that kind of thing.'

He tries out a spiteful pout.

'The shapes Kane's throwing have gotten all the urchins excited.'

And shows his teeth.

'He does tend to attract them,' he says. 'Little lost boys, ha?'

And suddenly, exuberantly chuckles.

'I'm only taking the piss,' he says. 'I know you're a hardworking sort who stands by your Dan. I still want to know all about it. What Kane has in store for Cork and why, young Cusack, you didn't think to tell me the story?'

'Nothing to tell.'

Phelan clenches Ryan's shoulder, oh, very companionably. 'Of course there's something to tell. Start' – he angles his neck as if he's trying to get a better look at Ryan's underarms – 'by confirming that you've decided after all to procure another batch.'

'No point in pretending otherwise, is there?'

'See?' Phelan says. 'That wasn't so hard, was it?'

But then he leaves unchecked a pause that pulls the sweat out through the back of Ryan's neck, so that Ryan has to say, 'Listen, boy, I can't tell you any more than that. That's as much as I know myself. He considered last time's fuck-up, weighed the odds and decided to give it another bash.'

'That's half a story, Cusack.'

'It really isn't, boy. I've never had anything to do with importation, I haven't a fucking clue what's going on.'

'Why would Dan Kane waste his time on someone who'll readily admit to being thick as two short planks? Come on, Ryan. I know you're not a dope. Haven't I seen myself what you're capable of?'

'I'm not fucking lying, J.P. Dan isn't generous with the details. Just that there's another batch due.'

'Due when?'

Ryan's head still shaking and Phelan's fingers still pinching and the light in the room flickering, or is it just Ryan's eyesight failing him, is he just shutting down as he's meant to in the beast's leather-jacketed, steel-toe-capped, burgundy-cheeked presence?

Phelan jerks Ryan closer.

'The start of April,' Ryan says. 'That's the plan but it's not concrete. I was told only expect them when I see them.'

Phelan softly repeats, 'Why would Dan Kane waste time on an idiot?' and smiles. 'Why would Dan Kane proceed at all, if he hasn't yet rained down judgement on the pricks who nicked his shipment?'

'How d'you know he didn't?'

'Didn't I just tell you I hear everything? All that's happened in your house is that your hick investor's gone storming out of your little fellowship.' Phelan makes a fist of his free hand and brings it to Ryan's chest. 'D'you know why I didn't follow up with you on the pills?' He extends his first finger to make an arrow to Ryan's throat. 'Because nice as they were, I believed your guff about the great rip-off. I took your word for it that that batch was all there was.'

'That batch *was* all there was.'

'So you're telling me now there's a replacement delivery on its way, with no fucking fuss made at all?'

'There was fuss made, boy, and I felt plenty of it!'

'Well, you'd think so. They were great yokes, Ryan, not too far off the shit we used to get in the nineties, and if you know your yokes like your mam and dad knew their yokes you'll grasp the enormity of what I'm telling you. It was instant love, boy. But too good to be true. Kane unearthed a cabal of genius chemists only to be shafted by his own shareholders. Like snaring an ould doll with a teardrop arse and perfect tits, only for her to lift your wallet and hightail it as soon as you look down to get your cock out. I was willing to let it go, on that basis. Not so much now.'

'What d'you want from me, boy?' Ryan's going for aloofness and going down in flames.

'For you to be more forthcoming, that's all.'

'I can't come forth with shit I don't know.'

'And I can't find use for a fella who knows nothing, and you, my boy, are no fool. Get me dates and locations for the arrival of those yokes, so I have something to hold over Mr Kane's head when I'm ready to make him share.'

'Listen, boy, I can't make decisions about splitting deliveries with you. You ask me to bring you fucking details and you're killing me.'

'You're babbling like there's something you can do about it,' says Phelan. 'You'll do as you're told – you've learned that much, at least.'

'You're not the one who tells me what to do.'

He's darkly amused. 'Yes I fucking am.'

There's no truce in the subsequent pause. He doesn't even release Ryan's shoulder.

'Ryan,' he says. 'There's a stink of bullshit off all of this, and I'm disappointed that you haven't picked up on it.'

Ryan looks down, like he's accepted he's failed the fucker.

Phelan tilts his head to catch his eye again. 'The alternative, of course, is that it's you who's shovelling the shit, but then you know what happens if you cross me, don't you?'

Ryan knows.

'Ryan.'

Phelan shakes his shoulder.

'Ryan.'

Ryan looks up.

There's glacial sincerity in Phelan. He's a man built for relaying bad news.

'The time is nigh for me to put a halt to Kane's gallop. He might take it well, if coke hasn't rotted what scant grey matter he started out with. He might not take it well, if he genuinely

156

doesn't know what's good for him. Decide on whose side you want to stand on that day, Cusack, because that's one decision I won't bother making for you. Once Kane's crushed, you lose your usefulness. Start thinking about where you want to divert it.'

At last, his shoulder's released. Phelan smiles.

'We'll let ourselves out,' he says, 'worried as we are that Danny Boy will twig that you're cheating on him, and chop you into tiny wee pieces, crying all the while. I'll swing by and see you again,' he calls from the hall, 'and I'll make sure you're alone, don't worry, unless you've really pissed me off. But speaking of piss . . .'

Ryan puts his hands on his knees and then stands straight again in a hurry, so sure is he that he will throw up his breakfast.

'. . . I don't think you pissed yourself,' Phelan continues. 'Made of strong stuff, are they? In Naples?'

Think, think, think, you stupid shit.

Ryan rolls a joint.

Think!

He got eight honours in his Junior Cert, three of them As, a triumph considering he spent the first half of the year in detention and the second half in Karine. He could have done the Leaving and he's sure he would have smashed it – someone who can secure and maintain a synthetically paranoid customer base to the point that he can buy a GTI with cash at the age of twenty would have no problem getting As and Bs enough for university. He's right, Jimmy Phelan. Ryan Cusack is no dope.

Think, for fuck's sake.

Then he gets the call. Its unique ringtone shatters his deliberations. He has a Pavlovian response to that sound: he startles, he salivates, he grabs.

'Ryan, I need you.'

Ryan wastes petrol taking the car for an unjustly short hop and she opens the door in a pretty tizzy, hair escaping from her high ponytail, hands churning round and over each other.

The monster sprawls in her bath. It ignores her white knight's approach. In response to its effrontery Ryan lifts his knee so as to stamp down hard and she cries, 'Ah, don't kill him!'

Ryan stands on one leg with his hand against the bathroom tiles and Karine cringes behind the open door and goes, 'Just put him outside.'

The spider shrinks in on himself, as if he knows that his life, like Ryan's foot, hangs in the balance.

'I put him outside and he might come in again and then where would you be?'

'Oh my God.' She disappears back onto the landing altogether, where she keens and takes exaggerated breaths and – he can read the pattern of her footfall – paces and shakes out her hands and puffs out her cheeks.

Ryan glances at the spider.

'Don't kill him,' Karine repeats, shakily, from the landing.

'Get me a glass so.'

He traps the spider and Karine squeaks and hurries behind as Ryan brings him down the stairs and releases him in her mother's flowerbed.

She stands holding on to the door with both hands, dishevelled with equal doses of the heebie-jeebies and sheepishness. She's in loose navy tracksuit bottoms and a blue tank top too pale to conceal a black bra; he stares at her and she stares at the spot where he ditched the spider. Satisfied, she holds the door open for Ryan to come back in. She shuts out the door behind him and brushes past and into the kitchen.

'Thanks,' she says, over her shoulder. She stops in front of the kettle and gets going on the brew. 'I know it's stupid. I didn't have anyone else to call.'

'Where is everyone?'

'Out.' She turns and places a hand on the corner of the work-top either side of her, and Ryan gets a kick of déjà-vu and wrinkles his nose trying to get his head around it. 'Leaving me at the mercy of that eight-legged freak.' She smiles weakly. 'Not that my sisters would have made great back-up.'

He sniggers as he's meant to and she accepts with a wider smile, turns back to the tea and deftly makes up his mug.

They sit at the kitchen table. She asks about Catalyst and Ryan tells her stories: last week's ejection of a local radio personality who'd pushed his knob against one of the girls trying to clear glasses, Sterry's appreciation of the Cork accent, the DJs they intend to secure for summertime parties.

'And of course Dan's part of it too.' There's no bitterness to this statement; she delivers it with a familiar resignation. 'I thought you were going to play,' she says.

Ryan shrugs.

'He wouldn't let you?'

'Maybe he knows I'm not that good.'

'That must be it,' she says, dryly, and laughs to herself. 'She's there too, of course,' she continues.

Their eyes meet and their mouths flatten and there's sparks in the silence.

Natalie, she mouths, exaggeratedly.

'She works with us, yeah.'

'Louise says she's a bouncer.'

'She's not a bouncer. She's a hostess.'

'The hostess' – Karine draws overly generous curves in the air over the table – 'with the mostest.'

Ryan can't help his smile. 'Jealous?'

'I am yeah.' She rolls her eyes. 'Dying.'

'You can be a little bit jealous. I don't mind.'

She sips. 'Hardly. In fact, I approve of you whoring yourself out to fat girls. Variety is the spice of life.'

'Yera yeah.'

159

She maintains that look of tart pleasure as she takes both mugs over to the sink. Ryan follows. They stand by the door to the hall. He feels that she's waiting for him to lay out how he's taking his leave, but that there's more to be said, too, though he's not sure what, or where it'd fit.

'Thanks,' she says, again.

She bows her head and gives him the upturned eyes. It gets him. Little blasts detonate from his belly to his throat.

'What else was I gonna do, girl? Leave you hostaged?'

'I know it's stupid to be scared of them.'

'It's not stupid.'

'It is, though. It's dopey. Dopey that you'll still come over, too. Right?'

She folds her arms and looks away and in a move befitting of a dope Ryan takes her chin and tilts her head back and kisses her.

She kisses him back. His hands push over her waist. Hers hook behind his neck. They open their mouths to one another. He pulls her firmly against him.

She takes his hand in hers. They go up to her room.

She lies underneath him. He kisses the tip of her nose and her mouth and her chin and her throat, she tastes just right, she always has, she's home in his mouth. He pulls her top and bra cup down over her breast and closes his lips around her nipple and she says, 'I'd feel better about this if it wasn't so easy.'

Ryan lifts his head.

'Did you even think about it before you kissed me?' she whispers.

'What did I need to think about?'

She stirs, impatiently. They sit up. She fixes her top.

'This must be what it feels like to cheat with you,' she says. 'It's just that that's a bit jarring.'

He slumps and she straightens. He pushes his palms against her pastel patterned duvet. She takes down her ponytail and ties it back up again. 'You have a new girlfriend,' she says. 'What are you *doing*?'

'I don't know.'

'Did you ever know? When I was the girlfriend and she was the temptation? Or before her? When it was other girls? Can you really just not stop yourself, Ryan?'

'With you? No.'

'Yeah, coz I'm so special.'

Ryan stands back. His heels knock against the wall. Karine hugs her knees.

'You are special, Karine.'

'Right, so special that after we broke up you had to immediately go dip your dick into some randomer. See, you talk the talk but you don't walk the walk, Ryan.'

'I don't get this,' he says. 'What you're doing.'

'This is how you used to cheat on me, isn't it?'

'This isn't cheating, this is . . . This is a compulsion.'

'Yeah, like I said. You can't stop yourself.'

'No, *you're* the compulsion, Karine.'

'Oh God, Ryan, I'm sorry. I had no idea I was so potent.'

'That's what it is, girl. You have me wrecked.'

'I have you wrecked? Ryan, I've tried and tried to fix the damage you do to yourself. I've never wrecked you!'

'You know that's not what I meant.'

'You gonna tell Natalie that too? When she realises what you're actually like? Coz it's fairly obvious, boy. That all you're doing is running away from me trying to fix you into the vag of some poor bitch who doesn't really know you.'

'Are you talking about the dealing? She knows that. D'you know what, she knows that and she doesn't think it's her life's mission to break my fucking melt about it.'

Karine goes red in the cheeks.

'So no fixing, that's the appeal. She obviously doesn't care about you, so.'

'She just knows there's more to me than bad news.'

'More to you than bad news? Does she know you've been in gaol? Does she know you're not allowed keep paracetamol in your house anymore? Have you ever pinned her to the wall, then?'

'See . . .' Ryan throws his hands up and pivots and wobbles his jaw and leaves the 'see' suspended in shame and resentment, because fuck her for bringing that up, fuck him for pinning her to a wall in the first place.

In a parallel reality he's fucking Karine right now and the light dims outside and blossoms in her eyes.

But if there's negativity hidden in a kind word or a light touch or a soul-searing fuck, Ryan will find it, he's trained to sniff it out, he's adept, now, in self-harm.

'If the only reason for this was to make a point about how awful I am, you can just leave me alone,' he says. 'I'm with a girl now who doesn't constantly make me feel like a man-sized shit. Let me get my head around that. I have better things to be doing than rescuing you from creepy-crawlies.'

'Jesus, Ryan. If she likes you just the way you are then she clearly doesn't know what you can be.'

She bites down on her lip. He throws her a pissy shrug and goes for the door handle, and she comes out with, 'Do you love her, so?'

'Fuck off, Karine.'

But, of course, it's Ryan who does the fucking off.

15

To Catalyst in that dangerous state of mind, through tracks overlaid with growling soul. Ryan hits the floor, shuffling, stumbling, sniffing it out. He finds it at the end of his second white line.

At the door he locates Natalie, clutching her clipboard and laughing with revellers. No Dan, though Ryan doesn't look hard for him. He bothers Dan's bit on the side. He stands with her and when she turns her head her lips come close to his cheek and he feels her breath on his skin.

'What are you doing?' Tonight there is a vein of emerald over her heavy eyelashes. Ruby lips, smudging out. Pink cheeks, goose pimples.

Ryan turns his head too, so his mouth is by her ear.

'I want to fuck you.'

'That,' she whispers, 'is a very bold thing to admit to here, isn't it?'

'Are you gonna follow me?'

'Where?'

'To the office.'

He hears her breath catch.

But she does follow, long minutes behind, through lasers and cast shadows; the dancers make a human shield. She joins him in the office and he locks the door behind her.

'You know Dan is here, right?' she says, as Ryan locks his arms around her and pushes his lips against her throat.

'I know he's here.'

'And you don't think he'd be a little suspicious of that locked door?'

'All we're doing is a line. Who doesn't lock the door first?'

'Maybe then, by way of insurance, you should line up?'

'You do it.'

He pushes a baggie into her hand and she turns to the desk and clears a space. He presses up against her and kisses her neck. He undoes the back of her dress and pushes its straps down over her shoulders.

'Oh God,' she says, 'we could get in so much trouble.'

'I'm already in trouble.'

In too much trouble to worry that she'll smell of him, and him of her; Ryan fucks because he's fucked. Jimmy Phelan has fucked him.

He pulls out and finishes on her arse. 'And if you'd missed?' she chides, breathlessly. 'If that went on my dress, or on the desk?'

'Fuck it,' is his response. He does his line with his jeans still unbuttoned.

He returns to the main room and Natalie overtakes for her spot by the front door. He finds Colm and nods as Colm shouts strings of sounds into his ear. Then Ryan nods to the beat. It's the wrong soundtrack altogether. A kind of hot funk, nostalgic and tough and thoughtful, and Ryan here waiting to drown. Two conundrums, as a breakdown leads to raised hands and a clapped, communal interlude: on whose side is he going to stand? Dan's, or Phelan's? Karine's, or Natalie's?

The lights come up too soon.

Dan reappears on Natalie's tail as she reaches the office with the night's takings. She hands the package to Ryan over the desk on which he's just fucked her. He sits in the chair and licks his thumb and begins to count. Dan engages Natalie in racy banter. She goes along with it. Ryan loses the count. He starts again.

164

The after-party's arranged. They go back to Colm's. They crowd into his apartment, dimming the lights and starting the beats immediately so as to stave off the comedown of the music-less hike. The usual suspects: the visiting DJ and his crew, some of the staff, a smattering of ould dolls. Colm, Dan, Natalie, and Ryan.

Dan holds court. Colm tempts a laughing girl onto his lap with half a bottle of Jack Daniel's. Ryan slinks off to the bathroom and locks the door behind him. Natalie knocks and calls softly as Ryan straightens after a senselessly fat rail. He lets her in and locks the door again. Natalie gives him a look.

'I guess you've no intention of getting tired tonight.'

Ryan takes a quick sconse at the mirror in case his nose is bleeding. It's not.

'What d'you mean?'

'Just . . .' She shimmies closer. 'I was thinking we could bow out, you know? Go back to yours.'

'You want more, do you, girl?'

Natalie kisses him and pulls away and asks, 'Are you OK?'

'Hmm?'

She curls an arm over his shoulder and around his neck and in her eyes he sees the counting of each individual coke grain, the judgement stacking. He endeavours to halt it. He starts to kiss her. He kisses her till she gets heavier in his arms.

'OK, we'll get out of here,' he whispers.

Dazed and beautiful she whispers back, 'Good.'

He unlocks the bathroom door and Dan is standing there with an open smile.

'What are you two up to?'

Natalie sidles out and crafts laughter unblemished by shame. It's great, in the way accomplished dictators or typhoons are great. 'Hiding from those who'd judge my inexperience,' she says. 'I live in fear that I might sneeze on someone's line. So I might have persuaded Ryan to give me a little, little bit in private. He's very good to me.'

'Is he now?'

Ryan looks towards the living room and out of the corner of his eye Natalie strokes the back of Dan's hand.

'I wish Colm was the kind of chap who kept champagne in the fridge,' she goes on, and walks back to the music and the light.

Ryan makes to follow and Dan reaches over and pushes his palm against Ryan's chest. He says nothing for a beat. Then, 'She's something else, isn't she?'

'Who? Natalie?'

'Yes, Natalie. She's something else, isn't she?'

Ryan shrugs. And sniffs. It echoes. Once he hears himself doing it he can't stop hearing it. He's sniffing like an ould wan in a doctor's waiting room.

'She must be something else,' Dan says, 'if she's persuading you to accompany her behind locked doors, when you know better than that, Ryan, don't you?'

'Better than what?' Ryan sniffs.

'You know what the fuck I mean. You can nose around a pile of gak, so long as you're not nosing around her.'

Ryan swallows and scalds the roof of his mouth. 'I just did a line with her, that's all.'

'Yeah, about that.'

Brief eye contact and a sudden twist in Ryan's gut; he wants to punch Dan. He wants to knock Dan's head off the wall behind, and then the wall opposite. Make proper use of this narrow space.

'How much have you been snorting?' Dan asks.

Ryan sniffs again, and as a response to his stupid question it irks Dan.

'What are you even doing here?' he growls. 'Haven't you still a cash delivery to make back to my gaff?'

'Amn't I supposed to be here? Isn't Catalyst my club too?'

'It's my fucking club, Ryan.'

166

He doesn't relax the pressure either in his palm or his voice. Ryan runs his tongue along the back of his teeth and sniffs again at the darkened wall.

'Make the delivery,' Dan says. 'I have two bottles of cava in the fridge. Bring them back with you. And don't let Gina cop you doing it.'

Ryan goes to move again and again Dan's palm stays flat and heavy on his chest, but he releases him a couple of seconds later, and Ryan goes back to the living room for his jacket. Dan, moving with him, too close, retrieves the cash roll. Natalie, leaning against Colm's breakfast bar with a tumbler of his Jack Daniel's, smiles at them, and Ryan ignores her as Dan steps back over.

'Are you leaving, Ryan?' Natalie. Smooth. Playful.

Dan answers for him. 'He's going to get you some bubbly. What the lady wants, the lady gets, and what Dan wants, Ryan gets, isn't that right?'

Ryan sees Colm lift his head.

'Natalie,' Dan says, 'have you ever met Ryan's girlfriend?'

'I don't think so,' she replies.

'Karine,' Dan says. 'Slender, very feminine, very pretty. Kinda like himself. You know the way they say owners start looking like their dogs after a few years? How long has it been, Ryan? A good five, anyway.'

Ryan sniffs malice back down his throat. 'We're not together anymore.'

Dan laughs raucously. 'How many times have I heard that? Five or six years,' he says to Natalie, in an overstated aside, 'which is why he's yet to show interest in any of the lovely ladies who gather around every Saturday night. Mind you, his relationship status has never stopped him pulling before.'

She manages a giggle.

'We'll introduce you to Karine as soon as he's done whatever penance she's given him this time,' Dan smiles. 'I think you'll like her, Natalie. And him better, too. He's not himself without her.'

He dismisses Ryan by redirecting his attention and Ryan leaves Colm's apartment and gets out into the cold air before he opens his mouth and bares his teeth and exhales – *Gaahhhh* – into the dark.

Before he starts the car he sends a message.

Did he see you get this text

The reply only comes through when he's a minute from Dan's place.

No. Are you coming back?

I have to. Don't you be there. Call a cab and I'll meet you with the key to mine

I've just told him I've done a line, how's he going to believe I suddenly want to go home to bed?

Don't care call a cab

Gina is expecting his arrival. She answers his knock quickly. She's in jeans and flat brown boots. Her hair is scraped back.

'I was expecting this around three,' she complains.

'Sorry, girl.'

'That's all right.' She tries to be funny. 'To the safe with you,' she directs at the roll, but a yawn stifles the joke. Ryan smiles, though Gina cannot maintain she's been inconvenienced if she's still fully dressed. She looks like she's only just gotten in.

'Goodnight, Ryan.'

168

He lets her shut the door. There's no point in picking up the cava because he knows he's not going back to Colm's until Natalie's out of there – not in a fit, not in a seizure.

He's just after a bump back in his car when she phones him from a cab. He intercepts the cab on the quay; he hands her his house key and tells her he'll be back as soon as he can. Back at Colm's Dan, as predicted, forgets to ask after the cava. Now that Natalie's gone he's back to his magnanimous self, witty fabrications and double-edged jokes. The clock ticks on, the bumps keep coming. Ryan gets away as the sun's coming up.

Natalie is still awake when he gets home. She lets him in, straight-lipped. She returns to his bedroom and curls on top of the duvet on her side, her back to him. Ryan tosses his car keys onto the desk and takes his jacket off. The sniffing's stopped. The panic's starting.

'That was stressful,' Natalie says.

'He knows something's up,' Ryan says. 'Despite your messing.'

She rolls onto her back and lifts herself onto her elbows. 'What does that mean?'

Ryan didn't intend to be so sharp. He shrugs.

She's not having any of it. 'No, Ryan. What does that mean?'

'You know. The hand-stroking. The giggles.'

'You'd rather I just told him I was kissing you in the bathroom? You'd rather I told him you'd fucked me tonight in his own club?'

Ryan kicks off his runners. 'It's not *his* club.'

'You haven't answered my question.'

'What, whether I'd prefer you burned him with the truth or buttered him up with a lie? D'you know what, girl? I'm not fucking sure.'

'Well I'm sure.'

'Yeah. Hence the softly-softly approach, is it?'

'We agreed on a softly-softly approach.'

'Did we, girl? I don't remember asking you to prick-tease.'

'I am not prick-teasing!'

'Oh, that rattles you. I mustn't identify what's right in front of me. All I'm supposed to do is lie down like a good boy and watch you lead him on every fucking weekend.'

She draws all of the air out of the room and up her nose.

'You better think about what you're saying to me, Ryan.'

'Think? How can I think if I can't get my head straight? How can I get my head straight when you keep leading him on?'

'I'm just being pleasant. And you can't talk, when . . .' She jumps off the bed and flings open his top drawer. '. . . you still have all of your ex's stuff here. Look! You keep all her bits around for when you eventually get back together, like Dan said.'

'Yeah, and you know why he said that.'

'Why did he say that?'

'Because he fucking knows there's something up, doesn't he?'

Ryan flops onto his chair and digs into his pocket for his grass and papers. Natalie sits on the bed as he starts to roll.

'Why do you still have all her stuff?' she says.

'Coz I fucking forgot it was there.'

'You?' Natalie extends a finger and draws it round the room. 'You're painfully neat, Ryan. How could you forget it was there?'

The spat spirals. Ryan sparks his joint and snaps back at her accusations.

'You are being really belligerent,' she cries.

'You said this was stressful,' he tells her. 'I'm stressed.'

'Maybe you'd be less stressed if you stopped hanging on to your ex's things.'

'I'd be less stressed if Dan wasn't pawing at you.'

She looks away and back just as quick, and says, 'So you're a cheat, are you?'

'What?'

'Your relationship status not mattering when you're on the pull, that kind of cheating. Was Dan on to something there? Did you cheat on Karine?'

'I cheated on her with you, Natalie.'

170

'Before me.'

They cannot get a rhythm going. They argue badly. They make ugly points. While they quarrel, about Dan and Karine, over definitions and parameters, the comedown takes hold over the half-buzz of Ryan's puny spliff and once it settles, he's finished. He cannot argue. He cannot stand up for himself. He starts thinking Natalie's going to take matters into her own hands and phone up Karine for the full story if he so much as leaves the room. He just wants to sleep – remove his head, place it on a shelf, throw a towel over it.

'And you don't,' Natalie says, 'need to tell me how dangerous this whole thing is, potentially. I know, OK? You know what Dan calls you? His Rottweiler. Fine thing to hear about the boy you've been sleeping with, isn't it?'

'That's just part of the poison,' Ryan says, but his voice is feeble. *She can hear the lie*, frets the cocaine. *She can see the truth.*

'Do you hurt people for him, Ryan?'

'I'm not an enforcer.'

'That's not an answer.'

'What d'you want me to say? I've never killed anyone.'

The fight goes out of her too, in a hushed breath. Ryan comes away from his chair. He gets closer to the floor as he moves, till he's on his knees by the side of the bed looking up at her.

'I knew you were a dealer,' she whispers. 'But you're more than a dealer. You're a gangster.'

Ryan thinks of Maureen.

'I'm no gangster, Natalie. I'm not able for it.'

'Well, what are you then?'

He feels the weight of the answer and under the heft he rests his forehead on the duvet beside her. She runs a couple of fingers through his hair, down onto the tip of his ear.

'I'm a musician.'

It sounds ridiculous. But it's all Ryan can get past his teeth.

*

Natalie sleeps. Ryan doesn't. He lies behind her with his fore-head pressed between her shoulders. The morning taunts from behind the curtains and he shuts his eyes, too tight. He speeds down black tunnels. He feels sick.

She stirs around midday and tells him that she feels manky and wants to go home.

'Are you able to drive?' she worries.

'Course I am.'

He feels like shit and he feels that he deserves it. Not for the coke, but for the answers he gave Natalie as she bit down on her thumb and stared at the wall, miles from him, but gaining.

I've never killed anyone.

He should've spun stories, assured her that all he does is make deliveries, countered Dan's canine classifications, retold their acquaintance in banal terms. She has a shower and Ryan drags himself to the kitchen and forces a pint of water down his throat. She joins him there; she slots herself into his arms but it's bother-ing her. He can see her imagining all sorts of what he gets up to at Dan's behest and he can't knock those thoughts off track because whatever she's thinking probably isn't that far off the truth.

Natalie shines so bright she might as well be a mirror. Ryan looks at her and sees what a scumbag he is. Everything that was ever said in the tabloids about dealers, everything a debtor ever called him, everything Karine ever walloped him with.

Dan phones him as he's driving. He is wide awake, purposeful.

'Come over, you're needed.'

'There in fifteen.'

Ryan drops Natalie off and heads for Dan's, praying for a short task or a long deadline.

Gina's coming out the door as he arrives.

'Hey, Ryan. I knew he had a meeting. I've been banished.'

That's how it must be: you get rid of the ould doll when work beckons, give her a few quid and shunt her in the direction of

Brown Thomas, bring her back again with a bottle of white wine and a long poking. That's the way, Ryan thinks, when you do things right. When you're not mocking loyalty with every load blown.

He shuts the front door behind him and Shakespeare's call directs him to the spare room. Walking down Dan's hall Ryan thinks that maybe he should decide to stand with J.P. in whatever clash is coming. He's fucked Dan anyway, might as well throw himself into the abyss.

The thought makes him red-faced and that's how he faces him: scarlet and shamed.

Dan's leafing through banknotes. 'Sleep well, Ryan?'

'Didn't sleep at all, boy.'

'I'm not surprised. You were wired.'

He smooths the notes into a tight rectangle, looks up, and smiles.

'And how,' he asks, 'did Natalie sleep?'

I'm a liar, you can't believe a word I say. Tell you how I know that. My dad told me.

He says it was inevitable that I'd grow into a maligning shit because I was brought up in multiple languages. He could never be sure of what I was thinking because he didn't know in what language I'd be thinking it. He couldn't read me, and he figured that made me foreign, and if I was foreign, then he mustn't have been able to trust me. Household xenophobia, a contagion released to fill the cavity you left. God, it's so fucking stupid.

I wasn't going back to one language just coz having more vexed my dad. After you died I read books, I read news sites, I watched films, I listened to podcasts, but you don't lose the everyday and make up for it in news reports. Thank God for my nonna, who still calls me and still pushes me, dashing in and out of Napulitano and taking long-distance swings at my accent.

Funny thing, my accent here is a bit off, too. My ts and ds are too soft and that's definitely Italy's fault. Like, it's still a Cork accent, and I only realised how strong a Cork accent at seventeen, when I went on my Dublin holiday. I didn't say much up there, partly because I'd invite headlocks with every C'mere timme and Aw ssstoppp and Like.

That first night I spent in gaol, oh fuck me, I don't think I could ever describe it properly, no matter how many languages I had. They put me in a committal cell that stank of shit and I sat on the mattress with my hands in my pockets, hyperventilating, scared I was gonna puke. I wasn't thinking of you then, Mam. You were gone six years and the everyday had changed.

But the next morning they brought me out to process me and the screw said, Did you phone home? and I hadn't, because no one told me I could have, and the screw said, You should have called your mam at least, and that's it, that's when I felt the absolute furthest from you. You, and my words, the way I thought and the way I gestured and the way everything used to make sense – all of it in the past, all of it gone.

It didn't stop me lying, though. Look at me now. Dan needs me steadfast and I'm not steadfast. I do J.P.'s bidding on the sly and I fuck someone I shouldn't be fucking because I don't mind telling lies to have what doesn't belong to me.

My dad had the right conclusion, but he started off wrong. It's nothing to do with the words you taught me or the blood you gave me. It's not your fault, how I turned out.

16

Ryan's forcing it. He's losing him. He's dead.

'Natalie?'

Dan confirms it, smiling.

'Dunno what you mean,' but Ryan's lie is frail as the washed-out daylight.

'She stayed with you last night, didn't she?'

'No.'

'Yes. I'm not going to tease this shit out for you, Cusack. I called her a taxi last night. I checked in with the driver afterwards. She was dropped off at your gaff. She didn't come out again until half an hour ago. When you dropped her home.' He sheds the smile. 'Didn't you just drop her home?'

A coke comedown shares symptoms with an unexpected bushwhacking; Ryan's skin is clammy, his mouth is parched. He has to swallow. 'It's not how you think, boy.'

'Well, yeah. I gave you the benefit of the doubt first, coz you'd be the last person on earth to do a number on me.'

He closes the gap. He takes Ryan's jaw in his hands and presses his thumbs into his cheeks.

'Tell me I'm right, Ryan.'

His eyes swim and he blinks and there are teeth now and words tumbling through them. 'I looked for an excuse for you, anything that would keep you clean. But in the end I had to draw the story from facts and not wishful thinking, didn't I?' He shakes Ryan's head. 'I don't get it.' He pushes harder. 'I don't get it! What the fuck were you doing? Trying to prove you were the bigger man with the bigger dick? I don't fucking get it!'

'Naw, listen,' Ryan says. 'Listen, it's not what you think.'

'Did you fuck her?' Dan's fingers stretch to the back of Ryan's neck and up the slope of his skull. 'Be a man if you're the bigger man. Fucking admit it.'

Their foreheads come together. 'Admit it,' Dan whispers. Ryan screws up his eyes. 'Admit it.' Still a whisper, but insistent, cracking. Ryan shakes his head.

'Listen, boy, I met her before I had any idea you knew her. I was already seeing her by the night you told me to get her home—'

Dan cuffs Ryan. He grabs his collar. He slams him back against the door. He punches him in the stomach. He lets him fall. Ryan coughs out over the wound, on his arse on Dan's off-white carpet with his back to the door.

'You hid this from me?'

Dan kicks out and gets him on the shoulder.

'You were fucking her since January and you hid it from me?'

Ryan gets his breath back. He gawps across the floor, at Shakespeare's shins, at the skirting board opposite, hand on his shoulder, afraid to press down with his fingers, sure he can feel the blood pooling under his skin.

Dan paces and tears at the air. 'And you had no idea I knew her? What, despite being there when I was out with her, you'd forgotten what she looked like, is that it?'

'I swear, boy, the night I met her I was on my own—' . . . but only just abandoned to his drunkenness by his boss, who was out for the night, socialising with a flame-haired girl and a counterpart who'd gotten the hump and fucked off in a taxi . . .

'You fucking knew,' Dan howls. 'And even if you didn't, she certainly did. I hope she was worth it, Ryan. I hope you've told her you'd die for her, just so she understands when you turn up a few weeks from now full of maggots.'

Ryan registers the gun advancing on him and presses back against the door. Dan pushes the muzzle into the bridge of his nose. 'Jesus, boy,' Ryan starts, then his voice goes. He puts his hands on the door behind him but his fingers slip on the gloss. His knees fold.

'What did you expect, Cusack? You must have pictured this when you weighed up your pros and cons. Or did you weigh it out at all? Pussy's just that fucking significant, is that it?' He keeps pressing, twisting, panting till Ryan's on his side on the floor, then he withdraws the pistol and applies his boot. Ryan gets it just below his ribcage. His lungs are emptied; he spasms and retches and curls up in reflex action. Dan falls back against the opposite wall. Ryan fights for air and once he gets a gulp he pukes on the carpet; he pushes at his belly; he cannot get up.

'D'you know the tragedy?' Dan gasps. 'No sinner on this planet is going to miss you, Cusack. I'm the only ally you had, and you just had to fuck me over.'

He lunges. He gets Ryan in the belly then the thigh then the groin. The impact goes from Ryan's crotch to his forehead. He vomits again. Water, then foam. His eyes spill over. He heaves.

Dan is back level with him. He pushes his fist against Ryan's throat. 'Open your fucking mouth.' He pushes the muzzle under Ryan's lip.

Shakespeare's voice, close. 'Dan.'

Dan breathes, 'I'll give the whore one for you later, will I?'

'Dan, you're not thinking, boy.' Shakespeare again. 'You're going to do him here? You're going to explain the brains all over the carpet to Gina, are you?'

'Gina swallows what I give her,' Dan says. 'So will you.'

Shakespeare shouts, 'Jesus, Dan, think about what you're doing!'

Think, a command enforced. Shakespeare pulls Dan away, and as Ryan dribbles out the taste of salt and metal he registers a quarrel at arm's length, a confusion of gestures.

178

Shakespeare and his way with words. Dan strides over and gets the boot in again, compensation for common sense.

Shakespeare takes the Ballyhooly Road and drives into a maze of lanes and hedgerows. They climb. Before them the vegetation takes on a dull brown and stubby conifers multiply. Shakespeare swings off the road and stops the Civic at the entrance to a forest track, blocked by a black and yellow boom barrier.

Dan has calmed to cruelty. He gets out of the car and pulls Ryan out of the rear passenger door and shoves before Ryan's found his feet. Ryan flies out of his grasp and onto the dirt. 'Get up,' Dan says. 'We've a ways to go yet.'

Ryan stands and immediately hunches. The only heat in him is behind his eyes, as far back as his temples, stretching to his hairline. He cannot clear the tears. 'Dan,' he says. 'A ways to go where?'

Dan jerks his shoulders. 'What the fuck d'you think is going to happen, boy? A ways to go meaning I've no intention of dragging your cadaver.'

'What the shit are you talking about?'

'Don't snivel, for fuck's sake. You think I want to see that?' Dan takes Ryan's shoulder and shoves him to walk ahead, kicks when Ryan stumbles.

Shakespeare, impassive, walks on.

Ryan is wide-eyed and shaking and cannot finish his petitions, though Dan is not deaf to them. He makes noises in response to Ryan's, sometimes in tandem. Snorts, curses, scorn, moans. They come off the track at Shakespeare's signal and trudge through trees planted in uniform rows. Shadows made by blueprints on some graduate's desk. Dense and dark, lifeless underfoot.

Dan pulls back on Ryan, fifteen minutes into the march. He takes Ryan's arm and knocks the barrel into the back of his head.

'Get on your fucking knees.'

Ryan gets on his knees. Dan grabs his hair and keeps him upright and Ryan looks at an earth corrupted by equations and industry.

'If I was going to bury you I'd pick bog,' Dan says, 'and you'd disappear. But I want to see how long it will take people to realise you're gone. How long then to find you? How long before there's another dead Cusack on the front page of the *Echo*?'

'This over a woman?' Ryan whimpers.

Dan loses it. He tugs at Ryan's hair before kicking him forward. 'This isn't about me and her, this isn't about you and her!'

'I'm sorry, boy. I just . . . I dunno, I'm sorry.' Ryan's sure now he's going to piss himself; he concentrates on that, as if by controlling his bladder he's not yet lost. 'I'm sorry,' he keens. 'I'm sorry, boy.' Even to himself, in this desperation, his apologies sound anaemic. He digs into the dirt and closes his fists.

'You did this,' Dan says.

Ryan screws up his eyes.

There is motion behind him. Ryan doesn't stir or open his eyes. The cold point of the muzzle rests on the back of his neck; it's teased up onto his skull; it is with such a light touch that as his shaking intensifies the muzzle's pressure becomes less perceptible. Ryan thinks of his father. He thinks of Karine. He feels profoundly separate, the sum only of his parts . . . he does not want to die knowing the last ever time he'd be held has come and gone without a ceremony.

He does not want to die.

Dan sinks to his haunches at his side. He grabs Ryan's hair again. His voice is contorted on the burst and bulge of Ryan's panic: 'Are you broken, Cusack?'

Ryan opens his eyes. Dan is blurred and warped. Ryan blinks. He tries to lift a hand to wipe his eyes but he cannot.

180

'Good,' Dan says. 'Because it fucking pains me. It pains me that I still need you and it pains me that I had to break you.'

He pulls Ryan up by his hair. Ryan has to grab Dan's wrist for balance. He feels the earth under his feet once more, the vertigo of height and exposure.

'She's a dirty bitch,' Dan says. 'So don't think I can't understand the attraction. But I promise you, if I hear of you sending her even another word, I'm going to finish what we started here.'

He opens his fingers. Ryan ends up back on his knees.

'Jesus, get up.'

The ache in Ryan's gut spreads as he straightens. Dan says, 'Gimme your phone.'

Ryan folds over one arm and pulls his phone from his pocket.

'Unlock it.'

Dan watches Ryan tap in the code and takes the phone.

'Now, everything that's in your pockets. Your keys.'

Ryan's key ring is light. Natalie still has his front door key.

'When you get home . . .' Dan tucks Ryan's things into his jacket. '. . . you're to bring me your pistol, and what ammo you've stashed. I'll take back what's mine.' Hands free once more, he grabs Ryan the way he did back at his house, holding his jaw, kneading his cheekbones. 'Everything.' His embrace intensifies. 'I leave you as I found you. Whatever you've lodged with me is gone. That pittance is fuck-all reimbursement for the years I've thrown away on you. You'll keep brown-nosing to your mafia buddies as I direct it. I made you, I broke you, I own you. Let that sink in, Cusack, on your walk home.'

A final belt across the mouth, bone against bone and salt on copper, and he leaves Ryan on all fours, spitting blood.

Ryan hears him retreat or he imagines him retreat; the ringing in his ears diminishes enough for him to register altitude and isolation; a car back on the road, moving away. He drops from all fours to the earth, right cheek to the ground, and lies there.

Get up.

Get up.

You can. You fucking have to.

Ryan pushes himself back onto all fours, retches, thrusts back onto his haunches, then onto his arse, curls one leg under him and stretches the other out and watches the undergrowth.

Come on.

He gets up and leans back against a tree. He fumbles with the buttons of his jeans and gets his dick out and pisses, at last, what remains from the pint of water he had in another lifetime. He gets some on his jeans leg. Damp on damp on dirt. Not that it matters.

It's a while more before he starts picking his way back to the forest track, slapping his weight against every second or third trunk. *I must look pissed*, he thinks. If there was anyone here to see him, he'd look pissed. If there was anyone here, way up the mountain on a sodden March afternoon.

He gets back to the boom barrier. Shakespeare's Civic is gone. Ryan looks around with one shaking hand on his mouth and realises that he doesn't know where he is because he doesn't spend his days executing people in the hills and picking out grave sites between collinear conifers.

I've never killed anyone. How wrong it is to be thinking that he should have gotten in some practice by now.

He starts to backtrack. His body aches, skull to soles. His jeans are wet. The collar of his shirt is sticky from the pastel broth of spit and blood.

He limps and reels for fifteen minutes down that mountain road, chest wobbling, lip bleeding. Here and there is a whimper, or weak malediction. 'Fuck,' he weeps. He turns, quivering. The world seems vast and ferocious, the sky thin.

There's a car. Ryan hears it before he sees it and knows that the driver isn't guaranteed to pay heed to him long enough to notice his frailty. He gauges stopping distance and staggers into the road.

182

The driver brakes and throws his hands up and rolls down the window.

'Jesus Christ! What are you doing?'

He's youngish, indignant. His forehead furrows under messy brown hair. 'What the hell's after happening to you?' He doesn't maintain eye contact for the response. He grips the steering wheel and looks out the window to his right, then to his left, then glances behind.

'Do I look able nick your car, boy?' Ryan says. 'I just need a phone for a minute.'

The driver produces a mobile and goes to dial, and Ryan yelps, 'Hold on, hold on!'

'You don't want the guards?'

'I don't need the guards.'

The driver grasps what's unsaid between Ryan's shallow breaths, and Ryan thinks he's going to take off again. 'Please,' he says. 'Please, boy, I'll just be a minute, I just need one call.'

'Don't try anything on me,' the driver warns, and Ryan says, 'Fuck, what d'you think I'm capable of trying?'

The driver passes his mobile through the window and locks his doors.

Ryan thinks it's going to ring out. He thinks he's going to sob if he only gets the voicemail, yet when Natalie picks up for a moment he can't speak at all, his back to his good Samaritan, on his haunches again at the side of the road.

Natalie is frantic. 'Dan just called me from your phone. He said all this stuff . . . Oh my God, Ryan. What's he going to do to me?'

Ryan puts his free hand to the tarmac and heaves.

To his right, in a tussock by the hedgerow, something stirs, and something crawls.

'You have to come and get me,' he tells Natalie. 'You still have my door key. I need you to go to my gaff first, I need you to bring me something.'

'Ryan, the only place I'm going is . . . I don't know. Bloody Canada!'

'Natalie, if you don't do this for me, I'm dead. Don't tell me now that you don't get that.'

With the reluctant help of the stranger whose phone Ryan's borrowed, they work out that he's in the forestry near Mallow, at least half an hour from where Natalie is. This pinpointed, Ryan hands the phone back through the car window and is abandoned again. He supposes the fucker didn't want him bleeding all over the passenger seat. He also supposes it may take the stranger only half an hour to do his civic duty, and prays that Natalie finds him before the guards do.

She pulls up on the arse of an hour and when Ryan falls into the passenger seat she grabs his arm. 'How did he find out? What did you *say* to him?' She's red-eyed and trembling with indignation.

'I said fuck all, Natalie. I didn't get much of a chance for a chat, I was getting the shit hammered out of me.'

'Yeah, well he had plenty to say to me. He called me, God, the worst things.' She knocks the tears from under her eyes. Her chin crinkles. She pulls back onto the road.

Ryan watches her grit her teeth and mirrors her and says once his breath evens, 'Did you know he was my boss? The night we met, did you know I was one of his—'

'Thugs?' She wipes her eyes again. 'You asked me that the time he made you bring me home from the restaurant. Do you think the answer's changed?'

'He says you knew.'

'He says a lot of things. He says he's going to kill me if he ever sees us together again.'

Ryan leans further over his gut. 'You wouldn't lie to me about that, would you, girl?'

'Yeah, go ahead and doubt me, Ryan! After me risking my neck driving up here for you! With a gun! A fucking gun, Ryan!'

184

He closes his eyes.

'And if I had been caught,' she cries, 'bringing that thing to you . . . Oh my God, Ryan. What would I do? What would my parents say?'

Ryan can still feel Dan's hands on his neck.

'Ryan!' Natalie goes. 'Ryan?'

Ryan needs to think. He needs to sleep. He doesn't need to be driven to doubt now that he's bled on his knees for her.

He sits up. The evening knots tufts of slate grey overhead. There's a break in the backdrop of trees and he sees the valley below him again, green under the clouds, a lushness sliced by ribbons of dark hedgerows and briar-coated walls.

Natalie shifts gears and makes a decision. 'I'm calling the guards.'

Ryan twists towards her. 'No guards!' he gasps; he holds his palm a centimetre from his shirt; his hand shakes as the pain of his sudden move hits him. 'You blab and the guards are going to come looking for me too, no sympathy for the likes of me, Natalie, not when I'm driving around in a GTI with a three-hundred-euro pair of jeans on.'

'Don't be stupid, you could help them arrest him or something.'

'Jesus Christ this isn't *Murder, She Wrote*, girl.'

'Like I don't know that? You just asked me to bring you a gun!'

They come back into the city on the Ballyhooly road and from there on to the Old Youghal Road, because now that Ryan has his gun he feels like he could collect his spare key and chance Dan's street to get his car, if he can drive. Natalie doesn't think so. She argues against every statement that comes from his busted mouth – anger at his doubt, denial of his capabilities, a presumptuous certainty that she can read this kind of shit better than he can. Ryan says he needs to sleep. She argues with him on that, even.

'You might be concussed.'

'I'm not fucking concussed. I'm fucking hungover and black and blue. I need to sleep.'

'And what about me, Ryan? What am I supposed to do?'

'Go home.'

'Go home? After his threats?'

'He's not going to hurt you, Natalie.'

'How d'you know that?'

'Because I know how this works, OK? He can kick the shit out of me because I'm nothing to no one. D'you really think your parents wouldn't notice if you were hurt?'

They approach his house. She starts crying again. She puts forward a new argument, but Ryan doesn't hear the details. He spots a car a few yards from his front door: David Cooney's Avensis. Dan's man Cooney, who's originally from down the road, but who doesn't live anywhere near Mayfield anymore.

'Check that grey Avensis going past, tell me who's in it.'

He bends double. His throat, scratched from repeated retching, fails to curb his cry. Through waves of convulsions his lungs take in just enough air to keep him lamentably, grievously conscious.

Like everything else, it passes.

When he manages to sit up, into a blurred landscape of greys and windscreen droplets, her hand moves onto his belly. She lifts his shirt. 'Oh God,' she says. Ryan prods his skin. There's no one spot more painful than the others. No bones broken, he thinks.

She parks up. She's managed to drive through the cross and out to Glanmire without his noticing. 'I can't bring you back to mine. My parents can't see you like this,' she whispers. 'What are we going to do?'

'The Avensis?' he asks.

'You didn't hear me? Two guys. In their thirties, maybe? The driver was, like, fat-faced, short dark hair. I didn't see the other one too well but I think he was bald, or he had a shaved head, I—'

'Cooney and Feehily. He really is expecting the pistol returned, fucking hell.'

'Returned? My God, were they there when I went to collect it? Did they see . . . did I just miss them? Oh God.'

Ryan folds his arms across his belly. 'I need to think.' A mantra, under breath. *I need to think, I need to think.* The pattern replaces any useful thoughts he might have had; the pattern becomes the thought in its entirety.

'We could go to a hotel or something.' Natalie reaches for the ignition. 'Down in West Cork maybe.'

Dan's got his phone, his car keys, his cash . . . his savings. And he's got two shams outside Ryan's front door.

'I need to load this,' he says.

She stiffens as he muddles a straightforward task.

'I have calls to make,' he tells her then. 'I need my other phone, and my other phone's in my car.'

'Ryan, no way am I driving back to yours, not with those guys there, not with that thing in your hand there, no way.'

A better idea dawns on him.

'I need to sleep and I need to think,' he says. 'Do you remember where Larne Court is?'

17

Open with a joke, he thinks, but the best Ryan can manage is a resentful, 'You didn't see this coming, did you?' when Maureen answers the door.

'Jesus Mary and Joseph. What happened to you?'

'I got caught doing something I shouldn't have.'

She holds on to his elbow, closes out the door behind him and leads him to the kitchen sink, from under which she produces a bottle of Dettol. 'Stay there,' she commands, as if there's power in him to the contrary. She returns with a wad of cotton wool.

'I'll do your mouth,' she says, 'and then you can talk, my lad.'

But the pause forced as she dabs at his lips gets him. He slouches by her kitchen sink and the ache in his belly and ribs and back and throat and jaw settles.

'Calm down,' she says. 'We'll fix it.'

'It can't be fixed.'

'Nonsense. I've a knack for these things, don't worry at all about it.'

'You don't understand, girl. He's gonna put me down.'

'No one's going to put you down.' She wastes a stern pause on him. 'You're not a dog, Ryan.'

So, like a dog, Ryan begs to differ. 'I fucked his girlfriend.'

'Language!' she snaps, and goes on, 'Whose girlfriend?'

'My boss.'

'Ah. And that's the kind of business bosses aren't fond of. Why would you go and do a thing like that?'

'I don't know . . .'

'You don't know. Does this one make a third girlfriend, so?'

'No . . .'

She grasps his pause in context. 'Ah no,' she says, dropping her arm. 'Not the posh girl.'

It is a bewildering thing to be lectured and mended together. 'You said she knew what you were like,' she carps. 'Obviously what you're like is *exactly* what she likes, the brazen . . .' Ryan takes a stand for Natalie's honour and Maureen knocks the legs from under him. 'How would it be a coincidence?' she says. 'Ah sure that's the way of things with young fellas, can't see past the length of your langers, but young wans? You wouldn't be wide to them.' She finishes with his jaw and glares. '*You* wouldn't be, anyway.'

'Sorry.'

'What are you sorry for?' Her frown wavers. She leaves the cotton wool by the sink and grabs his hands. 'Ryan. Stop it.' She presses her thumbs into his palms. 'Jesus, didn't I tell you you weren't able for this? Ah, the music got you too soon, boy.'

She goes to inspect his chest. She lifts his shirt and the gun's noticed. 'Jesus,' she says, vexed. She removes the pistol. Ryan's right hand comes up as far as his waist and clutches at the air. It's a protest so feeble she appears not to notice. She carries the gun to the coffee table and returns to pull her palms over his ribs. She affirms his belief that there's nothing broken and then she draws her thumbs along his lower lashes.

'Eejit,' she says, kindly.

Ryan wants to detect fluency in her coddling. He asks, 'Did you do stuff like this for your son?' but no such luck that his tearful stupidity would have a precedent.

'No,' she says, still smiling. 'No.' She pulls her thumbs in and out of fists, drying them. 'I wasn't around him enough when he was small. And as a grown-up, he's not like you. He's hard as

189

winter ground. Although, you know, he'd be well able for this kind of carry-on.'

'Coz I'm not.'

She shakes her head.

'I wish I had another shirt to give you,' she says. 'I'll wash this one is what I'll do. Settle in, like a good lad.'

She sits him on the couch and brings him a blanket to put around his shoulders. She makes a mug of tea and a rasher sandwich and from the kitchen she extracts the rest of his story, the revelation as Dan suffered it. Once she's convinced of Ryan's remorse she digs into his feelings for Natalie and lays them out in snapshots and songs and puzzles over them.

'Now,' she says, in the end, 'you've to sleep for me.'

She fetches a pillow and he lies stiffly across the couch. She *hmmms* at him and goes off to get a couple of tablets and a glass of water.

'I hurt my wrist last year,' she says. 'The doctor gave me these to help me sleep.'

Ryan takes the medicine. Maureen settles into the armchair across from him and tells him one of her tales, a ghost story this time, and he gets into it, so when the sleep kicks in he's invested and the words swirl and blur his vision, dull his hearing, and he's

talking to a man-shaped mass on the other end of the couch

who woke Ryan with a pinch and a low oath, whispered in his ear

and now he sits in murk and madness, asking how Ryan is going to make up to him the wrongs he's done, whether he's content to bleed and keep bleeding, whether he thinks a trough of crimson tears is half enough reparation to calm him.

Ryan tries to put his mind at ease.

'Dan,' he says, and he wants it to sound confident, but it's like his mouth's stuffed with cotton wool soaked in blood and antiseptic. 'Listen, boy . . . Listen . . .'

*

190

'Back from your holiday? Anywhere nice?'

Sure no, the last holiday Ryan was on he felt the earth split under him.

'What?' Gruff laughter above him. Ryan opens his eyes and sees nothing but bruised grey. There's a steady ache in his cheek-bone, pressed to the ground. There is fluid chill around his mouth and along his neck. He is cold, he realises; now the cold bites him over and over.

'It's not fucking English, I'll tell you that much.'

Ryan opens his eyes again. Iron and charcoal. He tries to lift himself onto his hands and knees and gets halfway and folds again.

Mi dispiace. Mi dispiace moltissimo. His mouth wraps around it, his lips fold over it, and it's all he can do to dribble into the tepid sorries already pooled under his cheek.

Stai tranquillo, cucciolo mio, she says, aeons away again.

'Tell Jimmy he's back with us.'

There's a man on his haunches by Ryan's head. He peers down from a scene steadily sharpening, nods, and stands up just as Ryan recognises him. The impression, first, of grizzled cheeks and quick eyes recessed in a full-blooded mask. The name, shortly afterwards: Tim Dougan. His position carried thereafter on a cold sweat: Jimmy Phelan's foreman, enforcer of the lord's whims.

Ryan gets his bearings.

He's still shirtless, lying on his right side with his fist curled by his nose on a concrete floor. It's a space made massive by empti-ness and by his slowly weakening dissociation. The walls, many feet away, are an identically dull grey. There are a couple of metal frames leaning against the wall to his right. There is a silver-legged table. And there is Dougan, in boots and black jeans and a worn leather coat that slaps his thighs as he moves.

Ryan centres his attention on his left arm and focuses on his watch, leans into his left hand and pushes himself up again and this time he thinks he might make it – his head is coming clear, like he's stepped into a winter's morning, and his arm's able to take his weight, but before he comes up enough to turn over there's pressure on the back of his head; it pushes him to the floor. 'Lie still,' Dougan says. 'There's a good boy.'

Ryan remembers Maureen first as the reason he's shirtless, and the rest of it unfolds from there: Dan, Natalie, punishment beatings.

'That woman I was with,' he says. 'Is she all right?'

He is slurring. He brings his right hand to his face and feels for the injuries Maureen salved. Her work's undone. There's a fresh graze on his chin, his lip's been split again. He wipes the moisture from around his mouth. Saliva's caked from the corner all along his jaw; his thumb is tinted when he pulls his hand back.

'Asking after her,' Dougan notes to someone behind Ryan, and Ryan becomes aware of other presences, moving and mute.

He tries to roll over again and again Dougan's boot pushes down on the back of his head.

'Didn't I tell you to lie still?'

'I'll lie still when you tell me what the fuck is going on.'

'It's Jimmy's place to tell you what the fuck is going on,' Dougan says, 'and after he's done that you'll be lying still for a long fucking time.'

He jerks his foot. The floor scrapes the tip of Ryan's nose.

'I'm hoping he'll let me finish the job. You're a lovely little thing.' Dougan's boot jabs again, this time at Ryan's cheek. 'You got a bit of a hammering, did you, boy?' A contented sigh. 'I like 'em tenderised.'

A door opens somewhere. There are footsteps making for him. 'How awake is he?'

Ryan is hauled upright and held crucified between two sturdy, dumb goons. He blinks and swallows and watches Jimmy Phelan stare back at him.

'Hello, Cusack.'

Gone is Phelan's cool superiority. He looks at Ryan instead with an irradiated hatred that pulls his brows toward his pupils.

'What's going on?' Ryan says.

'You tell me,' Phelan replies, through his teeth.

What Italian words counselled Ryan in his sleep dissipate. He claws at the hours, panicked. 'Why am I here?' he asks Phelan. 'That woman, what'd you do to her?'

'Are you trying to be fucking funny?' Phelan shakes his head, incredulous. 'Do you not understand what I'm going to do to you, Cusack?'

'Do to me?'

Phelan's reddening face twitches towards his steward's. 'How fucking much did you give him?'

Dougan says, 'Usual dose.'

'Well, just in case we accidentally broke you,' Phelan says, swivelling back, 'I'll lay it out in simple terms. Who told you about Larne Court?'

'Larne Court?'

'What the fuck were you doing at Larne Court?'

She made him tea and told him things were going to work out. Just another of Maureen's mantras, a spindly bone thrown for Ryan to catch. He sketches a desperate map of Larne Court's windows and doorways and tries to remember any unusual features, any periodic, nocturnal shuffling that might identify a neighbour's home as a stash house or a dealing spot, and the harder he pushes the looser his grip gets and the shallower and faster his breathing.

'Nothing. I was just visiting . . . What have you done with her?'

At Dougan, Phelan directs a ferocious 'Why does he keep asking after her?' before stepping up to Ryan and threatening, 'There's no game you can win here, Cusack. I am going to kill you. All you're doing is begging me to drag it out and you have no fucking idea, boy, how long Dougan can drag things out. So I'll ask you once more: who told Dan Kane about Larne Court?'

'Larne Court has nothing to do with Dan. I swear to fucking Christ, J.P., I swear to fucking Christ I don't know what you're on about!'

'Cusack, I was just called down to extract you from my fucking mother's sitting room. Did the ketamine hit you so fast that you don't remember that?'

Ryan gawps and Phelan widens his eyes in response.

'What?'

'Oh, fucking hell.' Phelan turns away and just as suddenly turns back and punches Ryan in the gut. Ryan is released, bones emptied onto the slab, a tumbling of bits and innards. He coughs out the very last of it and the pain dulls to a burning ache. He is allowed to catch breath enough to hear Phelan all over again.

His mother's sitting room?

One of Phelan's dogsbodies pulls Ryan's wrists behind his back, forcing genuflection.

'Talk, Cusack.'

'I swear to God,' Ryan gags. 'J.P., I swear to you, I had no fucking idea.'

Her son, who bought the apartment and stuck her in there and engaged her in stand-offs and acted the maggot and is hard as winter ground and well able for the kind of entanglements that reduce Ryan to a whimpering mess spits, 'You had no fucking idea? What, was she part of your community service? Volunteer with the elderly but don't forget a loaded gun as you've to return to being a hard bastard immediately after clocking off?'

'Jesus Christ, no.'

For long enough to track three rounds of Phelan's pacing that remains all the explanation Ryan is able for, and not even Phelan's promising 'You will die here' budges him.

194

'Jesus Christ!' Phelan finally parrots, and removes a pistol from his waistband, pulls the slide back and points it right at the centre of Ryan's forehead. 'Do you doubt me, Cusack?'

'I swear. No one told me about Larne Court. This has nothing to do with Dan. J.P., I swear to you. On my mam I fucking swear it!'

'Do you think I won't get this out of you, boy? This is for your benefit. Tell me now and I'll kill you quick. Keep teasing and by God you'll beg for the bullet.'

'Ask Maureen, then! Ask her! I never threatened her, boy, I never . . . She fucking found *me*!'

'She found you?'

'Months ago. She said she knew my . . .'

All she said makes very certain sense now. His mother, his father, his career trajectory. If he could fill his lungs Ryan would scream, out of fury and fear and *oh my fucking God che cazzo* . . .

'She said she knew what?' roars Phelan.

'She said she knew me!'

'My mother,' he says, 'tracked you down, out of all of the grandchildren of old buddies and biddies, out of all the boys in Cork, at the exact fucking moment you took a vicious hiding, just so she could petition me to help? Are you still down a fucking k-hole, Cusack?'

'I don't know, I don't know what's going on!'

'OK.' Phelan points and pushes out his jaw and raises his eyes to the ceiling. 'You're not frightened enough,' he says. 'Fine. We take the hard road. What d'you think, Tim?' He tilts his head. 'Feel up to a bit of butchery?'

'Jesus, Jimmy.' Dougan moves towards the silver-legged table with his hands in his pockets. 'I thought you'd never ask.'

Phelan approaches. The muzzle of his gun runs along Ryan's nose, over his mouth, under his chin, onto his throat. 'This one's a DJ,' Phelan says. 'With ambitions to match. Runs a gaff called Cat's Piss.'

'Sounds grotty.' Dougan's back is turned. 'D'you remember the craic we used to have with the decks, J.P.? D'you reckon this little twink is up to a bit of crack?'

'That's for him to know and you to find out, Tim.'

'Business first, boy. A DJ – he'd need his fingers for that.'

'Hold on.' Ryan chokes under the gun. 'Hold on.'

'Oh, you've not heard the half of it,' Phelan says. 'Before he was a DJ, he was a pianist. A virtuoso, this one. A proper little poof, down to the bone.'

Dougan looks over his shoulder. 'Oh, I don't need a bone from him, boy. Just his tight little arsehole.'

Ryan's chin bobs. 'That's not . . .'

'Are you feeling chatty?' Phelan feigns astonishment.

'J.P., boy, I have nothing to tell you, I swear, I'm not lying.'

'Y'know, I wouldn't have thought you'd be a tough nut,' says Phelan. 'You don't look tough.'

'He doesn't, does he?' Dougan says. 'I really hope he breaks before I have to score his face.'

'You've taken a fancy to this one, Tim?'

'Oh, he's just my type.'

He turns, swinging a knife with a worn handle and a long, curved blade.

'What're you at, boy? Don't come near me with that thing, Jesus!'

Dougan advances.

Ryan cries, 'I can't tell you anything else, boy, I swear . . . Please!'

'See, you should've said please first,' says Dougan. 'Manners as a last resort isn't pretty, even from a mouth as pretty as yours. Now, it makes it easier if you hold out your hand for me.'

'I never get used to this,' says one of the mountain-men, as Ryan's right hand is pulled out in front of him.

'Remember this later,' says Dougan, crouching. 'I got on my knees for *you*.'

196

Ryan's legs kick and slide behind him; he pushes back against whoever's pushing him forward; he mewls like a kitten, 'I swear to you, Dan had nothing to do with this! I fucking swear! I didn't do anything!'

'Arriving at my mother's house with a loaded gun is something.' Phelan catches Ryan's throat and pushes him back into suddenly empty air.

Ryan's head hits the floor. 'Ask her, for fuck's sake! Ask her!'

'And what insight could she possibly give me into the workings of your delinquent mind?'

'You'd be fucking surprised!'

A deft handover of the blade – Dougan's fist to Phelan's. He holds it now an inch below Ryan's left ear and horizontally across the mere membrane that protects his veins and his arteries.

'Don't you realise Dan Kane will never know how valiantly you fought to defend him? What you're about to go through, Ryan, won't protect him.'

'I'm not trying to protect Dan. I told you, I'm on the outs with Dan!'

'So I heard, from you and from my mother. Though my mother's not wide enough to understand, Ryan, how a man's desperation to climb back up his boss's hole will make him crafty. My mother does not know how vicious a runt you are.'

'I've known her since before Christmas! You think I'd build up to intimidating you over a few months? I'm not fucking mad!'

Phelan's knife presses the pulse back into his throat. 'If I don't find out in the next sixty seconds how you knew about Larne Court, I'm going to torture you, Cusack. I'm going to cut each finger at the knuckle, then I'm going to nail you to this floor, then I'm going to run a fucking train on you. You'll die only after playing bitch to half the city, and your father will break when he finds the video.'

'I swear to God above, Dan knows nothing of Larne Court.

Ask your mam yourself, she told me she knew me, I had no idea she meant anything to you!'

Blade, pressure and submission, gutless submission, spelled out in tears and snot and keening. Phelan takes the knife from Ryan's throat. He extends Ryan's arm and holds his hand flat on the floor. He raises his own.

'Italy, boy, Italy!'

Phelan gurns with the effort of turning his attention from Ryan's hand to his mouth.

'What?'

'Dan's new yokes. He has them coming in from Italy.'

'So?'

'From Salerno to Ringaskiddy, boy, two hundred thousand at the start of April, and I know because I brokered the whole fucking deal – quantities, price, methods, fucking everything. You want those pills? I can give them to you. Those fucking pills are the only reason Dan didn't shoot me dead already.'

Phelan drops the knife and straddles Ryan, both hands to his throat.

'And you're only telling me this now? Is that not equal reason to put you down?'

'Take them,' Ryan wails. 'Please, just don't . . . Please.'

Phelan looks back. Ryan cannot see what expression Dougan has for him, but the pressure eases. He retracts so that his hands rest now on Ryan's chest, and sits up.

'God almighty,' he says. 'If you're lying to me, Cusack . . .'

When he pushes off there's room only to breathe. Ryan can't even turn over. He lies on his back, curling his legs, gasping, damp from his hairline to his toes.

'Truss him tight,' Phelan says. 'I need to talk to my mother.'

Ryan is handcuffed to a pipe running along the back wall. He's left alone, the lights are turned off and he sits shivering, too afraid, even in his absence, to curse Phelan aloud.

198

When he gets back, Ryan has cut grooves into his wrists and can taste metal between his teeth and convulses, still, like he's doing cold turkey. 'Fuck me,' Phelan says. 'A few hours on your ownsome and it demolishes you. I thought you'd have appreciated the breather.'

The cuffs are taken off, and Ryan is pulled up to face Phelan, and Phelan speaks to him in echoes as they pull dark curtains on the room . . .

'Shock, maybe,' Dougan fades in. 'Or exposure. Sure he hasn't a pick on him.'

'Get O'Leary over. Lively.'

Ryan comes to again on the slab. Phelan comes into focus, on his haunches a couple of feet away.

'Fine lad like you, falling over on me. Can you get up?'

Ryan gives it another minute, then pushes himself up, totters halfway and finds himself back on his side, a few feet to the left.

Phelan's dryly amused. He lets Ryan wrestle with confusion and embarrassment for a few minutes more. 'Doctor's coming to have a look at you,' he offers, eventually.

'I don't need a doctor. I need to get back.'

'You say that like I should give a fuck, Cusack. Still, that you're so wildly off the mark makes sense. You must have common ground with my fucking crazy mother. Maureen's very fond of you, it seems.'

As Ryan makes it, at last, to his feet, Phelan tells him that after he fell asleep on Maureen's couch, she phoned her son and demanded his assistance in making short work of Ryan's woes.

'Of course, knowing what I know about you, Cusack, you can't blame me for assuming you'd pulled the wool over her eyes.'

Ryan had seemed nicely zonked but Phelan had Dougan administer a dose of ketamine, just in case. Ryan looks at his left shoulder on Phelan's gesture; there's a bruise, but there are bruises everywhere, 'which is why,' explains his assailant, 'we're going to give you the once over.'

After Ryan's offering Phelan the route, he returned to his mother, who ate the head off him, delaying him extracting the full story and, perversely, leaving Ryan to suffer even longer.

'So she tells me how she met you,' Phelan says. 'And I believe her. Because it's occurred to me that no man would admit to something so expressly mortifying if he wasn't absolutely desperate.'

His phone rings and he pulls it from his jacket pocket.

'Still, now that we've come to an understanding about new commercial endeavours, I'd say it's all been worthwhile, wouldn't you? Hello?'

More pressing matters, it seems. He leaves Ryan for another age and Ryan sits against the wall with his arms folded over his stomach, thinking of nothing but the cold; the cold is the whole of it, for so long.

Phelan comes back with a doctor, a fella of middle age, a tufted throat, a lavender shirt. Phelan has Ryan stand to meet him, but that's as far as the examination goes. The doctor glares, turns to the cleared tabletop, and scribbles a referral for A&E.

Phelan removes his jacket.

'Put this on,' he commands.

Ryan is guided to the back seat of an SUV. Phelan sits in beside him, and they're driven from a corner of a Little Island industrial estate back to the city.

They make a stop at Larne Court.

Maureen comes charging across the floor, shoots at Ryan concentrated misery and bawls at Phelan, 'You bould bastard!'

'Give him the rest of his clothes,' he says. 'I want my jacket back.'

18

'So what does Dan expect of you?' Phelan asks in the A&E waiting room, in the grey plastic chair beside Ryan's.

'He wants my piece.'

'Your portion of the transaction?'

'That too. No, my gun,' Ryan says softly; he hasn't the breath or the blood in him to correctly enunciate. 'He told me to bring my gun back to him. I guess he'll have instructions from there.'

'Because you're still his mouthpiece. Y'know, I feel for Mr Kane. Bad enough to be cheated by an accomplice, but it must smart to realise you've been suckling a Judas all these years. Fucking his ould doll.' He snorts. 'You really are Italian, aren't you?'

For a small while more he ponders. Then he says, 'It benefits me to keep things running smoothly for as long as I can. I'm not ready yet to take what you're offering me, and what you're offering isn't exactly guaranteed a smooth handover. Do we need to take our bitter middleman out of the equation, or do you think, being his very best friend, that he can be made see the necessity of paying his dues?'

'He's put too much work into it,' Ryan says. 'He won't share it.'

'How about O'Sullivan?'

Ryan thinks of Shakespeare, pragmatic and losing patience, concerned with the integrity of the route above all things.

'He could do.'

'That's something for me to think about then. You, Judas, proceed as you were asked. Bring him your gun.'

'You can't be serious, boy.'

'He just wants his equipment returned. Go do that. Once that's done, prostate yourself whatever way he asks of you. And come to a solid conclusion on Shane O'Sullivan's flexibility. I don't want a war, Cusack.'

He stands over Ryan and Ryan's chin tilts only enough to count the buttons on his shirt. 'Let me know if you pull through,' Phelan says, and slaps Ryan's shoulder heartily, and leaves him there.

Ryan has a longing, and he bears it only till he knows the bastard's not coming back.

He gets to his feet. He returns to the receptionist in the administrator's office. She slides back the window and Ryan asks if she can contact Karine D'Arcy, who's a fourth year student up there somewhere in the wards.

She's always been a sight for sore eyes, red eyes, tired eyes, black eyes. Today she's succeeded despite her best efforts; Ryan is so glad to see her, even though she's spitting fire.

'I suppose you'd call this workplace tension, would you?'

Adept at modifying her ire to fit her surroundings, she bawls him out of it under her breath and slides from exasperation to beatific patience whenever A&E staff appear. At least she's willing to explain the procedure: Ryan's suffered blunt abdominal trauma, so they're taking bloods to rule out internal haemorrhage, they're going to X-ray for fractured ribs, they'll arrange an ultrasound if they're not happy with the bloods. 'Y'know,' she hisses, 'this is the kind of thing that can kill you.'

He had half a story prepped before she found him in a cubicle: Dan lost the plot with him, handed him his arse and left him a long walk home. The doctor tells him to sit back out in the waiting room till he's called for his X-ray; Karine goes with him and

202

dredges for the rest of the tale. She pushes herself over her folded arms and her anger, like everything else about her, is so pure; she tears him down to a dirty, humiliated child. 'You tell me the whole of it,' she says, 'or I will call the guards. *He . . .*' *He* as a refined snarl. '. . . *He* does not get to do this to you.'

'It's so fucked up, girl . . .'

'I don't care how fucked up it is. Tell me.'

The last time Ryan was in A&E he wasn't conscious. There was none of this shamefaced explaining of his stupidity in a fluorescent amphitheatre, surrounded by peeling bulletins and daydreaming cleaners and other people's sweet wrappers. For a sour second, as he stands at the foot of the confession, he wishes Dan had killed him.

'Dan was with this girl.'

'I swear to God, Ryan, if you're going to say what I think you're going to say—'

'And I was with her as well.'

For a moment he thinks Karine's going to get up and leave him. For a moment he thinks she thinks so too.

'I suppose I shouldn't be surprised that your dick had something to do with it,' she says. 'And I guess Natalie's due a rude awakening—'

'It was Natalie.'

She needs time with this one, and Ryan has time, he has nowhere else to go.

'Ryan Cusack,' she whispers. 'What did you just say to me?'

'Dan was flahing Natalie. I didn't know till it was too late.'

'As in, you didn't know until he beat you up?' Karine pauses. She shakes her head and puzzles it out. 'No,' she says. 'Coz he wouldn't have done this to you for that. You didn't know until *I'd* found out. And once I'd found out and told you to fuck away off for yourself, you weren't going to give her up, were you? Coz God forbid you'd have to tug your own prick for a while, yeah?'

'If that's how you want to put it.'

She stands.

'D'you know what really, really hurts?' she says.

Ryan looks up at her.

'Realising,' she goes on, 'that I spent six years of the best days of my life sleeping with a fucking moron.'

She goes to take off but Ryan interrupts her flight.

'Don't leave me, girl.'

She rounds on him.

'Jesus, I'm arranging cover. I'm hardly going to leave you like this, am I?'

He's back in the waiting room after his X-ray by the time she returns, still in her tunic and not ready, so, to run away with him.

'Tell me the rest,' she says, likely hoping it can't get any worse, likely praying that his vulnerability in the face of eyelash-fluttering female attention is the endpoint of his sorry tale. Ryan hates to let her down but he's compelled to let her down. His pause widens her eyes and opens her hands. 'Ryan!'

'There's a project I set up for Dan. He still needs me for it. He's kicked me senseless but not kicked me out.'

'If you think you're going back working for Dan—'

'Listen. That new project has captured the interest of an old buddy of my dad's. Did you ever hear me talk about J.P.?'

'J.P. who?'

'J.P. Like, Jimmy Phelan. Dan, but like fifty times bigger. As soon as he heard I was on the outs with Dan, he hauled me in.'

'Hauled you in for what?'

'I'd to give it up to him. Dan's project. Phelan beat it out of me. I've got at best a couple of weeks before Dan finds out I've grassed him up. And then I'm dead.'

His voice is flat and hers dampens in response.

'What's that mean?'

'Dan won't give up what he's been working on and I've told Phelan everything. I can't see a way out of this, girl. I'm dead.'

204

So quickly it occurs to him that healing now is self-indulgence. He gets up and she hisses. He explains and he hobbles. She can move faster than him. She keeps pace under the burden of unused energy and she's ready to blow by the time they get through the doors.

'You can barely move, boy,' she cries. 'Where the hell do you think you're going?'

'I've to see Dan. I need to bring him something he asked for. That'll calm him down a bit and then maybe I'll have room to think. I need to get my phone and my keys back, I need to call Natalie and make sure she's all right—'

'Make sure *she's* all right?'

'I know what you think of her, girl.'

'You know I think she's an evil bitch, do you?'

'She didn't know either.'

'That's some coincidence, isn't it? Some trust fund pervert has a taste for drug dealers and just so happens to fuck you and Dan at the same time? And tell you then that it's just pure fluke. And you believe her?'

'I asked her, she swears to me—'

'Oh, she swears. Because girls like that are so moral, like; because they'd never go back on a swear. You are not leaving this hospital, Ryan.'

'I have to, girl. The longer I leave him wondering where I am, the closer he gets to exploding.'

'You are not leaving!' she bawls.

And so for all the breath in him Ryan bawls back. 'What's it to you anyway? You fucking ditched me, you pushed me away, even on Saturday you were hot and cold and . . . I have no fucking clue what you want from me, girl, why do you get to make demands?'

'Ryan, do you really not know I'm pregnant?'

Ryan opens his mouth again; he reaches down deep again; he begins to forge indignation again. The air goes out of his lungs again.

*

Fifteen weeks. The start of December. Ryan was just coming out of the doldrums so she wasn't being as consistent with the Pill as she would otherwise have been. Anxiety made her forgetful, and any spark at all from him was something to be fuelled. She was a bit all over the place while he lay still, she says.

'I don't understand,' Ryan says.

'What don't you understand, Ryan? You know how everything works, don't you?'

His brow furrows and hers creases in mocking consensus.

'Are you sure?' he asks.

This, she decides, is an unfathomably stupid question. 'Ah no,' she says. 'No, it never occurred to me that I should double-check. No, it's probably just wishful thinking.'

Ryan stands against the wall outside the doors of CUH's Accident and Emergency Department and is abruptly aware that he is standing, still standing so he has some strength left, in his legs at least and in his hard-headedness. Karine flits through emotions that bloom on her face then change in a single rise-and-fall of his chest. 'Say something that isn't moronic,' she commands, but her eyes swim and she rolls her thumbs over and over each other.

He can't coordinate lips, tongue and jaw.

She settles for anguish.

'Ryan!'

'Fifteen weeks means . . . '

It's a piss-poor attempt and she responds with appropriate agony.

'It means, Ryan, that at the end of August you're going to be a father.'

'That's five months away.'

'Oh God well done, Mr Grams-and-Ounces.'

Ryan pushes off the wall. Over her shoulders, the living dash down the rain-splashed paths in their scores. The hospital is a throbbing heart and he's a cog loose in an artery, something mechanical, something cold, foreign and corruptive.

'How long have you known?'

She's prepped for this. The chin goes up.

'Since the new year.'

They flow past, these breathing, shivering, oblivious cells, into and out of A&E or perpendicular to Ryan on the main thoroughfare, all with their own biology to contend with. Ryan looks down at his hands. They're red with the cold. There's life in him, whether or not he sees fit to believe it.

And in her. So he's now told. Behind the crisp panel of her tunic her belly seems the same shape as it ever was.

'Why'd you wait so long to tell me?'

She has an answer rehearsed for this, too. 'You don't tell anyone till you're twelve weeks at least.'

'OK, grand, but that was three weeks ago, and in any fucking case you're supposed to tell *me*.' But he has not rehearsed, and so his voice wavers. 'Who else knows?' he asks.

'My family. My course administrator. Louise. Emma. A couple of the other nurses.' Off his dejection she stiffens. 'I wanted to tell you Saturday, but that just went to shit. I could hardly tell you when you were flaking out the door in one of your little rages, could I?'

'Saturday? That's only days ago, Karine. You've had weeks.'

'Christ, it's not as if I didn't drop any hints.'

'You *didn't* drop any hints!'

'My mam was able to guess.'

'Your mam lives with you!'

'Yeah, well you might have noticed on Saturday, if you weren't so busy gawping at my boobs. I mean, look. Look!' She turns to the side, smooths her tunic over her belly, and there it is. There it is.

'You wanted it just to dawn on me?' Ryan says. 'Is this another test, like Saturday's . . . fucking . . . I shouldn't try to kiss you but I should just know when you're pregnant? Oh Jesus,' he says, 'don't give me this shit, you didn't want me to notice, you've been pushing me away since Christmas.'

'Yeah, you don't think for good reason? It's just chaos with you, Ryan. One bloody catastrophe after another. And I had plans, boy. Real plans that I now have to give up on and . . . Don't you think I had a lot to think about?'

'Like not wanting me to know about it?'

'Like considering whether I needed your lunacy wrecking my head on top of everything else, yeah.'

'That's comical, Karine, coz I think hiding a pregnancy from me for fifteen fucking weeks is lunacy, too. If it's mine, like. I mean, is it?'

For this toxin he needs to spread his arms, more to keep himself balanced than to stress the point. It's the wrong weapon to use, and he knows before he's finished brandishing it.

'Did you just ask me what I think you just asked me?' Karine says.

Ryan folds down the stupid, stupid defiance. 'I just need to be sure, like.'

'Do you really, in your wildest dreams, think that I'd tell you I was having your baby if I wasn't?'

A flurry of fingers. She reaches into the front pocket of her tunic and produces a folded card and a slip of paper.

'See?' She thrusts the card at him. 'Due date, right there. Count nine months back from that and let me know if you think I'd have had time, in between nursing you and petting you and trying to get you to move, to run out and be impregnated by someone else. You wanna see the scan pictures?'

She pushes the paper slip under his nose and more by impulse than evil he tilts his head back and stares out past her. She grabs his fist and opens it and inserts the slip of paper and pinches his fingers shut.

'You look,' she says.

Ryan looks.

More greys. Shadows shot through with silver. A little head.

'And you'll be lucky,' cries Karine, 'if that's not the last time you see it.'

'What, coz I questioned you? For fuck's sake, girl, you've been keeping the biggest thing in the world from me for fifteen weeks and I'm supposed to think that that makes sense?'

'You think I'd choose you to raise a child? Above pretty much anyone else on the planet?'

'Why would you say a thing like that?'

'Because it freaks me out, Ryan! Maybe that's why I didn't tell you. Because you're chaotic and you've a capacity for violence and you have no job and no prospects and no intention of ever changing. Because you're gonna end up just like your dad and don't you think for a damn second I can't see that.'

It doesn't make the poison easier to swallow that it hurts her as much to administer it. 'Couldn't be that bad if you stayed with me for six years, could I?' Ryan manages.

'Yeah, Ryan, coz I loved you.'

'What, past tense?'

She drags a hand across each of her cheeks. There's a nod or a headshake or a sob.

'Why are you having it, then?'

She narrows her eyes. 'Don't you dare ask—'

'I'm fucking asking! If you hate me so much why didn't you just get rid of it? Took you long enough to tell me. Isn't that what you were trying to decide? Isn't that something else I wasn't going to be fucking part of?'

She stands her ground. Inches apart, wet-cheeked, they stare at each other. 'I didn't particularly enjoy it the last time,' she says.

Ryan furrows up.

'I had a termination before,' Karine says, softly. She sags. She looks away. She sniffs and wipes her eyes again. 'When you were in Saint Pat's.'

Saint Pat's was nine months of panic and lonesomeness and degradation alleviated only by her letters, her love. Their separation was laughable in that it was merely physical, only physical, in that there was no other way to part them. It was laughable; he could never manage laughing, but he appreciated the sentiment. 'You didn't tell me?' he says.

'Ryan, you were in prison.'

'You could have called me. You could've . . .'

'But what input should you have had, Ryan? I had to think of my Leaving Cert, and the points I needed to get for my degree, and my life, my whole bloody life.'

'You had an abortion and you didn't even tell me?'

'You didn't check with me before you took up full-time dealing! You didn't ask for my advice before getting yourself caught with someone else's coke!'

But this makes no sense. Ryan and Karine were perfect when they were seventeen; they were beautiful; they were closer than the sand and the sea; she couldn't have kept something like that from him. Not while her boyfriend was on suicide watch behind bars, no, she could not carry that secret through the times they lay giggling in the middle of the afternoon, the times she came to him and wrapped his arms around her, the times he told her I love you, girl, I fucking love you so much, take every one of my mistakes and hold them, weigh them, crush them, crush me, if it means that you will know me . . .

He moves around her, using the wall. 'Where do you think you're going?' She takes his arm; he shakes her off. 'How far are you going to get, Ryan? You're going to shuffle four miles in the rain, are you?' He keeps moving. She moves with him.

'Don't touch me,' he says.

She steps in front of him and catches his forearms. She closes her hands over his elbows. He pivots. She pivots. 'Why?' she flares. 'Why amn't I to touch you?'

'I don't know you,' he tells her. 'How could you do this to me?'

210

'See, this is it, Ryan! You can march me right up to the hardest decision I'll ever have to make and just leave me there, but oh, I'm supposed to be perfect no matter what you throw at me. I'm sick of it. I'm sick of needing you and sick of being disappointed because you can't accept that it should ever be anything but you needing me.'

She steps back and her hands fall by her sides.

'Maybe I should just let you take off, Ryan. Maybe you'll be grand or maybe you'll get home and fall over and go into shock and die, but what difference would it make? It's always only a matter of time before you let me down.'

She reaches for composure. She swallows and pulls her lips inwards. When she walks away her gait is inappropriately steady, like all of the wracking had been confined to her throat and that's as much as Ryan is going to get out of her. He thinks that he should hold his arm out. Call after her, if his voice will hold. His shoulder blades press against the plaster. He pushes into the discomfort; he sways and feels the surface scrape the bone. His descent is just and painful. He slides down. He sits on the ground.

Minutes pass and a paunchy chap in a navy fleece slows to ask, 'You all right, boy?'

'Yeah,' because *yeah's* the instinctive response.

The fella notices the ultrasound pictures. Ryan has a thumb pressed to each end of the little shadow.

'Everything all right there?'

Ryan looks down at the pictures.

'I only just found out.'

'It's not bad news, so,' the man says, hopefully.

'No. It's not bad news.'

'Just that you're outside A&E, like.'

'It's me that's in A&E.'

'Heh. Chalk it down.' He offers a thick, pink hand.

The rest of him is equally florid. He has a congested, jovial face. He helps Ryan up and walks alongside him to the door, dawdling to keep pace, all the while smiling in awkward encouragement.

'Well,' he says, when they reach the reception hatch. He holds out his hand again. 'Congratulations.'

Ryan looks from the handshake to his runners to the rest of the waiting room and Karine is still there, in one of the plastic chairs.

She comes for him.

'You won't even let me have this one, will you?' she says.

So, freefalling, he rests his forehead on her shoulder and wraps his arms around her.

19

They don't admit him in the end. The doctor's happy with the X-ray. She enquires about the wait time for a CT scan, then settles for another blood test. She gets an ultrasound technician to pummel Ryan's belly for a bit, which he condemns through gritted teeth as fucking perverse. The doctor decides, on the basis of Ryan's not throwing up again and because his piss is the right colour, that he'll be fighting fit in no time.

'How have you been otherwise?' she asks as Ryan goes to leave; he assumes there's a note on his file, or an emergency room nurse has offhandedly said he's barely recognisable conscious. He's too goosed to be mortified. 'Grand,' he says, and the doctor lowers her voice and says, 'You should press charges.'

Back in the waiting room Karine accepts the ultrasound pictures, exhales, and hands him her phone. She wrinkles her nose. 'If it makes you feel better to know the brains of the operation is all in one piece.'

Natalie remains in one piece.

'My God,' she starts, as soon as she hears his voice. 'Where the hell have you been?'

She's fine, albeit a bit shaken, albeit a bit put out that slipping between the beds of dealers can have repercussions that look like loaded guns. Ryan doesn't think it wise to tell her the whole story so he tells her fractions: that he's been to sleep, he's been to the hospital, he's been examined for broken bones and bleeding organs.

'I'll sort this,' he says. 'Give me till the morning and I'll have a whole other story for you.'

'Oh yeah? What are you going to do?'

'Whatever he wants me to do.'

'And you think that'll sort it, do you?'

Ryan starts laughing, helplessly, madly.

'What's so funny?' Natalie shouts, and to his left Karine bounces from one foot to the other, taking a dim view of his sniggering.

Ryan covers his eyes with his free hand and laughs into the dark.

'Nawthin',' he tells them both. 'Nawthin' at all.'

Karine swaps her handset then for a twenty and tells him that he's to get a taxi home and go to bed.

'Dan can wait,' she says. 'Phone him and tell him what he's done to you. He'll probably be so pleased with his handiwork that he'll give you a rest. And then tomorrow hop on a plane and go to your nonna's for a while.'

'They even took Italy from me, girl.'

'How could they have taken Italy from you?'

Ryan drags down on the skin under his eyes and stares at the ceiling. 'I can't go anywhere,' he tells Karine and he tells himself. 'I'm caught between a pair of shams all set to go butting the heads off one another. If I go missing Dan's project will fall through. They'll both come for me, and if they can't find me, who d'you think they'll take instead? My dad, or my brother, or you.'

She ignores this. 'Why would Dan's project fall through without you?'

'I told you. I set it up for him.'

'And?'

And God, you're good, he thinks.

She folds her arms. She widens her eyes.

'And he's fallen in with the fucking Camorra. And it's not easy to find reliable translators. And this is big, Karine. This is really fucking big.'

She grips his hand. She brings it to her belly.

214

'No, Ryan,' she says. 'This is big.'

Well, both things can be big, can't they? Ryan tells himself on the blessedly silent taxi ride back to the city centre. He asks to be dropped at Larne Court. He is charged a tenner. He spends the other on a box of fags. *Both things can be big*, he decides. Life and death. Love and loss. Fucked and saved and fucked up and salvaged.

Maureen wants to talk. Ryan wants nothing but his gun back so he can proceed as her malevolent son directed. He stares at pieces of furniture in sequence in an effort to avoid her. He takes a red plastic Bic off the coffee table and lights up. He plays with the hem of the shirt she washed for him. In the end he looks at her and snaps, 'What?'

'What are you taking it out on me for?' she says.

'Because I'm in the shit, maybe. Didn't you read that in the tea leaves? You could have told me!'

'Told you that you're in the shit?'

'Told me that you're the mother of the biggest gangster in fucking Munster!'

Humph. 'And sure what good would that have done you?'

'Well, he wouldn't have shot me full of ketamine, driven me out to Little Island, punched the lining of my stomach out of me, pointed a gun at my head, threatened to cut my throat, tied me up half-naked in a warehouse, forced me to leak secrets about my boss, who's now going to pull me limb from fucking limb . . . that kind of thing.'

'I didn't do any of that,' she says. 'It gave Jimmy a terrible land, finding you here.'

'Is it not that you fucking told him I was here?'

'Is it not that being in the same trade yourself is what got you into so much trouble with him?'

'Oh yeah, a little gangster. Because you're that fucking insight-ful, isn't that it? Bullshit. Himself and my dad were buddies.

That's how you knew me. That's how you knew about my piano, my mam – fuck, Maureen! How could you tease shit like that out of me?'

'I only wanted to help,' she says. 'What good in having a terrible son, except using him for messes like this? I thought he could help you out.'

'What, I'm so lost that euthanasia seemed the best option?'

'I don't recall your father having a lip on him like that.'

Ryan deflates.

'My father's a prick,' he says. 'But I'm sure on some level you knew that, too.'

'I didn't and I don't believe it now,' she says. 'Fair enough, he's probably no saint, but I'd take him over Jimmy any day of the week.'

'Would you, now? My useless dad over your son, the man people fucking bow to? I'm dying while you stand here whinging about Cork's lord and master. My dad can do nawthin' for me, but you? Fuck, I bet you'd get away with murder.'

'And is being lord and master what you want, Ryan? There's no comfort where Jimmy is.'

'There's no comfort where my dad is, and his liver fucked.'

'Maybe not,' she says. 'But I'll tell you something, boy, I didn't need your family tree to know you're not able to play the gangster.'

'You did to know I could play the piano.'

Phelan's arrival puts paid to the spat. It's a kindness and a curse; Ryan needs more than bruises off his chest, but Phelan's placing Ryan's gun, still loaded, in his open palm is a push onto a one-way street. Ryan cannot put this off; Dan's been waiting now more than twenty-four hours.

'Now you listen to me,' Phelan says as his mother, in the gloom in the corner of Ryan's eye, shakes her head. 'You'll give this piece to Mr Kane. You will not use it on him. You are to protect my nest egg with every breath left in your body, Cusack, or I will come for you, and for all of the little half-blood, base-born shits who share your surname.'

Ryan has a fifteen-minute walk that takes him twenty-five. He slogs through the streets wringing pitying glances from strangers dismayed by the state of him. The flesh is just the face of it; Ryan is the assemblage of seven years of wrongdoings. He is the scourge of his own city. It's as well off without him, Cork.

Don't think I don't have the bones of you, it hisses, in cars growling past and radio piped out of shopfronts and the whirring of bicycle wheels, in the private conversations and decrees of hipster baristas and skinny suits and students surging round him.

Dan seems no closer to mercy, though he's had the span of a day to process Ryan's deceit.

'Where the fuck have you been?'

Ryan tells the floor rather than say it to his face. 'Hospital.'

'Who told you you could go to hospital?'

It almost feels like something Ryan could tell him. It would, ever so briefly, allow him the pleasure of seeing Dan baulk and blanch. Instead he tells him his dad made him go and Dan decides to get the boot in once more.

'Makes a change from putting you there himself, I suppose.'

He takes the offered pistol. He checks the magazine, then reaches out and cuffs Ryan.

'Fuck are you doing, going around with a loaded gun? You gonna use this on me?'

He doesn't take 'No' for an answer. That Ryan might have stumbled all the way here, trying to talk himself into murder and then resigning himself to his fate . . . Dan's eyes dilate. He gets a little tremor in his breathing.

He decides that a slave without the capacity to hear his master's voice or the means to get to him when summoned is fuck-all use to anyone but the most patient sadist. He hands Ryan back his phone and his car keys. Ryan clutches both in his right hand as he listens to him go on about how the Bank of Dan has seized all assets deposited and draw up new parameters for Ryan's business account. Seeing as he's lately destitute, Ryan won't be able to pay upfront at bulk prices any longer. No, he'll have to go on tick, he'll have to owe Dan interest, he'll have to run the risk, as all crawling street dealers do, of having his legs broken for financial infractions. Ryan does the sums as Dan harangues: Dan intends to ruin him. He wants to watch Ryan drown with one foot on his bobbing, gasping head. His is a child's ambition and Ryan is not in the right headspace to break it to him that he hasn't even started to feel the havoc Ryan has wreaked.

He'll baulk and blanch soon enough.

Dan sends Ryan on his way. He can't resist a final shove. The lurch forward triggers a spasm in Ryan's gut; he's tender and thin and the day's not done yet.

No sign of the man he really needs to speak to.

Ryan crumples onto the driver's seat of his car. He checks his phone for calls made, answered and dropped. The log lists calls to Natalie's number, one after another. Ryan thumbs the screen. There must be twenty of them, doled out in gluts from yesterday afternoon up to an hour ago.

He makes another one.

'I got my phone back,' he says.

'So now what?'

'I need to see you.'

'Have you lost your mind?'

'There's a lot we need to talk about. You think this is finished, or something?'

She submits.

Then he calls Shakespeare but Shakespeare has no intention of humouring delusions; he tells Ryan he has nothing to say to him, what could Ryan possibly feed him now but nonsense? Ryan warns that unless they come face-to-face this very evening,

Shakespeare will have no chance of surviving the coming clusterfuck.

Shakespeare hesitates.

His concession is voiced in curses. He tells Ryan to meet him at the entrance to the business park on the Mallow road and Ryan drives there with nothing more deadly than the second-hand word of Jimmy Phelan to protect him.

He arrives first and uses the time to lumber out of the car and position himself with his legs stretched and his arse on the bonnet. Nonchalance is not the guise he's after, but he's flahed out; he needs the breeze, lest he fold up.

Shakespeare pulls in ten minutes later. He strides over, his shoulders tilted back, and pushes his face up to Ryan's.

'Fuck d'you think I have to say to you, you dopey little prick?'

'I've a story for you.'

'Oh, you've a story for me? Cusack, I have fuck-all interest in hearing about your love life. Flahing the man's ould doll behind his back . . . It's the stupidest fucking thing I've ever heard, and this is gonna banjax everything.'

'It's a whole other tale I have for you, boy. And you're not going to like it.'

'Oh, I'm intrigued now, Cusack. What could be worse than pulling apart our enclave over some Southside whore? Ha? Are you an undercover pig as well?'

'Not a pig, no.'

Shakespeare's spittle hits Ryan's jaw. 'What the fuck does that mean?'

Ryan tells him a story he rehearsed on the drive over: befriending a nana who knew him through his family – Shakespeare's brows dip over the bridge of his nose – doing a few bits for her, getting comfortable enough in her presence to go there for a much-needed snooze after Dan abandoned him in the forestry, waking up on a concrete floor out in Little Island . . .

This last detail stitches up Shakespeare's snarl.

'See, it turns out . . .' Ryan pinches rucks of the denim on his thighs between his thumb and first finger. '. . . she's Jimmy Phelan's mother. So he wasn't too happy finding me panned out on her couch.'

'What did you just say to me?'

'The reason I was on the missing list last night is that I'd been pumped full of ketamine and handcuffed to a pipe in an empty warehouse. And I swear to shit I am not making this up.'

Shakespeare makes an unpleasant sound – a short 'ugh' – accompanied by the merest stagger backwards; he gets it before Ryan gets it out.

'He thought I was at her gaff on Dan's orders, and I had my piece on me, boy, and it was loaded. He threatened to kill me. He didn't just threaten – he made a good start on it. He had Tim Dougan with him and you know what that animal's like. You can imagine the kind of things they were promising me.'

'Go on,' Shakespeare says, through his teeth.

'And I gave him Italy, boy. He was gonna kill me so I did the only fucking thing I could think of: I gave up the route.'

In Shakespeare's silence Ryan has time to consider himself a lifeless pile on the side of the dual carriageway, a corpse enrapturing the tabloids, a cautionary tale.

'Let me get this straight,' Shakespeare says, and bounces his hands, pegging the weight of the confession. 'I save your fucking life to protect the route – like, you know that, don't you, boy? That without me there Dan would have done you, without me Dan would have painted his carpet with your insides . . . I save your fucking life to protect the route and you pay me back by selling that route to J.P.? On the ill-advised notion that your life could ever be worth as much as the channel? Do you not realise I'm going to put a bullet in you for this?'

'You could, boy. I couldn't stop you. Dan's taken my Glock. I'm weak as water.'

'So what's this? Deathbed confessional?'

'Or a message. Phelan has no interest in starting war. He just wants his due. He wants to talk to you.'

'So you come now to relay the word of God. Cap in hand, thinking I'm too cowed by him to kill you. Or is it that you expect me to be fucking grateful that you threw me a bone?'

'I expect you to make the right decision based on the scant options you have. Kill me, placate Dan, go to war. Or kill me, talk Dan round, and deal with Phelan. You'll still have the Camorra to talk down.'

'Are you repeating my logic back at me, Cusack?'

'You don't have a monopoly on cop on.'

'And you think you're the only Italian in Ireland, do you?'

'I might as well be.'

'See, I reckon your kid brother has the lingo too—'

'Yeah, maybe he could talk to them for you. If I haven't talked to them already.'

Now Shakespeare needs to turn the possibilities over, check for cracks and crawling things. He needs to listen to Ryan and he wants to lay hands on Ryan; when he pulls his lips back far enough to expose his gums Ryan's sure he's going to line him up for a third application of blunt abdominal trauma. But Shakespeare shoves his hands into his pockets.

'You've ended us,' he says.

'That's not the way it has to be.'

'Oh, you think?' He looks Ryan up and down. 'I knew it from day one, Cusack. What are you but a spoilt child, a boy running with men only because there's so little threat to you you can make grade selling to cowards and little girls? I knew one day you'd bite the hand that fed you, you black-eyed cunt.'

The night's numbed Ryan, or what ketamine's left in him is staging a resurgence on the basis of his having an empty stomach and a head on him for sleep. Anger makes Shakespeare's face a raw red, but Ryan's not afraid. He should aim for fear; it's only right. But he is just tired.

He tells Shakespeare that he'll set up a meeting and that he can choose thereafter how he wants to proceed.

'Aren't you worried that as soon as I deal with J.P., I'll come for you?' says Shakespeare.

'At least you'd be quick about it.'

'So you are worried,' he realises, 'that Dan will get to you instead. You don't think it'll occur to me to just tell Dan about your little coup d'état?'

'But what good would that do you?'

Shakespeare spits and the gobbet lands an inch from the scuffed white arc at the tip of Ryan's right runner. 'There'll be an end to all of this,' he says, 'and if you're relying on your language skills to keep you alive, I fucking pity you.'

He shakes his head again and turns away.

'I'm sorry, boy,' Ryan tells his back.

Dry laughter now and Shakespeare says, 'You're sorry, Cusack, only because you know as well as I do what's coming to you.'

20

Ryan gets home but doesn't pass the threshold. He parks, dredges for coins, pitches out of the car and does the road a couple of times, building speed and resilience, watching for informants and foes. He phones Jimmy Phelan as he does so. He tells him Shakespeare's waiting to hear from him. He passes on the number. He phones Natalie then, once he's satisfied he's not being spied on, and asks her to be ready to open her gate. He signals a passing taxi. It's a journey of less than fifteen minutes, during which he tucks his chin and hunches his shoulders.

When the gate opens he lamps her standing at the gable with her arms folded. She turns and moves around the back of the house and he follows. She stops on the decking by the patio door. She stands by slatted cherry wood furniture in what light bleeds through the smoke-blue curtains inside; colour pools at her feet and laps the landscaped darkness, her parents' land, earth bought and planted. When she decides he's close enough she says,

'Whose phone did you ring me from earlier?'

Ryan steps onto the decking and steadies himself with one hand on the treated timber railing. Natalie is rigged out in a navy tunic and dark jeans, with her hair loosely plaited over her shoulder. No warpaint to match the attitude, but her plainness makes her formidable; she's a caricature of an aggravated girl-friend made to stay up late to let in her misbehaving man.

'A heads-up,' she goes on. 'I called it back already.'

'If you called it back,' Ryan says, 'then you know whose it was.'

'I'm just wondering how it came to pass that you were able to use your ex-girlfriend's phone?'

'She's a nurse,' Ryan says. 'She was at the hospital when I was. I'd no phone, Natalie. I'd not a bob on me. What was I s'posed to do?'

A brushstroke of wind through branches. Natalie waits for calm. 'Oh, I'd probably have done the same. Just without giving her so many details, I guess. She's pretty mouthy for a healthcare professional.'

'We were together nearly six years. She knows to ask questions if I turn up in A&E with a busted lip and bruised ribs.'

'And so you told her all about why Dan was so cross.'

'So?'

'You don't think that's maybe something that should have been kept between you and me? I wasn't quite prepared for being berated by some Norrie slapper who's never even met me.'

'Excuse me?'

'Oh, don't play airs and graces with me, Ryan. I'm seriously not in the mood.'

'Don't call her a slapper.'

Her mouth stretches. 'Why not? She gets to call me names.'

'She got a bit of a fright, girl. This thing between you and me and Dan—'

'This thing between you and me and Dan is none of her business.'

'No, see, it is, and that's what I needed to talk to you about.' He turns out a brittle smile. 'Coz she's pregnant. Fifteen weeks.'

Her countenance flits from ice to tepid bafflement and then, in a magnificent swell, to scalding repulsion. She places a hand square in the middle of Ryan's chest and shoves him off the decking. 'You really are obvious,' she says. 'I suppose this is what a girl has to expect if she dates boys from the Northside.'

224

'What's that mean?'

'Maybe if you'd finished your education you'd be smart enough to know. What I mean is that you can go fuck yourself.'

'What, because Karine is pregnant?'

He makes to step up on the deck beside her. She pushes him back.

'Natalie, I didn't know she was pregnant. She didn't tell me!'

'Oh right. You tell her everything but she keeps secrets from you. Do you think I'm stupid, *bai*? There's only one of us here from a council estate.'

'Jesus, where's this coming from?'

He goes to take her wrist. She slaps him away. 'Oh, how am I supposed to react?' she says. 'Pat you on the back for proving me right? Do you have any idea what I've been through in the past couple of days?'

Ryan hacks out laughter and Natalie takes his convulsions as insult-on-injury. 'You're used to this!' she says. 'What's a slap to you? It's just more of what you dole out yourself. Aren't you the Rottweiler?'

'Rottweiler? Do I look able for this, girl?'

'Well, looks can be deceiving, can't they? I thought first day you didn't look like a drug dealer, and so why not proceed based on that inconsistency? But now here you are, showing up my naivety. Go back to Pramface, don't let me keep you.'

Ryan keeps her. He takes both of her wrists and pulls her close enough for her mouth to be a tilted kiss from his and she struggles, but there's strength in his insight and so strength in his grasp. ' "Like a drug dealer?" And you knew I was a drug dealer how?'

She wrinkles her nose. 'Oh, how do you think?'

Ryan drops her wrists. 'You knew,' he says. He steps back.

She has the grace to tear up. 'It's not my fault you didn't recognise me! That night we spoke, I was out with Dan, you saw me out with Dan, I smiled at you, for God's sake! You stared straight back! I thought afterwards you just weren't mentioning it because you didn't want *me* to remember.'

Ryan holds his head in his hands. He squeezes. 'Natalie, he could have fucking killed me!'

'You knew that months ago, Ryan! You chose to keep going! Why wouldn't I go with that? You were the one who knew what you were doing.'

'No, hold on . . . I knew only half the story. I asked you, Natalie. Tons of times. Did you know? And you kept telling me you didn't – what kind of sick game is that?'

'Game? Yet you're only telling me your ex-girlfriend's pregnant once she gets out of you my phone number and, oh, let me tot it!' She taps her fingers, she hams it up. 'Yeah, four months in, once she starts showing, once you can't really keep it quiet anymore. You're the one playing games, Ryan. Well, congratulations. You won.'

'I won? Explain that to me!'

'Do you have any idea what Dan's got over my head? I'm just starting a career, you know. Do you know what that is, Ryan? Is that an exotic concept?'

'The fuck, Natalie? Dan has nothing on you, what's he gonna do, tell KPMG he threw you a batch?'

'Jesus, Ryan, are you joking me? Do you really . . .?' She holds her hands splayed in front of her and raises eyes to heaven and shakes her head. 'You remember the night we spoke!'

'Course I do, night before Christmas Eve.'

'No Ryan. Before that. You gave me an account number for a guy in Italy. Oh my God. Oh my God, you really are that dense. Who d'you think's been doing the books for Dan on this Italy thing? Why do you think he was so possessive? Coz I'm just so good at blowjobs?'

Ryan has the bobs to get a taxi only back to Douglas village. There he leans for fifteen minutes at a bus stop, forehead against

226

a perspexed fast food promo, before he's whisked through colours smeared by speed and raindrops into the city centre. He hobbles to a second bus stop. He repeats the grind. His phone rings five minutes from his front door.

Karine. 'Ah, where the hell are you?'

'On my way home now.'

'You were supposed to be on your way home hours ago!'

'I'm nearly there,' he tells her, and then, mechanically, 'Don't be cross with me.'

She's in the sitting room with Joseph when Ryan comes through the door. Joseph jumps up and gives him a solemn hug that makes Ryan flinch, but it's as much her news for telling, he supposes.

'Well done, boy.'

The light from the television screen and the wall sconces makes Joseph look flushed and fervent. 'This is gonna be so good for you,' he declares, but Ryan's state of repair upsets him and it seems he's not sure what to say next. Karine, on the couch, curls one leg underneath her. She's rosy too, though whether that's the fault of Ryan's tired eyes or her physical condition, he doesn't know.

'Where were you?' she asks.

'I'd things to do. I told you.'

He thinks she's going to launch an investigation in front of Joe, but when she opens her mouth next it's to say, 'Have you eaten?' and so Ryan meekly answers, 'No.'

'Go have a shower,' she says. 'I'll make you something.'

Ryan's jeans are so dirty – wet and dried in cycles, stained with the various fluids knocked out of him – that it's a rough task to get them off. He stands in the shower for fifteen minutes, washes all over three times. The skin on the inside of his thighs is red and tender; his chest is a mess.

Whatever Karine tells Joseph, he beats a gracious retreat. By the time Ryan is out of the shower he's retired to his own room;

'Better Living Through Chemistry' is blaring and he's blaring along. Karine meets Ryan in his bedroom with a bowl of pasta pesto and chicken. He worries he's gone beyond hunger but he starts into it on the off-chance and manages the lot, so she, Irish-Mammy-in-Training, says 'Nothing wrong with your appetite, anyway.'

She brings the bowl back to the kitchen and on her return climbs onto the bed beside him.

'Show me.'

Knowing there's a mess been made of him, she helps him take his T-shirt off. She slouches and sighs. 'Oh Ryan,' she says. 'Oh Ryan.'

'It's getting better.'

She sighs again and says, 'So what happens next?'

'I haven't a fucking clue.'

There aren't many gaps to fill in; what details he's left out she's able to guess. She's appropriately horrified, so his update is appropriately faltering; she listens with her fingertips on his belly. The only part he keeps deliberately vague is Natalie's mania. He knows he'll need a run at it; he knows he can't enunciate something he doesn't understand; he knows Karine will morph from glowing-with-child to burning-with-rage.

He does ask what she said to Natalie to make the girl so incandescently irate. She shrugs.

'Seriously, D'Arcy.'

Her bottom lip pokes out. 'Probably told her she was a vampiric cunt or something.'

Ryan pinches his brows at their outmost edges and pushes them together and laughs under his breath. She shuffles forward and catches his wrist.

'So how long do I give you?' she asks.

Ryan knows his only hope lies in Shakespeare being able to convince Dan to pay *pizzo*, which is a tarnished hope if it glimmers at all. He tells Karine that he'll know more at the end of the week and that Shakespeare has the capacity to convince Dan to compensate Phelan, and he tells himself, and he tells them both lies, lies, lies and Karine being Karine doesn't believe any of it, but he guesses she feels sorry for him, propped on his pillows pulling faces with every move she makes.

They argue about flights to Naples, then flights to anywhere else. They argue about duty and rights. The argument winds down. Karine takes his hand.

He looks at her hand around his. His glance goes from there to her belly. He says, 'Show me something good.'

She gets him. She smiles.

She removes her hoodie, tucks her vest under her bra, straightens and turns to the side. The telling is a bow in the line of her body, quite high up, conspicuous now that she's stretching and framing with both hands flat on her sides. She cocks her head. 'Go on,' she says.

Ryan slides his fingers over her skin and she is at once familiar and new. There's a curve where there used to be none, that is all. But he can take credit for it; their bodies were meant to exist together; this proves it. He's in pain and he is light-headed, he is exhausted and he is rapturous.

'It's beautiful,' he says.

'It's weird,' she corrects. 'There's someone growing inside me. This week, about the size of an apple.'

'No way.'

She murmurs confirmation. She looks down and twists slightly, as if the bump and his hand on the bump is an outfit she's trying on.

Ryan slides his other arm around her waist and pulls her to him.

She settles, her head against his and her belly touching his side. Skin on skin isn't enough. He nudges her onto his lap and she gives in and straddles him and puts her hands on his shoulders.

229

'You need to rest,' she reminds him.

'I know,' under his breath, in desperate refrain, 'I know.'

'Coz I have zero intention of hurting you further.'

I know, I know.

One side of her vest has come out of the tuck and is beginning to fall back over her belly. He lifts it again and his fingers draw over her breast.

Again she reminds him that he needs to rest, but she doesn't move to stop him.

He says, 'I want to see.'

She stretches. 'You can see.'

'All of you.'

She smiles.

'I swear to God, girl, you've never been this beautiful.'

'Y'know,' she says, 'I thought so too? It kinda suits me.'

It's her weight on his lap and her belly grazing the bruises on his and her hands sliding from his shoulders to his neck: he kisses her.

'Does that not hurt?' she says.

'A small bit.'

He kisses her again and lifts the hem of the vest until she raises her arms for him. He straightens to kiss the straps away from her shoulders and it hurts; he freezes and screws his eyes shut; she says, 'See?' but the word comes as the clasp comes loose, much too late. Her breasts against his chest and below that, her rounded belly. Soft and half-hearted protest. She's afraid of damaging him. It's his breathing more than anything else: fast and shallow. She slips over him. She leans back. She ripples from where they meet right up to her throat. She takes on the task and she does it rhythmically and tenderly and even so, when he comes, when he holds his breath and the muscles across his belly contract and he pulls her hard down onto him, it feels like he's been kicked in the stomach all over again; it burns and wounds him but he doesn't give a fuck.

230

And it floods his brain with the feelgoods and lets him sleep.

He coasts from dreams to stupor and back again. There's a gathering of shapes and sounds, none enough to keep him awake. In darkness she's warmth curled up beside him. In the morning she's a guardian sitting up against his pillow, placidly scanning her phone screen. She lets him stir and snooze again. When he's properly awake, a bit after ten in the morning, she gets him painkillers and coffee.

'How are you feeling?' she asks.

'Pretty terrible.'

With no small degree of difficulty Ryan pushes himself from his elbows to a sitting position; he's stiff as a rusted gate.

Halfway through his coffee Karine turns and says, 'Is there anything downstairs for breakfast?'

'No idea.'

'I'll look,' she says.

He's loath to wash her off him but the shower gives him space to gather thoughts. It's all in Shakespeare's hands, he tells himself, and Shakespeare's the man for cold logic; if anyone can get through to Dan, it's him.

He thinks of Natalie. What she's admitted to will catch up with him; he hopes it will hold till he has the energy to hate her.

He thinks of holes in his and Karine's history, of sterile rooms and plane journeys, of decisions made outside of a locked cell. He thinks of fusings and flushings. He absent-mindedly cups his balls. He imagines himself a father at seventeen. This alternative Ryan makes better decisions, stays at home on the couch, makes peace with his poverty.

Karine's back is to him when he gets to the kitchen. She's doing scrambled eggs. He goes up behind her, thinking closeness will slow the reel in his head, but she stiffens in his arms and in that one action the nightmare retakes him.

'You all right?'

She jostles out of his hug and serves up.

'Y'know, it's occurred to me . . .' Her chin is trembling. '. . . I'm only all right when you're all right, and it doesn't go both ways.'

She places both plates on the table but she doesn't sit down.

'I throw up for weeks,' she says, 'and you don't even notice. Some gangland nut looks at you funny and my senses go haywire. I can't do this anymore. I get just the smallest taste again and I remember why I'm allergic. I can't do this, Ryan.'

She grips the back of the chair nearest her. She pushes her free hand over her forehead. She's wearing the T-shirt she took from him last night. The cloth is slack and the bump is hidden.

'I'll sort this,' he says. 'I'll burn the ends, it won't happen again.'

'You can't promise me that.'

He takes a step forward; his hands meet; he bows his head. 'I can swear it to you. I'll get my head together, I want to be with you, girl.'

'Yeah? And what about her?'

'What about her?'

She spits the words back at him. '*What about her?* Jesus Christ, Ryan.'

'I made a mistake.'

'Oh no,' she says. 'Oh, don't you dare.'

It's no task for her to cut past him; she's five months yet from labour and well able to move. She runs up the stairs and he trots after, making claws when he grips the banister. She throws his door out behind her. Ryan gently pushes it open. She's gathering the clothes thrown to the floor the night before.

'What did I say, girl?'

She holds up one hand. Sniffs, gasps, sniffs.

'Karine.'

He closes his hand around her wrist and she shakes him off. She steps too close and he falls back onto the bed; pain coils around his ribs. She continues readying to leave him. He could

232

have stopped her once. He did once. He trapped her between his strength and the plasterboard.

'I don't know what I said. What did I say?'

'D'you know what I've been through, Ryan? Can you imagine at all how I must have felt when I found out I was pregnant again, when the very reason I didn't have the first is because you were so all over the place, so bloody ransomed by Dan Kane and drunk on the rubbish he was filling your ears with?'

She wrenches off the borrowed T-shirt and gets into her own and there's no time, this time, to take in the form he's given her.

'D'you know I can't graduate without meeting my duty hours? D'you know I'll have to spend part of next year making up my maternity leave so that I'll get my degree? D'you know I'm stuck here now? There are zero graduate jobs in Ireland and I can't travel, I can't get experience, I'm so limited now, I have to put my whole life on hold, d'you know that?'

'But that's the thing, girl. I recognise that. What needs doing, I'll do—'

'Yeah, wonderful, and so all of this has been . . . what, Ryan? I asked you to quit this dangerous shit after it became obvious it was polluting you and you refused – oh, I didn't understand, I couldn't possibly get the intricacies. So I followed through with it and broke up with you and instead of sobering up and reassessing what I meant to you and giving me my boyfriend back, you pulled some reckless lunatic and forgot all about me. Because she didn't care how or when or why you got arrested or fucking killed, she was just the kind of girl you were after. I changed absolutely every-thing I was gunning for to accommodate your baby and you? What did you change, Ryan? Did you even change the sheets?'

She pauses to drag her hoodie sleeve across her cheeks.

'And now what are you telling me? That you made a "mistake". That you want me back, and that it's all going to be oh-fucking-kay despite your own admission that you're more tangled up in dangerous freaks than you ever were!'

It's all she can do then to stand and cry, and it's all he can do to stare and knot his fingers.

He recovers first. He pushes himself off the bed and she jerks back.

'I fucked up, Karine. I fucked up, I'm so sorry.'

'You're always sorry,' she says.

She goes for the stairs and he lumbers after her. She reaches the bottom and flops back against the front door. He steps up to her; he leans on the wood just over her shoulders; he rests his forehead on hers.

'None of this would have happened' – his hands slide down the panel; his thumbs rest against her neck – 'if I'd known you were pregnant. I'd never have stayed with her, I'd never have been so stupid.'

'It's not my role to keep you from doing stupid things, Ryan.'

'I know that. Just . . .'

Breathy – *just* . . . – and docile and yielding and grasping and frightened.

'I need to pull away from you,' she says. 'And it's perverse. Coz I should be with you. And I can't be with you.'

'What about last night?'

'Oh yeah, like if I could just hold you like that all the time, you'd be safe and it'd be perfect. What about me, Ryan? Am I safe?' Her hands go to her belly. 'Even if it's sweetness and light between us, there's still the guards. There's still the prick you work for. And if it's not sweetness and light, what then? With your temper? D'you know the amount of relationships that turn abusive in the first pregnancy?'

He doesn't think, he just says, 'This isn't your first.'

'Oh, bitter,' she says, after her eyes spill over, and oh bitter the taste of the words on his tongue. 'And your hands on my neck again. What am I saying, *turn abusive*? You started months ago.'

*

234

She leaves him and he returns to his room and sits staring out the window at the sky. The walls inch in. After a while he goes downstairs and does the ware. He has a smoke. He goes from the sitting room to the landing to the kitchen to his bedroom.

Joseph gets home from work. *What happened to you anyway? I got a dig. How come? Shit got out of hand; it's sorted now. Story with Karine? We're not getting back together. She'll come round.*

'Prove to her you've changed,' Joseph says, and laughs. 'Course, then you gotta do the changing.'

Ryan fakes amusement. Nods. Tsks through teeth as he nurses a joint. His head's gone.

This is going to be so good for you. This is gonna be the makings of you.

Joseph heads off to bed around eleven. He's got work, commitments, a role. His little girl is four years old. He tries to see her every single day.

Ryan retires to his room and stands in the middle of the floor. Around him are the tools of a lost trade. Black, blocky, blokey hardware. Dark plastics, weighted keys, pads and crossfaders. He gets the notion that he should pull the place apart. Wreck the gaff and in its wrecking make her a shrine. He lies on the bed instead. He turns on his side, slowly, gingerly, and reaches underneath.

Sound and Silence: A Human Obsession.

It's been a little under fifteen weeks since she gave this to him and he hasn't gotten past the chapter listing.

He turns the book from back to front. Whites and silvers, a clean font, starkly minimal.

It's supposed to do you good.

He hears her, sound in silence, and he grips the spine of her gift and curses himself.

21

Twenty-one years after being delivered into his father's hands Ryan steps quietly over his threshold.

He's timed it so that his siblings will have cleared out for school or college but his father won't yet have gotten stuck in on his thirst. Sure enough he's in the kitchen, hair standing in waves, wearing navy tracksuit bottoms and a bobbled hoodie. There's a wash on and there's ware drip-drying by the sink and there's a fella on the radio bemoaning homelessness.

'Hey Dad.'

'Jesus, the birthday boy.' Tony straightens and grins. 'You're out early.' And then, as he notices: 'What happened to you?'

'Got a dawk.'

'From who?'

'Some cunt. It was a stupid thing, sorted as soon as it started.' Though the tastelessness of his question makes Ryan want to ask *Why? Is it only you who's allowed hit me?*

Tony goes for the kettle. Ryan pulls out a chair, his grass, fags and papers. Early and all as it is he thinks they could both do with the cushion.

His father leaves the room as the kettle's boiling and returns with a silver gift bag.

'Happy birthday,' he says, and hands Ryan the bag and grips his far shoulder in the classic Tony Cusack hug.

It's an *Azzurri* track jacket. Ryan stands up again and puts it on.

236

'Suits you,' Tony says.

Ryan zips it up and smooths it down. 'It's me daza.'

'It'd kill you to wear an Ireland one, I suppose.'

But all in good humour. Tony goes back to the kettle. Ryan gets a knife from the drawer and cuts the tags off. They reconvene at the table. Tony gives Ryan a mug. Ryan gives him a pinch of grass. Tony takes another look at the track jacket and nods and wistfully says, 'How the fuck have I a twenty-one-year-old son?'

'I thought you'd have figured that out by now, Dad.'

Tony laughs as if he's not sure he likes the sound. 'Swear to God, Rocky, it's like it was yesterday. I was only a year older than you are now. I turn around then and I'm forty-three.'

It's a skit that Ryan is over here to report something that's going to make his father feel even older.

'I've something to tell you,' he mutters.

He doesn't focus but he knows Tony's crinkled up, paused part of the way through rolling himself a fat one. Ryan's forehead is in his right hand. He stares at a vague point on the tabletop to his father's right.

'What's the matter?'

Ehm . . . Ryan rolls into the palm of his hand and closes his eyes.

'Karine's pregnant,' he manages, in the end.

Tony goes still as stone.

'You fucking eejit,' he manages, in the end.

There's no malice in it; it's just stumped him, forty-three and barely able for his own fatherhood. He shakes his head. 'Jesus,' he says. He rubs green flakes from his fingertips and moves his hands from the unrolled spliff. 'I wasn't expecting that.'

'Neither was I, to be honest.'

'No? How'd you manage that in this day and age, boy?'

'Happens, doesn't it?'

'If you say so. Jesus!' again, as the shock spreads out. He manages to laugh. 'Well, that's a bit of news. How long is she gone?'

'Fifteen weeks.'

'That why she's been odd with you since Christmas, so?'

'Yeah.' It's the first time Tony's mentioned it.

'I knew you had to have done something,' he says. 'She's a great girl. Though I don't know what either of you were thinking, if you were thinking at all, like. What are you going to do?'

'I don't know.'

'You'd want to start thinking about it, boy.'

Tony's hands move to the joint, but hover over it. He flexes his fingers, draws his hands back and rests his fingertips on the tabletop edge.

'How d'you feel about it?' he asks.

'Scared.'

'Scared? What are you scared of?'

There's that flush of anger again. Like fatherhood's a simple thing. Like Tony was ever any good at it. *Why'd you come here, then?* Ryan doesn't know. He wanted to tell his father. His father is a stupid cunt but he just wanted to be around him. *Why?* He doesn't know. He doesn't fucking know. *Why?* Oh Christ, coz Tony is his dad and what if it's him who's taught Ryan how to be a dad and what if Karine's right and what if this whole thing is fucked, irreparably fucked?

'Why, Dad? Is there nothing to be scared of?'

'There's plenty,' Tony says softly; he's spotted the flame. 'I was only asking what was bothering you, boy. In particular, like.'

'I'll be lucky if she lets me have anything to do with it. Already she's her mind made up I'm worthless.'

'She's wrong then, isn't she?'

'How is she wrong, Dad? Didn't you say it yourself: all I want to do is chase my fucking tail?'

'Well, maybe this'll clear your head, boy.'

238

'What, you think I can get my shit together?'

'I do.' He frowns. 'I do of course.'

'She fucking hates me, Dad.'

'She does not.'

'She does. She told me already, no way is she taking me back. I can't be trusted. I'm bad-minded.'

Tony tosses his head and smiles at the floor.

So Ryan snaps. 'What the fuck would you know, anyway?' He gets up and takes his gear from the table and bundles it into the right pocket of his new track top. 'How the fuck would you know what kind of person I am? Apart from that if I'm fucked, I'm fucked like you. That's what she told me, y'know. On Monday. I was gonna end up like you. Is that funny, is it, Dad?' He makes backwards for the kitchen door. 'Monday. That's when she told me she was pregnant. Only on fucking Monday, as a last resort. Once she'd made up her mind to have it at all, like. She didn't with the last one, and I only found that out on Monday too. That's how bad I am, Dad!'

Tony stands to go after him so Ryan turns and barrels for the front door.

'That's why she was so odd with me when I was in Saint Pat's. Coz she'd gone off to England to have an abortion. Yeah, and only tell me years later. That's how bad I am, Dad. That's how fucking bad I am.'

Tony catches him before he reaches the handle. Strength in him still, though it's been years since Ryan's felt it. He takes him by the shoulders and Ryan shoves him off; his father stumbles and his back bumps the banister. 'Don't fucking touch me!' Ryan roars; novelty enough to bring his father to a standstill, he would have wagered, but that's Tony Cusack for you: a law unto himself, can't be trusted to follow reason.

He gets Ryan this time. First by the shoulders, then around the shoulders, and he hangs on even when his son stamps and quakes.

239

'It's all right, boy.'

'It's not all right. She fucking hates me.'

Tony pins Ryan's arms by his sides so he can't do anything but bow his head.

'It's all right,' he says again.

Ryan presses his nose against his father's shoulder and into his shoulder he goes, 'Am I that bad, Dad?' and Tony moves his arms up along Ryan's back and holds him tight and Ryan's done, he's fucking bawling. 'It's all I wanted,' he tells Tony. 'I know,' Tony says, and he rubs the back of Ryan's neck and again Ryan tells him, 'It's all I wanted, Dad.'

'I know, boy. I know.'

So Maria, here we are now.

Do you hear him? Telling me it's all going to be OK? Tony Cusack, the pushover lush, the weak-willed gom you married. There he is now, fucking expert in all things paternal, telling me that he was never as happy as the first time ever he held me, even though he's fucking punched me since, the two-faced prick, yeah, punched and shoved and knocked my head off walls. Telling me that I was the making of him. It's a bit cruel, isn't it, Mam? It's a bit cruel to fling shit like that at me if he doesn't mean it because I so fucking badly want him to mean it, that's why I fucking went over, isn't it? Karine's going to have my kid so I need to run up and tell my dad all about it coz I want his approval so fucking badly it hurts more than being punched. I want my dad. And I don't know why I want my fucking dad.

See, this is what you did when you decided to kill yourself.

Ah, yeah, don't think I don't know that. You made that decision, you got in the car, blind drunk and fuming. Don't think I don't remember you on the landing screaming at my dad, telling him you were gonna take us down to Youghal and drown us all if that's what had to be done. Do you think me talking to you is all forgiveness and fucking love? Naw, it's not. It's me telling you

Me telling you

Me screaming into the fucking void is what it is.

It's not like you can hear me. You couldn't hear Dad, could you, when he was bawling for you? You wouldn't know what it's like to see your dad like that but you made damn sure I'd know. I saw my dad fall to fucking pieces over and over again and where were you? Ah, fucking everywhere and nowhere.

Naw, fuck, what the fuck would I know about having a kid when everything I know is wrong? I know how to sit at the kitchen table with a can of crap lager and stare at the opposite wall in the fucking freezing cold because hey, only room enough in the budget for one type of fuel. I know how to fall down in the drive outside and stay crumpled there till a neighbour takes pity. I know that once my kid turns twelve I can punch the poor little fucker so hard I knock him to the tiles and that if anyone notices at all they won't make the tiniest fucking chirrup because God help us, the man's only going through a rough patch, he's been through enough as it is.

Do you hear him, Mam? My dad, the great instigator, the sack of spite, telling me that I'm going to be great at this? Telling me that I'm going to get her back? Telling me that Karine loves me, that he saw it clear as day last Halloween, when I was rushed to A&E because, like you, I thought I couldn't do it anymore and thought no one would give a single fuck if I was

Oh fuck, I'm afraid of what I'll do if I keep talking to you. See, Mam? You're still fucking me up.

22

'Saturday night I knew this was going to happen,' Colm yowls.

Ryan is in Colm's gaff because conscience told him he needed to admit to having fallen out with Dan and so making uncertain Catalyst's future. To tell him yeah, he was right, he'd been right all along, Ryan should never have believed he could bring two such disparate worlds as his and Natalie's together with the power of his cock.

Ryan hasn't been able to shake off the headache from his lapse into babyish blubbering in his father's hall. On top of that – or because of that – he feels nauseous, like there's a stale nub caught in a tonsil. He pulls the cuffs of his track jacket halfway down his palms and pinches them there. He rubs his covered wrists over his thighs, down over his knees, back again.

Colm walks to the breakfast bar and leans into it with his back to Ryan. 'Hawkish fuckers, aren't you, all the same?' he says, muffled between chin and worktop, between fear and rage.

Ryan says, 'Currency in it.'

'Yeah yeah.'

There is brief silence but for the dull disharmony of the night-time traffic outside before Colm starts again. 'I suppose you could say it's my own fault.' He rolls around. 'Searching for investors in the underworld, or whatever. But I've always thought in shades of grey. No good guys, no bad guys. All I wanted was a chance to make something of a very modest ambition. What was Catalyst, but a good start? And now look. Only weeks into it . . . Ah! This is my black and white payback for thinking in ambiguities.'

Ryan doesn't ask what he's at by complaining about black and white payback and Colm's not angry enough to stick the knife in unprompted.

'Still,' Colm grunts, 'you're all right.'

Ryan doesn't feel able to correct him. He does not feel all right. He does not think he would have been all right, even if Jimmy Phelan hadn't hitched his shitwagon to the tow bar, even if Dan had never figured out what was going on with Natalie, even if Ryan had never brought her home. The world is hostile. MDMA purity turns one-and-a-half-hour buzzes into vicious benders, his maternal heritage is corrupted for profit, a little person stretches secretly in a womb, already fearful of his father.

'It's Wednesday night,' Colm says. 'If he's about to dissolve this thing, he really should have said by now.'

'Say nothing,' Ryan says. 'Soldier on.'

He moves for the door and Colm says, 'Dunno if Triona told you – they're going to use your remix as the lead on that Aimee Keohane single. Rebrand her, the lot. So it's not like you don't have other shit going for you.'

'I sold that remix,' Ryan says. 'I signed it over for two hundred quid.'

'There's nine more tracks on that album,' Colm says. 'You think you'd pitch for it.'

'I don't think that's my path, boy.'

'Why? Where's the path you're already on taking you?'

'I think I need to stop altogether,' Ryan says.

He drives home, parks and thinks, *Well, if I'm not thirsty by now it's not for want of an occasion, ha ha.* He stands on the footpath, watching headlights slide by, watching a gaggle of kids a small ways up split and spill onto the road to avoid a bin and flow back together. After a bit Ryan starts walking. He takes the short stroll to the off-licence and buys a bottle of Jameson and back on the street and under his breath he wishes himself a happy birthday.

He doesn't jump when Shakespeare pulls up alongside in the Civic and drops the passenger window.

'What are you doing wandering around on your own, Cusack?'

'Going for a walk – what's it look like?'

'Foolhardy little fuck, ha? No more walks for you, boy. Dan knows.'

'Knows what?'

'That you've run crying to the big bad wolf.'

'Who told him that?'

Shakespeare shrugs. His mouth slackens but there's tension from his forehead to the tip of his sharp and skinny nose. 'Small city,' he says. 'In my experience, where there's an opportunity for mischief some cunt or another will take it. Doesn't matter now. I've never seen the man so angry, God he hates being wrong. I was right, he was wrong, you were the problem, not me, not Pender. You were always the problem.'

'I told you . . .' Ryan flexes his fingers around the whiskey bottle. '. . . J.P. only came in on this after the thing with his mam.'

'I believe you, Cusack. Dan, on the other hand . . .'

He spits out of the driver's window.

'I've been chatting with J.P. as per your intervention,' he says. 'But Dan's reaction to your infidelity is such that I don't need him finding out I've been keeping the same company in recent days, y'know? Given his cokehead-fuck history of doubting me, and all. So it seems to me we need to sort all of this shit out sooner rather than later.'

'What the fuck d'you expect me to do about it?'

'Do I have to spell it out to you, Cusack? He's looking for your head on a pike. You'd want to be ready. Like – and this is only a suggestion – by heading up your own offensive. You don't want a gang war, do you boy? Think of the crossfire.'

'How am I going to head up a fucking offensive, Shakespeare?'

'The how isn't my problem, Cusack. This is your mess.'

The Civic moves off with an animal suddenness that suggests its driver had only just been able to hold it back.

Jimmy Phelan, whose own mother suggests is a remorseless maggot-actor, hardly reacts to this news, telling Ryan that it's hardly his problem if Ryan can't keep his illegitimate activities to himself. Ryan has driven to see Phelan on his eventual say-so, his bottle of whiskey in the passenger seat of his car, thinking just straight enough to know that he needs to get out of Cork. He doesn't have the funds to stay gone. There's a modest few quid at home, taped under the bottom drawer of his desk, and there's a couple of grand in his dad's attic that Tony knows nothing about. Other than that Ryan is a pauper. In a near-empty, square white room at the front of the Little Island warehouse, he tries to explain this to Phelan. 'Either this route,' Ryan says, 'is a gold-bearing vein, or it isn't. D'you think I'm fucking codding you?'

'I don't think you're codding me,' Phelan chuckles.

'I need to get out of Cork. I can go to Naples, Salerno, wherever, and keep things moving there.'

'Do, then.'

'Yeah, well I need sponsorship to do it.'

Ryan elaborates on his newfound penury and Phelan is not moved. Not even a small bit. Oh, one needs to be prepared for such eventualities when one sells drugs for a living. No comebacks through the courts, no guarantees. This is Ryan's own fault; why should Phelan subsidise his stupidity?

'It's not like I spent it all on ould dolls and poker! Dan's got thousands belonging to me, boy.'

'And why in God's name would you let him hold on to so much money?'

'It was there for laundering—'

246

'Laundering. You don't know how to clean your cash? Jesus Christ, I suppose you drive past the bookies of a Tuesday morning and wonder what all the young shams are at in there.'

'I'm talking five figure sums,' Ryan says.

'Half a day's work,' Phelan says.

'This whole fuck-up is . . .' Ryan catches his thumbnail between his teeth, tucks the digit away again when he sees how it's shaking. 'I dunno, appalling timing.'

'No such thing,' Phelan says. 'You don't rely on timing. You spread your gains so you can shoulder your losses. But I guess you're young and still infected with the stupidity of adolescence, so we'll leave it there. Make a lesson of it. I've lost a lot more in my day, and I didn't have anyone to go *béal-bochting* to, either.'

'I'm not asking you to fund a fucking holiday, boy. I die here, and where does that leave you?'

'Worse off, but only temporarily. C'mon, Cusack. Don't be so naive.'

'What the fuck do I do, then?'

'You can afford the plane ticket, surely. Haven't you family out there?'

'I can't deal with the fucking Camorra from my grandparents' gaff!'

Phelan throws out another rumbling chuckle. 'OK, fine. Let's see if we can't quell Danny's murderous rage without wasting my money.'

'What's that mean?'

'Means I'll talk to him. Come on.'

Ryan pivots with Phelan's movements; Phelan takes his jacket from the seat of a blue-cushioned chair, he checks and smooths the blinds, he grabs his car keys and leaves his desktop bare. 'Listen, J.P.,' but he has no mind for listening. 'You don't understand,' but he knows that already and couldn't give the lesser of two shits.

247

'Are you seriously thinking that we can just go and find Dan and tell him to back off and that won't be confirmation enough to blow all of his fucking gaskets?'

'Cusack,' chides Phelan, 'I'm in this game a long time, and my say-so is heavier than a year's worth of Kane's expletives. I've been navigating tight spots and crushing gobshites for thirty years. What age are you?'

It's a rhetorical question but Ryan doesn't answer for Phelan's benefit. 'Twenty-one. Today.'

'Today?' Phelan turns back and makes signs of softening – kind of a smile, kind of a slope to his shoulders. 'Then let's see if we can't secure another twenty-one for you.'

Ryan follows Phelan back into town and by the time he parks, on the city centre end of Barrack Street, Phelan has located Dan through Shakespeare and demanded an emergency meeting.

'What, now?'

'Oh, you're an antsy little fuck until you're called to action, then you're asking *What's the rush*. Fuck's sake, Cusack. Yes now. Yes, here.' He lights a cigarette, snaps the hinge of his lighter shut and flicks a thumb at the pub three doors down.

Ryan has been here before. The pub is a dull and pokey place above ground but Phelan calls his assemblies below; it's in the cellar Ryan lied through his clenched teeth that he'd offed the girl Phelan wanted offed.

Phelan goes to turn and Ryan catches his arm, to a look of cool surprise.

'You don't expect me to be there, do you?' Ryan says.

'This is about you, isn't it? You're shitting bricks because you're sure Dan Kane wants to kill you. No, boy. You stand up straight and you face him. Twenty-one today, isn't that right? You're a man now.'

There are a couple of Phelan's cronies already in the cellar, one of whom is only thrilled to see how Ryan's skin crawls.

'Are we gonna make a pet of him or what, Jimmy?'

248

'That ship has sailed, boy. Mr Cusack here is twenty-one today.'
Dougan leers. 'They grow up so fast.'

'Get him a drink. Poor fucker needs it.'

Brandy. Straight. The smell hits Ryan's nostrils after the
liquid's down and he feels a retch gather and knocks his fist
against his sternum.

Dan shows up just after eleven thirty with Shakespeare in tow.
Maybe there are a few more from the crew outside, gathering as
they did when they waited for their leader to deal with Pender, a
long time back now. Dan sets a mild smirk on Phelan, but then
he clocks Ryan and the smirk slips off and he frowns in confusion. Phelan rests his knuckles on the table in front of him. Dan
stands a couple of feet from the other end with his hands in his
jacket pockets. Shakespeare watches Ryan; Ryan can see him
without turning his eyes to confirm it.

'We have a bit of a problem,' Phelan begins.

Ryan leans back until his shoulders hit the stone. He bows his
head and brings his hands up to his waist and stares at his
fingertips.

'I understand,' says Phelan, 'that Cusack has wronged you.
And believe me, Kane, I'm this close to telling you that it's your
right to take what compensation you can from the little fucker.
But this one's complicated. His father and I go way back. You
see my conundrum.'

It's a few seconds before Dan can reply, 'What the fuck is
happening here?'

'He fucked your ould doll,' Phelan says, helpfully. 'And you
gave him a hiding. But that's as far as I can let it go. I've drawn a
line and you're going to hurry your arse back behind it.'

Ryan's head drops till the back of his neck hurts, till his chin
hits the collar of his new track jacket. He's reminded of school,
of having to stand for a class's duration for some infraction or
another. *Can't you pay attention, Mr Cusack? Is it beyond your
capacity to* listen?

'This is ridiculous,' Dan says, 'so I'm compelled to assume you're joking me.' Blurred movement; he cocks his head towards Ryan. 'What the fuck are you at, Cusack, pulling outsiders into this?' Ryan makes fists. He conducts a thumb war with himself. He winces. He doesn't look up.

'I told you,' Phelan says. 'I'm a family friend. I couldn't look his father in the eye if anything happened to this young fella.'

'You're a family friend. You are yeah.'

'I am. And another thing I am is: very unlikely to want to play the long game with a fucking eejit like you. There will be trouble if so much as a hair on Cusack's head is turned over. Two things you need to ask yourself, Kane: are you so sure about this fucking child that you'll start something with me over him, and, more pressingly, do you want to walk out of here?'

Ryan counts and shuffles and blinks and all the while the weight of Shakespeare's glare pushes him closer to the cellar floor.

'Get away t'fuck,' Phelan says; shifting shadows tell Ryan that he's turned his back on Dan. There's scuffling as Phelan's men move towards Dan and Shakespeare in escort. Ryan watches his hands. He watches his hands.

The room begins to come back to itself. Voices rise and there's short laughter. A can snapped open. A phone call made.

Phelan's hand rests on the back of Ryan's neck. He flexes his fingers.

'You see how it's done?' he says.

He falls back and snaps his fingers under Ryan's nose. Ryan straightens. 'The man's angry,' Phelan says.

'Is he what.'

'But it's contained anger. I wouldn't much fancy being his missus tonight, but you're fine. And all done without once mentioning your friends in Italy.'

So Ryan reiterates, weakly, 'I need to get out of here.'

'When I'm ready to send you,' Phelan says. 'You've a few days yet. Maybe get some sleep. You look like shit.'

'Will you at least give me a fucking gun?'

'Violence begets violence,' Phelan says. 'If I give you a gun I'd be afraid you'd use it.'

'You'll wait till Kane takes a shot at me first? What, so's you can ID the bullet before you avenge the damage done?'

'Easy there, sweetheart,' Phelan says. 'He'll do as he's told, given who's told him.'

'Nothing would make me happier than to believe that, but in the meantime you're betting with my fucking life, boy.'

Phelan sighs. 'Would it make you feel that much better if I gave you a pistol?'

'A small bit.'

He looks back towards his boys, tilts his head, and one comes to serve him.

'Arrange to meet Mr Cusack in an hour's time so you can hand over one of the nines,' he directs, and to Ryan he says, 'Seeing as we're buddies now, let's say twelve-hundred.'

'Didn't I tell you earlier I haven't a bob?'

'G'way outta that, Cusack. Green and all as you are, I'm sure you have a few quid squirrelled away somewhere.'

Ryan's exit is a fiasco of knocked knees and false alarms. He is sure Dan's going to have someone waiting for him and he's ready to bolt and afraid then that bolting will only make him more conspicuous, and he twelve hundred euro and at least an hour away from any hope at all.

Ryan is at his father's house fifteen minutes later. He carries a kitchen chair to the landing, lifts the attic hatch, boosts himself off the landing banister, feels every punch and kick again. Tony is by the chair staring up at him when he looks back down through the hatch, his savings divided and tucked into his pockets.

'What're you doing up there, boy?'

'Looking for something.'

251

'Looking for what?'

'Doesn't matter. I didn't find it.'

'At this hour of the night? Ah, Ryan. Ryan. What're you at?'

Ryan drops down from the hatch and can't help but gasp out an *Aw fuck* as his torso rips and slams back together. He leans against the hot press door.

'What the fuck is after happening you?' Tony says.

'Think I pulled something is all.'

'Pulled something.' Tony looks like he's all set to well up. 'What were you looking for up there?'

'Doesn't matter, Dad, honest. Sorry. I didn't want to wake you, like.'

Tony shakes his head. Ryan goes to lift the chair again. He considers getting Cian out of bed to carry it back to the kitchen. His skin is on fire.

'Why don't you come home for a while, boy?' says Tony. 'Get your head together . . . I know you've gotten a land. I'd be happier to have you here.'

'OK.'

Surprise pulls at the points of Tony's face: eyes, mouth and nostrils.

'I'll be back in half an hour,' Ryan says, and lifts the chair and tries not to grimace.

Ryan is a motherless dealer who's done time and lived for years in a shithole with an unrepentant alcoholic who lays blame with his knuckles and kneecaps; Ryan is no stranger to fear.

He closes the unrepentant alcoholic's front door behind him. He sits in his car.

This fear is different. He feels that the skies have moved and he's a small thing but capable of great atrocities. He sees his potential shaped in Karine's belly, a wonder that could fix his past, present and future, and he is afraid he will never be allowed to hold it. It is the cruellest thing to offer him something so beautiful now when he's ravaged and lost.

252

He is only a few hundred yards from where he's supposed to meet Phelan's trader when he has to pull in and put his head to the steering wheel and huff out heat in pulses, like he's forgotten how to inhale deep enough to keep himself in traction.

He gets back to his dad's when the streets are silent.

He lets his father know he's home and sits then on the front wall and Tony probably stares out his bedroom window, wondering if his son is having a leisurely fag or a nervous breakdown. But there's nothing for it, Ryan has to watch the night. He sits with Phelan's pistol tucked under his jacket and stares up the street and jumps at engines and headlights swinging in off the main road. He hops off the wall and walks up to the top of the terrace and stares down a street of artificial light, black glass and brick, and returns to his father's front gate, afraid to turn his back and afraid to walk backwards.

But his tiredness catches up with him. It drives him back to his old bed and he lies, ears pricked, pistol under the pillow, balmed in the end by his brothers' breathing, and wakes then with a terrible start and light coming in through the curtains.

He pulls his jeans on and tucks the pistol at his waist and checks the rooms – his siblings have toddled out happily enough, according to the state of the kitchen – then the windows and the front and back door and he ducks outside, barefoot, and doesn't know what else he's supposed to do.

Tony's at the kitchen table, knuckles white round the handle of a lava-red mug. The radio's on, there's a drab voice as backdrop. Ryan thinks his head's going to come apart.

'What the fuck is going on with you, boy?' Tony asks.

'Nawthin',' Ryan answers.

His father might be up for taking that for a definitive answer; he might not. They are interrupted by the eleven o'clock news, where the victim of yesterday's shock shooting in Bandon town

253

is named as thirty-nine-year-old Jason Pender, a local father-of-two who was known to the Gardaí.

Ryan taps out a short pattern on the side of the sink and nods when Tony says, 'Bandon? Jesus Christ, Bandon of all places,' and trots up the stairs and goes into the bathroom and doubles up over the toilet.

Not that there's much in him to sick up, and soon he sits spent on the floor and listens to his father's fidgeting and wonders how the fuck, *how the fuck* is he going to hide from him the tremors of what's inescapable and absolute.

Right now, on this bathroom floor, Ryan could take the 9mm from his waist and put the barrel in his mouth and splatter his dad's tiles with his defective fucking brains and there'd be an investigation and a tie-in to the tragedy down in Bandon and something or another about his being known to the Gardaí. There'd be tutting over the front pages in the Centra around the corner, and Mrs Buckley across the road will stop at her front gate and give all the passers-by the same sorry story: 'He hadn't a hope after poor Maria, God help him. Another one gone coz of the drugs and what'll be done about it?' But it'll be forgiven and forgotten because at the end of the day Ryan is Known to the Gardaí. Twenty-one-year-old-almost-father-of-one and Known to the fucking Gardaí.

Almost-father-of-two, he thinks, *Jesus Christ*. He runs his hands over his thighs, down to his knees. He regards himself, the length of his body, the span of his chest, the bop off his father, in his cast and tints and his profligate fertility.

He gets to his feet only after Tony calls up the stairs after him.

'I've no coffee, boy. Unless you go down to Centra and get something from the machine.'

'I'll have tea.' There's a ceiling between them and God knows how many ages.

While his son sups Tony throws him bothered glances over a cigarette and asks, way too softly, if Ryan doesn't think that thing in Bandon was fucking shocking altogether and Ryan shrugs and barely sustains nonchalance . . . *Dad, Dad, I don't know what to fucking do, what am I gonna do?*

He heads upstairs. He's too giddy to lie down. He sits on the edge of his bed with his elbows on his knees. He whips up fury for Natalie, till slurs gather like a cancer in his throat. He wants to blame her for everything: her loveliness, his susceptibility to her loveliness, Phelan's exploitation and Dan's temper and Karine's deciding to hide Ryan's own potency from him. The anger buds and wilts and dies.

'I thought you'd have scurried off under a rock,' Shakespeare says, when he answers his phone, 'having heard your warning shots.'

'Didn't J.P. just tell him I was the inside man? What's he want doing the other fella?'

'Well, exactly,' Shakespeare says. 'Now that it's obvious the other fella lifted the yokes outside of J.P.'s say-so, and that I'm not the treacherous cunt he thought you weren't, the way was clear to take action. Sure Dan's livid. He didn't take J.P.'s directives well. Now he's after Italian take-out.' This with a drawl and a boisterous snort.

'What the fuck am I gonna do?'

'Jesus, you can't still be asking me that.'

'Oh, grand, yeah. You can't talk him down?'

'Did you talk him down for me?'

'Yeah, actually. Yeah I fucking did, because you'd have known nothing about it, would you, if I hadn't given you the heads-up? You can't want this shit, boy.'

'I'll tell you what I don't want is aggro with J.P.. Look, I'm covered no matter which of you crawls their way out of this. Sort it, or wait for Dan to clip you. I couldn't give two shits.'

Ryan phones Phelan and relays Shakespeare's warning and Phelan cuts him off.

'Hold on, are you actually dead? Are you calling me from the astral plane staring down at men in scrubs beating the fuck out of your chest?'

'I'm telling you the warning didn't have the desired effect. I'm asking you to get me out of here – Jesus, J.P., d'you want me to fucking beg?'

'You are begging,' he answers, distractedly, then clears his throat and says, 'I told you, you've a couple of days yet. Get yourself a slab of Dutch Gold and some skin flicks and hide under the bed or something. You're going on like you're Public Enemy Number One, rather than a suckling who's briefly pissed off some fat-lipped baytur.'

'Yeah, look, far be it from me to remind you I know the cunt better than you do—'

'For fuck's sake,' Phelan says, 'go find a burrow to back into, then. And stop pulling at my sleeve. I'm fucking embarrassed for you.'

'I'd be more fucking embarrassed,' Ryan tells him, 'if I thought myself commander-in-chief and it turned out Dan Kane thought of me more as a nagging old dame in a Barracka vault.' Though he can only tell him this because J.P. hung up on him.

Ryan thinks of burrows for a bit, of ceilings of crumbling earth, and weasels, and of being flushed out, whimpering, blinded by torchlight.

He can only think of one place Dan's sure not to find him and he doesn't think Phelan will be too thrilled about it.

Downstairs, Tony opens and closes a palm over his chin, running his fingers along his jaw, looking at Ryan like he's a magnificent puzzle he's too proud to admit to being stumped by.

'I'm off out,' Ryan tells him.

A powerful feeling on heading for the front door with his father a couple of feet behind: Ryan wants Tony to hug him. He wants him to pin his arms to his sides and rub the back of his neck again and prevent him from leaving. 'Listen,' he says, and

Tony prompts 'Go on' after a good long wait for his son to figure out what in Christ he wants to say.

'Are you OK with what I told you yesterday?'

Tony crinkles. 'Why wouldn't I be, boy?'

'Dunno. Can't imagine Gary D'Arcy's taking it as well as you are.'

'Gary D'Arcy's a miserable langer.' Tony grins, and his hand twitches. Ryan thinks for a second his father is going to grab his arm, but he doesn't.

'You're gonna be involved, aren't you?' Ryan asks, and Tony loses the grin and nods, slowly.

'Why wouldn't I be?' he says again.

'Coz it's as much your grandkid as D'Arcy's.'

'Yeah.'

'I wouldn't want him not knowing who his dad was.'

There's a moment where Ryan hopes his father will identify the panic behind the blurt, but he goes for something more reasonable: the notion that Ryan is afraid Karine will shut him out of his baby's life.

'Rocky, don't be daft. You'll be back together before you know it. Sure she's only mad about you.'

If Ryan hugs him, Tony will twig that there's something very wrong. Now there are images of Tony bereaved again, clutching a tumbler at the bar, slumped over the kitchen table, in a heap at the bottom of the stairs. Ryan holds eye contact till Tony looks like twigging; he brings him to the edge of understanding and looks away and takes his leave.

From the front door to the end of the drive doesn't offer time enough to process that this might be the last time he leaves home, nor time enough to trap an image of the concrete underfoot or the state of the lawn. Ryan drags his fingertips along the side of his father's car. He reaches the gate pillar. He steps onto public ground.

Once out of sight Ryan phones his brother and feeds him rickety shit about quick-fix spats. He asks him to avoid Dan and

257

Dan's boys, to stay sharp. Cian sounds earnest, demonstrates a diligent tone, and Ryan has to mask his panic yet again but the truth goads him. Continuing as he's going means he'll hide out for a couple of days before he's sent on to Campania and what then? Dan'll go for Cian. Dan'll go for Tony. Dan'll watch Karine grow. Dan'll never let Ryan home.

Maureen is surprised letting him in, recovered by the time she shuts the door.

'How are you?' she asks, detestably even-voiced, to which Ryan replies, 'Terrible.'

'Terrible?'

'Fucking terrible.'

He walks into her living room prepared to fold onto her couch, cross his arms and tuck his chin, but the Yamaha U3 in the corner opposite knocks the lot out of him, plans, terror and breath.

'What the fuck is this?'

'Well, you know what it is, don't you?' Maureen murmurs. 'Besides that I suppose it's a peace offering. I swapped it for a bookcase.'

Something from his chest, a sob turned into a snort or the other way around. The side of his dad's car to the length of his mam's piano. Ryan goes to it and stretches his arm and gives it only the very, very tips of his fingers.

Surrender checked, he turns on his heel. 'What fucking good is it to me now?'

'Ryan, if you can't find good in it, I don't know what to do with you.'

She blocks the route down the left hand side of the room, so he goes down the right. He reaches the couch. He sinks.

'I didn't think you'd be back to me,' she says, just visible out of the corner of his eye.

'Well, your son told me I'd better find myself a burrow to back into, so all I had to do was ask myself "Who's the biggest fucking weasel I know?"'

258

'If you're feeling that malicious, wouldn't you be better off finding some other home to haunt?'

'I figure you owe me sanctuary.'

'Do you, now.'

For a while neither says anything.

In the end her shoulders shift and she says, 'I didn't mean for this to happen.'

Ryan doesn't even snort.

Another pause of many tonnes and she says, 'I suppose it's very out of tune,' and makes a sprightly move for the piano and he stumbles over his crossed ankles in his hurry to intercept her.

'You don't touch it,' he says, and she curls her lip and says, 'Why not, if it's not going to do you any good?'

'Don't,' he warns.

'Oh this is what you'll take a stand over.' She opens her palm on the fallboard. 'A big fecking lump of wood.'

He opens his palm an inch from hers and leans towards her. 'I'm not taking a stand. It just turns my fucking stomach to see you touching it.'

'I wouldn't have said it was in you to be so vicious.'

'Coz I don't know how I'm going to stay breathing. And that's your fault.'

'If I remember right this is a predicament you got yourself into.'

'You don't remember right. I'd have managed your schizoid son and I'd have weathered this other thing, but you had to stick your oar in and now look. I'm fucking dead, Maureen. Forgive me if I don't feel up to playing you a jingle.'

'You're all over the feckin' place,' she says. 'And yet going nowhere. Sit down.'

She backs away and crosses the front of the couch towards the kitchen and when Ryan doesn't move she shrugs and says, 'Or stay there, sure, guard the thing. Hold on to the thing. Whatever keeps you upright.'

The telltale sounds of the ritual: the flick of the switch, the rumble, the cupboard doors. 'Don't make me fucking tea,' he tells her.

She returns with a mug in each hand and leaves one on the table.

'I don't want your fucking tea, I told you.'

'But you want my roof over your head.' She sits in the armchair and rests her mug against her belly. 'Ah, it's only half-board you're after.'

She takes a sip and eyes him through the steam.

'Ryan,' she says, and he's bruised by how his name sounds coming from her lips, because what if she's the last one from whom he's going to hear it? 'What use is your anger,' she asks, 'if you're determined to do nothing with it?'

'What should I do with it, girl? Nowhere good I can direct it. I'm fucked. Is that in your vocabulary at all? Fucked?'

'It's not, no,' she says. 'It takes a lot more to make me give in.'

'A lot more? Than this? I gave your son the only fucking thing that was keeping me alive and he can barely be arsed preserving it. This morning I talked to a fella whose last great favour to me was to tell me to make arrangements for my funeral, and what does J.P. tell me? To find somewhere to lie low while he thinks about whether it's worth the price of the ticket to get me out of here. Your son plays my life by ear and you give me a fucking piano!' Ryan slides his hand off the fallboard and then slaps it back down on the wood. 'Fuck you, girl. Fuck your meddling.'

'And feck your whinging. Do you think you're the first person ever to be backed into a corner?' She raises both voice and eyebrows. 'I've been knocked. I kept going. You'll keep going. Look at that yoke there.' She points, and Ryan stares as directed at his piano. 'What do you do with that? What's it for?'

He shakes his head at her.

'Not a hope in hell,' she says, 'your mother spent all those hours teaching you to play without there being a brain in your head.'

260

'See, the problem with you, girl, is you think this is about ráiméising my way out—'

'No it's not,' she says. 'If there's no way around it then you go through it, by God. Straight through and you stop for no one.'

'You don't know what you're talking about.'

'Don't I? I've been abandoned and robbed and exiled and all at the same time and if that didn't crush me, Ryan, back in the days when an Irish woman couldn't go for a piss without the say-so of the Catholic church, then this won't crush you. D'you think I don't understand evil? Sit down, drink your tea. Whether it's hiding or fighting you are, you need your fecking head for it.'

She gives him back his head. It takes her hours, it takes him strenuous effort. He does not tell her that Karine is pregnant; he will not trust Maureen with his bar-of-gold. But he believes she can sense that his fear is selfish in the most noble sense. He has given himself over to something tiny yet bigger than himself; she reads the primitive shapes of this devotion, she puts the notes right in his head.

When Maureen has withdrawn to her room, very late, when the pounding in Ryan's head has receded, he lifts the fallboard of his piano and brushes the keys.

23

Natalie meets him in the early morning, twenty minutes from the city, where a dull sea cuts into a silver sky. He stands a couple of feet back from the purl of the water, lulled by the wind, and so when she reaches him it's as a vague impression: indigo jeans, tousled hair and hesitance.

'Hi,' she says.

Ryan doesn't answer. He looks at the tapering world and tastes the salt.

'I'm actually glad you called me.' Natalie casts her voice just a fraction over the waves. 'I'm not happy with how we left things. Some of the stuff I said to you.'

'The truth will out,' Ryan says. 'Make it a weight off.'

He blinks and turns his head and she bows hers.

'I wasn't burdened by it,' she says.

'God forbid.'

'No, I mean . . .' She forces a sigh. 'You and me. It was very . . . natural. I stopped thinking of you as one of Dan's cronies very early on.'

'Cronies?'

She shrinks, then shoulders the error.

'I'm not so hot on the terminology, Ryan.'

'Why would you be?' He makes sure to catch her eye. 'There isn't much going on inside that head as far as I can make out.'

He wishes for the wind to grow wild. He plucks a pebble from the wash and hurls it at the grey.

'Did you ask me to meet you just so you could pull me apart?' she says.

'No. That you're a stupid bitch doesn't make me less of a stupid bastard.' He throws another stone. 'I guess I'm just mad to know what you thought was the point of all this.'

'You think I owe you an explanation.'

'Don't you?'

She comes round to the idea after two more pitched pebbles. She walks away, then pauses and looks back to make clear her surrender, and he throws another stone and follows her. She sits on a rock at the back of the beach and hugs her knees to her chest. He stays standing. He puts his hands in his pockets and watches the water.

She begins, 'There's something real about what you do. It's easy to fetishise authenticity when—'

'What the fuck are you talking about, girl? *Authenticity* . . . Did you practise that excuse?'

'Well, yeah,' she says. 'You think I didn't think about this? Over and over?'

This time unimpeded she launches into an account of her stupidity. She tallies a stack of native advantages: more swagger and sex in a boy like Ryan than in a fella peering down from an ivory tower.

'It sounds silly,' she says.

'You can hear yourself, then?'

'You're different to me,' she says. 'That's attractive. You can understand that, right? Why else would you be with me?'

He doesn't answer and she doesn't wait. She tells him that she had shallow, hare-brained ideas about him at first, but that he surpassed her expectations.

'Because they were so fucking low?' he asks.

Her pause exposes shame. She unhooks her hands and begins to draw one leg back and forth, tilling the sand with her heel.

'What was I gonna say at that stage, Ryan? That I'd only just remembered I remembered you? I didn't think it'd matter for a one-night stand or a Christmas fling. By the time I realised I wanted to be with you it was too late to say that yeah, I might have seen you with Dan before . . . I would have lost you.'

'Jesus, girl. If you knew how many times this week I was nearly lost . . .' He shakes his head. 'Anyway, that's only the half of it. You can sit there looking all sorts of sorrowful but it doesn't change the fact that when I told you Karine was pregnant you ate the head off me. I wasn't authentic then, was I? I was a thick Norrie wacker.'

'I lashed out . . .'

'Did you what.'

'. . . and I'm sorry. Just the idea of your ex still having this hold on you, and then the thing with Dan was so scary – *is* so scary – I just couldn't handle it.'

'*Having a hold on me*. Fuck's sake.'

She says nothing. She throws her arms around her shins again and presses her forehead to her knees.

'That's fucking juvenile,' Ryan says. 'And I years younger than you.'

'It's just I'm so upset you didn't tell me about it.'

'I didn't know about it, Natalie. I know you don't believe me, authentic and all as I am, but it's true. And I could have died without knowing it. Can you let that sink in? Coz I fucking can't.'

She says, 'Do you still have feelings for me?'

He faces her and the wind tosses serpentine trails on the sand at her feet.

'Oh, you're some ball-hopper, all right.'

He hunches his shoulders and walks to the water and kicks a clump of wet sand forward and spits in the froth and gives evils to the horizon and marches back to Natalie, still with his hands in his pockets, fingers splayed in temper.

'You know what, I was this close, Natalie. In the best possible way it wrecked my head that you were into me.'

'You think that because I didn't tell you the truth from the beginning, none of it was real?'

'Naw, girl, what makes me question it is how long you kept it going when not knowing the truth could have gotten me killed.'

'It was a few weeks, Ryan, and we barely left the house . . .' When his jaw falls she raises her hand and bobs her head. 'I'm sorry. I shouldn't be trying to defend it. If I could turn the clock back, oh my God, I'd do it in a heartbeat.'

'Can you prove that?'

She looks up again.

'You wanna make this right, Natalie?'

'Of course I want to make this right.'

'You still want to be with me, do you?'

On the way to the beach this morning Ryan tried to dismantle his resentment and until she stood at his side on the shore he thought he'd managed it. He knows that only a little of the mire he's up to his neck in is her fault. She was duplicitous, but so was he; he doesn't know if he'd ever have gotten round to telling her what he did with all the hours of his day. He might have been ignorant to how he was betraying Dan at the beginning, but Natalie's right, once he knew what he was doing he took charge and he kept going.

And yeah, once she snaps she knows what buttons to punch down on: call him a guttersnipe and watch him shudder. This is where the real resentment festers, and Ryan had buried the knowing till he got to the beach.

On that basis he expects her to go white and scuttle away, but she says, 'Yeah. I wouldn't have been so cruel otherwise. I know that sounds perverse.'

He shakes his head again.

'Wanting to be with me after all of this shit is what's perverse, girl.'

'I don't know . . . I thought we had something real enough to want to protect.'

He imagines his trials as one exaggerated pinch after another as she tries to determine just how real he is. Once he's bled and vomited he gets his certificate of authenticity: *he sure bruises like a bona fide boy.*

'I thought,' she continues, 'that we had a genuine connection.' She keens and rubs her forehead against her knees and once the anguish is out she says, 'Maybe we're as bad as each other?'

'You can't hold a candle to me, girl.'

She doesn't hear this admission of defeat. To the ocean she says, 'We never did any normal boyfriend–girlfriend things. Go to the cinema. Hold hands in Fitzgerald Park. Me drag you around Mahon Point on a wet Saturday. Instead we've just . . . smoked dope and had sex. Dope and sex shouldn't be the entirety of it.'

Dope and sex is all I know how to do, Ryan thinks, and it's succinct and dangerous and nearly buckles him, until from nowhere he adds: *music*. Tarantellas rehearsed and eventually, yes, perfected. Remixes made to order. Impromptu recitals and pianos that home, for fuck's sake.

So rather than buckle he agrees with her.

'Dope and sex shouldn't be the entirety of it,' he says.

He had accepted that he'd need to coerce her and worried about how he'd pardon himself afterwards, but Natalie needs no coercion. She tells him to follow her back to her house. They sit in the gloom behind closed curtains in her bedroom, her cross-legged on the bed with her laptop open in front of her, him on the floor with his back to the door.

They do business.

In her sphere now, he's put back in his box by the realisation of his profound ignorance. She picks through the fundamentals of evasive finance. They work through all she did on the sly for Dan, and how Ryan can slip into its intricacies. It's complex

266

stuff for a fella who was tossed out of school at sixteen and who keeps his savings in his dad's attic.

He leaves her to her machinations and forages for lunch in her kitchen. A few short months into their relationship, he hasn't been given many opportunities to learn his way around her house. He makes two coffees and nicks a leftover dinner salad, most of a baguette and a lump of blue cheese, and finds plates to divide them onto and stands then and presses his palms against the polished worktop; who'd have thought he'd find his feet in the manor?

He could land himself an airy fortress on the fashionable arse of the Southside the same way Natalie's parents did: hard work, steel nerves and flexible morals. Because maybe it's all run on blood. Natalie's knowing how to swaddle Dan's deeds in respectability is just one knowing from many millions; for every one of Ryan there's one of Natalie, someone upstanding laundering his profits, getting high on his drugs.

He thinks of Jason Pender, because here Ryan is in a marble kitchen, and where's Pender, the poor cunt? Not even in the ground yet. Having his bullet holes poked by strangers in sterile white while his children enjoy the eerie fondness offered by murmuring mourners. Ryan's been there.

He brings Natalie her lunch.

'So what now?' She stretches one leg and balances the plate on the inside of her thigh. She doesn't move to eat until he does.

'I dig up the sponds to do a legger. I go to Italy and I figure out how to break it to my nonna that I won't be staying with her and I find a gaff in either Napoli or Salerno and I dig a hole out of the wall and I jam myself into it and somehow over the space of the next five months I figure out how to get home again.'

'You hardly want company, do you?'

She says this just as he tears a chunk from his bread, and timed thus he can't even gawp at her.

'Ha?' he manages, through his mouthful.

'You think I wouldn't like to get out of Cork for a bit, Ryan?'

It's bamboozling that she thinks doing so with him would be a good idea, given their capacity for wrecking all around them, but she tackles this with typical Natalie logic, crooking and straightening her fingers, spinning reason from the thread of their mistakes.

'You really think we deserve each other.' And though he laces the summary in scorn she faces it with her chin in the air and says, 'I really think we have further to go.'

'Thirteen hundred miles further.'

'No one would question it,' she says. 'It'd look like a holiday at the end of my year off.'

'And what happens in five months' time?'

She answers with a question, delivered a couple of beats late.

'Do you still love your ex?'

'Of course I fucking do.'

She pulls her lips in and casts her glance as if she's seen a pest dash across her lovely walnut floor.

'Since you realised she was pregnant?' she asks. 'Or is this something you've been keeping from me all along?'

'You knew she dumped me. It was there to make sense of, so: I wasn't ready for the end of it.'

'So when you ask me what happens in five months' time, you're implying that you'll be going home to her.'

'But she wouldn't have me because I'm chaos.' Ryan puts his plate down and stretches and laughs softly. 'But I think,' he continues, 'she'll let me home to my kid.'

Natalie doesn't find the notion so natural. She rolls her eyes and says, too quietly, 'Five months is a good timeframe for me. I'll have an internship to start. I think Italy would make a good experience to mask a bad one. And who knows what will happen with us? I think we might regret it if we don't allow time to figure it out.'

'You want to come with me to Napoli.'

'We both need to get away.'

'Napoli.' Ryan winces, pleased and sickened. 'A baptism of fire, just before the Christening.'

Jimmy Phelan tells Ryan he likes him, though Ryan might not believe it. Safe in the cellar under Barrack Street, he fluffs his feathers and applauds Ryan's mettle. He appreciates how Ryan pulled himself together, and so that Ryan can keep that appreciation going he doesn't tell Phelan it was Maureen who made him rein himself in. Ryan's been busy. He tells Phelan that he has commandeered the financial channels and so the takeover will be as seamless as it can be. Without the purse strings or the translator, Dan's at Phelan's mercy. This will cut off the oxygen from his anger and force him to come round. When it comes to Phelan's turn to place an order, the machinery will be well oiled. The bobs will go from the account Dan set up specifically for the task straight to the sock puppets scattered in Milan.

All at a knockdown price: eighty-five cents a pill.

Which is a ten cent per pill gamble, and in order to hedge potential losses Ryan needs to be out of the country in case Dan and Phelan decide on an equitable merger after all.

Ryan is set for scheming. His pockets are empty, but his head's clear.

24

In the early hours of Sunday morning Ryan sits with his hands on the steering wheel and his shoulders hunched, marking time by the flagging carousers on their way past. First the bigger groups, on their way to parties: fellas in spirits too high for walking in straight lines, girls giggling at their messing, keeping to the footpaths. Then the stragglers, in groups of two and three, grousing or whispering. Then the lost boys shoulder-barging the walls. The gaps between them grow.

It's fifteen minutes after three when Colm texts to tell Ryan that Dan's left Catalyst, and almost half past by the time the man himself shows. He stalls outside and waits for the gates to open, but there's not light enough to see his expression. Ryan knows Dan can't see him either, watching from a few cars up on the street perpendicular to him.

He's gambling on Dan's not taking long. It's a bet calculated on last Saturday night's doings and made now only on a lack of other options. Ryan needs to get away. He has no money to get away. He cannot rouse patronage in Phelan. He's had money taken from him. He needs to get back what's his.

Natalie's already away; she drove to Dublin that afternoon. A couple of nights with friends, hastily organised, then they catch a flight to Naples via London. He doesn't know whether she's up for accompanying him because she's genuinely scared or because she feels guilty for her part in this fuck-up or because she's determined to cover her own arse. Maybe she'll stick it out and maybe she won't. Ryan doesn't care either way.

He rubs his palms off his thighs.

The first part of the wager comes through. Dan drives back past the gates and turns in the direction he came from. Ryan closes one fist inside the other. He waits.

Five minutes later, Gina's blue Mazda approaches the gates and turns left, away from the city centre.

Ryan drives after her.

Before everything was broken, this time last week, Ryan was sent out here to do the drop-off on Dan's behalf, and Gina took the money from him fully clothed and ready for the road. Ryan didn't understand it until Natalie went through what she knew of Dan's accounting procedures and there he had a notion: Dan doesn't keep the Catalyst takings at home. He has Gina tuck them away. Why else would she still be dressed and impatient? The woman owns daytime pyjamas, for fuck's sake.

He stays as far back from Gina's tail lights as he can, bearing in mind it's been only a few short months since she was last held up. It wrecks Ryan's head that he briefly shared Natalie with someone who forces his girlfriend to continue with tasks that, post-heist, must scare her shitless.

The city slips behind them, Gina and Ryan.

On the far side of Wilton she pulls into a clump of apartment buildings at angles to each other and with barely a border of car parking spaces. Her Mazda goes left; Ryan's Golf goes right. He pulls up as soon as he's rounded the corner and backtracks on foot. Between steps and hedges he spots her making for the glass door nearest her. She slings a tote bag over her shoulder and walks with her arms crossed and her eyes to the tarmac. She doesn't hear him coming.

She flicks a fob from her fist and presses it to a panel to the left of the door, so Ryan catches her from the right. He pushes the muzzle to her side, right into the curve, and with his left hand he holds her shoulder.

She freezes and in that stillness he hears his breath and it's jagged.

'Tell me you're doing a cash deposit, Gina.'

'God, Ryan, what are you doing?'

'Tell me.'

Like she's whispering prayers. Panting with syllables overlapping. *God helpme. Jeeschrist*. It's a struggle not to join in the hoarse refrain.

'Tell me it's a deposit, Gina.'

'You want it? It's all counted, it's in the bag.'

'It's not the Catalyst takings I'm after, girl. I've a feeling he has a small bit more here.'

In the brushed steel elevator she quakes and leans on him and for a second it's as if her cheek is going to rest on his shoulder. They take breaths, hard, in unison. The doors open. Ryan presses his thumb into Gina's shoulder blade.

Dan's deposit box is a one-bed flat, bitterly cold, grey even with the lights on. There's a closed oak door on either side of the hall; Ryan pulls back on Gina's shoulder and checks both. A bathroom with a blown bulb, and a bedroom empty but for a stripped double bed and a venetian blind closed tight over the window. He guides her forward again. She leads him into the living room and stands waiting for direction.

'Where does he keep it, Gina?'

She tries a 'What d'you mean?' and drags too hard at his patience. He bumps her sternum with the inside of his wrist. She cries out.

'Ryan, you can't ask me—'

'I can. I am.'

'You know there's no way you can come back from this . . . Let's just sit down and talk it out, OK?'

'Talk it out? Like I'm having some sort of fleeting fit? Jesus Christ, Gina, don't tell me you don't know I fell out with Dan. Don't tell me this hasn't been just as big a fuck-up for him.'

She spares him. She shakes her head. 'Of course it has.'

'Then you know what he's done to me. I just want my money.'

'You don't understand, Ryan, he'll never let that go, he'll never let you go.'

She won't meet his eyes. She tries to convince the floor that what remains of the man standing on it is making a terrible mistake and so he raises his gun level with her mouth and asks her if she thinks he's codding her or what?

Gina purses her lips and lines gather in yesterday's make-up. 'This can be sorted. I'll help put it right, Ryan. I know Dan.'

'You gonna petition him for me, are you, girl? He nearly fucking killed me! Had the gun up here . . .' He taps his temple. '. . . the whole lot.'

'He *didn't* kill you, though. He was only trying to scare you. I *know* him.'

'So d'you know what we fell out over? You'd guess, like. I'd have to be cutting the coke arseways, something like that?'

She winces.

'Naw, we'd been fucking the same woman. He nearly fucking killed me over that. Imagine. Do you know how much he cheats on you?'

'I'm not stupid,' she says.

'Well, if you're not stupid, girl, look at me and tell me how far further your dithering can push me.'

As she measures his desperation he measures her fear and knows that if he's still alive tomorrow he'll have new guilt to deal with. Gina's always been so good to him.

'Ryan. Please.'

His chest jerks; his misery imitates laughter.

'No one listened when I begged, Gina.'

It turns out the ugly wall-mounted boiler doesn't function. The real one is hidden behind a cabinet door, and the other is a dud. Its front casing comes away easily.

Gina leans against the worktop to Ryan's left with a hand on her forehead. Ryan puts the boiler casing on the floor, against the wall, and reaches again for his gun and his hand has just closed around the grip when he clocks them: three grey cash boxes, stacked, and wedged around them five stuffed bags of pills.

He takes one. He turns it over in his hand. Through the wrapper of the stained plastic he notes the logo stamped on each tablet. Through his grasp of maths – mass, numbers, probabilities – he feels out the tale. The tablets shift to make room for his fingertips.

'These are the missing yokes.'

Gina's response is a snuffle. Her palm moves from her forehead down over her eyes.

Ryan heaps the bags on the counter. Gina takes her hand away. She looks straight ahead, into the empty room, and widens her eyes as if warding off tears.

'Did he retrieve these when he got Pender?'

'I don't know about that side of things,' Gina says, and Ryan holds up his free hand and extends his first finger and she quietens for his conclusion.

'No. No, how would he? Pender never got these. You were never held up. These yokes never went missing in the first place.'

'I don't know the ins and outs of it, Ryan. That has nothing to do with me.'

'What the fuck, Gina?'

She shrugs, when a shrug won't do at all.

The gun takes the place of the pointed finger. 'You were never held up,' Ryan repeats, louder. 'You were never fucking held up, were you?'

'It wasn't my decision.'

'Pender's fucking dead, Gina! Why the fuck did that happen, if Pender had nothing to do with it?'

'It wasn't my—'

274

Ryan's hand on her neck and the gun at her cheek is enough to jolt her from her hymn. She makes that nightmare sound: a shriek noiseless but for strained whistling from the very back of her throat. Through his teeth Ryan says, 'This had nothing to do with Pender. So why is Pender dead?'

She's able for the chat, thinking the chat's all that's keeping her alive. In a manner Ryan demonstrated only days ago, when he gave up the route to a man all set to carve him up, Gina shudders and cries but makes sense when sense is needed.

'Jason started talking about bringing Jimmy Phelan in on things when the pills arrived. Dan thought he could have already approached Phelan, so we brought them here for safe-keeping. You know, till Dan could be sure. It wasn't supposed to go on as long as it did. Everyone got mad, and that complicated things. Dan told you all to be patient, didn't he? He just needed to work out who else was involved before he ditched Jason—'

'You're telling me that Dan staged a fucking heist because he was scared Jason Pender – fucking Jason Pender, the poor fucking cabbage – had an ear in Jimmy Phelan? You're telling me Dan staged all of this just coz . . . just coz he didn't have faith in the ranks?'

'It got out of hand . . .' Just as she gets out of hand, and slouches and sobs. Ryan grabs the worktop beside him. His gun slaps his thigh.

'Does he have even the smallest notion what he's done?' He blinks for focus. 'What does Shakespeare know about all of this?'

'Oh come on, Ryan. Obviously nothing.'

'Nothing. Like what Pender died for?'

'I don't know anything about that. He must have been talking, he must have been making things worse—'

'A,' Ryan tells her, standing straight, 'Pender wasn't talking and B, things couldn't fucking get any worse.'

On his command she unlocks the cash boxes and Ryan knows what he's owed but doesn't give a fuck what he's owed; he grabs her bag and stuffs the money and the packages into it. Gina stands making fists against her collarbone, weeping at the floor. 'D'you know how much these pills cost?' Ryan asks her, and asks again when she fails to reply. She shakes her head. 'Fifty fucking grand,' he says. 'That's the price of a man's life now, is it?'

He leaves the apartment block with a gun in one hand and Gina's bag in the other.

There should be theories that lead Ryan to a choice of conclusions, a story that comes together in his head. There are only mechanics. He drives to Larne Court and parks on the street outside. He stares out the windscreen with one elbow on the steering wheel and his forehead in his hand. He tries to force process. He tries to think of Jason Pender as anything but a note scrawled on the inside of his skull. The name rots to little noises. It starts to sound like nonsense.

Ryan sits up straight, takes a breath and looks at his passenger seat.

He counts. There's seventy-five grand.

His phone rings and he digs it out and says, softly, wryly to the sky, 'You took your fucking time.'

'My God, I'm going to savour fucking you up,' says Dan.

Ryan leans to look backwards, to his side, in all directions from which an army might approach. 'Nice yokes you've got there, Dan,' he says. 'What would Shakespeare make of them?'

There's the pause he was counting on.

'I'm going to kill you, Cusack,' Dan says. 'Well before you get to pitch your blabber. Do you hear me?'

Ryan stretches. 'Y'know, I shadowed your ould doll tonight just coz I'd a hunch she had to take the Catalyst deposit off-site. But did I know I'd end up coming away with this much? Did I suspect you to be as fucking mental a prick to have orchestrated this mess? Oh I hear you, boy. I see you.'

'You sit on your fucking conclusions now a while, Cusack, because you know a whole lot less than you think you do.'

'What's left for me to know, Dan? You nicked those pills, you piled the blame on Pender, you hid the lot from Shakespeare. What am I missing there, ha?'

'You come to me,' Dan says, 'so I can relieve you of a good bit more.'

'Don't fancy that much, to be honest with you.'

'You think I can't flush you out? I take this out on you or I take this out on your leftovers. Burn out your daddy, or . . .' as if the thought's just occurred to him, 'your sisters are old enough to turn out, aren't they?'

'See, boy, before tonight I'd have thought it wasn't in you to be an animal.' Ryan stuffs the money into the glove compartment and pushes his fingers against his throat. 'But I know the score now. You want us to put some sort of end to this, let's do it.'

'There's a good boy. Only know that it is an end. An execution. Don't think you can ransom yourself, either. You better have my money coming.'

'And our yokes?'

Another pause. Shakespeare's with him; there's no doubt in Ryan's mind.

'We'll put an end to it,' Ryan tells him, 'and it'll suit both of us. Don't think I won't tell Shakespeare all about your carry-on. Not like anyone could trust you now anyway, after what happened to Pender.'

'No one's gonna listen to your shit-stirring tall tales, Cusack. For every lie, I'll ram another one up Karine's cunt, and I fucking swear to you, Ryan, hand on heart, she's not going to like it. Up to you whether you want her to suffer alongside you. Shall we say . . . fifteen minutes?'

Ryan drops the phone and starts the car.

Ryan pulls in as directed at the entrance to his father's estate, where Shakespeare stands by some innocent's garden wall with his hands in his pockets as the wind casts shapes in the foliage behind him. Ryan goes to him and Shakespeare puts his hands on his shoulders and moves under his arms, along his chest and down his sides. Behind them is the thud of a car door closing. Ryan twists his head to watch Dan coming for him.

Shakespeare passes over the gun at Ryan's waist. He turns Ryan around and steps behind him and his fingers shove at the small of Ryan's back. He brandishes a second handgun. He holds it out to show Dan, then tucks it back wherever he got it.

'He's clear now,' he says, sullenly.

Dan swallows the lie.

'Where's my money?'

Ryan's response is a couple of seconds late and Dan takes it badly. He's at Ryan's throat before Ryan finishes telling him that he's not getting his fucking money.

'What d'you think will happen if you don't give it back, Cusack?' he says, fist to Ryan's windpipe. 'I'll gut you here and petrol bomb your father's gaff and if he makes it out at all, it'll only be on time to watch you bleed to death.'

Shakespeare, having conned Ryan the weapon concealed at his waist, doesn't like the idea of Dan attempting to gut anyone. He wedges an arm between them. 'We stick to the plan.'

'We do nothing till I get my money back,' Dan says, as close to Ryan's face as the pressure Shakespeare's laid on his chest will allow.

'We'll find the money!' Shakespeare hisses. 'We'll assume the cunt's stashed it with his old man and if that's not the case, I'm sure he won't be long telling us, lest we send Tony C into the ground after him. You told him not to ransom himself. Stick with it, we don't leave corpses on the fucking streets!' To Ryan, then: 'Get in the fucking car,' and Ryan knows he doesn't yet need to tell him about the pills, that Shakespeare has his mind made up about which of them he wants as the victor.

The wind ruffles Dan's coat. He seems to shiver from knees to throat. Ryan thinks that Dan's life is in his hands now and not

278

the other way around. He pleads with him. 'We can still work this out, boy.'

'That's pathetic,' is Dan's retort. 'You're fucking pathetic.'

It's Shakespeare who pushes Ryan into the back seat of the Civic. Dan sits in the passenger seat. Ryan watches the shifting black outside as Dan mocks and threatens and feeds him scenarios: where he's presumed Ryan's stashed his money and how he intends to get it back. Who he assumes will get in the way and what he'll do to them. Ryan blanks him. He tries to lose the warnings in courses of action plotted hard and fast. He tries to map his way home . . . On Dan drones. Ryan can't do what Shakespeare expects of him. Implausible. Impossible. The only solution is for Dan to calm enough to listen to Ryan's counsel. Equally implausible. Dan goes on about how he's going to replace Ryan with his brother, who's surely just as good at plámásing Italian hard men. Ryan meets his eyes then.

Shakespeare takes that familiar road out of the city and drives north towards the forestry.

Ryan's silence does damage. Dan's mouth twitches and his neck tips as the waiting nags at him; he so badly wants to refute the tale of the missing pills; he so badly needs it over with.

As they pull on to the mountain boreen Ryan at last says, 'I don't think this is beyond repair.'

'You'd be wrong then. You've made shit of my patience, Cusack. Don't think that your little heist was the sum total of ways your being alive has impoverished me. Or do you think I'm so daft as to believe you haven't told Phelan about my route?'

'I've told him,' Ryan says.

They get out of the car. There's a wind-whipped drizzle that gets under Ryan's collar and collects at the end of his nose. Shakespeare has a torch; its light is barely adequate. Dan wants them to move a little way in off the track. Not as far as the last time, he tells Ryan, for a man shouldn't have to die tired. If Ryan is a man at all. Dan muses about their history. He wonders why it took him so long to realise Ryan was a walking cancer – a liar, oh God yes, a liar, for fear Shakespeare might believe the revelations Ryan is bound to launch into any minute now.

But Ryan doesn't say anything.

'Right,' Dan says. 'This'll have to do.'

There's no light save for the circle thrown by Shakespeare's torch and the glow of Dan's phone screen. Scraps of charcoal between the ebony verticals of the conifers, that's all, and then only through the mist on Ryan's eyelids and lashes. It wouldn't be a bad place to die if you had mind for dying.

Dan moves between Ryan and Shakespeare and Shakespeare holds the light at his feet.

'We can fix this,' Ryan tells Dan, quietly, though the sound carries even over creaking bows and keening wind.

'Bollocks!' Dan's anguish comes out of shadow and catches Ryan's breath. 'Are you fucking goading me or kidding yourself? Because if it's the former, knock it off. You don't think this is the hardest thing I've ever had to do?'

'What, even after the trial run last weekend?'

'Still with the smart mouth.' Dan grabs Ryan's jaw and pushes his face to Ryan's face. 'Fuck you, Ryan. I've been your guide and your friend for seven fucking years – do you have any idea what this is doing to me?'

Ryan should keep one hand hovering over the grip of his gun, but now he must bring both hands up to pull at Dan's fingers. 'You? You kicked the shit out of me, Dan. You held a gun to my head. You took my money and you pushed me into work I'd never have seen a penny for and I'm supposed to feel bad for you?'

'What else was I supposed to do, boy? You made a fool out of me, and then would you take your punishment like a man? Yera yeah, running off crying to your fucking pal J.P. so he could barge in on all the work I've sweated through, so what do I do about that? I've to go to war over you, you sociopathic cunt.'

'I'm sociopathic? I'm not the one who finished Pender over—'

'Enough!' Dan shouts, and lower then, more urgently, 'I'll choke the life out of you, I'll watch till there's nothing left in you, and I do this because you made me do it.' He tightens his grip and Ryan pulls harder at his fingers and tells him, in what breath he's allowed, that he'll do what he can for him with Phelan, that though everything's crooked it can be put straight enough for them all to navigate; he swears they'll both get out of this; he hasn't said a word against him yet.

'Don't threaten me!' Dan bellows and tightens his grip on Ryan's jaw. Those features of Dan's that are hidden now by the dark Ryan knows well: the tones of grey in his eyes and his hair and more often than not his voice, so usually measured. Him slapping Ryan on the back or lightly shaking his shoulder, him nodding and grasping all of the shit that made Ryan, knowing him, almost as well as Karine knows him, and Ryan is nowhere near ready to lose another confidant. *I don't want to bring my kid into a city*, Ryan thinks and the thinking stuns him, *without both of us in it. I don't want a world of regret and missing pieces. I don't want my baby to ask me* Dad, who did you lose before you found me?

'Jesus, Dan, don't make me do this.'

'You'll be doing nothing—'

little the trees and the wind can do to mask the gunshot. Dan's eyes widen. His weight pushes Ryan back; Ryan stumbles over his own feet and lands on his arse on the ground. He scratches his palms; he hits one elbow. Dan falls unsupported and hits the earth knees first, then crashes on his side, then rolls face down. He makes a hoarse, juddering sound. His forearms shake. A deeper dark spreads on the left side of his coat. Shakespeare puts a second bullet in Dan's head.

'Jesus, Cusack,' he tuts. 'You're fucking useless.'

Ryan clambers up, both hands pressed to a tree trunk. He moves back further. His lips part and connect but he is breathless. His eyes sting with tears or with shock. It could be the rain. It could be some new, cruel climate.

'And to think I was worried you'd do him in the car,' Shakespeare says.

Ryan turns his back on the remains and walks.

'Hey!' says Shakespeare, and he sounds amused. 'Where d'you think you're going? We have work to do.'

Ryan chooses a tree to lean against. His heart keeps beating. His lungs fill and empty. His elbow aches.

25

There's a resting place for Dan and it's where he'd planned to bury Ryan. That's as much detail as is given as Ryan and Shakespeare fashion a temporary arrangement from earth and branches. Shakespeare tells him he'll do the rest, that Ryan needs to be back in the city. They sit in the Civic. 'Dan's car is in town somewhere. It can't still be in the morning,' Shakespeare says. 'Simple as that.'

'What am I supposed to do with it?'

'Drive it fucking home, of course.'

'Back to his gaff? But what about Gina?'

'Gina's a chance you have to take.'

Ryan sits in the spot Dan very recently vacated and gives his killer a nod and manages nothing else till they get back to the city. As they turn onto the Old Youghal Road he says, 'So what do we do now?'

'I thought what we do now is clear, Cusack? I go back and finish what we started. You move the car.'

'I mean after that. I mean . . .'

'You mean what kind of keening's most appropriate? Fuck's sake, Cusack. None. Nothing.'

'I could have found a way around it.'

'No, you couldn't. Get that notion out of your head, boy, before it starts multiplying. It would have been you or him.' He huffs. 'You think you'd thank me.'

The light's crept up on them. They drive into a world of downy grey silhouettes, a city that seems newly reclaimed from the sea. Shakespeare pulls in at the quay and hands Ryan Dan's keys. There's a weight in them, all that's left of seven years.

'This is fucking ridiculous,' Ryan says, softly.

'The game as it's played, boy.'

'He'd never have thought you'd leave me my gun. He'd have thought that ridiculous.'

Shakespeare looks out the windscreen. 'Listen.' He shifts in his seat. 'Things have worked out the only way they could have worked out. Decisions were made, hard decisions. You're still here, and if you want that state continued you better shut your mouth. Coz I tell you what, boy. From where I'm sitting you look like a prime suspect, and you are not half as indispensable as you think you are.'

'What d'you mean by that?'

'I mean, Cusack, you need to choke down whatever dithering's threatening to take hold, because if the Shades get wind of this, it's you they're gonna nail for it.'

'Why would they nail me for it?'

'I left you your gun for a reason, Cusack. Because you doing it makes the most fucking sense.'

This makes shit of Ryan's capacity for stepping lively into action. For a long while he stands in the drizzle on the footpath where Shakespeare left him, holding the keys in his fist.

He finds Dan's car down by the College of Comm and drives it back to Dan's gaff and parks in the space furthest from his door after twice nearly dropping the gate fob and dashes out of there so hot across the shoulders and neck that there might as well be a spotlight blistering him. It's an hour before he's back at his own car, with the light now coming as full as it will on this March-end morning in the mist.

He heads to his own gaff for a shower and to pantomime a rest; he lies on his bed and he stares at the ceiling.

After a bit he gets up. He stands by the window. He stares out at the rain. He feels the pain spread over his left ear. He phones Phelan.

Phelan answers only the fourth call in a row.

'Mr Cusack,' he says, hard, low.

'I've come into a bit of money,' Ryan tells the drizzle. 'I'm going.'

'Where are you going?'

'To hover around your interests, like I said I would. Why? D'you think I might have changed my mind?'

'I put nothing past you, Cusack. You're not always reliable as you should be.'

'Meaning what?'

Phelan affects the overblown surprise of an Infants teacher. 'Meaning I've to ask myself whether I should send Shakespeare with you on this, too, in case you get into the habit of shirking your shit.'

Nothing left in Ryan to say to that. He calls Shakespeare, and Shakespeare leaves it ring out twice before he answers. Sleep and irritation equally thick in his voice; he isn't having the same problem going under.

'What's up?' he says; the audacity of the cunt's indifference.

'That's done.'

'Well yeah, it'd want to be done. Not like you had room to manoeuvre any other way. Are you looking for reassurance? My bit's done too.'

'What about yer wan?'

Ryan means Gina. Shakespeare cops immediately. 'I'll talk to her.'

'You haven't yet?'

'Do *you* wanna talk to her?' He translates refusal from Ryan's pause. 'Then for fuck's sake, get a hold of yourself. After that thing in Bandon, the fucker's hightailed it. No doubt he'll come slinking back after a few months laid low in Spain.'

'What about me, though? She was there when I made the withdrawal.'

'Didn't you only withdraw what was yours? She'll be told that was unrelated. And if she doesn't believe it . . .' Shakespeare laughs. 'Well, that's your problem. You're still around to sort it out, that's the main thing.'

It hadn't occurred to Ryan that Shakespeare wouldn't know about his going to Italy. 'I've no desire to knock around here much longer,' he says.

'Don't you move, boy. We have work to do with the new fella. I can't go rebuilding anything without your contacts. I'm gonna need you to step in with the club.'

'How much rebuilding d'you think he's going to let you do, boy?'

Shakespeare laughs. 'You mistake this for an irrational world, Cusack.'

'I get the strong feeling that what happened happened to suit the new fella. Decisions were made, didn't you say? Didn't you mean with him? He just told me,' Ryan says, 'that last night he sent you with me. Meaning you were only following orders. Meaning there'll be no rebuilding, only a takeover.'

'An alliance,' Shakespeare corrects. 'A proportional way forward. How is it you're still underestimating me?'

'He was meant to be your friend, boy.'

'A friend fierce quick to doubt me after a decade of me backing him up and holding him up and patching him up.'

Ryan finishes their conversation wondering what role Shakespeare could possibly think him capable of now. He assumes that Shakespeare expects to replace Dan as the head of their scraggy crew and that Ryan will just fall into place under him with his arse cocked in the air.

He gets dressed again. He packs the bare minimum into one carry-on bag: a change of clothes, both passports, his laptop. He separates his windfall: forty k in one chunk, thirty-five in the other.

286

He goes to Maureen's place and tells her, 'I fucked it, Maureen. I fucked it.'

'You what?' She steers him to her couch and relieves him of his backpack. 'Will you not tell me?' Ryan has nothing left but truths many times removed. Shakespeare killed Dan and in so doing he ripped out Ryan's tongue. Ryan saw Dan die in front of him. There are no words left to him to shift the burden of it.

'Ah, craitur,' Maureen says. She puts both arms around him.

Ryan spends the night in Maureen's flat, unbeknownst to her son. In between arranging the next day's schedule with Natalie – Ryan will get the train to Dublin and she'll meet him at Heuston – he dozes and drinks tea and eats the chips Maureen toddles off out to buy for him. He sleeps in the end. If he dreams, he doesn't remember them. He wakes in the early morning before her and leaves a note on the back of an envelope on her coffee table. *Thanks girl. Tell Jimmy I'll call him if he's looking for me. I'll be grand.*

Tasks to do and fuck-all time left. Ryan catches his cousin before he leaves for work. Joseph doesn't take well to his hazy story or to his *quite fucking frankly, bollocksed* countenance. He doesn't take well to Ryan's giving him the remainder of the year's rent, but he takes it all the same. Ryan promises he'll tell Joseph the full story of the past week once he gets his head clear. Joseph erroneously thinks that Naples may well be the kind of place a man can clear his head.

Ryan drives home, up to his father's terrace.

Cian comes out to the passenger seat. They have a smoke.

'You all right, boy?' Cian says.

Ryan considers his home through the windscreen. Concrete scored by tyre marks, dirt trails carved through green; blemishes that clash with the bright brick walls just as Ryan and Cian clash with the neighbours who knock on past and take good hard looks in at the pair of them . . . *the two oldest Cusack boys, a right pair of shams-in-training, you'd want to give them a wide berth, like.* He tells Cian, 'The fucking game is crazy. I'm done with it, you're done with it.'

'What's after happening, boy?'

Ryan doesn't reply but for a headshake. He tells Cian instead that he's getting out of Cork for a few months and that he wants him done with whatever turds he juggles out there at the edges of his brother's empire of shit.

'I mean it, boy.'

'All right,' Cian says, and he says it sincerely and Ryan thinks of how bad things must look for his brother to respond exactly how he wanted him to.

He relays his instructions. Cian is to take a sum for Colm McArdle, an investment in a grand plan Ryan once made room for. He's to take another sum and hide it and use it only for emergencies and utility bills. He's not, for the love of God, to let their father know where it is. 'Course not, boy,' says Cian. 'D'you think I'm a gom or what?' Ryan tells him that Joseph will be collecting the GTI this evening and that he's under strict instruction never to let Cian borrow it. 'Ah, lousy,' Cian complains and Ryan says that he hasn't a quare notion of letting his little brother wrap his car around a tree or bailing him out if he gets done driving it without insurance. *Grand, fine*, Cian pouts. 'And sure I'll be back in August,' Ryan says.

'Why August?' Cian asks.

'Dad not tell you?'

'Dad told me,' Cian says. 'Just I was hoping you'd tell me too.'

Karine answers her parents' front door in pyjama bottoms and a vest and this time Ryan can see it, yeah, his small fella's there all right.

She doesn't greet him. She doesn't rebuke him. They look at each other, then he looks down. She lets him in.

She leads him to the kitchen and asks if he's eaten and he feels his face begin to screw up and Christ no, he can't be falling to pieces now. 'I'm grand,' he tells her and she says, 'Sure? I've got toast on, like.'

'I'm sure.' He even manages a joke. 'You're the one eating for two.'

They've got the place to themselves. The damage Ryan and Karine used to be able to do with that scenario, when damage was something gleeful and the scraps they tore from the walls of the world went only to strengthening their sanctuary.

She goes to wait by the worktop and to her back Ryan says, 'I'm off to Napoli. Dublin tonight, flight then tomorrow.'

She turns. 'Is that the best thing for you?'

'Yeah, and c'mere . . .' He slides his hands into his jeans pockets. 'I need to say this.'

She folds her arms but sternness in Karine is beautiful; the way she purses her lips, the way she juts her chin. She folds her arms and his heart jumps. She folds her arms, six years back, on the patch of grass and brush where they had their first kiss, she hides her hands, she hoists her breasts, she says 'It's cold' and he puts his hand on the small of her back . . .

'Natalie asked if she could go with me and I said OK. You were right, girl. It was stupid of me to say that Natalie was a mistake, or let on this was all done on a whim. I did this, I have to have done it for a reason.'

She narrows her right eye almost to a wink.

'So I go to Napoli,' Ryan says, 'and I see through this other thing I set up and I finish with all of that bollocks between now and August. You wanted me out. I said it couldn't be done overnight and I wasn't lying. But it's part done already and by August I'll be a different fella. I won't be me. I won't. I swear to you. I know it's too late for us but . . . I want to do a better job than my dad did.'

She takes a breath, as if she's about to speak, but lets it out again unspent.

'I can fix this.' This strand burns his throat. 'If there's no way around it then you go through it.'

She comes to him and if she'd have kissed him or looked deep in his eyes she'd have stopped him; he cannot see himself going if she does not play along. Instead she says, 'Well then you get five months, Ryan', and he agrees to those terms. Five months' penance, a rebirth for a birth.

And maybe it's not the end. But he owes it to her to at least try ending them.

He has a last task requiring the car. He hides the filched pills under his seat and drives to the Watercourse Road rental, the one Dan had set up as a stash house. After tipping out a handful he tucks the yokes into a coal box he finds in the old garden shed and sits back into his car and texts Joseph, telling him what time his train leaves and asking him to collect the car keys and, yeah, if he's up for it, maybe do Ryan one last great turn, maybe hide a tool worth twelve-hundred euro for him, as soon as he no longer needs it.

Then he sticks on a cap and pulls up his hood and draws it tight round his head and goes to meet Shakespeare, who says he wants to get a few bits straight, who says he has an update from Gina, who hints at plans in which he means to truss Ryan.

He's in his local, out the back by the poker machine, flanked at respectful distance by a couple of his own feens, and Ryan is sure he can smell it off them, too: bloodlust, haste and strange energy.

Monday, doleful air, talk radio, more light than is welcomed by midday drinkers, light enough to blink in. 'What the fuck are you doing, Cusack?' Shakespeare says. His runner hits the floor from the bar stool footrest. His eyes are the widest Ryan's ever seen them.

'A legger,' Ryan says.

'Didn't I tell you you weren't going nowhere, boy?' His rigidity betrays him, though. Neither he nor his boys have a piece on them but there's one in Ryan's hand cocked right for Shakespeare's head.

'Yeah, I knew you wouldn't be keen on it, boy, and I knew you wouldn't suffer me trying to talk you around, so I'm here now giving you a choice. I have too much here at home you can fuck with to get at me, so we have to part on certain terms. Ergo, you take what I'm offering you or I do to you now what you did to Dan. We finish our association today, whichever you pick.'

'Here,' Shakespeare laughs, 'in a fucking pub, in your own fucking back garden, in the middle of the day?'

'Ask yourself, Shane, what have I got to lose?'

Neither of his boys move but even so, Shakespeare holds up his hand as if to still them.

'I was waiting to jaw with you,' he says, 'coz I know you've laid your hands on much more than your fair share. Seventy-five kay, Gina tells me. What's yours out of that, Cusack? Twenty? You really think I'm gonna let you fuck off with fifty-five grand of my capital?'

'Yeah, I do.'

Ryan tilts his left hand so that Shakespeare finally focuses.

'Recognise these?' Ryan asks.

The knot in his throat bounces as he waits for Shakespeare's expression, and it comes, a slight frown as what Ryan's showing him makes sense. Ryan allows him to move close enough to see the logo. He gets it, quick as Ryan got it.

'Where are my pills, Cusack?'

'I'll tell you, boy. I don't want them.'

'*You* took them?'

'Hardly. Dan had them. Gina had them.'

Shakespeare's eyes go back to their slits. Still his lads don't move. Still the radio drones from the front room of the bar.

'You tell me where the yokes are . . .' Shakespeare's voice crosses from a grunt to a whisper; he wrestles with Ryan's treachery. '. . . and I let you away with the money? You must be fucking codding me.'

'I'm not codding you, but you're codding yourself if you think I'm believing Dan set those bobs aside for your inheritance.'

'He didn't,' Shakespeare says, 'but I'm still taking them.'

'A bullet, then. Or else you take my fucking generous offer and accept that we're square and we'll be square when I'm back too. Those pills make sufficient profit, considering you get your own crew and you get your scapegoat and you get a piece of the route and you stay alive, boy, which is more than some of us got.'

Shakespeare tries to break Ryan's stare with his own and when that fails his stare flickers and forks as he works out the players left and the moves they could yet make.

'All right,' he says. 'It's a deal. Tell me where my yokes are.'

'Once I'm standing on the platform in Kent station, boy, so we'd want to be making tracks.'

Shakespeare laughs. 'Jesus,' he says, and pulls a hand over his chin. He steps back again. His feens breathe as he gives them a twist of his hand.

'You're some piece of work all right, boy,' he tells Ryan, and much as it must pain him he can't help smiling.

There's no music here. No decks, no keyboards, no pianos. No room in my head. I'd like to get it back. My fingers itch for it but I can't relax, drop my shoulders, roll my neck. I can't imagine anyone'd feel sorry for me though, after all I've done, and it's a petty kind of complaint really, isn't it?

So Natalie is sticking it out. It's the end of June and she's still here in Naples in this short-term let fifteen minutes from your parents' gaff. She was thrilled that I got a flat with a balcony, she had notions that she'd be out on it in the evenings, guzzling vino and looking over the bay. You can't see the bay at all from the balcony, all you can see are other apartments. I tried to warn her but she ignored it and when I was proved right she shook off the disappointment. She's getting good at that.

She's disappointed your mam. Like, my nonna was delighted to see me and then appalled at the reason why. I mean naturally I didn't tell her about the networking and brainstorming that takes me into the city proper or all the way down to Salerno. As far as she's aware I'm only in Napoli because I won't have the chance to take a holiday in the sunshine, working on my tan and my tongue, after August, when I'm a dad. Still, though. I'm no kind of man to get a new woman as soon as I got Karine pregnant. I'm blue in the face telling her that the timing was a shitty coincidence, but she won't believe me. I might be her first grandchild, and the sun shines out of my arse more often than not, but this one? She's not so keen to forgive this one.

293

She demonstrated Italian hospitality, of course. She just did it giving Natalie the evils and Natalie, as Natalie does, threw it off.

Karine was fucking thrilled when I told her this over FaceTime and two bottles of beer on the balcony. She could no more hide her smugness than her belly. She's carrying it all to the front, which means, according to her nana, that we're having a boy. I don't need to be told. It's a small fella, of course it is.

Karine grows. My fortune grows too. Dan's shipment went through and Dan's money paid for the lot. Phelan immediately placed an order for the next: a quarter of a million pills this time. At the start of the month he had me arrange a meeting and he wanted it don-to-don and, convinced that Dan had been just a messenger who's probably deployed now elsewhere, the camorristi took to Phelan like flies to shite. Again the Irish were asked to pay upfront and again the money went into Dan's dummy account and Natalie skimmed ten cent per pill off the top and left me and her with twenty-five grand.

One time I said to her, Wrecks my head, maestro, as she performed some trick or another between bank accounts. You, she said, don't need to worry your pretty little head about it. Just know that together we are a devastating entity. No guilt in Natalie. She's it all planned out: we're gonna be entrepreneurs on paper, investors online. For now she's working with Colm. Catalyst chugs on, both a front for and a beneficiary of her brilliant mind.

No guilt in her at all, though she knows the full story. She knows that Dan is dead and that Shakespeare killed him and she carried that around with her for a while before she found the strength to ditch it. She's sweet to me, though. She knows it's hit me harder and because she's tied to me, she's mad to look after me. So mainly she lets me sleep, and I FaceTime Karine for as long as I want, and when I'm ready for Cork again she swears she won't gripe.

Me and Shakespeare don't talk at all except for one conversation after the delivery of Dan's batch. He told me that Gina's seen sense. He didn't tell her Dan was dead, hinting instead that

294

he might have done a legger after Pender was shot and sure, guilty as any of us, Gina's lumped for keeping the house, keeping the car, keeping the business fronts and keeping her mouth shut. I know from Phelan that Shakespeare's proved well capable of earning his keep.

I don't bother writing letters to Dan, but I come up with questions I might ask his pissed off ghost, if it ever comes for me. Like, Did you see that coming, boy? When you met Pender in O'Connell's pub by yourself that time, what did you say to him? I have the yokes, sit tight and shut up, no one's going to kill you? When were they going to reappear? Why didn't they reappear, after you realised I told J.P. about the route? Would you have killed me and then presented Shakespeare with the yokes? Look, boy, Cusack had them all the time. A little man with oh such big ideas.

It does my nut. I think about it all the time.

I've been writing it down then ripping it up and burning it.

I've been rewriting it and hiding it, in case something happens to me and my dad needs my side of the story.

It's the end of June, and this evening I was out on the balcony on the phone to Phelan. Phelan's gone pure giddy with the whole thing. He's thinking of selling yokes to the UK on the basis that no one would ever see that coming. The pills are tearing up dance floors, house parties and beach raves all over Ireland. Nobody but us seems to have a clue where all the MDMA came from, but they're not complaining. The street dealers are charging fifteen quid a pill in some scenarios. Clubbers are buying rolls and considering it an investment.

So I'd been thinking of the ten cent stealth tax and making this next shipment the last one I have anything to do with.

I put the idea pure respectfully to Phelan and Phelan the ringmaster says, Fuck no. Sure what am I to him, but a circus animal with a very limited anthology of tricks, allowed to live only because of my pedigree?

This can't go on forever, is all, I tell him, and I'm watching the courtyard below, under which grinds the earth itself. And I'm afraid it suits restless blood, this Neapolitan ground, so I don't know, when my blood is replenished, whether I won't be me, like I promised Karine, or if I'll be bad all over again. Coz you know what? I'm glad I'm alive. I'm glad Dan got it, and not me. And I'm so ashamed of being glad.

It'll go on till my say-so, Phelan says, almost kindly. He's in good form these days. Between Dan's and my frailties he's a minted man. You might think you're only a diplomat, Cusack. But you're more: you're a diplomat who knows too fucking much. Why wouldn't I keep you where I want you?

So when's my contract up, then? And I look over my shoulder and behind the glass my catalyst stretches on the couch with her laptop balanced on her belly, the laptop through which she can access a tapestry of our misdeeds, threads all over Europe.

Why would you want out of your contract? laughs Phelan, who knows so much of what I've done and doesn't give a fuck. You'd hardly leave me high and dry, Ryan, when there's still so much you owe me. Sure haven't I already saved your life?

Acknowledgements

Sincere thanks to Mark Richards, who is sharp as he is patient and who seems to be always right (sorry I lied about that crate of Tanora, boy).

To everyone else at John Murray, but most especially Becky Walsh, Yassine Belkacemi and the exceptional Rosie Gailer.

To Ivan Mulcahy, and to Sallyanne Sweeney and everyone at MMB Creative.

To the Arts Council of Ireland for its generous support. In general to the inspirational crowd of inventors and experimenters that make up the Irish writing community. To Tom Morris, orchestrator of so many of my opportunities, and a damn fine senator impressionist. To Kevin Barry. Always to Kevin Barry.

To my family and my friends, especially to Caroline Naughton, Louise Lynskey and Sami Zahringer. To the gang of Corkonian DJs 'n' dancers with whom I did so much essential research. I wish I could remember the guts of it.

As always to my bright and brilliant Róisín. And to John, who was there for every notion, every turn of phrase, every little defeat, every single step.

From Byron, Austen and Darwin

to some of the most acclaimed and original contemporary writing, John Murray takes pride in bringing you powerful, prizewinning, absorbing and provocative books that will entertain you today and become the classics of tomorrow.

We put a lot of time and passion into what we publish and how we publish it, and we'd like to hear what you think.

Be part of John Murray – share your views with us at:

www.johnmurray.co.uk

 johnmurraybooks

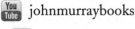 @johnmurrays

johnmurraybooks